Journey's Seekers

BK Parent
2014

Sommerhjem Journeys Series:

Journey's Middle: Winner of the Midwest Independent Publishers Association 2012 Midwest Book Award for Young Adult Fiction and finalist in the Fiction: Fantasy and Science Fiction category.

Journey's Lost and Found

Journey's Seekers

Journey's Seekers

B. K. Parent

iUniverse LLC
Bloomington

Journey's Seekers

iUniverse books may be ordered through booksellers or by contacting:

iUniverse LLC
1663 Liberty Drive
Bloomington, IN 47403
www.iuniverse.com
1-800-Authors (1-800-288-4677)

ISBN: 978-1-4917-2688-4 (sc)
ISBN: 978-1-4917-2690-7 (hc)
ISBN: 978-1-4917-2689-1 (e)

Library of Congress Control Number: 2014903885

Printed in the United States of America.

iUniverse rev. date: 03/19/2014

Acknowledgments

Many thanks to the Chapter of the Week Group who have been my main readers, critics, suppliers of ideas and support, and have kept me on track; to Celeste Klein who encouraged me daily; to my sister Patti Callaway, Flika Gardner, and Joni Amundson who insisted on their chapter every week and let me know if the cliff hanger at the end of the chapter worked; to René Carlberg, Cathy Carlson, Sarah Charleston, Glennis Cohen, Sarah Huelskoetter, Beth and Josh Irish, Vickie Keating, Jenni Meyer, niece Anna Perkins, Connie Stirling, and Robin Villwock for also being members of the Chapter of the Week Group and reading the story.

I would like to thank Eric Standen, retired Navy Supply Officer and present bosun of the tall ship The Friends Goodwill out of the port of South Haven, Michigan, for his expertise concerning boats and sailing. Any errors concerning boats and sailing in this book are completely the author's fault.

Once again, many thanks to my niece Katherine M. Parent for her cover art. I can only hope the inside of the book is as good as the cover she has designed. Thanks also goes to my niece Elizabeth M. Parent for her technical assistance on the Sommerhjem Journeys Series Facebook page.

A special thanks goes to Linne Jensen for surviving editing yet another book with me. I am extremely grateful for her knowledge of grammar, punctuation, and the ability to make sure the stories have consistency. Thanks also to Gale Stone for finding errors we missed.

To my father, Robert J. Parent, who taught me to appreciate a dry wit and to ask "I wonder" questions.

To CEK, always.

Introduction

Journey's Seekers was written originally as a serial. The chapters were each approximately four plus pages long and sent via e-mail to friends and relations once a week. A cliffhanger was written into the end of each chapter in order to build anticipation for the next chapter or, in some cases, merely to irritate the reader. You, as a new reader, have choices. You can read a chapter, walk away, and then later pick the book up and read the next chapter to get the serial experience. Another choice is to just read Journey's Seekers as a conventional book and "one more chapter" yourself to three o'clock in the morning on a work or school night. Whichever way you choose, I hope you enjoy the journeys of Chance, Ashu, Yara, and Toki.

Prologue

From the time the current folk occupying Sommerhjem arrived until several hundred years past, the country's rulers were chosen by the Gylden Sirklene challenge. That all changed after the extremely long reign of King Griswold. As he crept up in years, his daughter began to take over the day to day ruling of Sommerhjem, and when King Griswold finally died, she just assumed the reign. She also lived quite some time, and by then, it just seemed natural that her son would rule as the next King. He did not live quite as long as his mother, and his daughter, Octavia, then became Queen.

When the beloved Queen Octavia died, her daughter and heir, Princess Esmeralda, was not of age to rule. Following the death of Queen Octavia, there was a time of turmoil and intrigue as those who sought power vied for position. Eventually, Lord Cedric Klingflug was appointed regent from the time of Queen Octavia's death until Princess Esmeralda became old enough to rule as the next Queen of Sommerhjem. As the time came closer for Princess Esmeralda to assume the throne, rumors and rumblings began to circulate about Sommerhjem concerning power struggles between the Regent's supporters and those loyal to the Crown.

If Queen Octavia had not died when her daughter Princess Esmeralda was just a young lass, what transpired during the great summer fair the year she came of age to rule might never have happened. There would have been no reason to appoint a regent until Princess Esmeralda came of age, and no opportunity for Lord Klingflug to gain wealth, land, and power.

Unfortunately, during the intervening years, Regent Klingflug became overly fond of being in power. He set in motion a variety of plans which would continue to allow him to rule even after the princess came of age, if she managed to survive that long. One plan which worked well was to keep Princess Esmeralda isolated so she could not gain any popularity among the folk she would come to rule. Also, by keeping her from getting to know her subjects, she could not learn how upset they were with her and the Regent's edicts.

By his abuse of power, Lord Klingflug acquired more and more land and wealth for himself. His edicts and taxes caused a great deal of outrage from both the nobles and the common folk who were loyal to the Crown, but that had not stopped him. He levied higher and higher taxes and created special licenses, resulting in hardship for many in Sommerhjem. Those who aligned themselves with the Regent benefited greatly in coin and property while many loyal to the Crown lost their land and livelihoods.

The Regent was aware that there was one thing that could disrupt his well-thought-out plans and schemes. He knew, while many had forgotten, that the position of king or queen of Sommerhjem had not always been a hereditary position. Only in the last few hundred years, since King Griswold's reign, had the title been passed down from father or mother to daughter or son. Prior to that time, upon the passing of the old ruler, the new ruler of Sommerhjem was chosen by the Gylden Sirklene challenge. Regent Klingflug had had scholars loyal to him find out as much as they could about the Gylden Sirklene challenge. Then he had tried to find and destroy all of the parts and pieces needed for the challenge to be called and carried out.

On the day that Princess Esmeralda was to have been declared Queen, the Regent discovered he had failed in his quest to maintain power and to prevent the Gylden Sirklene challenge from being called. He was forced to relinquish his position as regent. Princess Esmeralda also stepped down from becoming Queen. An interim ruling council was formed to rule Sommerhjem for a year to the day the challenge was called, as was set out in the Book of Rules governing the challenge.

The challenge is directly linked to an object called the oppgave ringe, which is made up of nine pieces. All nine pieces must be returned to the capital of Sommerhjem by a year to the day that the challenge was called. By fall, four of those pieces had been returned to their proper place in the Well of Speaking in the capital. Two were placed in the vessteboks located in the sea wall in the Well of Speaking by the rover Nissa during the great summer fair. One was placed in the vessteboks by Greer, a former street boy from Havkoller, a rough and tumble border town in the country of Bortfjell, just across Sommerhjem's northern border. The fourth piece of the oppgave ringe was brought to the capital by Meryl, who came upon it by chance.

Five pieces of the oppgave ringe remain missing. On the day the challenge was called in the Well of Speaking, seekers, royal librarians, royal historians, and others were charged with finding out more about the Gylden Sirklene challenge and where to find the remaining pieces of the oppgave ringe. The missing five pieces of the oppgave ringe are being sought after by both those who would have them returned to their proper place so the challenge can proceed and by those who would prevent that from happening.

PART ONE

Chapter One

It must be almost time for me to stand watch, thought Chance, when he heard the ship's bell ring seven bells. That made it a half hour before he was to report for duty. Chance decided it was too soon to get up out of his bed that was swaying slightly with the rolling of the ship. Soon this trip would be over, he thought. Then, thinking he might have miscounted the seven bells, he sat up abruptly, which sent him flipping out of the hammock, landing face down on the deck. It was then that the wrongness of where he was hit him almost as hard as he had just hit the floor. When Chance lifted his head off the grimy floor, he saw he was in a very small room. Light was coming through the small barred window in the door.

This is wrong, so wrong, Chance thought, as he picked himself up off the floor and gave the tiny space a better look. He was obviously in a ship's brig, but how had that happened? He could not remember being thrown into the brig. For that matter, the ship he had been crewing on did not even have a brig. When he looked out the small barred window, Chance realized he was in the hold of an unfamiliar ship. The faint light he could see by was filtering down through a grate in the hatch. How had he gotten here?

Chance had left home over a month ago, setting sail for the country of Sommerhjem, and unless it had been a dream, he had landed in the port of Marinel. He distinctly remembered slinging his sea bag over his shoulder, saying his farewells to the crew, and disembarking. He had headed away from the dock area, and then what? What had he done after he had left the ship? Chance remembered he had felt hungry and was looking forward to some fresh food. He had headed up the street away from the docks to find a place to eat.

What had happened next? Chance felt so tired, and he had a terrible headache. Racking his brain despite the pain, he remembered he had been drawn toward a small eatery by the smell of fish chowder coming out of the open entrance. The weather had been decent enough that there were a few brave patrons eating at the small tables set out in front. He had gone in and had been directed to sit at a small table near the back. He had set his sea bag at his feet and ordered a large bowl of fish chowder and some fresh cider to drink. When he had finished and paid for his meal, he remembered he had felt dizzy. Chance had put the feeling up to being tired and not quite having his land legs yet. Then what had happened, Chance asked himself. Everything was still just a bit fuzzy and off kilter.

Chance knew he had walked down the street and had begun to feel more and more dizzy. Finally, he had found it difficult to keep moving forward. After that, it was a blank. Trying to figure out how he had gotten into a strange ship's brig was not going to get him out, so Chance took a second look around to size up the situation. Though he was slight of build, he was not small enough to fit through the tiny window in the door of the brig, so that was out. The brig consisted of just a hammock and an empty bucket with a rope handle. That was it. Chance wondered what had happened to his sea bag. Walking over to the barred door, he grabbed and turned the handle, but it was locked tight. He grabbed the bars of the door's window, pulled and pushed each one, and then tried twisting them. None were loose. Looking through the bars, he could see the hold was packed from deck to top with crates, bales, and barrels. Sitting on top of a crate across from him was his sea bag. Well, that answers that question, Chance thought. Unfortunately, the sea bag was too far away to do him much good.

From the sunlight filtering in through the hatch cover and what little he could see out of the window in the brig's door, it was obviously daytime. The question was: was it still the day he had left ship? The crew he had sailed with had told him what could happen if he looked for lodging or a tavern down by the docks, which was why he had climbed up higher in the town to find a decent place to eat. Thinking back, Chance remembered he had had the feeling he was being watched, but he had put that down to being in a new and strange port. Hindsight suggested that he should pay more attention to his instincts, if he ever got out of the mess he now found himself in.

Chance could hear the sounds of footfalls above him, and voices, but he could not make out what they were saying. No one came down into the hold during the long hours of the day. As the light from above grew dimmer and dimmer, Chance wondered if he was just going to be left in the hold to starve to death. A short while later, he heard the creak and groan of the hatch cover being lifted. He heard booted feet begin to descend the ladder down into the hold, and then a large man crossed over to his cell.

"Move back," the big man growled. "If'n it was just me, I'd let you rot in here, but Pivane thinks that's too cruel. He's bringin' you some water and hardtack. Wouldn't wants you ta starve ta death. Might be needin' yer strength fer where yer goin'." The big man laughed cruelly and headed back to the ladder. "You comin' down here with that grub, or what?" he called up to someone who was leaning in the opening.

Chance was starting to have an even worse feeling about his situation than he had when he had come to. He had figured out that he had been slipped some kind of concoction that had basically caused him to pass out, allowing him to be captured and placed on this ship. He had heard of folk being pressed into service on ships. Dragooned was what it was called. Unfortunately, Chance was beginning to feel that his being dragooned was the least of his worries. His attention was drawn back to his surroundings by the sounds of someone else descending the ladder.

"How hard is it to grab a small water skin and a couple of pieces of hardtack? What were you doin', makin' soup, too?" the big man asked.

"Ah, come on, Mako," Pivane said to the big man, "'tis the least we can do for the lad, considerin' his future."

"Tsk, tsk, tsk, Pivane. Sometimes I think you are just too soft for our line of work. You need to think more about the coin we're making and less about how we're makin' the coin. Besides, we need to make up for what that weasel Olwydd cheated us out of. We've gots expenses, you know. This little task is goin' to set us up good for a while."

"Sure wish we were makin' the coin on dry land. Never did like bein' on a ship," Pivane whined.

"Quit your complainin'. Only a few more days and we'll be to the Shadow Islands. After that, it'll be smooth sailin' back to Sommerhjem. This lad must be somethin' special that the folk that hired us also hired a small ship."

"Do ya trust the captain and her crew?"

"What's not to trust? She's one of the best smugglers along the Sommerhjem coast. I knows those that's payin' us made it worths her while to take us to the edge of the Shadow Islands. They're just as squeamish as you. I can think of easier ways of gettin' rid of a threat, but they didn't want that on their conscience. Why they think dumpin' him off the ship just inside the fog bank that surrounds the Shadow Islands is going to be more merciful, I can't say, but it's their coin, so's we'll just follow orders."

At the mention of the fog bank and the Shadow Islands, Chance saw Pivane visibly shudder and almost drop the hardtack. Chance was not liking what he was hearing. He knew a little about the Shadow Islands from his parents, who knew more than most about them, but that certainly was not very much. So much of the history of Sommerhjem, and those countries and islands closest to it, had been lost over the years. The Shadow Islands had a terrifying reputation. Very few who entered the fog surrounding them were ever heard from again.

Mako grabbed the small water skin and hardtack from Pivane and shoved it through the bars of the window of Chance's cell. "Here, take this, and don't try anythin' or there'll be no more. Enjoy yer meal," Mako remarked, and his laugh as he walked back to the hold ladder was less than kindly. "Come on, Pivane, there's a card game about to start, and I'm feelin' lucky."

While Mako and Pivane had been in the hold, Chance had tried to hold his panicked feelings in check. On shaking legs, he took himself back to the hammock and sat down. Before he had left home, he and his parents had talked about the possible dangers he might face, but he had felt they were just being worrywarts. After all, the Regent who had been ruling Sommerhjem had been forced to step down, and Sommerhjem was now under the rule of an interim council. It was finally time for one of his family to return home, and he had volunteered.

Chance had been feeling restless. Heading off to Sommerhjem had seemed like just the adventure his life needed. Usually, he was much more content spending his time reading books about history and other folks' adventures than working for the family trade company. Chance was the family dreamer. He wanted more than sailing between the islands of Havkoller. He wanted to live the adventures like the heroes of the books he read. Even so, Chance's dreams of adventure had not included being locked up in a ship's brig, destined to be dumped off in the mysterious and dangerous waters surrounding the Shadow Islands.

Oh why, oh why, had he ever left home? Why did he think that living in Havkoller, a country made up of many islands and his family's adoptive home, was not enough? Why was he not content, when he came of age, to follow in his brother's and sister's footsteps and to have his own trade ship? Why had he not let one of his other siblings come back to Sommerhjem when word had reached them that the Regent had been removed from rule and the Gylden Sirklene challenge had been called? Chance had plenty of time to ponder all of his questions, for other than the visit of the two who brought him food and water, no one else came down into the hold as day turned into night.

A number of years before, when he was just a boy, Chance's family had fled Sommerhjem. It had become apparent that unbeknownst to most of the folk, the Regent had begun to try to systematically eliminate the Høyttaier clan, of which Chance's family were members. When the ruling queen died, she left behind a single heir who was not of age to rule at the time of her death. A regent had been chosen to rule until the princess came of age. The Regent had done everything he could to try to maintain power, so he would not have to give up the ruling of Sommerhjem, if ever the princess attempted to become queen. Regent Cedric Klingflug's biggest fear was that someone would call the Gylden Sirklene challenge, which had been the way Sommerhjem's leaders had been chosen earlier in its history. Over the last several hundred years, most people had forgotten that the position of king or queen of Sommerhjem had not always been hereditary.

Regent Klingflug had had folk loyal to him finding out all they could about the Gylden Sirklene challenge. In the reports he received, it became clear that members of the Høyttaier clan posed a real threat to his plans to continue to rule Sommerhjem. If the Gylden Sirklene challenge was called, the Regent feared that someone would come forth with the Book of Rules that governed the Gylden Sirklene challenge. That in itself was not the real threat, for the Book of Rules was missing from the royal library and its whereabouts was unknown. In addition, it was written in an old, lost language. Lost to most folk, but not to members of the Høyttaier clan. The real threat was that the knowledge of how to read the old, and mostly forgotten, language had been passed down from one generation of Høyttaiers to another. Regent Klingflug felt it was better to be safe than sorry, so he had strung all of the ifs together and set out to eliminate the entire Høyttaier clan. If the challenge was called, if the Book of Rules turned up, if there were no Høyttaiers left, then he would have removed everyone who could read it.

Three things had stood the Høyttaier clan in good stead. The Høyttaier clan physically looked no different from most of the folk of Sommerhjem. In addition, they were very guarded about being Høyttaiers, teaching each new generation in secret. Finally, they had cultivated good friends in high places, who had warned them of the Regent's plans. Chance's family had left Sommerhjem to wait until such time as it was safe to return. His father had been a merchant in Sommerhjem and so became one in Havkoller. His family had a small fleet of trading ships that carried merchandise from one island to another. How Chance longed at that very moment to be crewing on his older sister's boat, or lying in a hammock on the front porch of home, reading.

The next few days were the same as the first day. Once a day either Mako or Pivane brought him water and hardtack and put it through the bars. Chance tried to engage them in conversation but had little success. Mako seemed to delight in taunting him as to what might await in his near future. Pivane appeared to be less inclined to give Chance a bad time but was reluctant to answer any questions.

Even though he could not see the sky, Chance was a good enough and a seasoned enough sailor to know when the weather began to change and the seas became rougher. When Pivane came to bring him his daily rations, he came through a door Chance had not noticed before, rather than coming down the ladder from the deck. He saw that Pivane was looking a little green and had some trouble navigating across the hold's deck. When Pivane left, he must not have closed the door he had come through tightly enough, for as the ship rolled from one side to the other, the door swung open, then closed, then opened again. Chance could hear snatches of conversation when the door was not banging loudly between the frame and the bulkhead.

"The weather is getting worse, and I tried to tell . . . ."

"Captain said she was going to . . . ."

"Don't see why we can't just toss the lad overboard right . . . ."

"Said we had to . . . ."

And then the door must have finally latched, for Chance could hear no more. The seas continued to rage, and the wind howled through the night. The now empty bucket rolled from one end of the tiny cell to the other, then back again with each roll of the ship. Chance's biggest fear was the ship would capsize or hit a reef, and he would be trapped in the cell. When morning arrived and a weak light filtered through the hatch grate, the wind had died down somewhat. The ship no longer felt like it was being lifted and tossed from one high wave to the next.

Several more days passed. It was midday when both Mako and Pivane climbed down the ladder. Neither was carrying anything. Pivane headed toward the crate that Chance's sea bag had been resting on. It had fallen off during the storm, and some of the contents had spilled out. Pivane hastily shoved Chance's clothes and gear back into the sea bag. Mako came over to Chance's cell carrying a ring of keys.

"Time for you to get out of that cell, stretch your legs, and get a bath," Mako said.

Chance thought that Mako's words sounded good, but the gleefully evil gleam in his eyes filled Chance with a feeling of dread.

Chapter Two

Mako unlocked the cell door and cautioned Chance to behave and not try anything. Since Mako was taller, bigger, and stronger than Chance, and Pivane also looked like he could hold his own in a fight, Chance took Mako's advice. Mako shoved Chance forward roughly, and he stumbled. It did not stop him from glancing about and trying to figure a way out of his dire situation. Chance was convinced that Mako's version of a bath was not the same as his version of a bath, other than it entailed water and getting wet.

Pivane went up the ladder first with Chance's sea bag slung over his shoulder. Chance was next, followed by Mako. When Chance looked up, rather than seeing open sky, all he could see was grayness. The fog that enshrouded the ship felt damp and muffled sound. Once he was on the upper deck, it was difficult to see even a few feet in front of him. He knew if he moved quickly enough, he would be swallowed up in the fog. Mako and Pivane would not be able to see him, not that that would do him much good. After all, he was on a ship. Once the fog lifted, he would be easy to find for it was not a very big ship, probably only large enough for a captain and a few crew.

A voice called out of the fog. "Hurry up, Mako. Get it done. I don't want to be in this cursed fog a minute more than I have to."

"Aye, Captain," Mako replied, giving a mock salute in the direction of the voice. Keeping an iron grip on Chance's arm, Mako told Pivane to give Chance his sea bag.

Pivane did as he was told and handed Chance his sea bag. Chance was instructed to sling the strap of his sea bag over his head and across his chest. Mako then commanded that Chance hold out his hands, and he tied them up tightly.

"Come this way," Mako directed Chance and dragged him a short distance until they reached the rail of the ship. Mako reached around Chance, unlatched the fastener that held the opening for the gangway closed, and opened it. "Time for your bath, lad," Mako said and shoved Chance through the opening in the ship's rail.

The last thing Chance heard before he hit the water was Mako's muffled laugh. The next moment found him sinking down into the dark, dark water, pulled under by the weight of his clothing and his sea bag. He had barely gulped a bit of air just as he hit the water, but it was not going to last for long. An overwhelming sense of sadness hit him when he thought of his family and how he had let them down, of how they would never know what happened to him. The regret that was weighing him down even more than his sea bag was the fact that he had failed at the very important task he had been sent to do. Chance had been so convinced when he left home that he was the right one to go, that he could handle the task. He had not lasted even a few hours in Sommerhjem. Some intrepid adventurer he had turned out to be.

With his hands tied, he could not remove his sea bag, which was dragging him further down despite kicking his legs as hard as he could. Chance's lungs began to burn, and he knew his air was running out. Suddenly, the sea around him began to light up. He could see the light even through his closed eyelids. A great feeling of calm overcame him, and he wondered if this was what dying was like. Something bumped his hip on his left side. Then something bumped his right hip. He felt himself being squeezed, held firmly, and being pushed through the water at a great speed. He was gulping air almost before his brain registered he had been pushed up to the surface.

Shaking his hair out of his eyes and treading water as hard as he could to keep himself from being pulled under, Chance wondered why his sea bag was not dragging him down. Something must be holding it up. Chance did not know if it was resting on a rock, or something else. He was, quite frankly, reluctant to either move or find out. It was dark again for the light Chance had thought he had seen when he had been underwater no longer glowed. He was cocooned in fog so thick he could have cut it with a knife. When Chance glanced to his left, he thought he caught a glimpse of a ship's running lights. He could hear muffled voices in the fog but could not make out what was being said.

While the water was not overly cold, Chance could feel himself begin to chill. He was growing ever more fatigued from lack of sleep and food. His legs were beginning to tire. Just when he felt himself slipping back down under the water, something nudged him up. Once again, he was pressed on either side by something hard, yet slightly yielding. While whatever it was was keeping his head out of the water, Chance did not know how much longer he was going to last. He did not dare call out in fear that Mako and Pivane would discover they had been less successful in getting rid of him than they thought. Besides, he thought, who else would hear him?

The cold was really beginning to get to him now and he could feel himself slipping away, no longer having the energy to kick his legs. Just when he felt he was through, that he had nothing left, he thought he heard the faint sounds of oars on the water, but it was hard to tell. He certainly could not tell what direction the sound was coming from. Was a dingy coming toward him from the ship he had just been thrown off of to make sure he was truly drowned, or was someone else out there?

Chance wished he knew more about the Shadow Islands. It just had not been a topic of conversation around the dinner table, and very little had been included in his studies. How he longed to be home now arguing with his mother or father that he had really studied enough for one day and should be let go to sail his small boat.

Chance had sunk beneath the surface and been buoyed up once again when he felt something grab the back of his shirt. Not knowing if he were facing a friend or a new foe, Chance tried to struggle. Even though he had very little strength left, he tried to fight, but whatever had him was too strong. Chance found himself being lifted up out of the water and across the side of a boat.

A very melodic voice whispered, "Settle down, or we will both end up in the water."

Chance was so numb, he did not feel the scrapes as his body was dragged into the boat. He was unceremoniously dropped to the bottom of the boat, rocking it. When the boat steadied, he felt his body being shifted upright. The fog was still so thick, he could not see his rescuer. As he heard the oars strike the water, he felt the boat begin to move. Chance lost track of time, for all his concentration was being used to keep himself upright and alert. He lost the battle and quickly slipped into that state between being awake and dreaming where he was not sure what was real.

When Chance was once again conscious of his surrounding, he became aware that he was wrapped up and could not move. When he struggled to free himself, he felt himself sway back and forth. He was wrapped up so tight, he could not free either his hands or his feet. Even his face was covered. This must be what caterpillars feel like in their cocoons, Chance thought with rising hysteria. He wondered if he ever got out of what he was wrapped in, if he would emerge with wings. Suddenly, something lightly brushed his forehead, and he stilled.

"Ah, good. Trying to thrash about will not help," stated the same melodic voice Chance remembered from the rowboat. "You were so cold and battered when I pulled you out of the water that I wrapped you up in a healing blanket. I am sorry I was not here when you came back to us. It must have been frightening. Try not fighting the wrap for you are in a hammock. If you keep struggling, you will find yourself upside down. Give yourself a little more time to heal. All will be well again."

Chance thought he heard that beautiful voice repeat that all would be well again, but he slipped back into a healing sleep before he was quite sure. When he awoke the next time, he found he was no longer constrained, but he was still in the hammock. He slowly opened his eyes and looked out the openings of the quarters he was in. He was surprised to find himself among some very familiar trees and flowers. His initial thought was the surroundings looked like home. Where was he exactly? Had the long sea voyage, landing in Sommerhjem, getting dragooned, and then being dumped overboard just been a highly imaginative dream?

When Chance took a closer look at his surroundings, he realized that only some of the plants, trees, and flowers were like the ones in Havkoller. Others were like none he had ever seen before. Chance carefully swung his feet over the edge of the hammock and sat up. He felt very rested and realized that he did not feel any sore muscles or bruises. Standing up, he took a few steps, which brought him out of the open-air thatched hut his hammock was in.

Chance jumped when he heard a voice coming from his right. Turning and looking in the direction of the voice, he saw a woman standing not more than a few feet away from him. He had not heard her approach. She was not a tall woman but striking, with a deep tan that contrasted with her white hair. Her eyes were the color of the sea that surrounded the islands of Havkoller, a brilliant deep aqua. While her hair was white, it was difficult to tell her age, for she moved like a young woman when she signaled Chance should follow her.

"You must be hungry for both food and knowledge. If you will follow me, please, I will try to answer all of your questions once we are settled."

Chance followed the woman, and as he walked after her, he began to realize several things. The air was warm, warm like at home. The air in Sommerhjem had been much cooler. The Shadow Islands where he had been dumped overboard were west of Sommerhjem and shrouded in fog. It struck him then that he was walking in bright sunshine. Where was he, he wondered.

Chance continued to look around, and when he looked up, he realized he could see sheer cliffs in the distance in any direction he looked. Waterfalls fell from great heights. Rainbows danced in the falling water. There was a peaceful, timeless feeling about the surroundings. Chance also became aware of a multitude of different bird songs and caught flashes of very colorful birds flitting through the trees. He also caught quick glimpses of furred animals in the trees but was hard pressed to name what he was seeing. He was brought out of his sightseeing when they entered a clearing next to a beautiful pond. Chairs and a table had been set near the edge of the pond.

Just as Chance was about to ask questions, the woman began to speak. "I think introductions are in order. I am Keeper Odette, and you are?"

"My name is Chance."

"And where do you hail from, Chance?"

Chance realized he could listen to this woman's voice all day, for it held such warmth and welcome. "I came recently from the islands of Havkoller, but my family is originally from Sommerhjem."

"And how did you find yourself in the waters of the Shadow Islands?"

"I can tell you how, but I don't know the why of it. I sailed to Sommerhjem on family business and then was dragooned onto a ship.

Two men, Mako and Pivane, seemed to indicate that I was to be disposed of and so threw me off the ship. I don't know why. Where are we?"

"Before I explain further, know that where we are is a secret which protects us, and we will do everything in our power to keep it. Know that now that you are here, you will have to remain here for the rest of your life. Should you wish to leave, in order to do so, you will have to go through a rite of passage that binds you to an unbreakable oath not to tell anyone of our location. You need to know that of those who chose that path, few survived."

Some choices, Chance thought to himself. Either he was destined to stay here, wherever here was, for the rest of his life, or he could go through a rite of passage that could kill him. He had mourned his family's loss when he thought he was going to drown, for they would never know what happened to him. Maybe that would have been easier. Since he could now be trapped here, he could be destined to live his life out knowing each day that his family would not know what had happened to him, and he could not get that information to them.

"I can see that what I have said saddens you. I am sorry. You have a right to know where you are. You are on one of the Shadow Islands."

Chance could not for the life of him imagine why the woman, who had identified herself as Keeper Odette, would lie to him. He did not think he could possibly be on one of the Shadow Islands. They were always shrouded in fog, and he had never heard any mention nor read anywhere in all his studies that they were inhabited.

Keeper Odette laughed at the look of sheer incredulity on Chance's face. "You have such a look of disbelief on your face! I can almost hear the words of denial going through your mind. I have not lied to you. We are sitting by this lovely pond, smack dab in the middle of the crater of a dead volcano."

This information was not very comforting to Chance. "How is it that this valley is so warm and not filled with fog?"

"I am sure some learned scholar will someday be able to tell us for sure, but our best guess is heat is vented into this crater from deep underground tunnels where lava still flows. Due to the sheer walls of the crater, the heat is held in. Our temperature is much the same year round and plant life thrives here. The crater walls rise above the fog, keeping the fog out, so we can see the blue sky on sunny days.

"Are you sure the volcano is dead?"

"Quite."

Just as the words left Keeper Odette's mouth, the ground shifted under Chance's chair, and he could hear a rumbling sound.

Chapter Three

Chance leapt out of his chair, spilling the goblet of cold fruit juice he had been about to drink down his front. He frantically looked this way and that, trying to figure out what to do and which way to go. It finally dawned on him that Keeper Odette was calmly sitting in her chair, and seemed not at all disturbed by the shaking ground or rumbling.

"Do not be alarmed, Chance. The shaking and rumbling is quite harmless. Just the islands readjusting themselves. Happens from time to time."

Chance did not look convinced. With great care he settled himself back in his chair. Keeper Odette handed him a small towel to wipe the spilled juice off his shirt as best he could.

"Again, I would suggest to you that a little ground shaking does not spell danger. If you stay as tense as you are now, you will surely twist yourself up in knots. Now then, I can understand that the news that you must remain with us for all of your days can be distressing, but it just cannot be helped. There is only one way into and out of this crater valley, and it is heavily guarded. Even if you could find your way to the sea and obtain a boat, the fog is impossible to get through without a guide. I am truly sorry, Chance. Know that we will do everything we can to try to make you feel welcome and comfortable here."

Chance sat back in his chair trying to relax, trying to absorb what Keeper Odette was saying to him. While Mako and Pivane had not succeeded in drowning him to get rid of him, they had still been successful. He was still being prevented from the task he had been charged with. To complete his task, he needed to get back to Sommerhjem. What had started out to be a grand adventure with sailing to Sommerhjem, carrying out his task, and becoming a hero to his family and the land of his birth, was not turning out to be so grand. An adventure to be sure, but certainly the grandness was greatly diminished.

He had to get out of here. By the time word got back to his family that he had disappeared, all might be lost. He had crewed on one of the last ships to leave Havkoller before the storm season. They would not expect to hear from him until spring, and by then, it might be too late to send one of his brothers or sisters to take his place. Now all he had to do, while sitting here sipping fruit juice, was to determine how very brave he was.

"If I have not done so before, I thank you for rescuing me from certain death by drowning. I can hear the sincerity in your voice when you said that you would try to make me feel welcome and comfortable," stated Chance.

"Why do I feel like I hear a 'but' coming on?" Keeper Odette asked. "Not, mind you, that I am surprised. Be assured that all who come to be with us always feel that theirs is a good reason why we should just send them off on their merry way. You are no exception. Again, let me reiterate that the way out of here involves great risk. I urge you to just take a deep breath and accept your fate. You need to give us a chance."

Could Chance tell this woman that the future of Sommerhjem depended on him? That sounded melodramatic even in his own head. All of a sudden, Chance was immensely tired and completely overwhelmed. His tutor had always told him that sometimes he needed to gather as many facts as possible before trying to solve a difficult problem. Good advice, Chance thought to himself. He needed to get the lay of the land, get more information about who lived in the crater, and if there was any way at all to get out of here besides risking his life in some rite of passage.

Chance spent the next several days learning about what would be his new home if he could not find a way out. The folks were friendly and did try to make him feel welcome. Nights were the hardest, for lying in the dark alone gave him way too much time to either be mad at himself for bungling the task he was charged with or being overwhelmingly homesick.

When he had been on the island for a week, he was informed that Keeper Odette wished to meet with him right after breakfast. He was instructed to meet her at the spot where they had first talked. Chance found he was a little nervous concerning the meeting, but could not quite figure out why.

"Now that you have had an opportunity to settle in a bit, we need to discuss your future here. While nature provides an abundance of food so we have substance for our bellies, everyone needs something to occupy their hands and minds. What skills have you acquired in your young life?" Keeper Odette inquired. "Were you apprenticed?"

"In a sense. My family owns and runs trading ships between the islands of Havkoller. I crewed on my sister's ship and was learning the trade."

"Was this what you wished to do?"

Chance needed to think about how to answer Keeper Odette's question. He had followed his brothers and sisters into the family trade because it seemed the thing to do at the time. None of them knew how long they would be in Havkoller since it was not the home of their birth. His family needed to earn a living and trading was what they knew. While the family business had been successful, he knew his parents and older siblings longed to return home to Sommerhjem. They had had such hope when they had heard the Regent had been forced to step down. Even so, they were realistic enough to know that the danger was not over for members of the Høyttaier clan.

"Chance? Chance?" Keeper Odette called.

Chance started and pulled himself back to the present. "I'm sorry. I was just thinking."

"Thinking is always good. It must have been very deep thought, for you seemed to be miles away. Now my question concerned whether you had wanted to become a trader. Did you see being a trader as something you wanted to do for all of your life?"

"No," Chance said, so softly Keeper Odette almost did not hear his answer. "No," Chance said, with a bit more conviction.

"Let me try another question. If you could choose any way to make a living, any way at all, what would you choose?"

"No one has ever asked me that question. Before we left Sommerhjem, I thought I might want to be a seeker. I really like puzzles and mysteries to solve. Knowing the why of things, but that was just a young lad's dream." And one that will never become reality unless I can get off this island, Chance thought to himself.

"How interesting. I imagine you are thinking to yourself that that option is now null and void since your area to travel as a seeker is severely limited. Perhaps not. Come with me."

Keeper Odette led Chance down a side path he had not noticed before. Coming out of the dense foliage, Chance found himself looking at a low stone building that was built right into the side of the crater wall. There were tables and chairs set out in front of the building. Upon closer inspection, Chance could see that the tables more resembled desks. He looked at Keeper Odette inquiringly.

"This building houses all of the knowledge that has been gathered over many years by many people. I am the present Keeper here, charged with maintaining the old knowledge. Much of what is here has been recovered from ships lost in the fog of the Shadow Islands, and much comes from those who have come here to live out their lives with us. We have recorded each of their tales. Seekers spend their lives trying to gather and hold the old knowledge and find that which is lost. You need to do nothing more than walk through that door, and there is a lifetime of work awaiting you."

"Why do you call yourself a keeper? Are you really not a seeker?" asked Chance.

"That is a good question. My task is to make sure the form which holds the knowledge does not deteriorate, fall apart, or get chewed on by mice or bugs. I make sure that the knowledge is preserved in its original form. If it comes to us damaged, then I may have to copy it into a new form. You have to have a flair for tedious detail to do a keeper's job. Each day I hope one of the other residents will want to take up that task with me. Maybe one of the children. Alas, I do not think it is your calling."

Chance felt that Keeper Odette was probably right. While it might be interesting to learn how to preserve old parchment and books, he would find the exacting work tedious after a time. Having a chance to delve into what was preserved was another matter entirely. For a brief moment, Chance let himself think about what it might be like to have the opportunity to look at what was housed in the building in front of him. Then reality came crashing back. He needed to get away from here. He needed to get back to Sommerhjem.

A new thought occurred to Chance. Perhaps there were maps or other information on how he could leave this crater and make it out to open water. He had nothing to lose but time by entering this building and checking out what was stored within. With that idea in mind, Chance followed Keeper Odette inside.

What struck Chance first was the amount of light in the large room they had entered. He looked up thinking there must be skylights, or a glass dome, but saw neither. What he did see were irregular openings in the ceiling through which light poured.

"I see you have noticed our lighting system. Most ingenious. Because of the occasional shaking of the land, glass windows would be both impractical and dangerous. Imagine sitting under one of those openings during a ground quake. No, not a very good idea. Some clever folk a long time past figured out a way of using a shiny metal tube and a very hard crystal lens. You would have to ask someone more knowledgeable than I how that all works. Follow me, please. The archives are through this door here. Because they are stored in the dry cave system inside the crater wall, most all of what we have here stays pretty well preserved. Is there anything in particular you are interested in?"

Maps that will show me the way out, Chance thought, but said instead that he was interested in ancient writings. Keeper Odette lit a lantern and led him down a branch off the main corridor.

"Here you will find books, parchments, old ships' logs, and other material dating back hundreds of years. You are welcome to take any material out to the main room, or outside in good weather for that matter. Many of the items here are in languages I have no knowledge of, nor do others here. Are you versed in ancient languages?"

Chance did not know what to tell Keeper Odette. How had he not thought through his answer to her when she had asked what he was interested in? What would happen if he just boldly said that yes, he was versed in at least one ancient language and was a member of the Høyttaier clan. He did not know enough about the folk here to trust them with that knowledge.

Just then someone hailed Keeper Odette and she excused herself, saying over her shoulder as she departed, "Good seeking, Chance. Who knows what you will find."

Since it was not going to look right if Chance immediately left the shelves he was standing by to wander about the corridors looking for maps, he thought he might as well spend some time looking at what was in front of him. The shelves stretched quite a ways back so he pulled a book out at random. It looked to be a ship's log. The date on it indicated it was from about thirty years prior, but it was in a language Chance had never seen. Certainly not one he was familiar with. He closed that book and moved farther down the shelves, pulling books here and there at random, and checking their contents. Sometimes he got intrigued by what the author had written and had to force himself to close the book and move on.

Chance jumped in surprise when someone tapped him on the shoulder. Turning, he saw the Keeper was standing behind him. Just as he was about to say something, his stomach growled quite loudly.

"Ah, I could have saved myself a trip for your stomach is giving you the message that I was about to deliver. It is way past mealtime, and you should pull your head out of that book and follow me. It will all be here after you have eaten."

When Chance stepped outside, he was surprised to note by the position of the sun how much time had passed since he had followed Keeper Odette into the archives. How had he let that happen? He had wasted hours when he should have been doing something to find a way off the island. Chance found he had lost his appetite. He excused himself and began to walk, not choosing any destination in particular, but letting his feet take him where they would. The crater valley was quite large and he certainly had not explored all of it.

Chance was so lost in thought and angry at himself that he did not notice right away that he had wandered into a grove of enormous quirrelit trees. Suddenly, he felt a whack at the back of his head and spun around to see he had been hit by a low-hanging branch. What Chance could not figure out was how the branch, which he had ducked under and passed beyond, could then hit him on the back of his head. Staring at the branch, which was still quivering slightly, Chance caught movement out of the corner of his eye.

Chapter Four

Chance's curiosity was piqued by the quick glimpse he had had of what he thought was a furred animal with a ringed tail. He had seen it so briefly, because it had darted away so fast through the overhead branches, that he could not be sure. His thoughts soon turned back to his continued worries. As enticing as the archives were, he could not let himself be distracted from his primary goal again. Chance needed to get off the island, away from the Shadow Islands all together, and back to Sommerhjem.

When word had come to Havkoller that the Regent had been forced to step down because the Gylden Sirklene challenge had been called, word also reached Chance's family that one of their clan had been present. The Book of Rules governing the challenge had been produced and translated. That certainly had lessened the overt reason the Regent might still seek out Chance's family. However, besides his family being keepers of the old language, as were other members of the Høyttaier clan, they also were the keepers of one of the nine pieces of the oppgave ringe, a small misshapen gold ring with irregular markings. All nine pieces of the oppgave ringe needed to be in the capital city of Sommerhjem a year from the day the challenge had been called.

When Chance's family had left Sommerhjem to escape the hunt for those of their clan ordered by the Regent, his father had determined that the piece of the oppgave ringe had to be left behind. It would not do, he had said, if the ring were misplaced or lost on the voyage to Havkoller. Chance's father had put the ring in a safe place. It was Chance's task to retrieve the ring and get it to the capital city of Sommerhjem. The urgency of that task came crashing down once again on Chance. He felt like such a failure. It was one thing to let himself down, but he had let his family and the country of his birth down as well. An overwhelming sadness began to weigh him down, and he tilted his head back to rest on the trunk of the tree he was sitting under. The stress and strain of near drowning, being told he was trapped forever on the Shadow Islands, and feeling like a colossal failure had taken its toll. Soon Chance was asleep.

As Chance slowly became aware of his surroundings once again, a slight weight pressed on his chest, and something tickled him alongside his face. He was afraid to move. Though no one had warned him of any dangerous creatures living in the crater valley, he was going to take no chances. During his sleep, his head had tilted forward, with his chin coming to rest on his chest. Slowly, Chance opened his eyes and glanced down. Staring up at him were two huge gold-colored, black-ringed eyes which almost overwhelmed a small red furred face. Pointed tufted ears on the top of the animal's head twitched several times. A longer look revealed that the animal was clinging to his shirt front with small hands and feet. Chance could just make out that it was probably the animal's ringed tail which was tickling the side of his face.

Chance had never seen an animal like this one. Not on any of the Havkoller Islands, or that he could recall, in Sommerhjem. He did not know if he was looking at a young one or a fully grown adult. He did not know if he should be worried that it would attack or just what would happen when he needed to move, for he could not remain still forever. When he looked back into the animal's eyes, Chance had the strangest feeling that he was being laughed at. In the next moment, the animal bared its teeth, and Chance could only hope he was being smiled at, for those teeth looked wickedly sharp. The animal then reached up with its small hand, patted Chance on the cheek twice, quickly climbed up Chance's shirt, leapt to the tree trunk, and in a flash was gone. Chance looked and looked, but he could not spot the ring-tailed animal anywhere in the trees.

After the strange encounter with the animal, Chance wandered back toward the archives, hoping to find Keeper Odette. He felt more comfortable with her than the others who lived on the island. Luck was with him, for he found her sitting outside of the archives, having what appeared to be an afternoon tea. She waved him over.

"Care to join me?" Keeper Odette inquired.

It occurred to Chance that he was now quite hungry, and so he sat down and helped himself. For some reason, he felt more at peace and refreshed since his short nap. He could not understand why. He had certainly not been either at peace or relaxed before he had gone into the quirrelit grove.

"I see you have been in the quirrelit grove," Keeper Odette suggested.

Chance looked at her in amazement. How had she known, he wondered.

Keeper Odette laughingly explained. "No, I am not clairvoyant, nor can I read minds. It is just that you have several pieces of quirrelit bark in your hair. Quite fetching really." When Chance looked appalled and quickly ran his fingers through his hair, Keeper Odette began to apologize. "I hope I have not offended you. Is it a custom, then, to wear bark in your hair in the Havkoller Islands?"

"No, not a custom. I was just embarrassed that I didn't notice." Chance quickly changed the subject. "I was wondering about something. May I ask you a question?"

"You are welcome to ask. I do not guarantee that I will have an answer."

"While in the quirrelit grove, I saw an animal that I have never seen before. It was small . . ." and Chance held out his hands to show what size he meant. ". . . reddish fur, golden eyes with a mask of black around them, ringed tail, and paws more like hands. Do you know what it is?"

"You must have gotten quite a glimpse of one of the halekrets. We know they live in the quirrelit grove, but they are rarely seen. Very shy animals. I think in all my years, I have caught sight of one of the halekrets only a half dozen times."

"Are they native to the Shadow Islands? I have never heard of halekrets either in Sommerhjem or Havkoller."

"I am not sure I can answer that question. They are not found on any of the other islands, and I have not found any record of them in the archives earlier than a couple of hundred years ago. I would be happy to show you what I have found, if you would like."

"I would like that very much," replied Chance.

Keeper Odette was glad to see the lad become interested in something. She always worried about those new to the islands. While she had no desire to be anywhere else but where she was presently, she knew that the loss of home, friends, and family weighed heavily on the newly arrived. Chance had been no exception.

"Grab the tea tray and follow me. I can show you where you can begin your education about the halekrets."

Chance picked up the tea tray, being careful not to bump into anything that would send the teapot and cups crashing to the ground. He was relieved, when once inside the archives, he was directed to set the tray down on a table just inside the door. He then followed Keeper Odette down a different corridor and into a fair-sized room filled with floor-to-ceiling bookshelves.

"What little information there is about the halekrets can be found in one of the journals on this shelf. One of the folk here took an interest in them about two hundred years back. Not much information, I am afraid," Keeper Odette stated regretfully. "Here, this one has something about halekrets in it."

"May I take the journal outside?"

"You are welcome to do so. Just make sure you put it back where you found it when you are finished for the day. I'll just leave you to it then."

Chance nodded to Keeper Odette absentmindedly, for he was already walking and beginning to read the first page in the journal. He had to stop reading for a few minutes because he had gotten himself turned around in the archives by not watching where he was going. Once he found his way outside, he sat down at the nearest table and began to read once more. By the time it had begun to be too dark for Chance to read, he knew a great deal about the writer of the journal and only a little more about the halekrets. Keeper Odette had been mistaken that the slim journal was a study about halekrets, but it had intrigued Chance enough that he had continued to read.

It seemed the writer of the journal, one Laron Karmoris, had been the black sheep youngest son of very major merchant family. He had been of a more scholarly bent than the other members of his family and had little interest in the family's merchant company. His father's solution to his love of books and learning was to apprentice him to the company bookkeeper. Spending day after day inside pouring over dry account books had driven the journal writer to desperation. Facing a life of living under his father's thumb and the daily dullness of looking at bills and accounts, Laron had chosen to run away from home and seek adventure.

Chance could certainly relate to the writer of the journal, and the irony of the similarities did not escape him. He thought he might have liked and have become friends with Laron if he had met him. In his journal, Laron had gone on to describe how he had ended up in the Shadow Islands. On a rare day off from the family company, he had packed his small skiff with the intent to run away and seek his fortune. The morning he left had been bright and clear. Unfortunately, he had been caught in a freak summer squall, which had blown him out to sea and shredded his sail. His small boat had been tossed about for several days before the storm blew itself out. After that, the currents had finally taken him to the Shadow Islands. In retrospect, it had been a really foolish idea, Laron had written. He suggested he probably would have returned home in a few days, if he had not been caught by the summer storm.

Laron went on to describe his gratitude at being rescued by the folks who lived on the Shadow Islands. When told he could not return to Sommerhjem, he had had mixed feelings of guilt and relief. Laron wrote of how he had found the archives to be a place where his scholarly yearnings were happily fulfilled.

Most of the rest of the slim journal was filled with notes about Laron's early life in the valley. It was in this part Chance found the information about the halekrets. It seemed the animals were not native to the islands, and according to information Laron had obtained from old timers in the crater valley, the halekrets had first been spotted in the quirrelit grove not many years before Laron's arrival. No one knew how they had arrived there, or exactly when. The halekrets, from what anyone could tell Laron, were extremely shy and avoided folks completely. They seemed to subsist on fruit, nuts, berries, and grain. The rest of what Laron had written was about the physical description of halekrets, which matched what Chance had seen.

There was more to the journal, but the light for reading by was gone, so Chance stood up and stretched. He had become stiff sitting on the hard bench and reading. Tempted though he was to move inside and read by lamplight, Chance went and put the journal back where he had found it. Sensing that the archives were empty, Chance lit a lamp and began to wander the corridors hoping he might find a room that had maps. What his wandering did teach him was the archives were far bigger than he had imagined. Disheartened that he had not discovered a map room, Chance felt some comfort in the knowledge that if he were to be stuck in this valley for the rest of his life, he would at least have the archives to fill his days. He could be like Laron and keep a journal. Maybe he could add to the knowledge about halekrets.

That night while Chance lay in bed, he began to think about what he had read. The name Karmoris sounded very familiar to Chance. Where had he heard it before? The answer did not come before he fell asleep, but when he awoke, he remembered. When he had been very young, his great grandfather had been alive and had lived with his family. It had been Chance's duty to spend time each day with his great grandfather while everyone else in the family was busy with company business. Chance had never minded, for his great grandfather was often more in the past than in the present, and Chance had been fascinated by the stories his great grandfather told. He had talked about the great merchant families, and that is where he had heard the Karmoris name before.

Chance really had to think back as to what his great grandfather had said about the Karmorises. He knew they were not among the great merchant families now. His great grandfather had told him that the head of the family had made some very bad decisions, which had severely reversed the fortunes of the family. In trying to recoup the family fortunes, his sons had taken up smuggling and had not been very successful, for all had been caught and punished. There were a few members of that once great family left, but they no longer had much wealth or position. No wait, Chance thought. There was one daughter who had married well, and her branch of the family had been a little more successful.

Chance did not know why this obscure piece of information mattered, and so got out of bed. After a quick breakfast, he headed back to the archives. Maybe today he would be more successful. Again the archives appeared empty, so Chance thought he would continue to search for a room or shelves that held maps. He surprised himself when instead of exploring new corridors, he headed toward the shelf that held the slim journal he had been reading the day before. Chance rationalized his actions by telling himself that he was just going to take another look to see if he had missed any references to halekrets. When he sat down outside to finish reading the journal, he found he was less looking for information on halekrets and more curious about what Laron Karmoris had felt guilty about.

Reading through the last pages of the journal told Chance no more about either halekrets or what Laron felt guilty about. As he was about to close the book and put it back, Chance noticed part of the back cover had peeled away from its binding. He wondered if he should find Keeper Odette and mention it to her, since she seemed to be the one who kept the material in the archives in good repair. Curiosity got the better of his good intentions however, and Chance gently lifted the corner that was loose. Inside was a folded piece of paper.

Chapter Five

Chance quickly checked around to see if anyone was nearby and watching him. Not seeing anyone, he carefully worked the folded piece of paper out. Just then, Keeper Odette hailed him from down the path. Chance quickly and surreptitiously tucked the folded piece of paper into his pocket. Keeping his head down, he slowly closed the journal and pretended he had not heard Keeper Odette. When she called again, he raised his head and waved. He did not know why he had taken the paper out of the journal, nor could he explain to himself why he did not want Keeper Odette to know about it.

"Did you find what you wanted to know about halekrets in the journal?" Keeper Odette asked.

"I found a little information, but not much. I thought I would go try to see if I could see one again today." Now, why have I not told Keeper Odette about my close encounter with the halekrets yesterday, Chance wondered to himself.

"I wish you luck with that. Like I said, they are rarely seen, but you can give it a try. I am never one to discourage learning and discovery. I just wanted you to know I will be off island for a few days. Feel free to visit the archives as much as you wish."

"Th-th-thank you for that," Chance replied, stumbling over his words.

After getting over his amazement that folks could leave the crater valley at will, Chance then called himself a dunderhead. Of course, the trusted folks who had grown up here traveled from island to island. He wondered if someone like himself would ever be trusted enough to be given the knowledge of how to travel off the island. It then occurred to Chance that with Keeper Odette gone, he would not have to worry so much about where he was found in the archives.

"I need to excuse myself, for I have a great deal to do in the archives this afternoon. I can put that journal back for you," Keeper Odette offered.

"No, I need to get in the habit of returning things to where I found them," Chance told Keeper Odette.

His reasoning sounded good, but he just did not want Keeper Odette to discover the loose flap on the back cover of the journal. He felt even more guilty when she told him that his actions were very commendable. Chance had always been honest with himself and in his dealing with others, yet here he had taken something out of the journal and intended to take it away from the archives. In addition, he had not told Keeper Odette about the damage to the journal and had covered that up with politeness. His guilt followed him all the way to the quirrelit grove.

Once in the grove, Chance headed back to where he had been sitting the day before. He was glad when he made it under the branch that had previously whacked him on the back of the head without further injury or insult. Once he made himself comfortable, Chance glanced around to see if he could catch a glimpse of any of the halekrets. Nothing stirred in the foliage. Reaching into his pocket, Chance took out the folded note he had taken from the journal. He was very careful opening the note, for it looked to be as old as the journal and was extremely brittle. He was afraid he would damage it. Once he had the note opened, Chance gently smoothed it out on his pant leg.

His first reaction after reading the note was to laugh. Here he was, trapped on an island with the knowledge of where to find one of the rings of the oppgave ringe, and now, he had what appeared to be the beginning clue of where to find a second one. There was considerable irony in the situation.

The note, written by Laron Karmoris, was a confession. In the note Laron stated he had taken the oppgave ringe piece out of the secret compartment built into the parlor fireplace in the family home located in the seacoast town of Willing. He had learned about the ring when his father had shown it to his older brother. His father was bestowing the knowledge of a family secret on his older brother, but not on him. Laron confessed that that act, which he had accidentally witnessed, had made him angry. He had felt left out. In a rash moment, Laron had taken the ring. When he had gone to Tårnklokke to visit his older sister, he had hidden the ring. He had figured that when the ring was discovered missing, his older brother might get the blame.

Laron went on to confess in his note that he felt great remorse. When he had taken ring, it had been just an immature lapse of judgment. He felt if he had not been stranded on the Shadow Islands, when he had grown older and smarter he probably would have fetched the ring and returned it, with no one the wiser. At least he hoped that would have been the case. Laron had then written in his note that he was leery of telling anyone straight out where he had hidden the ring, so he was leaving a clue in the form of a riddle.

Chance thought the clue was, at the very least, a very bad rhyming verse. The note read:

As the clock strikes the midday hour,
Before the cat can devour the mouse,
Slip unnoticed into the musical tower,
And snatch the clue from inside the mouse's house.

Chance just sat there staring at the note, and then he began to laugh. The joke had to be on him. Here he thought he had found a real clue to the location of one of the pieces of the oppgave ringe, but this Laron fellow must have been bonkers. Or maybe he just went bonkers trapped here on this island with no way out. Was that what was going to happen to him, Chance wondered.

A great weight seemed to settle on Chance's shoulders. If even a little part of Laron's note was true, if he really had taken and hidden one of the rings before he was lost from Sommerhjem, then would it really make any difference whether Chance ever left the island? Even if he could get off the island and retrieve his family's piece of the oppgave ringe, it wouldn't matter. All nine pieces had to be found and brought to the capital before the end of next summer. How was anyone ever going to discover what had happened to Laron's family's piece of the oppgave ringe?

Would Chance's family find out that Chance had been unsuccessful and have time to send another member of his family from Havkoller in time? What difference would it all make now? He should just resign himself to his fate and get on with his life here. No more looking for a way out.

Chance was tired, so very tired and discouraged, that he just slumped down where he was sitting and let his mind go blank. He soon drifted off into an uneasy, troubled sleep. Chance began to dream of Sommerhjem, but not the one he remembered from before his family left. This Sommerhjem was a dark, dismal place filled with the stench of burnt-out buildings and fear. As he walked down the streets of the town of his dream, folks huddled in doorways, and no one would meet his eyes. As he glanced around in his dream, he saw shattered glass from broken windows littering the streets. Shutters on buildings were askew, window boxes empty or filled with debris. A glance down a side alley showed Chance several folks huddled around a small fire. He did not even want to think about what he glimpsed they were roasting over the fire.

Chance walked another block, stepping carefully over garbage and around a broken-down cart. No children could be seen playing in the road, no old men sitting outside shops swapping tales. Chance would catch furtive movement out of the corner of his eye, but when he turned to look, he could not spot anyone. When he came to a deserted crossroads, Chance stopped. It was then he became aware of the sound of boots marching. At the same time, he realized what little life he had seen on the mostly deserted road had vanished. The stomping of boots became louder and louder, closer and closer. Everything inside Chance was screaming that he should run, but he found his feet frozen to the road.

A voice in Chance's head was telling him he had to move, move now. He needed to find safety, he needed to find home. It was time, time, time. You can't stay here. You must go, go now, the voice kept urging him over and over, telling him he had to move, and move quickly. The sound of stomping feet kept getting louder and louder, closer and closer. Chance's heart began to pound in his chest, thump, thump, thump, matching the sound of the pounding boots. He turned and frantically looked this way and that, not knowing which direction to go, which direction was the way to safety. One moment it sounded like the marchers were coming from behind him, the next moment it sounded like they were coming from the right. They kept coming closer and closer, and still his feet were frozen to the road.

Suddenly, Chance's fear shifted to anger. His dream of this strange and frightening Sommerhjem became mixed up with the present. He was tired of being at the mercy of others. First, Mako and Pivane had snatched him off the streets of Marinel and left him to drown. Then, Keeper Odette had welcomed him to the crater valley but told him he could never leave. Oh, he could leave, but only by going through a rite of passage, which would most probably result in his death. In his dream, Chance turned and faced the direction he thought he heard the loudest stomping coming from. No more letting others control his life. No more letting his family down. He would find a way off this island, through the fog to open water. He would find his way to Sommerhjem. He would retrieve the ring and get it to the capital.

With great determination, Chance began pulling himself awake and out of the dream. The sound of stomping boots began to retreat, and the last thing Chance remembered from his dream, before he awoke, was the sight of a single flower blooming in an otherwise empty window box.

The cool breeze that caressed Chance's face felt good. He realized he was very hot and sweaty, and was just about to reach into his pocket for a handkerchief, when he froze. Sitting across from him was a halekrets watching him. Chance did not know if this halekrets was the same one he had encountered the day before, or if it was a different one. Chance kept still, and out of the corner of his eye, he caught movement. Another halekrets moved into his line of vision and came to stand next to the halekrets in front of him. This one was taller and bigger, standing almost a foot tall.

When the third halekrets came to stand with the other two, Chance got the distinct impression he was being looked over and measured. Not measured as to his height or weight, not that kind of measured. It was as if the halekrets were judging him. Some of the anger left over from the dream began to well inside of him. He was torn. Did he give in to the anger or try to remain calm? He did not want to frighten the halekrets, for who knew what they would do? On the other hand, he did not like the feeling that he was being judged. It was like taking a test he did not know he was supposed to study for, Chance thought to himself.

Time ticked slowly by as Chance and the three halekrets stared at each other. Suddenly, the halekrets turned, and in a blink of an eye, they were up the tree trunk behind them and hidden by the foliage. After the halekrets had gone, Chance stood up, wondering what that meeting had been all about. What a strange afternoon it had been. As he dusted himself off, Chance reflected on the dream he had had. With renewed determination, he headed out of the quirrelit grove and made his way toward the crater wall. He was determined to find a way out of the crater valley.

By the time the sun had set, Chance was more discouraged than ever. He had checked out every cave opening, crack, and fissure along one section of the crater wall and had found no way out. After a quick evening meal, he headed toward the archives, determined to find where the maps were stored. Once again, he had no luck. The next two days followed the same routine. As long as it was light enough to see, Chance explored the crater walls. He came across several openings, but they led nowhere. He found one that was guarded. It certainly was the way to get out to the sea from the crater valley. Unfortunately, he had not come up with a reasonable idea of how to get past the guards. He thought of trying to befriend one of the guards, but while they were always polite and friendly, none of them seemed to invite a closer relationship. Chance also realized that if he were to try to follow any one of them, or was overly curious about their routines, they might notice.

As Chance worked his way along each section of the wall, he looked for a place he could climb to the top of the crater. After a while, he abandoned that idea, realizing that even if he did reach the top, who knew what was on the other side? There could be a sheer cliff or more rocks to scale down. If he reached the bottom and sea level once again, there was no guarantee he would find anything other than fog and water. It wasn't likely there would be a beach with a convenient boat tied up just waiting for him. In addition, there was still the problem of finding his way out of the fog.

Each day, once night fell, Chance returned to the archives and searched a new corridor or two, a new room or two. He had had no luck finding even one map, or even a reference to any maps. What he did discover in the archives made him long for the chance to spend hours there. Chance often found himself distracted by a volume here or a journal there. He would have to drag himself away and push himself to keep on searching for a way to leave the Shadow Islands.

By the third day, after Chance had been delving into every nook and cranny along new sections of the crater wall, he began to run out of determination, not to mention steam. Deciding he needed a break, Chance packed some food and headed toward the quirrelit grove. It was not as if the others who lived in the valley were not kind. They always tried to make him feel welcome at mealtime, but they were also content living in the crater valley. Chance just needed some time to think things through.

Chance needed to talk to Keeper Odette one more time about leaving the Shadow Islands. He needed to decide if he should tell her why he so desperately needed to leave. Maybe he could persuade her that he should be allowed to leave because he knew where to find one piece of the oppgave ringe, and quite possibly two. If she did not know what the oppgave ringe was and how important it was for selecting the next ruler of Sommerhjem, he would need to explain. He just had to convince her to let him leave and not have to go through the rite of passage. His leaving was too important to be delayed.

When Chance settled in to eat his midday meal, he was not surprised when one of the halekrets showed up. He thought it was the smallest of the three he had seen before, but could not be sure. Because Chance was feeling in a funny mood, he looked at the halekrets and said, "So, would you care to join me for the midday meal?"

Chapter Six

The halekrets tipped his head slightly to the left and just stared at Chance. Chance stared back. Then, the halekrets surprised Chance by cautiously moving forward, until he was just a foot away from where Chance sat.

"So, would you prefer some bread and cheese, or would you rather have some fruit?" Chance inquired, feeling very foolish talking to an animal.

To cover his embarrassment, Chance tore off a bit of bread, put it on a leaf, and set it on the ground in front of him. He also set a slice of fruit on a leaf. The halekrets quickly turned, jumped up onto the trunk of a nearby tree, and swiftly disappeared.

"Not to your liking, then?" Chance said, and found himself unexpectedly sad that the halekrets had left.

Just minutes later, the halekrets returned. He walked over to where Chance had set out the bread, cheese, and fruit, and set two nuts down on a leaf he had carried with him. The halekrets then picked up the bread and cheese and began to eat. Chance took a chance and reached down to pick up one of the nuts. The halekrets just kept on eating.

"I beg your pardon, I don't think we have been formally introduced. My name is Chance. What's your name?" Chance asked. The halekrets gave no answer. "I think I'll call you Ashu because you are so quick."

Since the halekrets did not seem to have an opinion one way or the other about a name, Chance addressed him as Ashu, and continued to carry on a one-sided conversation until all the food was gone. When the last small piece of bread had been eaten, Ashu brushed the crumbs off his fur, bobbed his head in Chance's direction, and once again swiftly departed.

"Thanks for joining me for a meal," Chance called after the halekrets. "How about joining me for the evening meal?"

The halekrets did not answer back. Feeling somewhat bemused by the encounter, Chance stood, brushed himself off, and headed back toward the cliff wall.

The afternoon brought no more success than the morning had, and Chance was very discouraged by late afternoon. He had been greeted by the others in the crater valley when he had come upon them. They were always polite, always friendly, and always helpful, but somehow distant. If he did not find a way off the island, he hoped he would be able to make some friends. Otherwise, it was going to be a lonely life, Chance reflected.

Since Chance really did not want to be with others, he once again packed a meal up and headed toward the quirrelit grove. He realized he felt more at peace in the grove. He also had to admit to himself that he really hoped Ashu would join him for the evening meal. He was delighted when he did. At least he thought the little halekrets was the same one he had shared lunch with.

Chance talked to Ashu during the meal, telling him all that had happened to him since he had left home. He even told Ashu why he needed to get away from the Shadow Islands and back to Sommerhjem. Ashu sat quietly and listened. When Chance finally wound down, he found he did not feel silly talking to the halekrets. He wanted to linger, but the sky had begun to darken, and Chance could smell the hint of rain on the wind. He thought if he hurried, he could get to the archives before the sky opened up.

Chance made it to the archives and slipped inside, determined to find maps. Though he searched and searched, shelf after shelf, room after room, he had no luck. Under other circumstances, he would have been delighted to spend hours studying what was contained in the archives, but a sense of urgency kept pushing him to keep looking for a way out of the crater valley during the day and for maps in the archives at night.

Chance's eyes began to burn from trying to read book titles by lamplight, and he felt so weary. Chance decided to give up his search for the night and head back to his quarters. Once he reached the archives' front door however, he almost changed his mind. A strong wind had blown in. Chance could hardly see a foot or two in front of his face through the torrential downpour. Faced with having to sleep on a hard bench in the archives for the night or rushing through the pouring rain, Chance just stood in the doorway, undecided.

In a few minutes the rain lessened, as squalls often do. Chance saw the break in the storm as the window of opportunity it was. He made a dash for his quarters and almost made it without getting drenched. Once he dried off and climbed into his sleeping hammock, Chance tried to stay awake, fearing the unsettling dreams would come again. He was asleep in minutes, but his was a troubled sleep.

In his sleep, Chance once again found himself in a dream of Sommerhjem. Dark clouds hung low over the landscape. It was early dawn, and at first, Chance thought he was in a winter woods but soon realized he was in a forest that had been ravaged by fire. As he walked in among the trees, he saw that the pines were just burnt spears. The other trees had fared no better. Dry burnt branches cracked underfoot. That was the only sound Chance heard. He did not hear the sounds of birds greeting the dawn. There were no sounds of smaller critters rustling through the leaves, but then there were no leaves to rustle through.

Chance walked farther and came upon a grove of quirrelit trees. Here too, there had been damage, but the grove had not been destroyed like the rest of the surrounding woods. When he entered the quirrelit grove, he found himself almost dropped to his knees by the overwhelming sense of sorrow he felt. Suddenly, he heard the flap of wings and looked up to see several scavenger birds silently circling overhead. Soon they were joined by more. They began to glide slowly down, heading straight toward him. They kept coming closer and closer, and Chance found his feet frozen to the forest path.

Once again, Chance's fear turned to anger. He yelled at the scavenger birds, "Not this time. You are not going to stop me. Not ever." Chance shook his fist at the birds. He reached down and grabbed up a stout branch of quirrelit wood, prepared to beat the birds off. Another part of Chance's mind began a second battle, trying to pull himself out of the dream and wake up.

Suddenly, Chance woke up covered in sweat, gripping something in his hands. He carefully sat up and swung his legs over the edge of his sleeping hammock. What he was holding felt like a walking stick, but that was impossible. He did not possess a walking stick. Carefully standing, Chance moved toward the small table to find and light the lamp. He was indeed holding a walking stick, a beautiful and intricately carved walking stick, made of quirrelit wood. Just as he held the walking stick closer to the lamplight to examine it, he caught a flash of movement out of the corner of his eye. When he turned, he thought he caught a glimpse of a small ringed tail.

Chance shrugged his shoulders, dismissing what he had seen, and went back to examining the walking stick. In his opinion, the walking stick was an old one, not one that had been freshly carved. It was in a pattern he was unfamiliar with. Someone had lovingly cared for the walking stick, for it was well oiled. Strangely enough, it felt like it had been made for him. Chance was abruptly jolted out of his thoughts by a very loud boom of thunder. Setting the walking stick aside, he crawled back into his sleeping hammock and tried to go to sleep.

For the next several days, Chance continued to walk the crater walls during the day and take his meals to the quirrelit grove. The halekrets he thought was the one he had named Ashu joined him for his meals. He no longer felt foolish sharing his meals or his thoughts with the little animal. Each evening, Chance explored more of the archives, but with little success. He wondered what had happened to Keeper Odette, but then maybe her definition of being gone for several days was different from Chance's idea of the word 'several'.

Chance stayed later and later in the archives each night, for he had begun to dread bedtime. He knew he could not stay up night after night and avoid sleeping. Every night, his dreams had been filled with fearful images of a Sommerhjem so very different from the one of his memories. One night he dreamed he was in a fishing village, but the small fishing boats were all pulled up on the beach, large holes in the sides of every boat. The village was deserted except for a few old men. Another night, he was in a mine, chained to a line of very small men and women, being forced hour after hour to swing a pickax, chipping away rock. That morning he had awakened to the sound of metal on rock ringing in his ears. In the middle of another night, he pulled himself out of a dream shaking, for he had dreamt about starving children on farms because all that the farmers raised was harvested and carted away, leaving only the spoiled and rotten produce for the farmers' families. What had pulled him out of that troubled sleep was the image of being chased across a stubbled wheat field by a group of hooded horsemen.

Each morning, Chance dragged himself out of his sleeping hammock, finding himself more and more angry and determined. In each dream he found himself turning back on whomever or whatever was chasing him and declaring he was not going to be stopped. The images from his dreams haunted him during the day. The only peace he found was in the quirrelit grove, where he continued to share his meals with the little halekrets.

Late at night on the evening she returned, Keeper Odette found Chance asleep in the archives. His head was cradled in his arms, resting on the desktop. The lamp was sputtering and had almost burned out. She had heard the concern about Chance in the voices of several of the valley folk. As soon as she had been able, she had gone looking for him. She was worried that they were going to lose him. She had been informed that he had been spending his days searching the crater wall for a way out and his evenings in the archives. It concerned her that he had withdrawn from having meals with the others. They mentioned that the lad did not look like he was sleeping well. Keeper Odette had seen others follow the same pattern. Almost all had chosen to go through the rite of passage. Only a few had survived. This Chance lad was so young, too young to lose his life. There was nothing she could do to prevent him from choosing the rite of passage. She was bound by tradition and rules. The Shadow Islands' history had proven that exceptions to the rules endangered them all.

Chance came awake with a start in response to a hand gently shaking his shoulder. "Just five more minutes, okay? It's too early to get up."

"You might want to try those five more minutes and the rest of the night sleeping in your own hammock," suggested Keeper Odette.

"Oh, ah, I must have fallen asleep," Chance replied, hoping he had not been caught drooling on the book he had been reading.

"You should go and finish your sleep. Join me in the morning for breakfast, if you would."

"Yes, ma'am." Chance rubbed the sleep out of his eyes and stood up. "I'll just put this book back and be on my way."

"Just this once, I think you can let me take care of the book and the lamp. Go on with you now." Keeper Odette could only shake her head as she watched Chance stumble and weave wearily down the hall out of the archives.

When Chance awoke in the morning, he remembered that he was supposed to meet Keeper Odette for breakfast. He felt less weary, for surprisingly, the rest of his night had not been filled with dark and frightening dreams. He found himself anxious to talk to Keeper Odette, and yet reluctant. He had awakened knowing he could not stay on the Shadow Islands for the rest of his life. He did not know what his dreams had meant, but his determination had grown each successive morning. He would not be able to live with himself if he did not try to determine his own fate.

It was not until breakfast was over that Keeper Odette asked Chance to join her in a stroll. "We can walk and talk. I feel you have had some very troublesome days while I have been away."

Chance was not sure just what he was going to say before he opened his mouth, but once he started talking, his wants and feelings all came tumbling out. "I have to leave here. My family sent me to retrieve one of the pieces of the oppgave ringe, and I cannot fail in my task. You have to let me leave. Just tell the guards to let me out of the crater. All I need is a small boat and a way out of the fog. I promise not to tell anyone what I have learned about this valley."

"Ah, Chance, what a burden you carry. I know of what happened in Sommerhjem this summer and appreciate how vital it is for you to be able to complete your task."

"Then you'll let me go? No going through some rite of passage?"

"I would if I could, but I am bound by a set of rules."

Chance came to a halt, as did Keeper Odette. He drew himself up. Hoping his voice sounded steadier than he felt, he addressed her. "It is with respect that I request to be allowed to leave this island. If the only way to leave is to choose to go through a rite of passage, then I choose to do so."

"It is your right to choose the rite of passage. Is there any way I can dissuade you from your choice?"

"No, ma'am. I have to leave."

"So be it then. We will meet tonight at the quirrelit grove after the evening meal. Take the day to prepare yourself. May luck ride your shoulder tonight, young man."

After Chance left Keeper Odette, he had gone back to his quarters. He was a little shaken that his request to go through the rite of passage had been set for this night. He had thought, well, he didn't know what he had thought. His course was set now, and there was no putting off what was to come next.

Chance spent a few short moments packing his sea bag, for he had so little to pack. He wanted to have everything ready. At the last moment, he remembered the walking stick and laid it across his sea bag. Chance looked around his living quarters one last time and then left. He had decided if he was to have only one day left in his short life, he would spend it in the quirrelit grove with what he considered his only friend in the crater valley.

Chapter Seven

Dinner was a quiet affair. Folks on the island had undergone others choosing to go through the rite of passage before. They were respectful, and when the meal was over, many came by the table and wished him luck.

"It is time, Chance," Keeper Odette stated. "No one will think less of you if you want to change your mind."

"Thank you for your kindness and for leaving the door open, so to speak, for me to not go tonight. I will not be changing my mind. I know this is something I have to do. So, what happens next?"

"You will need to leave your possessions with me. I will take care of them until you return. Do you have your things gathered and packed?"

"Yes, they are still at my quarters. I'll go get them."

"One more thing. You are allowed to take one thing with you, as long as it is not a knife or a weapon. Many take a talisman or something that is special to them. I will wait for you here."

When Chance returned to where Keeper Odette was waiting, he realized he had one more important question.

"Keeper Odette, I have a request."

"Yes, Chance. What do you wish?"

"If I do not return, will you get a message to my family? Will you let them know I'm gone? I know this is a lot to ask. I don't want to put any of you in jeopardy. Maybe you would just let them know I drowned. Would you do that? Please. I don't want them to wonder."

Keeper Odette almost did not hear Chance's request, for she was looking at the intricately carved walking stick he carried. She had seen only two others of its like. One had been carried by her older sister when she had chosen to leave their island home, more years ago than Keeper Odette wished to count.

"Keeper Odette?"

"What? I apologize. I am sorry. Yes, we will try to get word to your family if you do not make it through the rite of passage. Of course, we will let your family know. We are not cruel folk, Chance. Protective of what we hold in trust here, that much is true, but not intentionally cruel."

While Keeper Odette had been speaking, half a dozen other islanders had gathered. They formed up in two lines with Keeper Odette and Chance at the rear.

"It is time, Chance," stated Keeper Odette. "Do you remember the instructions I gave you over dinner?"

"Yes, ma'am. Once we are where the rite of passage is to take place, and after all of you leave, I'm to collect the pack of food and the water skin you have left for me, and then begin following the path that will open up before me. I don't really understand what is going to happen after that."

"And I cannot tell you. I am sorry. Do you need more time?"

"No, I'm ready," replied Chance. He was surprised that his voice held steady. He was also surprised that he really did feel ready, that his choice was the right one.

"If you are sure then, we need to head into the quirrelit grove now."

Chance nodded his head, and the procession went into the quirrelit grove. He realized that, other than the sound of soft footfalls, the grove was very, very quiet and still. It was so different from how it had been earlier in the day when he had sat and talked to Ashu. To be more accurate, when he had talked at Ashu. Chance felt a sudden pang of loss. He was going to miss the little halekrets.

Chance's attention was brought back to the present when he noticed the group had turned onto a path he had never noticed before. It surprised him, for he felt he had already walked every path and lane in the whole crater valley. The path wound its way around quirrelit trees, never going in a straight line. Finally, the group arrived at the base of a huge quirrelit trunk that had grown flush with the crater wall. The six members of the group ahead of Chance and Keeper Odette parted, forming a corridor. Keeper Odette motioned for Chance to wait, and she stepped forward.

He did not see what she did, but a section of the tree trunk swung open, creating a doorway.

"It is time, Chance. From here on, you must go alone. Or perhaps not," Keeper Odette said, unable to keep the surprise out of her voice.

After the door had swung open, Chance gripped the walking stick tighter and was preparing to move forward when he felt the walking stick shift slightly. He looked down just in time to see a little halekrets begin to climb up the walking stick. In less than a blink of an eye, the halekrets was sitting on Chance's shoulder, his ringed tail gently curled around Chance's neck.

If it had been quiet before in the quirrelit grove, it was unnervingly silent now. All seven of the folk who had accompanied Chance into the grove were now looking at him with a mix of emotions showing on their faces. Keeper Odette finally broke the silence. She spoke so quietly, as if to herself, and Chance was not sure exactly what she said. Something about it being a long, long time since one of the Neebing blessed had walked the paths of the valley. He did not know what she was talking about, or if it was a good or bad thing. It did not seem like it was a good time to ask.

The others in the group seemed to have shaken off their astonishment and had broken ranks. They were standing in a bunch, carrying on a whispered debate. Keeper Odette had to clear her throat several times to get their attention.

"I think we need to get back to the task at hand. Chance has chosen the rite of passage, and we need to let him get started," stated Keeper Odette quite firmly.

"But, Keeper Odette, there is no precedent for what to do concerning the halekrets on the lad's shoulder," one of the group suggested.

"Very true. I cannot recall there ever being any story or tale of a halekrets having anything to do with any of the folk here in the valley. In our lifetimes, most of us only catch a glimpse here and there. Amazing," Keeper Odette said, just shaking her head in wonder. "As to precedent, I feel the matter is moot. It looks like the halekrets has chosen to sit on Chance's shoulder, and I do not think it would be wise to try to remove him. Chance, do you have any explanation as to why one of the rare halekrets is sitting on your shoulder?"

"I don't. At least I don't have a way to explain why he is sitting on my shoulder any more than I can explain to you why he has chosen to spend part of each day with me. I think this is the halekrets I call Ashu."

A gasp was heard from one of the women who had been part of the escort, interrupting Chance from saying more. A quiet murmur ran through the group. Chance looked up to see what they were looking at. On the lower branches of the surrounding trees were eight more halekrets of various sizes. Two of the halekrets swiftly descended, walked toward Chance, and flanked him. Upon reaching him, the taller of the two halekrets took his hand and tugged him forward toward the opening in the tree trunk.

"I think precedent or no precedent really does not matter," Keeper Odette said, somewhat bemused. "It would seem Chance has a new escort."

Chance barely heard Keeper Odette wishing him luck. His whole focus had turned toward the opening in the tree trunk. He halted just at the opening, thinking that the halekrets would surely not be going to accompany him. The one sitting on his shoulder scrambled down the walking stick, but did not drop off. Instead, he reached out a hand and brushed it just under the eye of the halekrets who was standing next to the walking stick. Had the one Chance called Ashu just brushed away a tear on the face of the other halekrets, Chance wondered. The other halekrets, who had been standing a pace back, walked up to the one clinging to the walking stick. He reached out and patted the smaller halekrets on the cheek. The two bigger halekrets then stepped back. The little halekrets climbed back up the walking stick and resumed his seat on Chance's shoulder.

"Good luck to you, Chance, although I have a very strong suspicion you might literally have luck riding on your shoulder," Keeper Odette commented. "If the halekrets you call Ashu wishes to take this journey with you, it would appear to be his choice. You need but to step through the opening in the tree trunk. Your fate awaits. I hope I will see you again."

"I thank all of you for your kindness. I want you to know that my feeling so strongly that I have to leave is no reflection on anyone in this valley. I just know the right thing for me to do is to leave," Chance said sincerely.

There was just nothing more to say or do, and so Chance stepped through the opening with Ashu on his shoulder. When he looked back, he saw Keeper Odette and the others turn and walk away.

"Ashu," Chance addressed the halekrets, "you don't have to go through this rite of passage with me. It's kind of you to want to keep me company." He reached up as if to remove the little halekrets off his shoulder, but the halekrets just tightened his tail around Chance's neck. Hearing something just outside the opening, Chance saw the two bigger halekrets still standing there. They nodded their heads once, then turned, as if to leave.

"Wait, please. Please." Chance pleaded, not at all surprised that he thought the two before him would understand what he was saying. "I've told him he doesn't have to go. He seems to want to stay with me. I, well, I, well, thank you. I'll do my best to keep him safe."

The two halekrets looked at Chance and Ashu for a long moment, nodded again, and walked away.

"I guess this is it, Ashu. If you are going to insist on coming with me, we had better get started."

Remembering Keeper Odette's instructions, Chance looked around the inside of the quirrelit tree trunk, which seemed larger on the inside than it had appeared on the outside. Across from the opening, leaning against the far wall of the trunk, was a pack and a water skin. What he did not see was the path he was to follow. Chance stepped away from the opening to pick up the pack and the water skin. When he did so, he heard a click coming from the direction of the portion of the floor he had just stepped off. When he turned back to look, he saw the opening in the trunk of the quirrelit tree close behind him, leaving Chance and Ashu in darkness.

Chance turned the rest of the way around, hoping he had not turned too far and was facing the doorway. Taking careful steps forward, Chance found the wall of the tree trunk, but standing where he thought he had entered the quirrelit tree did not produce another click or open the door. He tried pushing on the wall, stomping on the floor, but to no avail. He turned around once again and shuffled forward, trying to get to where he had seen the pack and the water skin. His foot came in contact with the pack first. Chance crouched down and his hand touched the water skin.

"I'm going to have to have you move so I can put the strap of the water skin over my head," Chance said to Ashu.

He was surprised at how calm he was feeling, considering he was shut inside a huge tree trunk in complete darkness. In addition, he was talking to a halekrets as if the little animal understood every word. Chance felt Ashu clamber down the walking stick. Chance leaned the walking stick against the wall of the trunk, picked up the water skin, and drew the strap over his head. Once he had the water skin settled, he reached down and tried to pick up the pack. It was stuck. By feel, Chance determined one of the straps was caught on a tree root, or something similar. He unhooked the strap. When he picked the pack up, he heard another click.

Several things happened simultaneously. A portion of the tree trunk wall in front of him swung outward. His walking stick, which had been leaning against the wall, clattered to the ground. Ashu swarmed up the full length of Chance's body and clung to his hair. Chance just stood there staring. Ahead of him was a very dimly lit corridor of smooth rock.

Reaching up to loosen Ashu's tail from around his neck, Chance remarked, "It would seem that is the path we are supposed to follow. Now, if you could release the stranglehold you have on my neck so I might breathe better, that would be good."

Chance was not sure if it was his hands gently trying to move Ashu's tail or his request, but the little halekrets unwound his tail. Once Chance was more comfortable and could breathe again, he asked Ashu to climb down for the moment. Chance bent down, picked up the pack, adjusted the straps, and put it on his back. He then bent back down and retrieved his walking stick. When he straightened back up, he squared his shoulders and prepared to step forward. Ashu clambered back up onto Chance's shoulder and settled himself. Chance had taken no more than three steps down the corridor when he heard the portion of the tree trunk they had stepped through swing shut.

"Well, my friend, this seems to be it. We have only one way to go, and that's forward."

Chapter Eight

Chance did not know where the dim light was coming from that allowed him to see where he was to go, but he was very glad he was no longer in total darkness. He took a moment to open the pack and check what it contained. Inside were packets of dried fruit and hardtack. It was a meager amount, but if doled out sparingly, it might last the two of them a number of days, Chance thought. In addition, the pack held a long coil of rope, a cup, a bowl, several candles, matches, and two small sealed bottles. One was labeled a salve good for cuts. The other was marked poisonous. The one marked poisonous worried him a great deal.

After repacking the pack, Chance and Ashu set off down the corridor. He noticed tool marks on the walls, which suggested the corridor had either been carved into the rock or a natural opening had been expanded. The corridor he was following took a number of twists and turns, went up for a while, and then down. He saw no side corridors. As he headed downward, he became aware that it was getting warmer and warmer. The corridor he had been walking through had turned into a round smooth natural tunnel. He also noticed a flickering red glow had begun to reflect off the tunnel's surface.

It had become so hot that Chance stopped and took off his pack and water skin, in order to remove the light jacket he was wearing. Ashu waited patiently for Chance to put the pack and water skin back on before he resumed his seat on Chance's shoulder. The two then continued down the tunnel. The heat continued to increase. Though tempted to guzzle water to relieve his thirst, which was increasing with the rising temperature, Chance refrained. He did not know if he would have an opportunity to refill the water skin and knew he needed to conserve their supplies.

With each step the heat increased, as did the red flickering glow. The tunnel took a sharp turn to the right, and Chance cautiously rounded the corner. He found himself standing on a ledge in a large cavern. Before him was a deep narrow gorge. Heat came out of the gorge in waves. When Chance looked down, he could see the glowing red molten lava flowing sluggishly by. He looked left. The ledge he was standing on ended just a few feet from where he stood. Ten feet beyond the end of the ledge, the wall took a curve to the left and he could not see where it went or what was beyond. To his right was a narrow ledge barely a foot wide that hugged the wall. He could see the ledge continued on for about fifty feet. After fifty feet, the gorge took a bend to the right, and Chance could not see where the path went after that.

Since going back did not seem to be an option, Chance took a deep calming breath, and was just about to step forward, when Ashu clambered down the walking stick. Chance had forgotten he was holding it. He would need both hands to cling to the gorge wall as he moved down the narrow path. He was reluctant to leave the walking stick behind. For some reason it seemed very important to him that it remain in his possession. Once again Chance removed his pack, in order to tie the walking stick to it. When he looked up from his task, he became aware that the halekrets was gone. A chittering sound made Chance look up. Ashu was sitting on a ledge that Chance had not noticed before, about five feet above Chance's head and to his left as he faced the opening to the tunnel.

Chance was about to open his mouth and ask Ashu to please come back down, when the halekrets did exactly that. Oddly enough, Ashu did not come straight down like he did when coming down a tree trunk, but took a diagonal route. It was then that Chance noticed regular protrusions sticking out of the wall. The protrusions formed a diagonal ladder. Was Ashu suggesting Chance climb up and go left down the gorge rather than following the path to his right, Chance wondered.

Chance was torn by indecision. Should he take the path to the right, which he could clearly see, or climb the diagonal ladder to the left? While he was debating, Ashu climbed back up and disappeared. Ashu's move took the decision out of Chance's hands. He could not lose sight of the little halekrets. After all, he had promised to look after Ashu. Maybe that was a foolish notion. Ashu was just an animal after all. Chance should just let him go and follow the path to the right. It looked less risky.

Chance turned to his right, but found he just could not take the first step down the trail. Instead he turned back, reached up, grabbed the first of the rocks sticking out, and climbed. When he reached the narrow ledge Ashu had been standing on, he discovered it was even narrower than the trail he had not taken to the right. Very carefully, Chance slid his feet along the ledge. He was more than aware that one bad move, one slip, would send him falling down into the lava flow. Chance had been concentrating so hard, it took him several minutes to become aware that the ledge he had been shuffling along had become wider. Ashu was standing about twenty feet ahead of him on a path that was almost four feet wide and fairly level.

Even though the path was wide, Chance took the time to untie his walking stick from the pack. He used it to thump the path ahead of him, making sure it was solid. Ashu's slight weight hardly disturbed the dust on the dry path. After walking for several more hours, they came upon a tunnel opening in the cavern wall. Ashu, who had been ahead of Chance, stopped at the mouth of the tunnel and waited. Even at the entrance to the tunnel, there was a marked difference in temperature. Chance could feel the cooler air flowing out of the opening.

"I don't know about you, Ashu, but I could do with a bit of cooling off. Even if this tunnel leads to nowhere, it might be a place to get some rest."

Ashu cocked his head as if he were really listening and understanding what Chance had said. He then turned and entered the tunnel. Chance once again found himself following the little halekrets. The tunnel twisted and turned for about five hundred feet and then ended. Chance could still feel the cool air, but now it came from above him. When he looked up, he thought he could see stars, but could not be sure. There was some light at the end of the tunnel, which seemed to be coming from a fungus growing on the walls.

Chance removed his pack and the water skin. He put a small amount of water in the bowl for Ashu and took a small squirt of water for himself. Opening one of the packets of fruit, he took out several pieces, broke off a small piece for Ashu, and bit into another piece. When they had both finished, Chance put everything away in his pack and leaned his back against the tunnel wall.

"I'm sorry there's not more. Well, there is more, but I think we should save it. I don't know how long we're going to be here. I think we should call it a day, for it has been a long one. We need to get some sleep. Is that alright with you?"

Ashu gave a last lick to the fur on his paw making sure any stickiness from the dried fruit was gone. He walked over, climbed onto Chance's lap, turned around several times, and then settled down.

"Do make yourself comfortable," Chance stated wryly.

Exhaustion soon won the battle against wakefulness, and Chance slipped into a troubled sleep. His dream was different from the ones he had had recently. Instead of taking place in Sommerhjem, this dream took place in the crater valley. Trees had been cut down to build new buildings and they had bars on the windows. Smoke from several forges was causing a haze in the valley. More striking were the folks he could see from his perch in one of the few remaining quirrelit trees. They were a mixed group of rough-bearded men and tough-looking women. Here and there Chance could see areas where folks looked to be practicing sword fighting and other types of armed combat.

When Chance looked in a different direction, he noticed a crudely-made cage. Small tree trunks had been cut down and lashed together. Gathered inside were folks he recognized. Keeper Odette was there, along with others who had seen Chance off. All of their clothes were in rags, and they were dirty. One man was lying in the dirt, and Keeper Odette appeared to be pleading with one of the men who was outside the cage. The ground shook under Chance almost throwing him off the branch he was perched on. He grabbed a hold of the branch above him and set his feet more firmly. The ground shook harder, and Chance could hear a loud rumble. Then, something descended from above, and he felt himself being strangled.

Chance snapped awake and halted abruptly. He found himself no longer in the cool tunnel. He was standing on the path mere inches away from the edge of the lava pit. One more step and he would have plunged into the lava below.

"Thank you, my friend," Chance told Ashu, who once again had a stranglehold with his tail on Chance's neck. "Now, that you have saved me from being roasted, could you let me breathe a little easier, in more ways than one?" Ashu loosened his tail.

Chance turned and walked back into the cool tunnel all the way to the end where he had been resting. He wanted to be as far away from the lava flow as possible. The sweat that was running down his back was not just from the heat of the lava, but from fear. He could not remember ever walking in his sleep. He could never even remember being told he had ever walked in his sleep.

Because he was shaking so hard, Chance wasted two matches trying to light the candle. He felt a great need for more light. Once he got the candle burning, he huddled close to it, as if it would give him some protection. It took several moments before he settled down and looked, really looked, at what the candlelight revealed. The candle's light reflected off two sturdy metal rings fastened into the tunnel wall. A short bit of rope was hanging from one of the rings. Chance knew he would make very little progress if he was to try to carry on with as little sleep as he had had. He knew when he was very tired he did not think well, and he could make a costly mistake. Chance opened his pack and pulled out the coil of rope. It did not take very much time to securely tie himself to the two rings. He hoped he had not added knot untying to his abilities while sleeping. Once settled as comfortably as he could be under the circumstances, Chance drifted back to sleep. His sleep was deep and dreamless for the rest of the night.

When Chance awoke, he felt it was morning and that his internal clock had awakened him at its normal time, but he could not be sure. Surprisingly, he felt rested, even considering he had slept sitting up. Ashu was still curled up in a tight ball on his lap. He gently moved the little halekrets off his lap and began to untie the ropes. After coiling up the longer rope, Chance put it back in his pack. He once again put a little water in a bowl for Ashu and broke one of the hardtack in half. Ashu took the hardtack and put it in his bowl. Chance followed suit by placing his hardtack in a cup with a bit of water. It was much easier to eat when soft, but not any more palatable.

Since lingering over breakfast was not going to serve any purpose other than to delay leaving the cool of the tunnel, Chance gathered up his meager supplies, settled Ashu on his shoulder, gripped his walking stick with determination, and headed to the mouth of the cool tunnel. Not far beyond the tunnel entrance, the path took a wide swing to the right, ending at a narrow arch over the lava flow. Narrow was a generous description of the arch, for it was less than a foot wide in places. He either had to cross over the lava flow on the very narrow path or turn back. As Chance stood debating the wisdom of going forward or turning back, Ashu zipped across the arch, turned, and hunkered down.

"Easy for you to do. You run along tree branches all of the time. This must have looked like the royal road to you. Not so easy for me."

Chance had once seen ropewalkers walk a narrow rope strung high between two trees at a summer fair. They had made it look easy. The ropewalkers had strung a low rope between two other trees and put plenty of hay underneath to soften the fall of those adventurous fairgoers who wished to try their luck walking the low rope. They had said it was just a jump up onto the rope, then one foot in front of the other, using a long pole to help with one's balance. Chance had tried it and had been an abysmal failure. Even with the walking stick to act like the ropewalker's pole, there was no soft pile of hay awaiting him, should he fall.

Setting one foot gingerly on the arch, Chance found himself frozen in place. He could not seem to go forward, and he could not seem to go back. It was like all those situations in his dreams of late, this inability to move his feet. Chance tried to grab onto the determination and the anger he had felt in his dreams when he had stood up to what he feared, but was not successful. Ashu chittered encouragingly. Chance stepped back and let go of any dignity he might have possessed. He got down on the ground and scooted forward on his seat. Once he was fully on the arch, he put his legs over either side and slid himself across. He had concluded that living was far better than dying at that moment, and who was going to see him besides Ashu? Once across, he just lay prone on the stone floor, letting his heart settle back into its normal rhythm.

It was only a short distance down the path before Chance and Ashu entered a new tunnel. Again, there was a slight bit of light to see by, and soon the two came into a circular cavern. Leading out from the cavern were six tunnels. Now Chance faced the decision as to which one to take.

Chapter Nine

Chance stood looking at the six tunnel entrances for a very long time. Other than slight irregularities in shape, there was nothing to distinguish one tunnel entrance from another. There certainly were not any signs hanging above any of the openings saying "Right tunnel, ignore the other five." Ashu had remained on Chance's shoulder and offered no suggestion. It seemed to Chance that rushing off willy-nilly would serve no purpose. He had had no indication from Keeper Odette that there was a time clock ticking, other than the one imposed by a limited amount of food and water. Just randomly picking a tunnel would be one way to go, but Chance decided to take a closer look at each entrance before proceeding. He was glad he did.

As Chance checked each tunnel entrance, he began to notice symbols scratched into the rock walls just outside the openings. He also began to notice a pattern, once he chose a particular symbol and looked for it at each entrance. One symbol struck him as something he had seen before. As he stood there trying to think of where, it came to him. The symbol he was looking at on the tunnel walls was similar to one carved on the walking stick he was holding. The symbol scratched on the wall was a crude rendition of the symbol carved on his walking stick, but Chance was sure they were the same with one exception. The symbol scratched on the wall, though crude, was the same as the one carved on the walking stick with the exception of having a slash mark through it. Chance decided to check out an idea that was forming in his head.

He walked back to the tunnel entrance on his far left and noted the walking stick symbol, as he had begun to think of it, had a slash mark through it. The same was true of the symbol mark on the next three openings. On the wall next to the fourth opening from the left, the symbol mark did not have a slash mark through it. Opening number five from the left had the slashed symbol, and opening number six did not have the walking stick symbol, slashed or otherwise, anywhere near its entrance. Chance looked over the entrance to the sixth tunnel several more times and could still not find the symbol he was looking for, though there were other symbols, marks, letters, or combinations of letters on the wall outside the sixth opening. He needed to think about what it all meant.

It seemed obvious to Chance that others before him had been faced with the decision of which tunnel to go down. Due to the repetitive pattern of some of the marks he had seen, he had a strong suspicion that some, if not most, of the tunnels led back to where he was now standing. If that assumption were correct, then one opening should have more marks than any other, but Chance had not found that to be the case. That could mean several things, none of them very reassuring, the most dire of which was that some folk who had made the marks did not return to find the right passage. That brought Chance's thinking back to the walking stick symbol. The mark was beside five of the six tunnel openings. Either the maker of the mark had been successful and tunnel four was the correct one to go down, or he or she had not survived tunnel four to come back and try tunnel six.

"Well, what do you think, Ashu?" Chance asked the halekrets, who had draped himself across the top of the backpack. "We can take tunnel four and hope the symbol maker was successful, which is why I cannot find that symbol scratched in the wall next to opening six, or we can try opening six."

Ashu did not seem to have an opinion one way or the other.

After debating with himself for several more minutes, Chance decided to go down tunnel four. Gripping his walking stick tighter, along with his resolve, Chance set off down the tunnel. Again, his way was lit by a soft glow coming off some type of vegetation growing sparsely on the walls of the tunnel. He had walked for what he estimated was an hour or two when the tunnel split. Chance took the time to examine the area around each opening and then went over it a second time. He was glad he had, for he found the walking stick symbol scratched into the walls just inside each opening, but the one on the left had a slash mark though it. Chance really did not know if his choice to follow the walking stick symbol maker's path was the correct one, but for some reason he felt it was right. He had no way of knowing the fate of the folk who made the marks, but Chance figured he had either made a brilliant choice, or he would share the unfortunate fate of the symbol maker.

Chance remembered back to a time he had traveled with his family to a summer fair. He couldn't quite remember where it had been, but at any rate, there had been a hedge maze on the fairgrounds. His brothers and sisters had dragged him along, even though he had not wanted to go. They had thought it was a grand joke to walk him deep within the maze and then run off leaving him there. The tunnel he was walking through now with all its twists and turns, splits and branches, reminded him of that maze. He also remembered how panicked he had felt as a wee lad left alone by himself in the maze, which was very similar to how he felt now.

Chance did not know how long he had been walking through the tunnels when sheer exhaustion finally caused him to stop. He had come upon a beautiful side grotto and decided it would be as good a place as any to get some rest. As he settled in, trying to get comfortable on the hard rock floor using his pack for a pillow, he felt Ashu curl in beside him. Just having Ashu's warm little body snuggled up next to his gave Chance a great feeling of comfort.

The dreams began almost immediately. Once again, Chance found himself in the crater valley, or what was left of it. The valley had the feel of having been abandoned for quite some time. What was left of any of the buildings was just tumbled down walls and occasional roof beams. Trees grew up out of the buildings through what was left of the roofs. The paths Chance had once walked were overgrown. He found his way to the archives, and to his horror, saw that the doors were hanging ajar. He was afraid to go inside. Steeling himself, he stepped through the door. The sheer destruction of what had been housed within was more than shocking. Paper littered the floor in torn sodden clumps. Books were torn apart, and many of them looked half-burned. Fragile parchments were crumpled. The smell of decay, rot, and rodents was overwhelming. Chance began to hear screaming as he tried to pull himself out of his nightmare.

Once awake, Chance found the screaming had not ended with his dream. Added to the screaming was an undertone of moans. When the screaming and moaning would stop momentarily, the whispers would start, rising in crescendo until they were drowned out by renewed screaming. Chance's first impulse was to leap up and rush to the rescue of those who were screaming. He did not act on his first impulse because of Ashu's reaction. The little halekrets was alert, but neither frightened by nor frantic from the sounds surrounding them. When Chance sat up, Ashu clambered up his shirt front and positioned himself on Chance's shoulder. Chance took it as a good sign that Ashu had neither grabbed hold of his hair nor wrapped his tail tightly around his neck.

Cautiously, Chance stepped to the entrance of the grotto and into the tunnel. He walked about fifteen steps away from the grotto opening and was surprised to discover that while the screaming and moaning had not stopped, it was not as loud in the tunnel corridor. Experimenting, Chance walked back into the grotto, and the cacophony of sound increased in volume. Chance realized the beautiful grotto was a trap. Anyone would be drawn to the translucent columns rising up from the floor and hanging down from the ceiling. When he had entered the grotto, it had felt like a sanctuary to him. It would probably have felt that way to others, Chance thought. Like me, others first impulse would have been to rush out, trying to find the source of or to escape from the screaming and moaning. In their mad dash, it would have been easy to have become disoriented and lost.

Reasoning he and Ashu would get no more sleep in the grotto, Chance went back in to retrieve his water skin and backpack. The noise was almost deafening in the grotto. Strangely enough, Chance caught the scent of rain, and the air in the grotto felt slightly damp. Returning to the main tunnel, Chance made sure Ashu was settled on his shoulder, turned right, and began to walk. The farther the two of them got away from the grotto, the more the sounds of the screams, moans, and whispers decreased, until he could no longer hear them.

At each new branch or opening, Chance checked for the symbol he had been following. He was drawn up short when he came to a small cave that had three tunnels leading out of it, for he could not find the walking stick symbol scratched on any of the tunnel walls. Had the one whose path he had been following been fooled by the screaming? Had something happened to the symbol maker before he or she got to this point? Or had he missed a mark along the way? Chance decided to retrace his steps, hoping he could remember the way.

It was disappointing and very frightening to find that he had arrived back at the grotto once again without finding the walking stick mark. So far, following the walking stick symbols had seemed as good an idea as any, and Chance was loath to follow them back to where he had started in order to choose another of the six tunnels to go down. Maybe he had missed something, he thought, feeling very discouraged. He was also beginning to get concerned. He and Ashu could wander aimlessly for days and not find a way out. At some point their food and water would run out. Then, it would only be a matter of time until they perished. He was brought back from his downward spiraling thoughts by a sharp yank on his hair.

Brought back to the present, Chance was not mad at the situation he found himself in, but at himself. Once again, as in the dreams, he felt the anger rising within him along with determination. He was not a quitter. As long as there was strength in his body, he would go on. He had made a promise to the two halekrets that he would take care of Ashu, and that is just what he was going to do.

Throwing his shoulders back, which almost dislodged Ashu, Chance turned around and started back down the tunnel toward the three openings. He walked much more slowly this time, and even then, almost missed the symbol. Surely this could not be right, he thought, for the symbol was scratched on the tunnel wall next to a very narrow fissure in the rock. The symbol had no mark through it and it matched the ones Chance had been following.

Chance was not sure he could fit through the narrow fissure. He was reluctant to even try. What changed his mind, however, was that, once again, he became aware of a draft coming out of the fissure that carried the hint of rain. After leaning his walking stick against the wall, he gently nudged Ashu off his shoulder, and slipped off the backpack and the water skin. Setting them next to the opening, Chance turned himself sideways and just barely squeezed through the opening. He found himself in another tunnel. Lying down, Chance reached back to grab his backpack and pull it through, only to have Ashu travel up his arm and perch on his head.

"Not helpful, Ashu," Chance admonished the halekrets, now having to draw back his hand in order to brush his hair out of his eyes.

It was not difficult to snag the water skin and draw it through the narrow opening, but the backpack was another matter. Finally, Chance had had to squeeze out of the fissure, unpack half of the items, and push them through the opening. He, then, pushed the half empty pack through the opening, grabbed his walking stick, and squeezed back through the fissure. The tunnel they had just entered felt different to Chance, but he could not quite put his finger on just what it was. He spotted the walking stick symbol right away. Actually, he spotted two of them. Chance was surprised by what they indicated. His first inclination was to turn left and head the direction he thought the three tunnels were in. The symbol on the wall, which would have directed him left, had a slash mark through it.

"Even though I thought we should go left, Ashu, I guess we should go right. Sort of feels like we are heading back the way we came, but maybe not. I am so turned around now I couldn't guarantee we are not a few feet away from where we started. I think maybe we should pay attention to drafts and the smell of rain."

Ashu had no comment one way or the other. He had draped himself across the top of the backpack and had settled in for a nap.

"Some help you are," Chance said, but then thought about what he had said. "I apologize, Ashu. Just by being with me you have been a big help, and I think you have probably saved my life more than once."

Ashu let out a soft snore.

Chance and Ashu wandered the tunnel maze for hours. He began to worry that he should have made his own mark on each new tunnel entrance, but he had not. Finally, the fatigue from lack of sleep, little food and water, and continuous walking began to slow his footsteps. He began to look for someplace to rest. Once again, he almost missed a small opening. He stopped to catch his breath, for he had been climbing steadily uphill for quite some time. Chance bent over, placed his hands on his knees to give his back a rest, and felt a slight draft across his hands. Looking to his left, he spotted a hole in the wall about knee high. Right above it were two metal rings, and above that was the walking stick symbol. Was he supposed to go through the hole or tie himself to the rings?

Chapter Ten

What to do? What to do? What to do? The question kept tumbling around and around in Chance's head. He finally decided to put his pack, water skin, and walking stick on the floor of the tunnel and tie the rope to the rings that were solidly attached to the wall. He tied the other end of the rope around himself. Chance had decided to check what was through the hole before he made any decisions.

Entering the hole feet first, Chance was glad he had tied himself to a rope, since once he had his whole body through the opening, the surface he was lying on dropped down at a steep angle. Chance slipped downward at a fairly rapid rate through a very narrow tunnel before he pulled himself to a stop by grabbing the rope and holding on tight. Moving slowly and carefully, one by one he wriggled his hands above his head and began to pull himself up and out of the hole. When he crawled out of the hole, Chance did not even bother to stand. He just stayed down on the floor to give his heart a chance to slow down; it was beating so fast. Chance began to doubt the wisdom of continuing to follow the walking stick symbol marks. Had the one who had made the marks gone through the hole and perished? He was just too tired to figure it out now. Taking a small portion of food out of his pack, he and Ashu ate. Not even bothering to untie the rope, Chance lay down and was soon asleep.

The dreams began almost immediately. This time the dream was about Chance's family. It took place in the harbor on the island where they lived in Havkoller. The family had just boarded a sailing ship loaded down with provisions for a long sea voyage. The whole family was aboard, along with all of the possessions that were important to them. They were not sailing away toward Sommerhjem. As Chance looked around, he could see the family's trade ships all moored in the harbor. It looked like his family was leaving everything behind, including him. He found himself running, running down the beach toward the water, waving his arms. He kept calling out to them to wait, please wait, but they did not even seem to notice him. Chance had just reached the water's edge when he was yanked up short and startled awake.

Where he would have run to, if he had not been too tired to untie himself from the rope he had used earlier, Chance could only guess. He slowly walked back to where he had been sleeping and made the decision he would follow the symbol maker's path once again. Untying the rope from the rings in the wall and himself, he looped it through one of the rings. To one end he tied his backpack, water skin, and walking stick. This bundle he pushed through the opening first. Grabbing a hold of the other end of the rope and calling to Ashu, Chance settled himself on his back inside the opening. Ashu crawled onto Chance's chest, flattened himself against Chance, and took a firm hold on Chance's shirt. Very slowly, Chance eased himself forward, pushing his gear along with his feet.

When Chance's gear went over the edge of the sharp incline, it almost pulled Chance along with it, but he held on tightly to the rope. Soon his body began the descent, down, ever downward to the point that Chance worried about two things. He worried first and foremost that he would run out of rope. He would know that when his gear bumped against his feet and started going upward instead of down. He could, of course, at that point let his gear drift upward and hope he would reach the bottom of the chute he was sliding down before his gear got caught at the top. His other fear was he would have to untie his gear or let go of the rope, sending his gear, Ashu, and himself careening downward for who knew how far and how fast. Chance feared the loss of his gear far more than the loss of the rope, but hoped he would lose neither.

Chance's arms were beginning to tremble with the effort of keeping their progress down the chute a slow and steady one. Unfortunately, he felt his pack bump against his feet. Chance hoped it was because his gear was hung up on something, but when he pushed it with his feet, he felt the rope go taut. He decided that if he were going to make a rapid descent, he wanted to have all of his gear with him. Tightening his grip on the rope end that was tied to his gear, Chance very reluctantly let go of the other end of the rope.

The chute Chance was in was now too wide for him to be able to put his feet and hands against the sides to slow his speed, which picked up with each passing moment. He began shooting down the chute at an ever increasing rate, until, unexpectedly, he was not. The chute had changed direction. Instead of traveling downward, suddenly Chance found himself traveling up a gradual slope, which began to slow him down. Then the chute flattened out, and he slowly slid to a stop. He was glad no one was there to greet him, for his arrival had been less than dignified.

Sitting up, Chance looked around and discovered he was now in a tunnel where he could stand up. Standing up, he dusted himself off, untied the rope and repacked it, and slung his backpack and water skin back on. Ashu had climbed down and was sitting next to the walking stick.

"Well, that was quite a ride, don't you think, Ashu? Once is enough for me though. How about you? No comment?" Chance inquired.

Reaching down, Chance picked up his walking stick, and invited Ashu to climb back up. He was surprised with the little halekrets when, instead, he began walking down the tunnel.

"Too bad you can't give me a ride for a while."

Ashu just gave Chance a long steady look before turning back and resuming his walking. Chance was not surprised when they came to a fork in the tunnel. Once again, he looked for the walking stick symbol and discovered it at both openings. The symbol on the right tunnel was crossed out so Chance signaled to Ashu that they should take the left tunnel. The rest of what Chance assumed was the day continued in the same vein, as did the next day, and the day after that. Each night, Chance found something to lash himself to. Each night the dreams came. Sometimes they would be about Sommerhjem; sometimes they would be about the crater valley. He did not dream about his family again.

Fatigue and very small amounts of food and water began to take their toll. Chance lost all track of time. More than once he missed seeing the walking stick symbol and had to double back to find it. Just as he was about to collapse from sheer exhaustion, he felt a strong wet breeze on his face. Ashu began chittering, swiftly leapt down off Chance's shoulder, and ran down the tunnel.

"Wait, Ashu, wait!" Chance called out frantically, as he tried to get his tired body to move at more than a snail's pace. Rushing, he stumbled and almost fell several times before he caught up with the little halekrets, who was standing in an opening that was covered by a sheet of falling water. Chance slowed himself down just in time to slip to a stop on the wet rock floor. At first, he could not get his exhausted brain to figure out just what he was looking at, or what he was hearing. It finally dawned on him that he might be seeing the backside of one of the many waterfalls that fell into the crater valley.

The more time Chance stood there taking in what he was looking at, the more convinced he was that his guess was right. As he cautiously moved forward along the wet floor toward the curtain of water, he became aware of a slight damp breeze coming from his right. The water was more of a mist than a fall there, so Chance headed in that direction. Ducking under a low overhang, Chance stepped through the mist and found himself in a short tunnel. Ahead he could see a light brighter than the dim light he had grown used. The breeze now carried the smell of green growing things, which caused Chance to quicken his pace. Ashu had already disappeared ahead of him around a corner. What he saw when he stepped out into the early morning light brought him up short.

Chance found himself standing on a two foot wide ledge twenty feet up from the crater floor, looking out at the trunks of several quirrelit trees. Ashu was nowhere in sight. Ah, to have a halekrets' climbing ability, Chance thought to himself. Twenty feet down was too far to jump safely. There was nothing on the narrow path on which to tie the rope, and the closest tree limb was too far away. It would be too cruel a joke to find himself so close to being out of the tunnels, to actually be in the crater valley, and then not be able to get down off the ledge. Chance began to pace the narrow ledge, admonishing himself to think.

Chance rejected going back to the curtain of water, passing through, and jumping off the ledge into the shallow pool at the bottom of the waterfall. He rejected jumping off the ledge period. He definitely did not want to return back into the tunnel maze. His tired brain finally began to function, and he took the time to lie down on the ledge and look over. In the low light it was difficult to see, but he thought he could see some hand and footholds. Chance tied his gear once more onto the rope and lowered it down, being careful to leave most of the rope on the ledge, in case he had to haul everything back up again. He then swung his legs over the side of the path and felt around for the first foothold. It took a long time, on shaking limbs, to cautiously get himself half way down, when his left foot slipped, leaving him hanging by his fingertips. He no longer had the strength to hold on and slid down the cliff face, scraping his hands and hitting his head. Chance collapsed at the bottom of the cliff.

Chance was only out for a few moments. When he came to, he found himself looking into three pairs of golden eyes. At first, he thought he was seeing triple. Finally, he was able to bring his eyes into focus and discovered he was not seeing triple, but rather seeing three halekrets. Ashu was there with two others. Ashu was pulling on his hand.

"Give me a minute, if you will, Ashu. I need to make sure I'm all of one piece."

Taking a moment to slowly and gingerly move his limbs, head, neck, and back, Chance concluded he was battered but not broken. When he had started to move, the halekrets took off. Chance felt bereft that his movements had scared the animals away. Just as he was about to stand up, the three halekrets returned with paws full of fruit. Chance had never tasted anything so good. He did not even notice the juice running down his chin.

After he finished eating and before getting up, Chance took the time to reflect on his time in the maze of tunnels. He did not know how long he had been inside. He did not know if how he got out was what he was supposed to have done. He worried that he had not fulfilled the rite of passage, and after all he had been through, he would still not be able to leave the Shadow Islands.

"Well, I'm not going back, I can tell you that much," Chance told the three halekrets who looked at him quizzically. "I'm not going back," Chance said to himself softly.

Chance continued to sit where he had fallen, making no move to stand or go and find someone in the valley. He needed time to think. What had the whole maze ordeal been about? And what about the dreams? Were they just his tired brain making up stories, or was he somehow being shown the future? He hoped not, for the future in his dreams looked pretty dismal. Chance could not imagine that he was so important as to be the one folk whose actions, or lack of action, would cause the outcome of the future to match his dreams.

Surely his never getting to Sommerhjem would not cause such a dismal future for the country. Surely, if he were forced to give away the Shadow Islands' secrets, the valley here would not fall to ruin. Why would his family sail off and leave him behind? These thoughts kept going round and round in his head, and he could find no clear answers to his questions. With a full stomach for the first time in days, and a head full of unanswered questions, Chance finally gave in to his fatigue and slid into sleep, sitting there at the base of the cliff, lulled by the sound of running water.

When he awoke, the sun told him it was toward late afternoon. Ashu was curled up on his lap. The other two halekrets were nowhere to be seen. As gently as he could, Chance lifted Ashu off his lap and was about to set him down on the ground when Ashu woke and scampered up Chance's arm onto his shoulder. Shifting himself onto his knees, Chance grabbed his walking stick and used it to lever himself up into a standing position. Every muscle in his body screamed in protest, he was so stiff and sore. He almost overbalanced himself trying to bend over to pick up his pack and water skin. Once everything was settled, including Ashu, Chance began to walk toward the archives, hoping to find Keeper Odette there.

A part of Chance was fearful that somehow one or more of his dreams of the valley had become reality while he had been gone. It was with great relief that he saw that the doors to the archives were not hanging from their hinges and that Keeper Odette was sitting outside as he approached.

Chapter Eleven

Chance did not know what to expect from Keeper Odette when he approached her. What he had not expected was to see her leap up from her seat and rush toward him. He did not know whether he should run, or be prepared to defend himself. Shifting his weight and taking a tight grip with both hands on his walking stick, he stood his ground. Keeper Odette's first words caused Chance to relax his grip just a wee bit.

"I cannot begin to tell you how very happy I am to see you and your small furry friend alive and standing here. I have been so very worried. Come, sit, before you fall over. I will call for some food. Wait, I am being selfish. Would you like a bath and a nap before you do anything else?"

Chance laughed for the first time in days when he thought of what he must look like, let alone what he must smell like. The little part of him that was still angry with the island folk, and especially Keeper Odette, for putting him through the ordeal of the maze, for not just letting him leave the island, felt that making Keeper Odette sit downwind of him would be just revenge. Chance thought better of it, however.

"Actually, a bath and a change of clothes would be nice, but I will hold off on the nap," Chance told Keeper Odette.

"I will gather a meal together and let us meet back here shortly, if that is alright with you."

Chance returned to the archives a short while later, feeling better than he had in days. He had washed the dust, sweat, and grime off. He had cleaned up his scrapes and cuts. Chance had been surprised, when he had jokingly invited Ashu into the bathing pool, and the little halekrets had jumped in the water and paddled about for a few minutes. Now in clean clothes, Chance found he did not mind that his shoulder was a little damp due to an almost dry halekrets sitting on it.

Keeper Odette had laid out a limited buffet for Chance to choose from. The fresh food was a welcome sight, especially compared to what he and Ashu had been eating for days.

"I did not know what the halekrets ate, so I brought a variety of fresh fruit, berries, and nuts."

"He seems to like all of those. I thank you for your thoughtfulness. I had worried that once we returned to the valley, he would go back to his family. Well, I think of the two who were with him as his family at any rate."

Chance fell silent at this point for his main concern at the moment was not whether the buffet would provide Ashu with a meal, but rather, what was going to happen next? Would he be allowed to leave the Shadow Islands?

"I have no facts to support what I think, but I think the one you have named Ashu is supposed to be with you. Call it intuition or an old woman's fancy, but I really feel that is true. I suspect, however, Ashu's continued companionship is not what really concerns you at the moment."

"You are right. I need to leave the Shadow Islands and get to Sommerhjem. I, well, I . . . ." Chance trailed off not really knowing how to explain all that was circling around in his head.

"What did you learn during your time away from us?" Keeper Odette asked gently.

Chance took a moment to really think about what Keeper Odette had asked. What had he learned? He had learned he had more strength and more courage inside himself than he had been aware of. He had learned that he never, ever wanted to be a victim or be told he could not do something. He had learned how to harness his anger and use it to overcome his fears. He had learned that sleep was something he needed, but wanted to avoid due to the dreams.

The dreams, Chance needed to take another moment to really think about his dreams. Were they just something he had created out of his imagination, or were they something more? Either way, were the dreams a message? Were they trying to show or teach him something?

Chance first thought about the dreams he had had before he had taken up the rite of passage. They had all involved places in Sommerhjem. Was that just his guilt for failing to carry out his task in Sommerhjem manifesting itself? Pretty puffed up of him to think his not retrieving the piece of the oppgave ringe would cause Sommerhjem to fall to rack and ruin, he thought. Chance recalled he had pulled himself out of each of the terrible dreams by gaining the courage to stand and face his fears rather than by turning and running. Maybe that was the lesson of the dreams.

But what of the dreams he had had in the tunnel maze? Had the lesson been the same, Chance wondered. They had showed the destruction of the crater valley, of it being taken over by much less peaceful folk than those who now lived here. The most horrifying dream had been the one about the destruction of the archives and the abandonment of the crater valley. Were the dreams trying to show Chance what would happen if the secrets of the Shadow Islands were revealed?

Keeper Odette held silent and waited patiently. She could see a host of emotions crossing Chance's face. It would be interesting to be in the lad's head, she thought. He had made it through the rite of passage, and that was important. More important than surviving the rite of passage was the answer to her question. His answer would seal his fate more than the ordeal he had just endured.

"My time here in the crater valley and during the rite of passage has taught me a number of things," Chance began.

Keeper Odette was encouraged by the words Chance had just spoken. She was even more encouraged by the sense that the lad in front of her had grown up a great deal in the last several weeks.

"When I left home, it was because I thought I was heading off on a grand adventure. Like the heroes in the storybooks I have read, I would overcome each and every obstacle easily. Nothing would ever come close to harming me, and I would, well, you get the idea."

"Having read some of those types of books you mentioned, I can well understand what you are saying," suggested Keeper Odette. "Reality didn't quite match the stories, yes?"

"Reality has been an eye opener to be sure. When I first came here after being unceremoniously dumped overboard, I was determined to leave. After a little while, I gave up. I tried to convince myself I could be content being here, mostly because of what the archives held. They are a great temptation," Chance laughed, a bit self-consciously.

"From what I heard, that stage did not last long."

"No," Chance said, hesitating, for he was not sure about telling Keeper Odette about the dreams.

"Go on."

"It was the dreams," stated Chance in a rush.

"Dreams?"

"I started having dreams each night. Frightening dreams about a Sommerhjem I didn't know. The dreams showed a land that was filled with poverty and darkness. The common folk were beaten down. The land scorched. I know it is foolish to think I could singlehandedly be responsible for Sommerhjem's future turning out like my dreams, but they made me more determined to leave the valley. I don't know if the dreams were caused by guilt because I had failed to do what I had set out to do, or something else. With each dream, I found I no longer wanted to feel sorry for myself, no longer wanted someone to control my future. In each dream, I got angry and turned to face what was frightening me. With each passing day, I became more and more determined to leave the valley and find my way back to Sommerhjem."

"And so you chose to go through the rite of passage, even though your chance of survival was very narrow," said Keeper Odette.

"Yes. I just couldn't stay. At least not just now." Now, where had that thought come from, Chance wondered.

Keeper Odette daintily dabbed at her mouth with her napkin to hide a slight smile.

Clearing his throat, Chance went on. "During my time in the tunnels, I had more frightening dreams, but this time instead of being about Sommerhjem, they were about this valley. They showed me possibilities of what might happen here, and I presume the rest of the Shadow Islands, if somehow the wrong sort could find a way to enter here. I now understand why you don't want your secrets to get out. I can only promise you that I would tell no one. I do, however, need to leave."

Keeper Odette was silent for a very long time. It was all Chance could do to sit and remain silent. The waiting for her to speak was almost harder than the rite of passage.

"Would you be willing to take an oath of honor that you would never reveal the secrets of the Shadow Islands, even under threat of death?"

"Yes," Chance answered, without a moment of hesitation.

"I will arrange for the oath giving to happen tonight at dinner. It will take a few days for you to learn what you will need to know to leave and return to the Shadow Islands. We will give you all the assistance we can. If you will excuse me now, there is a great deal to do. You have done well, you and your furry friend. Take your time over the rest of your meal, and then, you might want that nap. Your friend Ashu has a head start on you already."

Chance looked down at his lap. While he had been talking, he had not noticed that Ashu had climbed down and settled himself on his lap and was fast asleep. When Keeper Odette left, Chance took a deep breath and relaxed his shoulders. Along with the relief he felt knowing he had passed some sort of test, and would be allowed to leave the Shadow Islands, came a huge wave of fatigue. Chance covered a giant yawn with his hand and decided to forgo any more food. Keeper Odette had been right. He needed a nap. Gently cradling the sleeping halekrets in his arms, he walked back to his quarters.

From where Keeper Odette had stopped just within the shadows of several pines, she had a clear view of Chance. She saw he did not last long sitting and watched him walk toward his quarters. Little did he know it was not the rite of passage that had earned him his way off the island, nor was it his great need to leave. It was not his professed newfound courage or determination. All of those reasons were certainly necessary, but it had been one telling sentence that had earned him the most approval. It was when he had said he could not stay for now. He just did not realize that he was now a member of the Shadow Islands community. Time would tell what role he would play in their future, but Keeper Odette had a pretty good idea.

Chiding herself that she did not have time to waste, Keeper Odette hurried down the path to talk to others. Much needed to be done over the next few days. It was with a lighter heart that she went about her tasks. She was relieved that Chance had survived his rite of passage. Also, she was even more relieved that he would now be able to try to complete the task in Sommerhjem he had set out to do. Keeper Odette knew how important it had been for him to succeed when he had landed on the shores of Sommerhjem. The importance and urgency had not changed. It had been so hard to stick to the traditions and rules concerning new arrivals to the Shadow Islands. It was certainly one of the most difficult decisions Keeper Odette had had to make in a great long while.

Chance woke to the sound of someone clearing his throat. Slowly, he opened his eyes and found he couldn't see anything. Reaching up, he moved Ashu's tail from across his eyes. Now able to see, he saw that one of the islanders was standing just outside his sleeping quarters.

"Your pardon, Chance, but it is near mealtime. Keeper Odette sent me to let you know."

"I thank you. I'll be there shortly."

Chance lifted Ashu off his chest and sat up. It was then that it struck him that Ashu had not disappeared when their caller had come.

"Are you going to go with me to dinner?" Chance inquired.

Ashu climbed up and perched himself on Chance's shoulder. Chance took great comfort that the halekrets was going to be with him, for he did not know what was going to happen next. As he entered the communal dining area, he was surprised by both the number of people who greeted him and how welcoming they were. In fact, he was a bit overwhelmed.

Keeper Odette greeted him warmly and said, "There are many here from the other islands whom you have not yet met. Those who primarily reside in this valley are most happy you have survived. Many have watched other newcomers come to the valley and not be content. They, like you, chose to go through the rite of passage. Most did not survive. You can understand, perhaps, that while the folk of the crater valley try to be caring and welcoming, it is difficult because they fear for each newcomer. Loss is always hard, and it is especially hard when you have grown to know someone. But enough talk. Come, let's get the oath taking out of the way. Then we can enjoy this celebration, thrown on your behalf."

When Chance finally found his way back to his sleeping quarters hours after the meal, he was very tired, but he did not want to go to bed right away. Instead, he sat outside his quarters with Ashu on his lap and tried to recall the last few hours. Most of it was a blur. So many new faces and names. Chance chuckled to himself, for he had a great suspicion that many of those who sought him out to talk to him were much more interested in seeing Ashu.

"You were a pretty popular fellow this night, Ashu," Chance told the halekrets.

Ashu seemed unimpressed, as he continued to clean a bit of fur on his leg.

Just before Chance finally stood to turn in for the night, he remembered what Keeper Odette had said to him just before he left the communal dining area.

"Get a good night's sleep, for the next few days are going to be intense and very tiring."

Chapter Twelve

As Chance pulled in the main sheet to adjust the sail of the boat that was carrying him toward Sommerhjem, he reflected on the last few days. Keeper Odette had not been fooling when she had told him his days were going to be full. He remembered every detail of those last few days on the Shadow Islands. From sunrise to well after sunset, he was given a crash course on how to enter and leave the Shadow Islands, and how to navigate in the dense fog. He now knew a little more of what was hidden in the fog, and what the fog protected. What astonished him most was how the folks had treated him since he had survived the rite of passage and taken the oath of honor. They had always been kind, but now they were even more welcoming and helpful. In addition, they were very open in their conversations with him.

Chance found that when the time came for him to leave the crater valley, he was reluctant to do so. The most obvious reason was he really did not want to be parted from Ashu, who had not left his side since their return from the tunnel maze. The second reason was he felt, strangely enough, more at home in the crater valley than he had ever felt in Havkoller. He wondered if he would still feel that way after he spent some time back in Sommerhjem.

Chance's first task on the day he was to depart took place early in the morning. He got up at dawn, and with Ashu on his shoulder, he walked to the quirrelit grove. He wanted to be able to say goodbye to the little halekrets in private. Chance headed to the base of the quirrelit tree where he had first met Ashu and took a seat.

"So, my little friend, I'm going to have to leave this valley today. I'm going to take a sea voyage and go to the land of Sommerhjem. I find I'm reluctant to leave here, but I must. My biggest regret is, well, is . . . ." Chance stopped talking at this point because he was not quite sure what to say to Ashu, or if the little halekrets even understood what he was saying. "Your home is here, and your family. I wish I could take you with me, but I'm not sure it's right. You have been a true friend, and I'm going to miss you."

With that said, Chance lifted Ashu off his lap and set him down on the ground. When he stood up to brush off his pants, Ashu, without a backward glance, swiftly climbed up the quirrelit tree and disappeared into the foliage. It was with a very heavy heart that Chance, after trying to catch a last glimpse of Ashu, finally drew his eyes away from the quirrelit tree and headed back out of the quirrelit grove. He found himself dragging his feet as he walked back to his quarters, but he could no longer put off packing. His supplies had grown, and he needed to organize them.

Just as Chance was tightening the strap on the last pack, he caught movement out of the corner of his eye. Turning, expecting to see one of the islanders come to help him move his things down to the dock, he was surprised and delighted to see Ashu and two other halekrets standing just outside his sleeping quarters. Ashu touched each of their faces with his hand, and they in turned touched his face. The two nodded to Chance, turned, and were swiftly gone. Ashu entered the sleeping quarters and climbed up Chance's body, taking his familiar spot on Chance's shoulder. Chance found himself lifting a slightly shaking hand to first brush away a tear that was sliding down his face, and then, to gently stroke Ashu's fur.

"I hope this means you're going with me," Chance said to Ashu. "I'm not sure how good an idea it is, but I'm sure not going to try to convince you to stay here."

Chance was pulled out of his recollections by a shout from another folk aboard the boat.

"Bring her a little more to port, if you would please. A little more. That's good. Now hold her on that course. Ashu, get back here, do you hear me? Come back off that bow sprit."

Chance just laughed. It felt so good being on the water once again. He had worried how the little halekrets would do on a boat, on the open water. Would he be seasick? Would he be frightened? So far, Chance had been more afraid for Ashu. The little halekrets had shown absolutely no fear of clambering about the rails and the rigging as if the sailing boat was just an oddly shaped tree. His favorite place was at the tip of the bow sprit. He seemed to revel in the view and the sea spray.

Chance had thought he was going to be given a small sailing vessel and sent on his way, once he had finished his training on how to maneuver between the Shadow Islands and how to get in and out of the fog bank that surrounded them. He had been surprised when he had been introduced to Skipper Nereo. Skipper Nereo was, Chance had been informed, one of the Shadow Islands traders.

"We cannot grow or produce all that we need," Keeper Odette had informed him. "Skipper Nereo here has the trade route to Sommerhjem. He acquires what we need and also picks up information. It is important to our safety here on the Shadow Islands to be aware of what is happening in the countries closest to us. Most folk know only the legends or stories about the Shadow Islands and do not realize folk live here. It is in our best interest to keep it that way. However, it is also in our best interest to know as much as we can about the world outside the fog bank that surrounds us. Living in a fog bank is one thing, but living in a fog is quite another thing altogether."

When Chance, Ashu, Skipper Nereo, and his one crew member left the Shadow Islands, they did not leave from the east side of the Islands. The Skipper had explained that there had been an increased number of ships lingering on the edge of the fog bank on the east side of the Islands, the side closest to Sommerhjem. Since it would not do to be noticed by any of those ships, they had instead sailed west for about a day and then north.

Instead of heading for the port of Marinel where Chance had landed before, they were heading for the port of Willing, which had a good deep harbor into which the Travers River flowed. The Travers was a very deep navigable river from the port of Willing on the coast to the town of Tverdal and provided an easy way to move goods from the sea to the interior and back.

The plan was for Chance to sail up the Travers River in the small skiff that was being towed behind the ship. Skipper Nereo had not asked where Chance was going to go once he got to Tverdal, nor had he wanted to know. He had been informed by Keeper Odette that Chance had a task to accomplish and it was important that the less anyone knew the better. It had been arranged that Skipper Nereo would drop anchor each month at the time of the half-moon in Litenhaven, a small seaport farther down the coast, and be there for several days to reconnect with Chance and Ashu, should they need transportation back to the Shadow Islands. In great need, the skiff they were towing was seaworthy enough to get Chance back to the Shadow Islands, but that should only be attempted when other options were not available.

The fact that Keeper Odette and others assumed Chance would return to the Shadow Islands did not strike Chance as odd. At first, he had convinced himself that he would return because he would need to bring Ashu back to his family. Now that he was away from the Shadow Islands, he had felt a pull as if the Shadow Islands themselves were calling him back. In the quiet of the night, holding the ship on course in a steady wind, with Ashu curled up on the bench next to him, he asked himself the question Keeper Odette had asked him about what he really wanted to do in the future. He had come to the conclusion that continuing in the family business as a trader was not what he really wanted to do. Now that he had leave to come and go from the Shadow Islands, Chance knew he could choose what he wished to do.

Chance wanted to try to become a seeker. He was not quite sure how to go about it, but once he completed what he was headed to Sommerhjem to do, he was going to find out. He would not be a seeker in the traditional sense where he wandered the land to seek knowledge, for he wanted to spend his days exploring the archives. He did not need to become a seeker to continue to do that, but he also wanted to be part of a group, not just an isolated learner. He wanted to be part of the seekers and be able to exchange ideas, share what he had learned. Being a seeker would also allow him to be away from his family for long periods of time, yet connect with them from time to time without having to give away that he lived on the Shadow Islands. Chance knew his family would wish him well, for they had always encouraged their children to seek their own paths.

Chance had more immediate issues to think about this day, for Skipper Nereo had informed him they were but a day out from the port of Willing. He hoped there would be no one waiting for him this time. Chance had wracked his brain long and hard trying to figure out how Mako and Pivane had known about him and when he was to arrive. He did not think anyone in his family would have discussed it with anyone. Chance did not think his cousin Clarisse, who was a member of the Glassmakers Guild, would have given him away either.

The first time he had landed in Sommerhjem, he was supposed to have headed to the Glassmakers Guildhall in Marinel and make contact there. His cousin was supposed to have had transportation and gear arranged for him. Since he never made it to the Glassmakers Guildhall, it occurred to him that his cousin had probably been notified by now that he had not arrived as expected. He hoped against hope that she had not sent a message to his family that he was missing. Chance especially did not want either of his parents to be worried.

No matter how his last arrival in Sommerhjem had been discovered, he did not think anyone would be aware of his arrival this time. Chance's intention was to separate his small skiff from Skipper Nereo's ship when they were about a half day out from the port of Willing. Chance was then going to sail into the harbor and on up the Travers River to Tverdal.

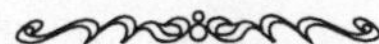

Master Clarisse was torn. The latest bearer of a piece of the oppgave ringe had arrived in the capital, and she knew she should stay to be part of the group to prepare the ring bearer as to what was going to happen the next day at the Well of Speaking. However, word had reached her that her cousin Chance had still not arrived at the Glassmakers Guildhall in the Port of Marinel. Even accounting for bad weather, he was several weeks overdue.

"You are going to wear that rug out if you don't stop pacing. Besides, you are making me even more tired than I already am. Carz and I have traveled practically night and day to get here with some important news for the council, and we are exhausted," stated the rover Nissa. Her hunting cat Carz was stretched out at her feet, asleep. "Things seem to be progressing well. With the fourth piece of the oppgave ringe about to be placed in the vesstebeks, more and more folks are becoming convinced that the Gylden Sirklene challenge is real. Is there something wrong with this latest arrival?"

"No, yes, no . . . ."

"Well, that certainly makes everything clear."

"I am sorry. I am not making sense," Master Clarisse said apologetically. "I am sure everything is fine concerning the oppgave ringe and its bearer. My problem is my cousin Chance. As you are aware, our former regent Lord Klingflug tried to prevent the successful calling of the challenge by eliminating members of the Høyttaier clan because we are the keepers of the ancient language. Without anyone who could read the Book of Rules, Lord Klingflug might have been able to convince the folk that the Gylden Sirklene challenge was a sham."

"What does this have to do with your cousin Chance?" Nissa inquired.

"Fortunately, the royal librarian got word that Lord Klingflug had ordered the systematic elimination of members of the Høyttaier clan. Before his agents could come looking for the list of who was in the clan and where they resided, she pulled the rolls listing their names. Without the rolls, it became much more difficult to determine just which folk were actually Høyttaiers. A very brave and gutsy thing to do. Pretended to be all in a dither when Lord Klingflug's agents came demanding to see it. She then got word out to some of us, and we spread the news quickly. Most of us were fairly safe since we are very close mouthed about being Høyttaiers. Some felt less safe and fled the country. My cousin Chance and his family fled to the Havkoller Islands."

"Did Lord Klingflug's agents track them down and harm them?"

"No. I have had word that they are not only fine but thriving as traders between the Havkoller Islands. In response to my message to them that the Regent had been removed from power, I received word that Chance was returning to Sommerhjem. He should have arrived at the Glassmakers Guildhall in Marinel by now. I had arranged for a horse and gear to be waiting for him there. Even with bad weather, he is several weeks overdue. I have tried not to worry, thinking that I would hear from him soon, but this morning a message arrived that the ship he was on had already docked, unloaded, and departed. Chance, it would seem, arrived in Sommerhjem when expected, but never made it to the Guildhall."

"What can you do?"

"I need to head off to the port of Marinel and see if I can pick up his trail. I have asked Seeker Eshana to accompany me. Lady Esmeralda is also insisting I travel with a patrol of royal guards."

"Don't you need to be here for the ceremony tomorrow?"

"That is what is tearing me apart. How do I fulfill my duties as the Høyttaier representative to the interim ruling council and my obligations to my clan and family? My best solution is that you take care of the newest ring bearer and get her through the ceremony while I go to Marinel."

"Me?"

"Who better than you? After all, you have been in her shoes. I know I cannot be gone long, but Seeker Eshana said he would continue on if we can find any clue as to what has happened to Chance."

There is something she is not telling me, thought Nissa.

Chapter Thirteen

Master Clarisse and Seeker Eshana had ridden hard to reach the port town of Marinel. Once there, they had gone straight to the Glassmakers Guildhall to see if any more information as to what had happened to Chance had been discovered.

Both Master Clarisse and Seeker Eshana had been greeted warmly by the resident Glassmakers Guildmaster of Marinel. "Be welcome, Master Clarisse, Seeker. I wish I had better news for you. I've had further inquiries made, and I'm afraid the news is not good. Come now, let us not stand here in the Guildhall. You must be tired from your ride. Come, let us get comfortable, and I will tell you what I know."

Once all three were settled in a small parlor off the main entrance, the Guildmaster went on. "Your cousin Chance did indeed arrive in Marinel at the time you had anticipated him arriving. Unfortunately, he did not make it as far as the Guildhall. Through some discreet inquiries, I've found out he made it as far as one of the eateries a good ways up from the docks."

"In my letter to his family, I had suggested that the dock area was not as safe as it might be."

"All too true, I'm afraid. Chance appears to have followed your directions. Unfortunately, it seems someone anticipated his arrival. From what I have come to know, they slipped something in his soup or drink, which caused him to become quite disoriented after he left the eatery. At first, it appeared that your cousin had been dragooned."

"Oh, this is indeed not good news," exclaimed Master Clarisse. "Wait. It first appeared he was dragooned?"

"Yes, and then the tale gets stranger. There was a witness to what happened to your cousin, and she was quite willing to be forthcoming for a bit of coin. Seems two less than savory characters grabbed your cousin and hauled him aboard a ship captained by a known smuggler."

"What would a smuggler want with my cousin? I would think a smuggler would want crew members who were very loyal, knowing the captain's business."

"Well, here's where things get complicated. The smuggler's ship returned to port . . . ."

"That's good then. We can get Chance off that ship," stated Master Clarisse beginning to rise.

"Would that that were possible, but it's not. I am sorry, I'm not telling this correctly. Yes, the smuggler's ship returned to port, but Chance was not on board. In addition, the two who snatched Chance in the alley, disembarked and vanished before we could question them. I do have one other piece of information. However, it is not encouraging either."

Master Clarisse looked at the Guildmaster questioningly. Seeker Eshana remained quiet.

"A reliable informant let me know about a conversation he overheard from one of the smuggler's crew. The crew member was bragging that he and his skipper had been to the Shadow Islands. Dropped something off, he said. The informant stated the crew member was hinting that whatever they had dropped off was a very special cargo. 'Didn't even make 'im walk the plank, just dropped 'im off,' is what the crew member said. I'm afraid that Chance might have been that very special cargo."

The ashen look on Master Clarisse's face made a strong statement as to how she was taking the news. Seeker Eshana reached his hand out and gently placed it on Master Clarisse's arm.

"It would seem that the first thing that needs to be done is to question the smuggler and the smuggler's crew," stated Seeker Eshana very calmly.

"Unfortunately, she and her crew left the very next day after the conversation was overheard. Word has been sent out to try to locate her, but she has not been in the business of smuggling as long as she has without being caught for no reason. Unfortunately, she is very good at the business of eluding authority. She could be anywhere by now," stated the Guildmaster.

"Then, I guess we need to go to the next plan," suggested Seeker Eshana.

"You have a next plan?" questioned Master Clarisse. Both men could hear the discouragement in her voice.

"Of course. I also think finding the two who put your cousin on the smuggler's ship would give us some answers."

"Do we know who they are?" Master Clarisse asked.

"Ah, yes, we do. They are two lowlifes named Mako and Pivane, who are basically for hire to the highest bidder. My feeling, from the information I have gathered, is they earned a goodly sum for this job. As far as I know, they are no longer in the port of Marinel, nor did they leave by ship."

"Those two again!" exclaimed Master Clarisse. Both men looked at her questioningly. "Seeker Eshana and I left the capital the evening before the fourth piece of the oppgave ringe was to be placed in the vesstebok in the Well of Speaking. Before I left, however, I had the opportunity to hear how it had come into the possession of a young woman named Meryl. To make a long story short, those two men were somewhat peripherally involved in her adventure of getting the ring to the capital. We think they were not aware that she carried the ring, and were not actually after her but after another who was following her. But that is a story for another time. Now, it would seem that our best chance of finding out what happened to my cousin Chance is to find those two."

Seeker Eshana could see the wheels turning in Master Clarisse's mind as to how she was going to go about being in two places at once. She could not be away from the capital for very long, for she had duties to her clan and country she could not fulfill otherwise, and yet, she felt responsible for finding out what had happened to her cousin.

"Here is what I might suggest. I know you have obligations back at the capital but also feel responsible for your cousin. Why don't you let me try to find Mako and Pivane? I can be quite persuasive when it comes to finding out information. Would you trust me to find out what I can?" Seeker Eshana held up his hand to halt Master Clarisse from speaking just then. "If I get a lead on what might have happened to him, or where I might find him, I will follow up. Besides, who is better suited for this job than a seeker?" Seeker Eshana said, trying to make himself look haughty and overly important to lighten the mood.

Master Clarisse gave a slight chuckle. "Good try at the superior-to-all-others act, and your offer does have merit. I know finding a lost folk is not quite what seekers do, at least not living lost folk, but I suspect you would be better at it than I would. I thank you for your offer." Turning to the Guildmaster, Master Clarisse inquired as to whether the Marinel Glassmakers Guildhall had any messenger birds to spare.

"As a matter of fact, we just got restocked with messenger birds whose home roost is at the Glassmakers Guild at the capital. I can make a few available. Do you need anything else?"

The three talked for a little while longer before the meeting broke up. Master Clarisse was anxious to head back to the capital, and Seeker Eshana wanted to begin looking for any information concerning Mako and Pivane before the trail grew any colder. They parted ways with Seeker Eshana promising a very anxious Master Clarisse that he would send a messenger bird off the minute he knew anything conclusive concerning her cousin Chance.

The news that Chance might have been set off the smuggler's ship somewhere in the vicinity of the Shadow Islands had given Seeker Eshana pause. That the smuggler and her crew would chance getting even close to the Shadow Islands suggested to Seeker Eshana that someone with a worrisome source of information and a large amount of coin had hired the two lowlifes and the smuggler's ship. It seemed clear that Chance had not been a random target. It was important to find Mako and Pivane to get some questions answered. First and foremost was the question of how the two even knew Chance was to arrive in the port of Marinel. The second question was whether they knew why Chance was coming to Sommerhjem, which was a question Seeker Eshana also wanted answered. He had his suspicions.

Seeker Eshana took some time sorting through what he knew of the area surrounding the port of Marinel. He also tried to think about what someone in Mako or Pivane's line of work would do if they were feeling flush with coin. From all the information the Guildmaster had been able to gather, the two were no longer in the port and had not left by ship. That meant they had traveled off by land. Since they made their living being muscle for hire, one way to track them down might be to send word out that there was a lucrative job available and appeal to their greed. It would not do to send word out that a seeker was looking for the pair, so Seeker Eshana enlisted the help of an acquaintance he trusted. Several days later he had the location where the pair had settled to enjoy the fruits of their last job.

It took two days of hard riding for Seeker Eshana to reach the inn where Mako and Pivane had set themselves up. After leaving his horses and most of his gear in the inn's stable, Seeker Eshana entered the inn and took a table in a shadowed corner to wait. He wanted to observe Mako and Pivane before he approached them. It was closer to mid-afternoon when the two came strutting in as if they owned the place, yelling for service. A good amount of coin makes some people arrogant. The two Seeker Eshana was observing certainly seemed to feel they were entitled to immediate service because they had coin to throw around. No setting anything aside for a rainy day for this pair.

Seeker Eshana did not have time to wait for them to eventually run out of coin before approaching them, for that might take several more weeks. He needed to get their attention, and then, get some answers out of them as quickly as possible. After several hours of observing the two, Seeker Eshana came to the conclusion that the innkeeper, the rest of the inn's staff, nor the regular patrons were all that pleased with Mako or Pivane. They were loud and demanding. Just as Seeker Eshana was about to get up to approach the two, three men entered the inn and headed straight toward them.

"Well, lookie what we have here," sneered one of the men approaching Mako and Pivane's table. "Just the two cheating, lying lowlifes we've been looking for."

The man who had spoken grabbed a chair, turned it around, and straddled it facing the pair. The other two men had positioned themselves behind Mako and Pivane. When Mako had attempted to stand up, the man behind him had placed his hands on Mako's shoulders and pushed him back down. Mako began sputtering and protesting. Seeker Eshana could tell that this impromptu meeting could turn ugly fairly quickly. He unobtrusively got up and slipped out a side door of the inn, walking quickly to the stable where he retrieved his walking stick.

Walking to the front door of the inn, Seeker Eshana stood in the open doorway blocking the light. He made an imposing figure standing there, tall, staff in hand. Seeker Eshana just stood there looking over the room for a moment. He then walked straight to the table that held the five men.

"Your pardon, good sir," Seeker Eshana addressed the man seated across from Mako and Pivane, "but I have a need to speak to those two before you continue your business. I promise I will not detain them, but it is urgent. You will be well compensated for your time. I would also suggest that we escort the two outside, so as not to disturb the other fine folks present."

Seeker Eshana's request and suggestion was said in the mildest of tones. Whether it was his imposing stature, or the fact that all of the men had recognized him as a seeker, the man in charge signaled the others to allow Mako and Pivane to rise. There were a lot of tales circulating around Sommerhjem concerning seekers, many of which were just smoke and mirrors, but most folk would rather not test them out. Seeker Eshana had been counting on that.

When all of the men were outside the inn, Seeker Eshana suggested that they move to the stable, where it would be more difficult for Mako and Pivane to slip away. Once the two were placed in a stall and the door closed behind them, Seeker Eshana turned and addressed the leader of the three.

"I would have a very private word with the two you have an interest in. I have no wish to spend very much time with them. I give you my word, I will not let them get away before you have your discussion with them. Will that suit you?"

"That'll be fine, Seeker. Me and my men will be just outside the stable."

Seeker Eshana nodded his thanks and headed back inside. Once the man guarding the stall door had left the stable, Seeker Eshana entered the stall.

"Now then, gentlemen, and I use that term loosely, we need to talk."

What Seeker Eshana subsequently learned from Mako and Pivane was both disturbing and not very helpful. It was clear that they had no real knowledge as to who they had been working for. They were just hired lackeys. They had been offered a great deal of coin to snatch Chance when he arrived in the port of Marinel. They had been given a very accurate description of him, and the name of the ship he was to arrive on. They had followed him from the docks to the place he had stopped to eat. Slipping a sleeping draught into his soup had been quite easy. Pivane had distracted him, and Mako had taken care of the soup. They had then waited outside and followed him. Once he was manageable, they had carted him off to the smuggler's ship.

They did not know who had hired the ship, but when they got there, the captain had informed them that they had been left specific instructions as to what was to happen to Chance. Seems whoever was behind the hiring of both them and the smuggler's ship did not want Chance killed outright. He was to be dumped overboard just inside the fog bank of the Shadow Islands. Mako and Pivane did not know why they were supposed to drop him overboard there, but with what they were getting paid, they were more than willing to follow instructions.

"What about his gear?" Seeker Eshana inquired.

Mako and Pivane looked at each other, and there was a long pause before Mako spoke. "We was told to look through it for anythin' of value or anythin' odd. We was also told to look for any journals or books."

"And what did you find?"

"Look, we've been helpful answering your questions . . . ." Mako stated, realizing he had only a little more information to use as a bargaining chip, "but you gots to help us get away from those men outside the stable."

Seeker Eshana rose himself up to his full height and pounded his staff on the dirt floor of the stall. "You will tell me what I want to know, and you will tell me now," Seeker Eshana commanded.

Pivane stumbled all over his words to give the Seeker the information he wanted. "We, we didn't find nothin'. Just clothes and thin's. No books or any of thems other thin's thems that hired us wanted. He just had a sea bag, that's was all."

"And what happened to the sea bag?"

Both the men again glanced at each other, and then away. It was Pivane who again broke the silence first and told Seeker Eshana just what had happened to the sea bag. With a look of disgust, Seeker Eshana turned and left the stall, calling to the men outside the stable that the pair was all theirs. He knew where he needed to head next and hoped he was in time.

Chapter Fourteen

Seeker Eshana made it to the small seaport of Litenhaven in record time. He hoped he had remembered Skipper Nereo's route and routine. Luck rode with him, for he arrived just before Skipper Nereo's ship was set to leave port. He gave the reins of his horses over to a stable lad and swiftly strode to the dock.

"Permission to come aboard, Skipper," Seeker Eshana called out.

The Skipper, looking down at the man standing on the dock, got a delighted look on his face. He waved an arm, indicating that Seeker Eshana should come aboard.

"Welcome, my old friend. What brings you upon my ship's deck once again?"

"I'm hoping you have some information for me. If not, I'm hoping you can break away from your route and take me home."

"Why don't we take this conversation below to my cabin, my friend."

Once the two had settled themselves into Skipper Nereo's cabin, Seeker Eshana explained what had brought him to Litenhaven. "Master Clarisse of the Glassmakers Guild, and member of the Høyttaier clan, was expecting her cousin to arrive at the port of Marinel. When he was way overdue, we came looking. He was apparently intercepted. She had to get back to the capital, and I said I would try to find out what happened to him. It would seem that he was literally dropped off at the Shadow Islands, but unfortunately, he was weighted down with his sea bag. Is there any chance that you might have heard of a lad being rescued in recent weeks?"

"Funny that you should mention the word chance, for a young lad by that name was plucked from the sea with a little help from our guides and friends. He was taken under Keeper Odette's wing."

"That news is a mixed blessing then. Master Clarisse's cousin is alive, but still out of reach for her. Under the circumstances, I am hard pressed as to how I will be able to let her know."

"Actually, I need to clarify. This lad, Chance chose to take the rite of passage." Skipper Nereo looked up to see the look of grave concern on Seeker Eshana's face. "He's fine. Made it through relatively unscathed. As a matter of fact, I dropped him off about a half day's sail out from the port of Willing several days ago."

"Do you have any idea where he was heading?"

"Sorry, I'm not going to be much help there. He was going to sail up the Travers River at least as far as Tverdal. I don't know if he was going to travel beyond that point."

"It will be a place to start then. Can you give me any help on how I might recognize him? Master Clarisse gave me a general description, but anything you can add would be helpful," suggested Seeker Eshana.

"Well, now that you mention it," said Skipper Nereo, giving a hearty laugh, "there are two things. One, he's carrying a staff that looks very much like yours. Second, he has a traveling companion."

"He is traveling with someone? Anyone I know?"

"I don't think you know him . . . ."

"Someone new since I was last there?"

"Sorry, I have not been clear. His companion is a halekrets."

Seeker Eshana sat back, and the look of astonishment was quite something to behold, for Seeker Eshana did not get fazed by much.

"A halekrets, you say?"

"A halekrets."

"Oh my."

"Oh my, indeed. Is it important that you actually catch up with him, or just find out he is alright?"

"It is important that I catch up with him. Seems he has an important task to complete for his family. Someone discovered why he had come to Sommerhjem and waylaid him. It seems to me that either someone Master Clarisse trusted has betrayed her, or somehow information is being acquired in places conversations should be safe. Regardless of how the information was obtained, it is important that Chance's identity is kept as quiet as possible. It is imperative that he be able to complete what he came here for. Right now, he is relatively safe, but there are eyes and ears everywhere who will be trying to stop what he needs to accomplish if it is discovered he is back in Sommerhjem."

"You would get there fastest by ship. There is a good fresh wind blowing."

"There is the matter of my horses and gear."

"How are your horses' sea legs?"

"Tolerable."

"We can sail within the hour."

Chance had not made good time sailing to the port of Willing because the winds had been light much of the afternoon. Since it was so late in the day by the time he had arrived at the port of Willing, Chance dropped anchor in the shelter of the harbor and chose not to go ashore. The night was warm and relatively clear. It would not be the first time he had spent the night sleeping on a boat. Ashu seemed content, and so, the two settled in after a cold dinner and watched the sun set and the stars come out. The gentle rocking of the boat was comforting. For the first time in days, Chance felt a moment of peace. He knew that that feeling was only temporary, but for this night he was going to hold onto it.

Tomorrow would be soon enough to do what he needed to do next. He needed to sail at least as far as Tverdal before leaving the skiff behind. After that, he would need to acquire a good horse, but perhaps not right away. He was glad that Mako and Pivane had only gone through his sea bag and not looked too closely at its handles. He was also glad they had not searched him very thoroughly. If they had, he would not have the means to purchase a horse and saddle. He could probably find a meal and a place to stay at the farms along the way he needed to travel, and he was used to hard work. It was not uncommon for lads of his age to do a walkabout before they settled down. Farms always had chores needing to be done, and many would welcome an extra hand in exchange for a meal and a place in the hayloft to sleep.

Feeling like he at least had some type of plan in place, Chance was soon asleep, lulled by the gentle rocking of the boat. He awoke at dawn. The day was somewhat overcast, and there was a good wind blowing. Although the clouds continued to gather throughout the day, Chance and Ashu made steady progress up the river. About mid-afternoon Chance passed through Tverdal. During his sail up the river he had determined that he did not want to stop in the large town, being somewhat leery after his experience in Marinel. Instead, he continued on and dropped anchor near dusk, once again sleeping on the boat. The next morning he awoke to a dark and dreary sky. Looking down river, Chance could see the storm clouds were continuing to build.

"We had best pull up anchor and skedaddle, Ashu. I don't like the looks of those clouds coming in. I don't think the darkness out there is just a fog bank. Never good to be caught in a storm, and I would like to get as far up river as I can this day."

As the morning wore on, the sky became darker and darker, and the wind increased. Fortunately for Chance, he had the wind at his back and was able to move along at quite a good clip. When thunder began to rumble and he could see lightning in the clouds behind him, Chance decided it was time to look for a place to get off the river and tie up. Up until that point, the river had held a pretty straight course. Chance noted that just ahead the river took a turn, and once he had rounded the turn, he spotted a small fishing village nestled in a sheltered cove.

"Looks like we're in luck, Ashu."

Chance turned the bow of the boat into the small cove and deftly pulled up the centerboard. A short moment later the keel of the skiff scraped against the river bottom. Chance leapt out and began to pull the skiff farther up on the shore. He was surprised when another pair of hands grabbed the side of the skiff and helped him haul it completely out of the water. Looking up, he saw a man of middle years dressed in fisher garb.

"Best pull her a little higher. This storm that's a comin' looks to be a nasty one. Ye can tie her to that iron ring in that large boulder yonder. We don't get much tide surge here, but ye never know what twist nature will take."

Chance thanked the fisher and tied the skiff up as he had been directed. He quickly furled the sails and laced them tightly to the boom. Once the skiff was battened down, he grabbed his pack and walking stick out of the boat. Ashu had surreptitiously tucked himself into the pouch-like pocket that had been built into the front of Chance's pack. The fisher had indicated that Chance should follow him up a path, over a low dune covered with marsh grass. Ahead of them, set on stilts, were several small cottages. The two of them stepped through the door of the largest of the cottages, just as the skies opened up. A huge clap of thunder caused Chance to jump.

"It's a good thing ye got off the river when ye did. This storm is goin' to be a bad one. I can feel it in my bones. Ye wouldn't have been able to sail much farther up river in any case. River gets a mite narrow and shallow about a quarter of a day beyond here. I'm Devisser, and ye are welcome to wait out the storm here. What . . . ." Devisser stopped speaking when Ashu poked his head out of Chance's pack. "I was goin' to ask ye who ye are, what brings ye to my neck of the river, but more importantly, what is that animal?"

"I will try to answer your questions in order of importance," Chance answered, taking an instant liking to the gruff fisher. "My furry friend here is a halekrets and I've named him Ashu. He's a little shy. My name is Chance, and I'm beginning a walkabout. My folks thought I should get it out of my system before I joined the family business."

"I'm familiar with walkabouts. Took one myself in my youth. I must confess I'm not familiar with halekrets."

Chance knew that the little halekrets was going to cause comment, so he and Keeper Odette had discussed what he could say.

"I don't know very much myself," stated Chance, which was the truth. "I found him adrift on a plank when I was sailing along the coast. Could have been on a ship. He seems very comfortable on the skiff. Anyway, he seems content to be with me, and quite frankly I like his company."

"Always good to have a companion with ye on a walkabout. Like I said, ye are welcome to wait out the storm here. Ye intend to sail farther up river, and then head back to the sea?"

"Actually, now that I know I couldn't go much farther upriver, I'm wondering, could I leave my skiff here? It's time to begin the walk part of my walkabout."

"Can't see as that would be a problem. Make yerself at home. I need to go check if the last of our boats has made it home. Be back shortly."

The floorboards shook as the latest series of thunder claps rumbled overhead. Chance did not envy Devisser being out in the pounding rain. The cottage had grown cold with the increased damp, so Chance added a few more logs to the fire. Then, he filled the tea kettle and swung it over the fire. Steam had just begun to rise when Devisser returned. Rain and wind followed him in the door, along with another fisher. Chance was surprised when the second fisher pulled back the hood of her rain cloak, revealing her as a woman of middle years.

"So glad to be in off the river. That's quite a storm brewing out there. So, ye must be Chance. I'm Berrimilla, Devisser's wife. Welcome to our home. Let me get out of these wet clothes, and then maybe we can talk Devisser into putting a meal together. Ah, I see ye put the kettle on. I certainly thank ye for that. Oh my, who is your little friend?"

The wind favored the sail back to the port of Willing, and Skipper Nereo pulled up to the town dock midmorning. Close scrutiny of the boats in the harbor suggested that Chance's skiff was not moored there. Once Seeker Eshana had unloaded his horses, he thanked Skipper Nereo and his crew.

"Thank you for the quick and safe passage. I hope this has not disrupted your schedule too much."

"Not to worry. Our schedule can never be set in stone because we are always at the whims of nature and the sea. I will be back in Litenhaven, barring weather, around the half-moon, should you have need."

"Thank you, again. Give my greetings to your family when you are back home."

The road was a good one from the port of Willing to the town of Tverdal, and Seeker Eshana made good time, until he had to seek shelter during a heavy storm. Once he reached Tverdal, he headed to the docks to see if Chance had moored his skiff there. Having no luck spotting the skiff, Seeker Eshana was just about to depart, when he caught a snatch of a conversation.

"'Twas the cutest little animal ye ever did see. Lad called it a halekrets."

Seeker Eshana edged closer to the pair who were talking. The woman fisher was telling one of the fishmongers about how this lad had pulled his skiff up at their cove in order to get off the water before the storm.

"Nice young lad, he was. Most polite. Husband said he handled that skiff like he had been sailing all his life. Said he found the little animal adrift on a plank off the coast. Shy little thing. He named it Ashu. Never seen the like. Just another one of those odd mysteries the sea gifts one, that's what I say."

"Did he come to town with you, so as we's can see the, what did you call it, a halekrets?"

"No. He asked to leave his skiff with us and set off on a walkabout. Got my husband reminiscing about his own youthful walkabout. Husband had us in stitches. I was a little worried he was going to pack a knapsack and head off with the lad, the old fool," the woman fisher said fondly. "Said maybe before he got too old, he would take a chance on Chance. Thought he was pretty clever making a joke about the lad's name."

When the fishmonger looked at the fisher questioningly, she explained the lad's name was Chance. Both women had a good chuckle over that. Seeker Eshana had moved close enough to enter the conversation at that point. He introduced himself and asked if the fisher knew where Chance had been heading, suggesting he had been supposed to meet him but had been delayed.

"He didn't say, but the best lane out from our place heads toward the village of Elvebredd. He might've been goin' that way. He's on foot."

Seeker Eshana thanked the woman and headed back to get his horses. He was in such a hurry he did not notice that there was another folk on the dock who had paid close attention to his conversation with the fisher and had left the dock just as swiftly.

Chapter Fifteen

Seeker Eshana made two stops before he left Tverdal. He stopped in at the Glassmakers Guildhall and had a brief talk with Master Meriter. Seeker Eshana used one of the Guildhall's messenger birds to send a quick coded note off to Master Clarisse. He also obtained the name of a good horse trader. Once he left the Guildhall, he purchased a good sturdy horse and saddle. As he was leaving the horse trader's place, Seeker Eshana became aware that he was being followed. Curious as to why someone would be following him, he turned down a side alley, tied the reins of the pack animal and the new horse to his horse, and sent them farther down the alley. Stepping into the dark shadows, he stood silently and waited. He did not have to wait long. The scrawny street lad, who had been following Seeker Eshana, found himself dangling a foot off the ground with a very surprised look on his face.

"Now then, lad, it would be in your best interest to explain quite quickly why you are following me," Seeker Eshana stated quietly, but with authority in his voice.

The street lad found he could not look away from the Seeker's eyes. A half dozen reasons flashed through his head to explain away why he was in the alley. He discarded all of them almost before they formed. There was something about this man who was dangling him off the ground that frightened him more than those who had hired him. He did not even try to negotiate a few coins for the information.

"A man from the docks, sir, he gave me a copper to follow youse."

"And . . . ."

"And I was to report back to him where youse went and what youse did."

"How long were you to follow me?"

"'Til youse settled for the night, or youse left town."

"Anything else?"

"Well, ah, could youse set me down, sir?" asked the street lad, who was beginning to recover from his surprise and fright.

Seeker Eshana could see the lad was beginning to get a slight look of cunning back, and so, changed tactics. Before he set the lad down, he whistled for his horses. When the horses returned, effectively blocking one end of the alley, Seeker Eshana placed himself so he cut off the other direction out of the alley, and then, set the street lad down, keeping a firm grip on his arm.

"Well then, now that your feet are once again back on the ground, do you think that and a few copper coins might help your thinking? The information you give me is going to be free. The payment is for you to forget we had this conversation, and that forgetfulness will be pledged on your honor. Are we clear?"

"Yes, sir."

"Pledged on your honor?"

The street lad took a look at the Seeker's face and knew if he pledged, he would not break the oath. There was something about the man holding him that told the lad that there was no weasel room with this situation.

"Yes, sir."

"I would hear you say it."

"I pledge on my honor that nothing of our conversation in this alley will be told to anyone else."

"Fair enough. Now, what else can you tell me?"

"Well, that same man as hired me, also hired one of me lads to run off and carry a message to some other man. I don't know the other man. He's a stranger in our town. Been here about a fortnight."

"Go on."

"Me lad was to take a message to him."

"Do you know what the message was about?"

"Don't know, sir. Honest. Just me lad was to fetch this man quickly. Something about the package they's was looking for had arrived."

Seeker Eshana had a very bad feeling at that moment. He flipped the street lad the coins he had promised and mounted up.

"When you get back to the man who hired you, tell him you followed me to the Guildhall, to the horse trader's, and then lost me when I took off on horseback with my pack horse and an extra horse. You don't really know where I was heading, and that will be the truth."

Seeker Eshana then wheeled his horse around and headed back the way he came. The street lad was wise enough not to try to keep up and follow him. It had not worked out so well the first time.

Seeker Eshana thought to himself that if he had overheard the conversation on the dock, it meant others may have also. Not only that, the telling about the halekrets by the fisherwoman to the fishmonger might not have been the first time she had told that tale. As Seeker Eshana began his quick journey out of town, he berated himself for not being quicker in his thinking. Just because Mako and Pivane had found Chance and thought they had disposed of him, it did not mean others who were to be on the lookout for Chance had been given the word to stop looking. While it appeared that Chance was expected by his cousin Master Clarisse to disembark at the port of Marinel, weather and other circumstances could have prevented the ship he was sailing on to pull in there, so he might have had to dock at any number of ports along the coast. It stood to reason, the port of Marinel was not the only one being watched.

Seeker Eshana put some distance between himself and the town of Tverdal before he slowed his horses down. He did not doubt that there might have been someone else alerted to which way he had headed out of town. He had been torn between heading directly east toward the village of Elvebredd, or trying to misdirect anyone who had an interest in where he was heading. The fact that others were interested in Chance had given Seeker Eshana a very bad feeling, so he had chosen to head toward the village of Elvebredd. He hoped he was either not too late or Chance had become much more careful in his journey. If only the lad had not been so trusting with his name.

As Chance began to walk away from Devisser and Berrimilla's cove on the lane that headed toward the village of Elvebredd, he had some time to reflect on what had happened in the last week. In thinking over his journey, he realized he should have used much more caution when pulling into the cove. He had had a plausible story as to what he was doing there and an explanation about Ashu. That was all well and good, but he had made an erroneous assumption that no one would be interested in him since he had been picked up and supposedly taken care of by Mako and Pivane. As he walked, it had occurred to him that Sommerhjem was not a small island or a small village where everyone knew your business. It had not been rational for him to think that others might not know of him and had not been alerted to look for him. Chance was not all that common a name, and here he had just introduced himself to the fishers with his real name. Once again, he berated himself for being so unprepared and, quite frankly, very bad at grand adventuring.

"Those characters in storybooks always seem to know instinctively what to do and make the right decisions, Ashu. Me, I just keep bumbling my way along, and look where that has led me so far. I need to learn to be much more cautious."

Ashu made no comment.

Chance had been walking about a half day and was looking for a place where he might take a break. Just off the road he spotted a small spring and decided it would be a good place to rest. He was rooting through his pack, looking for his drinking cup, when he heard the sound of horses approaching from the direction he had just come from. He did not know what caused him to quickly grab Ashu and put him on a low branch of the tree he was standing next to.

"Quick, Ashu, hide," Chance directed the halekrets in a quiet but urgent voice.

For some reason, Chance wished he could also scramble up a tree and hide in the foliage, but none of the trees by the spring were big enough to conceal him. Trying to look casual, he went back to his pack, located his drinking cup, and was just dipping it into the spring when two riders pulled up on the lane by the spring.

"You lad, you Chance?" one of the riders asked. "Master Clarisse of the Glassmakers Guild sent us looking for you."

It was all Chance could do to hold steady. He had to think quickly. How would his cousin even know he was in the area? Before he had left the islands of Havkoller, he had been given instructions as to what he was to do when he disembarked at the port of Marinel. If for some reason the ship he was on was unable to make it to the port of Marinel, Chance was supposed to stay along the coast, find another means to get to Marinel by water. He didn't think his cousin would have sent word about the countryside for folks to be looking for him, should he be delayed or missing. His chances of getting to where his father had tucked the oppgave ringe piece away for safekeeping, without being stopped, rested on the idea that very few folks would even know he was in Sommerhjem, or why. No, this did not feel right, and he was glad he had hidden Ashu.

"I'm not who youse are wantin' sirs. Me name's Sorley. Who'd youse says youse was lookin' for?

Neither of the two riders looked convinced by Chance's answer. "We're looking for a lad named Chance. You certainly fit the description we were given. Where are you from, and where are you heading?"

"Well, I'm headin' to me granmere's house. I'm her main helper yah sees. I'm good with the animals, I is."

Chance was now getting a very bad feeling about the two sitting astride their horses. He had two hopes. One was that Ashu would not suddenly decide to come down out of the tree and show himself. Second, he hoped that the two riders would believe him and head off.

"Why don't you swing up behind me? My horse can easily carry two, and we can get you to your granmere's house all the sooner."

"Ack, that's kind of youse, sirs, but this bein' me half day, I'm in no hurry to get anywhere. I thank youse, though."

"Your half day is it now? And just what are you doing with your half day off?"

Chance's mind was scrambling for an answer while his eyes were desperately seeking a way to run. He was finding neither an answer to the man's question, nor was he finding an escape route. If he tried to run, he would not get very far on foot against two men on horses.

"I'm thinking this lad is not telling us the truth."

"Yer right, sir," Chance stated.

The man who was beginning to swing down off his horse, reversed his progress and sat back down in the saddle. "You're the lad Chance?"

"That were not what I were lyin' about sir. It's not really me half day, but, well . . . ." and here Chance tried to look really embarrassed. "Well, the truth is that there's this lass, see . . . ." At this point Chance put his head down, his hands behind his back, and dragged his left foot back and forth in the dirt, trying to look as shy as he could. He hoped it was working.

"I, for one, think we should escort the young lad back to his granmere's place," stated the man, who again began to dismount. "We are honor bound to make sure his old granny gets a full day's work out of him."

"Or, we could just take him back to the fisher's cove and have them tell us if this is the lad that left his skiff moored in their cove, the lad called Chance," suggested the other man.

"Really, sirs, I'm not this lad yer looking for. Yer've no call to just go around bullying any lad ye run across." Chance had never been very good at lying, at least that is what his mother had told him. These men, besides frightening him, were also making him angry. "I might be skippin' out on a bit o' work for me granmere, but youse has no call to drag me home. What's what between granmere and me is none of youse's business."

By now the larger of the two men had completed swinging down off his horse and began walking toward Chance, who was steadily moving back away from the man. In a sudden move, the large man made a grab for Chance. His having older brothers and sisters and learning how to dodge them when they roughhoused helped. Unfortunately, while he was trying to dodge another grab by the first man, the second man dismounted and came toward him. Now, he found himself playing keep away from both men. Chance did not know how much longer he would be able to elude the men. Just when he thought all was lost, the two horses the men had been riding suddenly fled the clearing. Chance and the two men paused in their game of keep away and watched the backsides of the horses disappear down the road. Chance thought he saw a ringed tail flying out behind the mane of one of the horses.

Chapter Sixteen

Seeker Eshana was berating himself. Sometimes being smart does not always suggest one also possesses common sense, he thought to himself. He should have left Tverdal the minute he had overheard the fisher talking about Chance. Since leaving town, he had held his horses to a steady ground-covering pace, but he would need to stop soon. How much of a head start others had, who might be after Chance, was a big unknown. Whether he was even following the right lane was another big question. He had just begun to slow his horses down to a walk when he heard the thunder of hooves approaching. Seeker Eshana shifted in his saddle to prepare himself.

Rounding a bend in the lane gave Seeker Eshana a clear view of the two rider-less horses that were galloping toward him. He quickly released the lead rope of the pack horse, knowing it would not wander off. The new horse he had acquired would stay tied to the pack horse, he hoped. Seeker Eshana then turned his horse around and prepared to try to snag the reins of the lead horse that was charging his way. He hoped the two running toward him were tired, for so was his horse. Just as the lead horse approached, Seeker Eshana urged his horse forward. As the lead horse came along side, Seeker Eshana made a quick shift of his body, leaned down, and grabbed the trailing reins of the lead horse, which were fortunately hanging down on his side. Slowing his horse and pulling the other horse to a slow walk, and then to a stop, did not take too long. Fortunately, the second horse slowed and stopped at the same time. Seeker Eshana dismounted, tied the reins of the lead horse to his own, and walked back to secure the second horse that had been running free.

As he approached his second horse and pack horse, he thought he heard something racing through the trees overhead, but could see nothing. Having traveled extensively throughout his life and seen a great deal, not much surprised Seeker Eshana anymore. Looking back at his horses, the sight of a halekrets perched on his pack horse with a small hand resting on Seeker Eshana's walking stick, however, caused him to pause.

"Well, now, you're an unexpected surprise. Been a long time since I've seen one of your kind. A bit far from home aren't you?" Seeker Eshana spoke in a quiet gentle voice to the little halekrets, whose ear tuffs and fur were standing straight up. "I'm looking for your friend, Chance, and I am thinking he is in trouble. Give me a moment while I tie these horses up, and then, we will go see. That alright with you?"

Seeker Eshana walked over to the pack horse and took out a coil of rope. Ashu did not move from his spot. Seeker Eshana then moved off the lane and tied the rope between two sturdy trees. He took the two horses he had halted and led them off the road, tying them to the rope. He did the same with his pack horse and the spare horse, all the while explaining to Ashu that they would be able to move faster if not burdened down with a small herd of horseflesh. Once the horses were secure, Seeker Eshana invited the halekrets to join him, not knowing if the little animal would understand. Ashu reached Seeker Eshana's horse and scampered up onto the saddle before Seeker Eshana arrived. He did not know how far the two horses he had captured had run, but he hoped wherever they had come from was not so far away that he would be too late to help Chance. He had no doubt in his mind that the horses and the halekrets were linked to Chance's whereabouts.

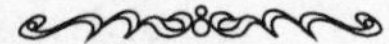

The horses running off momentarily distracted the two men who were trying to capture Chance, giving him an opportunity to put some distance between himself and the two men. Now, however, he was facing two very angry men, and the very serious game of keep-away began again. Chance had quickness on his side, but they had numbers. He did not think he could outrun them, but he needed to try. The men had worked themselves to either side of him and were moving in. In a desperate move, Chance began to run toward one of the men as the other one chased him. In a last minute maneuver, he abruptly pivoted and made a desperate dash, barely missing being caught by the man's outstretched hands.

Chance found himself running toward the lane and decided that the levelness of the lane might be to his advantage. At least he hoped he would be quicker than the two following him. If not quicker, then perhaps he would find a place he could veer off the lane that might provide some cover. Maybe there would be a farm up ahead, and he could appeal to the farmer to help him. Glancing over his shoulder, he became aware he was not lengthening the distance between himself and those who were chasing after him. Now, if he could just find a river he could dive into. He was a very good swimmer and could only hope the men chasing him would not be.

Running long distance was not something he had done very much of, and he was beginning to get a stitch in his side. His breath was coming out in ragged gasps. To add to his problems, he became aware of the sound of a horse coming up from behind. When he took a look over his shoulder, he saw that the two men who were chasing him were gaining, and so were the horse and rider. Unfortunately, while he was looking behind, he did not notice the deep rut in the lane. When his foot hit the rut it threw him off stride and off balance, causing him to go down hard, knocking the wind out of him.

The horse and rider who had been coming up behind Chance passed the two men who had been chasing him and pulled his horse up just short of Chance. One of the tallest and largest men Chance had ever seen dismounted, reached down, helped Chance up, and then turned to face the two men who had drawn up a short ways away from them.

"Can I help you gentlemen?" Seeker Eshana inquired.

"You can step away from that lad. He, ah, he tried to steal our horses."

"If he tried to steal your horses, where are they?"

"Well, they ran off when he was trying to steal them."

"Then why are you not chasing after the horses rather than the boy?"

"We were going to catch him and take him back to Tverdal to the peacekeepers. We're hoping his horse," the man stated pointing to the other man, "will return to his home stable. Hopefully, mine will follow."

"So, let me get this straight. You are suggesting that this lad somehow overcame the two of you long enough to untie your horses and then run them off?"

"Well, see we were, ah, napping, yes napping, and so, while we were asleep, this lad here, ah . . . ."

"I can only hope that you do not make your living as a storyteller, for the one you are trying to tell me is way too unbelievable. Two men caught napping by a spring just off the lane are chanced upon by a thieving youth who is so inept at horse stealing that he sends them charging down the road. Seems he would just have untied them, mounted up and ridden off with you both chasing after. So lad, I would hear your side of the story."

"I were just gettin' a drink when these men says they's lookin' fer some lad named Chance, or Charles, or some such. I telled them I weren't him, but they weren't believin' me. I knows it's was wrong to trys to take me half day when I shouldn't, but that don't give thems no call to tries to grab me and take me back to me granmere's. That 'taint right now, 'tis it? I was just tryin' to see this lass I's sweet on . . . ." Chance tried to put a bit of whine into his voice.

"You can't be believing the lad, now, can you?" one of the men asked.

"I see no evidence that the lad tried to steal your horses, and fortunately for you, I managed to catch them. They are tied up down the way. Let me have a chat with the lad here. You two can start your trek down the lane, and I will join you in a moment."

Both of the men took one look at the look Seeker Eshana gave them and decided that there was no point in arguing. They would just have to cut their losses here, and once they had their horses, regroup. Once the two were well out of sight and hearing, Seeker Eshana turned to Chance.

"Your little halekrets has had quite an experience riding, but I think he prefers trees. He is really quite quick. I don't think the two men who were after you ever saw him, which is a good thing. Look to your right about half way up that pine at the edge of the road."

Chance tried not to look startled and wondered if he should stay in character as the farm lad off on his stolen half day, or look. Ashu took the decision out his hands by chittering loudly as he scrambled down the tree trunk. He fairly flew across the short distance from the tree to Chance and was on Chance's shoulder almost before he could blink, much less react.

"Perhaps introductions are in order, but we need to make it quick. I need to reach the place where I tied up the two men's horses before they do. I want to make sure they have a very long walk back to Tverdal," Seeker Eshana said with a wink. "I am Seeker Eshana and am acquainted with your cousin Master Clarisse, if you are Chance. She has been very worried about you. I know you have no reason to believe I am even a seeker, or that I have your best interest at heart. Just know I count Keeper Odette and Skipper Nereo as friends. Think on that while I take care of our two acquaintances. I will be back shortly. If then you choose not to stay in my company, that will be your choice."

Chance watched the man, who called himself Seeker Eshana, ride off. There was much to be said for waiting for his return. The man claiming to be a seeker knew that Ashu was a halekrets, but then, he could have learned that from the fishers in whose cove Chance had left his skiff. While the Seeker somehow might have run into Skipper Nereo, Chance did not think the Skipper would have volunteered information about Chance, but that was possible. The name that was hardest to explain away was that of Keeper Odette. How would the Seeker know, or know of, Keeper Odette?

Chance was torn. So far, he had not been smart in his choices. He did not want to make another mistake. Those two men who had tried to capture him were looking for him specifically. He did not think for a minute that he might have seen the last of them. He should get himself as quickly as he could to the nearest village or town and try to get some means of transportation other than being on foot. On the other hand, if the Seeker really was a seeker, he would certainly seem to be a good ally to have around. Chance finally decided he was going to get that drink that had been interrupted, repack his pack, retrieve his walking stick that had been dropped in the fray, and begin walking. The Seeker Eshana could certainly find him on this lane, and the Seeker had left the choice of whether to stay in his company up to Chance.

Chance had been walking about half an hour when he heard the sounds of several horses approaching from behind. He could only hope it was not the two men returning, or someone else who was looking for him. The land was too open for him to find a hiding place. A sense of weariness settled over him, weighing his shoulders down like a heavy winter coat. He knew he could not outrun whoever was coming up from behind.

Seeker Eshana had mixed feelings about leaving the lad Chance, but he needed to make sure the two men who had almost captured Chance would not just turn around and follow him again. The men did not have too much of a head start. He was sure he could overtake them, and even pass them by, if he pushed. He needed to figure out a way to really delay the men without being accused of being a horse thief.

It did not take long for him to catch up, for the two men were moving even more slowly than Seeker Eshana had anticipated. One was now limping, and the other did not look to be in much better shape. Neither of the men looked like walking and running was something they did on a daily basis, so this day's exercise had taken its toll. An idea began to form up in Seeker Eshana's mind. He pulled his horse up alongside the two men.

"Gentlemen, and I use that term loosely, the more I have thought about your version of what happened and the lad's story, the more I have become convinced that you were not telling the truth. A thought occurred to me that perhaps you are in the business of 'recruiting' young lads to serve on ships without their leave. What is to prevent me from turning you over to the Tverdal peacekeepers?"

"Now, just wait a darn minute. You've got no call to accuse us of being involved in dragooning nobody." The man who spoke had no illusions that the big man riding the horse beside him was more than capable of overpowering him and his companion.

"If not trying to press the lad into service, just why were you after him?" Seeker Eshana asked, hoping to gain some information that might be helpful. "I don't believe for one minute he was trying to steal your horses. A young lad, no matter how sweet he is on a lass, would probably not resort to horse thievery. His sweetheart is probably on the next farm over, or over a hill and around a bend. Certainly within walking distance."

The two men looked at each other. Both were reluctant to answer the rider's question.

"I would suggest you do not continue to lie to me," Seeker Eshana stated with authority in his voice.

"Look, times are hard, and so's work on the docks. This man, see, he gave us some extra coin to keep our eyes and ears open. We were to report to him if we learned anything about a lad called Chance. We overheard this fisherwoman talking about a lad of that name and some little animal he had, so we took the information to the man. He sent us off looking for the lad with a promise of several silvers if we found him and brought him back."

"Does this man have a name?"

"Calls himself Adok."

"And where might a folk find this Adok?"

"He spends his time at the Leather Scupper down by the docks. He's a nasty piece of work."

"So, why do you work for him?"

"Likes I said, times have been hard. All those taxes and special licenses the Regent imposed shut a lot of jobs down. We both have families and mouths to feed. This seemed like some easy coin, though I was having second thoughts."

"I am inclined to believe what you are now telling me. I think what you need to do is let this Adok know the lad you chanced upon was just a farm lad and not the lad Chance. If he had been this Chance lad, I wonder where the little animal was? Did you see this lad with an animal?"

"No, sir."

The two men and Seeker Eshana continued down the lane until they arrived to the place where Seeker Eshana had left the horses. He told the men to stand back while he dismounted and untied his pack animal and extra horse. He then untied the rope he had strung between the two trees and took the reins of the other two horses. Looping the reins over the horses' necks, he gave each of them a slap across their rumps, sending them trotting down the lane. The two men began to protest, but Seeker Eshana stopped them with a look.

"While I'm inclined to believe you, I'm also not so trusting as to think that you might not just turn around and try to snatch that poor lovesick lad back up and claim he is the lad Adok wants. I figure it's a long walk into Tverdal, and by then, the lad might be more difficult to find. Now off with you. If you hurry, you may just catch up with your horses."

Still protesting, the two men hurried down the lane after their horses. Seeker Eshana tied the lead ropes attached to his pack horse and extra horse to his saddle, mounted his own horse, and turned it to head back where he had left the lad. He only hoped the lad was still waiting for him.

Chapter Seventeen

Chance was somewhat relieved when he looked behind and saw that the rider that was approaching was the man who had introduced himself as Seeker Eshana. He was still not sure about the man, and he had not made a decision as to what he wanted to do next. He did want to ask a few questions, however. As the rider drew closer, Chance saw that he had a pack animal with him and an extra horse that was saddled. He could only wonder why the man had an extra horse. Had he stolen it from the two men who had tried to nab him?.

"Now then, lad, you made a wise choice to keep moving on down the lane. I would like to take a moment to rest my horses and have a long conversation with you. However, I'm not really trusting our two acquaintances. If they manage to catch their horses, which I sent down the lane toward Tverdal, they might try to follow you, or me, or us. Perhaps you can trust me enough to mount up and put some distance between us and those who might attempt to follow."

"Do you always travel with an extra horse fully saddled?" Chance asked, for he was still undecided as to what to do.

"A good and astute question. No, I do not, but I had hoped to catch up with you. I caught a fisherwoman's conversation at the docks concerning a lad named Chance who traveled with a halekrets. Skipper Nereo had informed me of your companion. I caught up with the good Skipper at Litenhaven, and he gave my horses and me a quick trip to the port of Willing. From there, I rode to Tverdal looking for you. After I overheard the conversation concerning you at the dock, I took the time to pick up an extra riding horse, thinking it might make your travels easier. I also sent a coded message via messenger bird to your cousin, Master Clarisse. It was a calculated risk, for we are both concerned that there is someone who is passing on information best kept quiet to the wrong sort. Obviously, your arrival was rather important to someone other than your cousin. Perhaps with time, you will trust me with that reason. Meanwhile, why don't you mount up? We can continue this conversation farther on down the road. Oh, and you might want to tie your walking stick to the pack animal."

Chance weighed his options and could not see the harm in taking the offer of a horse. What had made Chance feel better about his choice to go with the Seeker was what he had found on the pack animal when he had gone to tie his walking stick onto the back of the pack. As reluctant as he had been to let go of the walking stick, he could see the wisdom of tying it onto the pack animal. It would have been awkward to try to ride, carry the walking stick, and make sure Ashu was secure. What he had found tied to the top of the packs on the pack horse was a walking stick that could have been the twin of his. If nothing else, he wanted to know where the Seeker had acquired his walking stick.

Chance swung himself onto the saddle. While it had been quite some time since he had ridden, he did not think he would embarrass himself as the horse moved into a trot. He would be sore when the ride ended this day. Ashu, however, had positioned himself in front of Chance and was holding onto the front of the saddle as if he had ridden horses all his life. The lane they were traveling on was reasonably flat, and it was not a challenging ride, for which Chance was thankful.

This close to the river, the land was fertile farmland. Though he had spent about half his life living in Sommerhjem before his family fled to Havkoller, he was surprised he did not feel any sense of homecoming. Neither had he felt really at home in Havkoller.

After having ridden for several hours, Seeker Eshana called a halt. "Let's dismount and walk the horses for a while. I, for one, need to stretch my legs, and my horse could use a rest. Let's walk them to cool them down, and while we are walking, perhaps we can get acquainted. I'm sure you have questions. I have made the assumption that you're the lad named Chance who is the cousin of Master Clarisse. When she had word that you had arrived in the port of Marinel but had not made it to the Glassmakers Guildhall, she became very worried. I accompanied her from the capital to find out what had happened to you. She is aware that you were dropped off at the Shadow Islands. I persuaded her to return to her duties in the capital and offered to try to locate you."

Chance dismounted, and Ashu took up his customary spot on Chance's shoulder. Chance took his time sorting out just how much to tell this Seeker, and what questions he wanted to ask.

"How do I even know you're a seeker?" Chance asked, because he wanted to know, and to give himself a bit more time to sort out his thinking.

"That's a good question, and one that really doesn't have an answer. Seekers don't come with identifying marks or letters from the Crown. I could unpack my formal seeker robes or show you the medallion I wear around my neck, but I could have had them made just as well as earned them. I could introduce you to folk who would vouch for me, but then you don't know them either. There's neither a reassuring nor satisfactory answer I'm afraid."

"Would you tell me where you got your walking stick?"

"Now, that's a question I can answer, and you are one of the very few folks that I can give an honest answer to, for I know you won't betray me."

Chance stopped walking and turned to face Seeker Eshana. How would he know he would not betray him, Chance wondered.

"I was born and grew up on the Shadow Islands. As mysterious as the Shadow Islands are to many, to me they were just my home. That surprises you. Not all who dwell on the Shadow Islands drifted there on the tide, never to leave again. At any rate, while I found the archives fascinating, I felt a call, I guess you could call it, to seek out the old knowledge and learning so I could add to the archives. To do that, I needed to leave the islands and apprentice with a seeker. When I first arrived in Sommerhjem, I stayed for a time with Keeper Odette's older sister, who had left the islands before me. When I had finished my training and was about to strike off on my own, she gave me the walking stick. Why do you ask?"

"I guess it's the one thing that has me leaning toward believing you. You might want to take a close look at the walking stick I tied onto your pack horse."

Seeker Eshana walked back to the pack horse and looked at the two walking sticks tied side by side. It was obvious that they were made by the same carver. In point of fact, except for very few variations, the walking sticks were a matched pair.

"Interesting. May I ask how you acquired your walking stick?"

Chance thought it sounded too farfetched to tell Seeker Eshana that he had acquired the walking stick in a dream, so he just told him it had been left in his sleeping quarters in the middle of the night. It was the truth, if not quite the whole story. Seeker Eshana did not press Chance to elaborate.

"It would seem that we have a place to start, then," stated Seeker Eshana, when he returned to take the reins of his horse back from Chance. "The offer still stands to travel together for as long as you wish. I told your cousin I would try to find you. Do we need to get you to the capital and her?"

This Seeker keeps asking questions I really don't want to answer, Chance thought to himself. He could go to the capital and meet up with his cousin, but then more people might become aware of him. He could just thank the Seeker for rescuing him from the two men and part ways with him. He could take a chance and stick with the Seeker. The latter seemed the best course for now.

"I think, since there seem to be some really undesirable folks trying to find me, going to the capital at this time would not be in my best interest. I would like to take you up on that offer to travel a ways with you."

"Fair enough. I suggest we mount up and put a little more distance between us and Tverdal. Any particular direction you need to head?"

Once again, Chance was torn as to how much information to give this man. Though he had spent but a few hours with him, there was a feeling growing in Chance that he should trust the Seeker. He had heard about seekers most of his life. His brief time on the Shadow Islands and in the archives had reinforced the idea that he wanted to have the opportunity to become a seeker. Was it just coincidence that this Seeker had entered his life at just this time, Chance wondered.

"Direction?" Seeker Eshana asked again.

"Oh, sorry. I need to head southeast and avoid the capital. I realize the first time I arrived in Sommerhjem, ports farther south might have been more convenient, but it was felt that if I came into the port of Marinel, that would be unexpected, if anyone was looking for someone of my family to be returning to Sommerhjem. You can see how well that theory worked out. Skipper Nereo dropped me off a half day out from the port of Willing because that was where he was headed."

"Southeast it is, then. Now, while I think you did a credible acting job as a lovesick farmhand, we cannot count on those two men being convinced. They also heard about the halekrets but didn't see him. Since I know you don't want to abandon the halekrets, somehow we need to confuse those, if any, who might be sent to find us. Do you know much about seekers?"

Chance found himself a little confused by the abrupt change of subject. He knew seekers spent their lives in pursuit of the old knowledge and trying to find that which had been lost. They were folks who sought out the land's mysteries. A seeker was someone who was a scholar, and it was said, so much more. Chance told Seeker Eshana what he knew about seekers.

"So, you have a general idea, but have you ever wondered where seekers come from, or how they make their living?" Seeker Eshana inquired.

"I guess I never really thought about that. I have never personally met a seeker before you, just heard about them. I always thought it was something I wouldn't mind becoming. I like learning, mysteries, and solving puzzles much more than trading and adding figures. Probably just a lad's daydream," Chance said, feeling quite embarrassed. He wondered why he was telling the Seeker this.

"So, you once wanted to become a seeker, did you? Interesting. Sat daydreaming about it, did you, instead of studying your boring old lessons?" Seeker Eshana said with good humor.

"Truth?"

"Truth is always helpful."

"You're right. I did distract myself from the more boring lessons by thinking that being a seeker would be a grand adventure and certainly better than sitting inside on a beautiful day learning my letters and numbers. Granted the learning part still calls to me, but I'm not so eager for grand adventures anymore," Chance said ruefully. Trying to get the subject away from himself, Chance asked, "How do seekers earn a living, if I may ask?"

"A long time past, a very wise woman began to realize there was more to Sommerhjem than we knew. She was aware that others had occupied this land before your ancestors settled here. For that matter, little or nothing was known as to where we came from or why. These mysteries both bothered and intrigued her. She set about creating the Order of the Seekers and used her holdings to provide funds for the first several scholars to begin to try to find the answers to her many questions. In her lifetime, she continued to gather several more like-minded folk, and they became the first seekers. At the time of her death, there were about ten to a dozen seekers. When she died, she willed her holdings to the Order of the Seekers. There always seems to be one or more among us who, after a time, wants to get off the road and has an affinity for managing the holding. We ingather several times a year to share what we've found and to resupply."

Seeker Eshana could tell he had caught Chance's interest and that he felt was good, for several reasons. It took the lad's mind off of those thoughts which were troublesome, and it prepared him for what Seeker Eshana was going to suggest next.

"The seekers are always small in number. It's not an easy life, for we are on a permanent walkabout as it were. It's difficult to have a family when one is constantly on the road. It's a life that has its rewards, however. I have an idea how we might solve our dilemma concerning what to do to make you less traceable."

"What do you have in mind?"

"I've a mind to offer you an apprenticeship. I've been looking for someone who might want to try the seeker's life. In addition, those who might be looking for you might not be looking for a seeker and his apprentice. Take your time, and think about it."

"A-A-Apprentice, you want me as an apprentice?" Chance stammered. Inside his feelings were like a small boat tumbling through rapids, swinging this way and that, spinning in circles, caught in backwaters. Had he heard Seeker Eshana right?

"Take your time. Think it through. A good seeker looks at a question from as many sides as he can."

Chance really did not want to think it through. He wanted to say yes. True, he had thought that being a seeker would be a grand thing when he was younger. It was his recent feelings about the idea that Keeper Odette had directed him toward that was making him want to agree. However, the Seeker had given wise counsel. Chance needed to think the offer through carefully.

After several minutes of silence Chance said, "It would be my heart's desire to become a seeker, and I thank you for your kind offer . . ."

"I think I hear a 'but' coming here."

". . . but I can't at this time. I have an obligation I need to fulfill before I can do anything else."

Seeker Eshana had watched Chance carefully while he had thought through his offer and during his answer. He could see the lad was genuinely torn between what he wanted to do and what he needed to do. Seeker Eshana could not help feeling that this meeting between the lad and himself was more than just him finding Master Clarisse's cousin. Several times in the past, Seeker Eshana had had a feeling, a knowing, that something was right, and he had learned to trust his feelings. He and this lad's lives were meant to cross, and they were meant to travel awhile together.

The two rode in silence for the rest of the day, each wrapped up in their own thoughts. They had traveled until well past the time for an evening meal when they reached a crossroad. There was a small inn nestled in a stand of very tall pines. Seeker Eshana suggested they grab a meal and see if there was an available room for the night.

"No matter what you decide in the long run, for tonight you are my apprentice. If anyone is still looking for you, it might muddy the trail. Do you think Ashu would be willing to hide in your pack until we can get settled in a room?"

What astonished Chance even more than Ashu's cooperation was the transformation that came over Seeker Eshana once he dismounted. Chance did not know what the Seeker did, but somehow he made himself appear older, smaller, and somewhat frail. No easy task for a man that size. By dark, the two were settled in their room. Chance had much to consider before sleep came. It was very dark when a rough hand shook him awake.

Chapter Eighteen

"I would strongly suggest you not make a sound and very quietly lie back down. No, don't look to your friend, for he will be no help to you. Ah, that's better. All comfy cozy now? Good. When I tell you to, you will get up, and then, you will pack your gear, and be prepared to come with us. There will be no fussing or whining. Am I clear?"

Pivane knew better than to argue with someone who was holding a very long, sharp, pointed, wicked-looking knife directly at his heart. Now what, he asked himself. Seemed like his luck lately never even lasted until the coin ran out. First, after the Seeker had made them talk, they had lost half their earnings for grabbing the lad Chance when the Seeker had left them at the mercy of the men they owed coin to. In addition, the Seeker had not given them anything for their information. Now this. Pivane nodded his head that he understood the cloaked and hooded figure, who was pointing the knife at him. Upon being given the command to get up, Pivane sat up and swung his feet over the side of the bed. He glanced across the room and saw that Mako was being similarly threatened by another cloaked and hooded figure.

"I would strongly suggest that the two of you move lively now. Our Lady does not like to be kept waiting."

Mako exchanged a glance with Pivane which communicated that he was less than pleased to be dragged out of bed by two men. It was even worse that they seemed to be working for one of the nobles. Pivane shot him a questioning look back. It did not take either man long to stuff their belongings in their packs.

"I took the liberty of having your horses saddled. Once your gear is loaded, be prepared to ride and ride hard. We have a great deal of ground to cover."

When Mako and Pivane emerged from the inn, they noted that dawn was just breaking. All thoughts of trying to make a break for it were quickly dashed when they saw the two men escorting them were not alone. Six others waited, already astride their horses.

The group traveled throughout the day with very few breaks. It was late afternoon when the leader turned his horse down a side lane that led to what turned out to be a hunting cottage. He ordered Mako and Pivane to dismount and led them into the cottage. Standing with her back to the mantle was a woman of stern bearing, dressed in hunting clothes. Her face was hidden behind the veil attached to her hunting cap. She did not look like she suffered fools gladly, as she stood there tapping a riding crop across her left hand.

"Are these the two bunglers, then?" the woman questioned the leader of the group.

"Yes, M'lady."

"M'lady . . . ." Mako began.

"Silence!" the woman said coldly, as she made a slashing motion with her riding crop. "I will get to you two in a moment, and you will have an opportunity to try to convince me not to drop you down the nearest very deep well. Get these two out of my sight for now."

The leader of the riders directed several of his men to escort Mako and Pivane out to the stables and tie them up.

"What have you found out?"

"Near as my sources could find out, Mako and Pivane were hired to snatch Chance when he arrived in the port of Marinel. It would seem that either there are more than one folk gathering and selling information in the capital, or your informant is making coin on the side."

"That will be dealt with when we get back to the capital. So, whoever else is in this game got there before us."

"So it would seem."

"I think it is time we had a chat with those two you brought in."

Mako and Pivane fell all over themselves answering the questions posed concerning their involvement in grabbing Chance and what they had done with him. The when and where they could answer, but they did not know who had hired them nor why. When the interrogation was over, Mako and Pivane were informed that they would be spending the night in the stable, but would be released the next day after most of the others had left. It was strongly suggested that they would be best advised to locate themselves in another part of Sommerhjem and not speak a word about this meeting. They agreed.

Once back in the hunting cottage, the Lady spoke. "How much credence do you put in their story?"

"It is just convoluted enough to be true and matches the rumors we have heard, but on the other hand, folks don't get dumped at the Shadow Islands and then appear in Sommerhjem a few short weeks later. I wonder if those two and their smuggler friends didn't just take the coin, sail several days out, and dump the lad. Some fisher or passing ship could have picked him up."

"That would certainly explain his possible arrival back in Sommerhjem. More so than that fanciful tale about braving the Shadow Islands. Now, tell me again what those two bunglers you hired in Tverdal told you about a lad named Chance."

"A woman fisher was overheard talking to a fishmonger concerning a lad named Chance, who had sailed into their cove. The lad said he was on a walkabout and asked to leave his skiff in their cove. She said his name was Chance, and he had a small animal with him the likes of which she had never seen before. Some sort of reddish furred animal with a ringed tail. Said the lad rescued the little animal off a piece of flotsam."

"So, you think this lad is the Chance we are looking for?"

"Chance is a name not often heard in Sommerhjem. The two bunglers that I hired," the man said ruefully, "caught up with a lad that fit both our description and the fisherwoman's description of the lad named Chance. My bunglers did not see any animal with him, however. In addition, the lad said his name was Sorley and he was a farm lad."

"But you look like you think something else. Why?"

"There was a seeker who arrived just as my men were about to detain this Sorley lad. He had been seen on the docks and probably had overheard the fisherwoman's tale also. He seemed unusually interested in the farm lad and did not believe my men when they tried to suggest that this Sorley had tried to steal their horses. The Seeker even went so far as to send their horses running down the road with them chasing after. You could speculate he did that so they would not try to go after this Sorley lad."

"But you don't think so."

"No, I do not. The Seeker's actions seemed suspicious. Besides intervening and making my two hires walk, after he heard the fisherwoman's tale and stopped at the Glassmakers Guildhall, he purchased a spare horse. Makes you wonder who that spare horse was for."

"Makes you wonder indeed. On the off chance that this lad Sorley is indeed the Chance we are looking for, it would be best if you personally set out to find either Sorley, Chance, or the Seeker."

"You know I am loyal to you, Lady Farcroft, and I will do as you ask. I'm concerned with the fact that one of the three folk is a seeker. I heard Master Clarisse's declaration concerning the grave consequences that could happen to any who might interfere with a seeker. This next move comes with much higher risk, if it truly involves a seeker."

"Then we will have to be very, very careful."

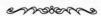

"Sorry lad, didn't mean to startle you, but it's time to go," Seeker Eshana told Chance. "I appreciate it's the middle of the night. Leaving now with no one watching might make it more difficult for others to find us."

Chance quickly packed up and quietly followed the Seeker down the stairs and out to the stable. He was amazed at how quickly and quietly Seeker Eshana could move for such a big man. It took no time at all to saddle the horses and be on their way. Chance was surprised that instead of heading south, they took the lane that headed due east. It was just before sunrise that the Seeker turned his horse onto a very narrow track heading into a dense woods.

As the track wound its way deeper and deeper into the woods, Chance became just a bit concerned. As he had lain in bed awaiting sleep the night before, he had been going back and forth in his mind about what he should do. On one hand, he was still leery of the Seeker. Was this man he was following really a seeker and did he really know his cousin Clarisse? If he really was a seeker, should Chance tell him about where he was going, and why? He was shaken out of his musing when Ashu leapt off his shoulder and ran up a tree trunk. Chance swiftly pulled his horse to a halt. He was concentrating so hard trying to keep Ashu in sight, he did not even notice that Seeker Eshana had halted his horse also, but not because of Ashu.

"Greetings, Seeker Eshana, what brings you to our home forest?"

"Just cutting through and could use your help. We would like to quietly disappear in your forest."

"Of course. Any particular direction you are heading?"

"South for now, and then east."

"Do you need a quick route or a very hidden route?"

"Don't suppose you have both?"

"Sorry, no."

"I think hidden would be better."

"I suppose you want your back trail to disappear, too," the forester queried, giving Seeker Eshana a long suffering look.

"If that wouldn't be too much trouble."

Chance watched the exchange between Seeker Eshana and the forester. Unless this was some kind of elaborate ruse to convince him that the Seeker was who he said he was, it would seem Chance's luck was changing. He was distracted from this line of thinking when Ashu unceremoniously dropped down out of the tree onto the rump of Chance's horse, causing the horse to side step and dance a few steps. The horse's movements attracted the attention of both Seeker Eshana and the forester.

"Well, that's one way to make an entrance," the forester said, chuckling. "Let me set things in motion, and then, perhaps you can introduce me to the lad and his companion. I think we are going to need to take a slight side trip." With that said, the forester slipped away as quietly he had appeared.

Seeker Eshana turned to Chance, and then began to chuckle. "It is always good to have something unexpected and memorable happen in the middle of a stressful time. That little halekrets certainly can be entertaining."

Chance found himself beginning to chuckle, too, and he felt lighter somehow. "I think my heart, which has finally returned to my chest, could do with a little less entertainment."

The forester had returned to where Chance and Seeker Eshana waited. He indicated that they should follow him and apologized in advance that their passage through the forest was going to have to be delayed a bit. He explained that they needed to take a slight detour, for he wanted to consult with an elder of the clan before they traveled on. They would, he assured them, still be heading in the general direction they wanted to go.

It was several hours later when Chance noticed the forest begin to change. The trees were more spread out and the underbrush had changed from thicket to ferns and low-lying plants. Chance did not know why he was surprised when he began to notice young quirrelit trees. Their ride ended when they arrived in the heart of the quirrelit grove and a small forester village.

Their guide dismounted and walked toward them. "You can tie your horses here in the shade. Chance, there is someone here I want you to meet. Or perhaps that's not really correct. There is someone here I would like to introduce to your companion."

The forester led them to the center of the village to a home that was attached to what had once been a huge quirrelit tree. Chance was torn between looking at the home that was part cottage and part tree and looking at one of the oldest folk he had ever seen.

The woman sitting on a bentwood rocker, who was later introduced as Elder Nelda, was tiny, and her feet barely touched the ground. Her face had a touch of red on both cheeks, and there was an air of suppressed excitement about her. On her lap, held in her gnarled hands, was a very old fragile-looking book.

Elder Nelda motioned that Chance should come closer. At first, he thought that she was inviting Seeker Eshana to come closer and had to be prodded by the Seeker. Chance moved to stand in front of the old woman, who looked at him for quite some time. Chance found himself looking everywhere but at her. She made him feel a bit uncomfortable. When Chance finally did look into her very dark wise eyes, he felt himself captured by them, falling into their depths. When the woman finally spoke, Chance felt like she must know everything there was to know about him.

"They say that when a number of Neebing blessed walk this land, it will be a time of great change. I had heard there have been several in the capital this summer, but had not thought to meet one. Come sit beside me, lad."

Chance had no idea what the woman was talking about, but felt compelled to do what she asked. He sat on the bench beside her rocker. She indicated to the forester who had brought them that he might wish to show Seeker Eshana around the village. The Seeker nodded to Chance that his sitting with Elder Nelda would be alright. Chance was not so sure.

Once Chance and Elder Nelda were alone, Elder Nelda continued to rock, her hands running tenderly across the cover of the book she held. As the silence lengthened, Chance was surprised that instead of becoming more nervous, he began to relax.

"I'm glad my great grandson remembered his childhood lessons and tales," Elder Nelda told Chance. "It's your companion who is of great interest to me."

At first Chance thought Elder Nelda was talking about Seeker Eshana and looked in the direction he had gone.

Elder Nelda let out a quiet chuckle. "No, lad, not the Seeker, but that little one who rides your shoulder."

Chapter Nineteen

Much to Chance's surprise, when Elder Nelda reached over toward Chance, Ashu quickly, but softly, jumped from his shoulder onto her arm. When she moved the book to the side, Ashu dropped to her lap and settled in. Chance was a bit disconcerted that the halekrets, who up to this point had been so shy around others, just made himself comfortable on Elder Nelda's lap. Elder Nelda did not seem surprised, as if small animals did that all the time.

"My mother, and her mother before her, and her mother before her, and so on back into the mists of time, have been the holders of the history and stories of our clan. Each generation passed down the stories and their wisdom to the next. At first, it was only by the spoken word, and then later on, both the spoken and the written word. I, in turn, have tried to pass this learning on to each successive generation, to both the lads and lasses of our clan. Seems at least the stories about the animals stuck when it comes to my great grandson."

While this insight into the forester's way of life was interesting to Chance, he wondered what it all had to do with Ashu.

"I suppose you're wondering what that has to do with your small companion here?"

"I am curious," Chance replied.

"In this old, old book are descriptions and drawings of animals. It was made by some long forgotten forester who had both a talent for sketching and a talent with words. I often would entertain the children of the clan on dark stormy days with this book. I would read the description of an animal, show the sketch, and then, we would all tell what we knew about the animal. That worked pretty well for the animals that lived in our own forest or had been seen and described by foresters from other forests who visited. When no one had seen the animal, or knew of it, we tried to figure out what it might be like based on what it looked like. Your little friend is here in my book."

Chance was astonished by Elder Nelda's revelation. No one that he had talked to on the Shadow Islands knew very much about the halekrets. In addition, he had not been able to find very much in the archives, other than they did not seem native to the islands. While he did not know every animal that resided in Sommerhjem, he had never heard of anyone speak of them during the time he had lived here. He also was not aware that they lived on any of the Havkoller Islands.

"What does the writer say?"

"She suggests that a little ring-tailed animal might once have lived in abundance in the forests that covered Sommerhjem. They had a particular affinity for the quirrelit groves. When the writer of this book was living, only a few remained, and were often paired with very special folk. What do you call this little one?"

"Ashu."

"No, I'm sorry. I was not clear. What do you call the type of animal he is?"

"I call it a halekrets."

Chance began to worry that Elder Nelda would ask him where he had acquired the halekrets. He really did not want to lie to this Elder of the forester clan, but he also was honor bound not to talk of the Shadow Islands. Suddenly, something struck him that he had not really ever thought about. How had those on the Shadow Islands known that Ashu's kind were called halekrets? Had someone on the crater island named them? The next thought he had made him glad he was sitting down. Halekrets was a word from the old language, the language that he, like other Høyttaier children, learned from the minute they began to talk. Had a member of the Høyttaier clan lived on the Shadow Islands several hundred years ago? Did that mean there might be books or writings in the old language in the archives? It was certainly something to think about. Elder Nelda began to speak, drawing Chance back to the present.

"Just between you and me, the halekrets, as you call them, appear to be somehow related to another from the time before we came to settle Sommerhjem, and to be equally rare and elusive. They, too, live in the quirrelit groves and forested land. Very few know of them, and even fewer talk about them. I'm referring, of course, to the Neebings."

This was the third time Chance had heard the word Neebing. He had to think back. He had heard one of the escorts, who accompanied him to the entrance of quirrelit tree that led into the maze, mention something about being Neebing blessed. Now this Elder of the forester clan had mentioned something about him being Neebing blessed. Just as he was about to ask what that meant, Seeker Eshana and the other forester returned.

Elder Nelda addressed Seeker Eshana. "There is a reason this lad and his companion walk this land at this time. There are ancient stories which tell of when there is great need, Neebing blessed will walk the land and change will come to Sommerhjem. He has riding on his shoulder one who has not been seen in this land for time out of mind. An omen, I would say. Guard him well, Seeker. His journey, like that of the other Neebing blessed, has just begun. I'm tired now, so you need to excuse me. Travel well and safely, lad."

Elder Nelda motioned to her great grandson that he should help her up, and she retired into her home.

Chance turned to Seeker Eshana. "Do you know what she's talking about?"

While Seeker Eshana could hear the confusion and concern in Chance's voice, he could say little that would reassure the lad. "Only a little. I think, however, we need to have a serious talk about what really brought you back to Sommerhjem. I have a fairly good guess, but I think it is your story to tell. Think about it. Here comes our guide. We need to be on our way."

Though the going was slow because their guide led them along animal trails and narrow paths, by late afternoon the trio came out of the woods to where a narrow lane ran parallel to the edge of the forest. Opposite the forest edge were meadows as far as the eye could see.

"This lane edges the forest for several miles and then meets up with a more well-traveled lane. The land will continue to be rolling but cultivated. You will pass by a number of farms and eventually get to a small village.

The pub keeper there has several rooms for overnight guests. He is a good man and loyal to the Crown."

"We thank you for your assistance and directions."

"It was our pleasure. Travel safe."

The forester slipped back into the woods, and to Chance's mind, seemed to vanish. All the while he had been following the forester, Chance had had one part of his attention fixed on the ride, and the other part mulling over what to tell Seeker Eshana should he ask again about Chance's purpose for returning to Sommerhjem. He did not think Seeker Eshana would believe him if he told him that he was just coming back to get his family's old home ready for their return.

"So, lad, don't you think it is about time you talked to me about your real purpose for returning to Sommerhjem?"

Up until that very moment, Chance had not known what he was going to answer. "Yes sir, I think I do owe you an explanation. My family, down several generations, has been charged with keeping safe one of the pieces of the oppgave ringe. When my family left Sommerhjem, my father did not think it was wise to take the ring out of the country. He hid it carefully. I have been chosen by my family to retrieve it and take it to the capital."

"Ah, that begins to confirm much. Since you have been out of the country, you are probably unaware that the interim ruling council has charged the seekers with finding the whereabouts of the pieces of the oppgave ringe. I was diverted from that task when I set out to find you. I have often found that when I look for something else, I discover what I originally set out to find. Well then, lad, I would be honored if you would let me continue to travel with you."

That the Seeker would be honored to travel with him struck Chance as an interesting turn of events. Here he was, still slightly in awe of seekers, and one was honored to travel with him. He did not have much time to dwell on it, for after giving his consent to travel on together, Seeker Eshana urged his horse to a ground eating pace, and Chance could only follow.

When the two arrived and dismounted at the small inn the forester had mentioned, Chance noted that Seeker Eshana strode briskly toward the door.

"Come along, lad, lest you miss out on a meal. I'm hungry enough to eat a small deer all by myself."

This jovial, loud seeker was quite different from the one Seeker Eshana had portrayed at the last inn. Whereas before, he had appeared smaller, older, and frail, this time he portrayed a hale and hardy man. Chance wondered as to why and was determined to ask Seeker Eshana before the night was over.

After the evening meal, Seeker Eshana sent Chance out to take care of the horses. He had determined that they would stay at the small inn for the night. Just as Chance was finishing up grooming the pack horse, Seeker Eshana joined him.

"If you are done, I would suggest we take a short walk. I have just had a very interesting conversation with the innkeeper."

The two left the stable and began to walk at a leisurely pace down the lane. To any who might be watching them, it looked like two folk who were out stretching their legs. Once they were far enough away from the inn, and hopefully out of ear shot, Seeker Eshana began to tell Chance what he had learned.

"It would seem that there are folks who are mighty interested in finding me. Seems they have some important information they want to give me. Can't imagine who might be looking for me, or even know I was in the area for that matter. Struck me as just too coincidental. It does pose a problem, however. We have some options."

"Options?" Chance asked. He wondered what those options might be. Seeker Eshana was for the most part someone who would normally stand out in one's memory due to his size. Chance also suspected those who were looking for either of them probably had a pretty good description. Whether he traveled with the Seeker or alone, there were those who knew who they were looking for.

"There are always options. We could go our separate ways and hope for the best. Not an option I'm immensely fond of, but a choice nevertheless. We can continue to travel together as seeker and lad, or seeker and apprentice. I suspect, however, that those who are looking for either one of us have fairly good descriptions. We need to change our appearances somewhat."

"How do we do that?"

"I think we need to make both of us older."

"I've seen you do that, but I don't know how you did it."

"Well, my lad, if you are truly interested in becoming a seeker, now would be the time to let me know. If so, I can begin your lessons, including how I made myself go from a strong, strapping man to a stooped-over frail old fellow."

Seeker Eshana had asked Chance if he might want to become a seeker hours back. Off and on, Chance had thought about whether or not he truly wanted to follow the seeker's path. All of his thinking had led him to one conclusion. Becoming a seeker was truly his heart's desire, but he was still not sure he could accept the Seeker's offer.

"I would truly like to apprentice with you, but I am not sure I can say yes to your offer at this time. You are aware of what I need to do before anything else."

"That should not be a problem, lad, for remember, we seekers are charged with finding the whereabouts of the remaining parts of the oppgave ringe. Since you know the location of one, that makes your quest my quest, and in a sense, my quest is you. In both cases, we both want the same thing. We both want to find and deliver the piece of the oppgave ringe to the capital. I want an apprentice, and you want to become a seeker. Works out very nicely don't you think?"

Chance thought it sounded too good to be true. Part of him was still trying to hold close the idea that he might be about to become an apprentice to a seeker. Another part of him, the part that was almost overly cautious, was wondering if something seemed too good to be true, then maybe, it really was.

Chapter Twenty

Blaxton walked down the dimly lit corridor taking in the rough stone walls. This old keep built of the local black stone, which sat atop a hill, had been the ancestral home of the Farcrofts. The family had built a magnificent manor house on their land when Sommerhjem had become more settled and peaceful. The old keep had been kept in good repair over the centuries, however. The Farcrofts were not a trusting clan, and even in times of peace were always prepared to defend their ancestral home. Never the rulers of Sommerhjem, but always an influence behind the scenes. Always plotting and scheming.

Blaxton was not looking forward to his meeting with Lady Farcroft this night. He did not have the news she wanted. The sounds of his footsteps echoed back from the bare walls of the corridor leading to the great hall. The hall itself had a high cross-timbered ceiling. Torches jutting out from the support pillars burned dimly, casting flickering shadows. There were others in the room, but all of the attention was focused on the woman sitting in the high-backed chair directly in front of him. She had a commanding presence.

There were two sides to the Lady before him. They matched the two dwellings on the Farcroft land. Those who visited the manor house met a woman who was often thought of as a silly, dithering dowager more interested in the latest court fashions than what was going on in Sommerhjem. Those who held clandestine meetings with her at the ancient keep knew a woman who was strong willed and commanding. Lady Farcroft had worked tirelessly behind the scenes on behalf of the former regent. Her plans for her future wealth and power had been crossed by

Lady Esmeralda and others loyal to the Crown. Some of the best plotters in Sommerhjem for the former regent had been bested by a rover girl, a hunting cat, the former princess, and others. All that planning and plotting had been thwarted, and Lady Farcroft's rage simmered just below the civilized surface she presented to those who were gathered.

"Report," Lady Farcroft commanded.

"I'm afraid I don't have good news. As you know, a seeker was seen with a lad after the confrontation by the bunglers out of Tverdal. We suspect the lad is the one who is being sought, the Høyttaier Chance. It is clear from new reports that the two continued to travel together, but their trail was lost when they entered the Smale Stier forest. It's difficult to track anyone in one of the forests if the foresters don't want you to. Lord Klingflug didn't do us any favors when he moved the foresters out of their home forests. It has made them very loyal to the interim ruling council, who restored them to their traditional home forests."

"So, we have lost their trail, then," stated Lady Farcroft.

"Temporarily. As you are aware from all we have been able to learn, there is a strong possibility that Chance's family has held one of the oppgave ringe pieces in trust. We also think they knew what they held. We suspect that the lad Chance has been sent by his family to bring the ring to the capital. It would seem that he was not carrying it on his person or in his gear when he was picked up in the port of Marinel."

"Another bungled plan. If I had been in charge, he would have been brought here, and we would have gotten the information we needed out of him fairly quickly," suggested Lady Farcroft.

No one in the room doubted that she would have accomplished that task, nor did they ever want to be in a position where she thought they were withholding information.

"I have no doubt you would have had the information we need, had they put you in charge in the first place," Blaxton placated.

"Be that as it may, it does not change the fact that their trail is now cold," stated Lady Farcroft, barely controlling her anger.

"Based on what our folks have been able to learn, the lad's family left Sommerhjem quite quickly after the word was sent out that Lord Klingflug was tracking down members of the Høyttaier clan. We do not think his father or mother had much time to travel very far from their home, other than to leave the country. Unfortunately, they could have hidden the ring at their home or anywhere along the way to the coast. Leaving it in some random place along the way seems fairly risky, however. They also could have entrusted the ring to a friend or relative, but in that instance, it would be fair to assume that that folk would have brought it to the capital by now."

"Do not forget that they were traders and could have contacts along that route to the coast."

"I stand corrected, M'lady."

"I think they would not have left something the family has kept safe and secret for several hundred years some random place, nor do I think they would have entrusted it to anyone else. No, they would have wanted it to be in a safe and accessible place, but one that they were very familiar with. I think they hid it at their home."

"As you are aware, our agents have torn that home apart practically brick by brick and have come up with nothing. However, I agree with your logic that the piece of the oppgave ringe is somewhere in the area where their home is located."

"You have sent folk out to watch all the ways into the area, then?"

"Yes, M'lady. In addition, I intend to leave at dawn and head that way myself. I have cautioned our folks to be on the lookout, but not stop or capture the lad. I thought it would be more prudent to let the two retrieve the ring. That way we can dispose of all problems at once."

"I concur. Remember, however, there can be no connection between the mysterious disappearance of the Seeker, the lad, and us. I do not think Master Clarisse's declaration at the Well of Speaking, that no harm come to the ring bearers or any seeker, was an idle threat. You will need to use the utmost caution and stealth. No trace can be left as to what happened to the two you are going after," declared Lady Farcroft.

"It will be done, M'lady, as you have requested." Blaxton made a slight bow, turned, and strode quickly out of the great hall.

Seeker Eshana raised his hand, indicating that Chance should rein his horse in and stop. Chance almost missed his signal in the dim dawn light.

They had been traveling by night and resting by day for the last several days. Chance could only remember one other time he had been this tired, and he really did not want to spend very much time thinking about his time in the tunnels during the rite of passage.

Seeker Eshana dismounted and motioned that Chance should do likewise. "It is time to begin our change," Seeker Eshana stated. "You think we are but a half day's ride from your former home?"

"Yes, Grandfather," Chance replied, just as he had been instructed to do by Seeker Eshana over the last few days. Language, Seeker Eshana had said, was the first part of a good disguise. He had told Chance that he needed to be really comfortable with the role he was about to play. They were about to ride into Chance's hometown looking to all who would see them like a frail elderly grandfather and a dutiful grandson. Both had let their beards grow out, and while Chance's was still a bit sparse, it did change his appearance. Seeker Eshana had pulled a blond and silver wig out from the recesses of one of the packs. His beard was so light that it appeared almost silver anyway. As for clothes, Seeker Eshana had taken a solo visit into one of the larger villages along the way and purchased suitable clothing, which was fine enough to suggest that the two of them were fairly well to do.

When they had stopped and camped, Seeker Eshana had had Chance practice helping him dismount from his horse. Chance had also practiced how to help the tottering old man Seeker Eshana became by taking his arm and helping him walk. Seeker Eshana had told him that for a really good disguise to hold up for any period of time, one had to become the role one was playing.

Their plan was to go to the town of Raskfoss, where Chance's family had lived before exiling themselves to the Havkoller Islands, settle in at the best inn in the area, and stay for a day or two under the pretense that Seeker Eshana needed to rest, the trip being hard on him. Their story was that Chance was accompanying his grandfather to his aunt's home farther to the south for a visit. Once they were as sure as they could be that their disguises held, Chance would try to retrieve the ring from where his father had hidden it. They would then leave the area, but remain in disguise for a while, before switching to something else. It was a risky plan at best, for neither could predict whether there were folks on the lookout for them. Their biggest difficulty with the whole disguise was Ashu. He had certainly proven to be an attraction whenever he had been seen by the folk of Sommerlijem.

The two changed clothes and went over their plan one more time. With no better plan and nothing to delay them, the trio headed toward the town of Raskfoss. As he rode toward the home he once knew, Chance thought it was fortunate that of all his brothers and sisters, he was the one that looked most like his mother's side of the family. His father was quite well known in Raskfoss, having grown up there as had his father before him. Chance's mother, however, was not from the town and her brothers had rarely visited. As they moved closer to the town of Raskfoss, the more familiar the land began to look to Chance.

"I remember this farm on our right," Chance commented to Seeker Eshana. "We used to get our eggs from the grandmother who lived here. See that grove of trees ahead? There is a quirrelit grove in the center. I remember it well. Whenever I was upset, or just wanted to get away from my brothers and sisters, I would ride out to the grove. It was always so peaceful there. My siblings found their solitude and peace on the large lake next to the town, but not me. I always headed toward the grove."

There was such a look of longing on Chance's face that Seeker Eshana did not think he was aware of that the Seeker decided a slight detour was in order. When they came to the edge of the grove of trees, he turned his horse into the woods. It was refreshingly cool in the shadows of the trees. Seeker Eshana dismounted and indicated Chance should also dismount.

"Let's tie the horses up and stretch our legs a bit before we ride into the town. Why don't you show me your quirrelit grove?"

Chance was all too happy to agree to the Seeker's suggestion. With Ashu on his shoulder, he led the way through the trees until they entered the ring of quirrelit trees. A sense of calm came over Chance as he entered the grove, and it brought back good memories. He was so lost in thought that it did not register that Ashu was no longer on his shoulder.

Much as Seeker Eshana would have liked to extend this visit to a place where Chance felt comfortable, it was time to move on. He gently touched Chance's shoulder and indicated they needed leave.

"Where did Ashu go?" Chance asked, when he realized that the halekrets was no longer on his shoulder. He looked all over, up and down, trying to spot the small halekrets.

"One minute he was on your shoulder, and then, suddenly in a flash he was up that tree you are standing next to. He was so quick, I lost sight of him almost instantly."

A horrible crushing feeling of loneliness filled Chance's heart at that moment. Of all that had happened to him since he had left his family, nothing caused him more fear than the idea that perhaps Ashu had left him.

Chapter Twenty-One

It was all Chance could do to keep the panic he was feeling at bay. He had not realized how dependent he had become on Ashu's companionship. He kept frantically looking for the little halekrets, but to no avail. Finally, a firm but gentle hand on his shoulder stopped him from anxiously turning in circles, searching every branch of the quirrelit tree.

"Turning yourself around and around until you are too dizzy to stand up is really not going to help," Seeker Eshana suggested kindly. "Take a deep breath. That's it, and now another one. We are in no rush here. Why don't you sit down and be still? I'm going to go back and tend to the horses. Take time to listen and watch. Ashu may just have gone in search of something to eat."

Chance did as the Seeker had suggested. Finally, once he could hear over the beating of his heart and his breathing was not coming out in ragged gasps, he realized that the peacefulness of the quirrelit grove still remained. As he calmed down, he could hear the rustling in the leaves, the bird songs, the quiet skitters of small creatures in the grass. Chance thought about his reaction to Ashu leaving him. Had he panicked because he felt he was letting the two halekrets back in the crater valley down, for he had promised he would take care of Ashu, or was he being selfish? Maybe Ashu had found a new home in the quirrelit grove and would want to stay.

Chance settled into a more comfortable position with his back to the quirrelit tree and waited. He did not call out. As he sat there, the calm and peace of the grove fell over him like a gentle spring rain. Chance tried to convince himself he would be alright if Ashu decided to stay in the grove,

After all, it was not like he owned Ashu. Chance sat very still and waited. He hoped Seeker Eshana would take his time with the horses and not come right back. Minutes passed and nothing changed. Chance was still sitting alone at the base of the quirrelit tree. He was about to stand up and stretch his legs when he heard a faint sound just above him, and then, the familiar weight of Ashu on his shoulder. If anyone had been watching at that moment, Chance's grin might have lit up the whole quirrelit grove.

Ashu scampered off Chance's shoulder and onto his lap. When Chance looked down, he saw that Ashu was holding something that looked like a small scrap of cloth dangling from a tightly coiled up cord.

"I'm so . . ." Chance had to clear his throat which suddenly felt tight before he could go on. ". . . I'm so glad you decided to come back down out of that tree. What have you got there?"

Chance took the offering from the halekrets and looked it over. He was holding in his hand what appeared to be a small pouch attached to a cord. It looked neither old nor worn. Chance could not imagine how such an object would have wound up in a quirrelit tree. He did not think posing the question of the pouch's origin to Ashu would produce an answer. Just then Seeker Eshana reentered the grove.

"Ah, I see our little friend has returned. Good. What is that you are holding?" Seeker Eshana asked.

"I was just wondering that myself," Chance replied, as he held the object out to the Seeker.

"Ah."

"Ah?"

"It's a pouch made of golden pine spider silk. Have to admit I have never seen golden pine spider silk in quite this reddish brown color before. How odd that Ashu should find one here. Looks new." Seeker Eshana turned the pouch over and over in his hands before remarking, "How fortuitous that you happen to come into possession of a small golden pine spider silk pouch at just this time."

"Why is that?"

"Apparently, some folk who are sensitive to such things can detect if someone is carrying an object of power, like one of the rings of the oppgave ringe. If the ring is wrapped in some way in cloth made of golden pine spider silk, the silk somehow prevents detection."

Handing the pouch back to Chance, Seeker Eshana led the way out of quirrelit grove. While Chance took the time to check his horse and re-cinch the saddle, Seeker Eshana gave him a long thoughtful look. Once both were settled in their saddles, Ashu settled in the pack Chance had rigged onto the back of his saddle for times when the halekrets got tired of riding on Chance's shoulder or in front of him tucked in behind the saddle horn.

As they rode toward Raskfoss, Seeker Eshana went over their disguise one last time. "Now remember, I am Sennett . . . ."

"Yes, Grandfather."

"Quiet youngling, I am not through with my instructions," Seeker Eshana stated, giving Chance a look of mock sternness. "Do you remember where we are from, and where we are headed?"

"Yes, Grandfather."

"Good. Do you think Ashu will be content to stay hidden until we reach our rooms at the inn?"

"I have asked him to do so, but I'm never sure how much he understands. I do know that I would rather take my chances keeping him with me than to ever lose him. His sudden disappearance in the quirrelit grove taught me that."

"Then, we will just have to trust to our cunning and luck."

It did not take long to reach Raskfoss. Chance thought it had not changed much in the time he had been gone. He had thought he might have a feeling of homecoming and was surprised when he did not. He realized he had not really left much behind in Raskfoss except memories. He had not had a best friend or schoolmates, for he had been taught at home. He and all of his brothers and sisters had worked from their early years on in the family business. They all had kept much to themselves, he realized. When they had moved to the Havkoller Islands, not much had really changed, other than their location. He wondered if his family might even return to Sommerhjem once a new ruler came to power.

Chance was pulled out of his reflections when Seeker Eshana halted his horse at the town gate. Seeker Eshana inquired of the gatekeeper concerning a decent inn, and they were given directions to several.

"We should go to the Hawser House," Chance told Seeker Eshana. "From the directions the gatekeeper gave us, I think it is the inn that used to be called the Eight Bells Inn. It's not far from where we used to live, and we can reach my old house by walking the beach, if the lake is down. Folks would often stroll by the house on the beach on an evening walk, so we would not look out of place if we chose to take a stroll on the beach. It's not where I will need to go eventually, but I would like to take a look at the old home place."

"It would also be a wise idea to see if anyone is watching the place, or is particularly interested in those who might stroll by."

The two traveled in silence, seemingly lost in their own thoughts. Had anyone looked closer, they would have seen that both the riders were very alert and aware of their surroundings.

Seeker Eshana was pleasantly surprised by the Hawser House. It was not a fancy establishment, but it was well maintained and clean. Right on the water's edge of the large lake, it was a two story timber building. The grounds were well groomed, and the stable sat on the adjacent parcel of land. A large vegetable garden was growing between the stable and the inn and looked healthy and well-tended. After tying their horses to the hitching post outside the main entrance of the inn, they entered the lobby. They were greeted immediately by the innkeeper.

"Welcome, welcome to Hawser House. Are you here for a meal, or are you seeking a room?" the innkeeper asked, as he look the two over. He could see that the elderly gentleman before him look quite tired and was being steadied by the young man next to him.

"We would like a room for several days," Seeker Eshana told the innkeeper in a voice that was raspy and filled with fatigue. He was bent over and appeared to sway slightly, as if standing up was a major effort.

"Do you have a first floor room, sir? My grandfather does not scamper up stairs the way he used to," asked Chance.

"Now Gershón, I'll be fit as a fiddle after a good meal and an hour off that horse."

Chance gave the innkeeper what he hoped was a look of appeal, trying to get across that his grandfather was a stubborn old man, but he really did not need to be climbing stairs. The innkeeper took the hint.

"I happen to have an excellent room just down the hall here, last door on your left. Why don't we go take a look at it?"

Once Seeker Eshana had given the room his approval, he settled himself into one of the chairs in the sitting room with a great sigh. "Might we have a meal sent to the room?" he asked.

"I will arrange it right away. Do you want me to send one of my lads to take care of your horses?"

"No, no, Gershón will take care of everything. Will our gear be safe in your stable?"

"Everything will be well looked after," replied the innkeeper.

"Very well, then," Seeker Eshana replied. "I think I will just rest here. A meal in about an hour's time would be appreciated."

Both the innkeeper and Chance exited the room and walked abreast down the hallway and outside where the horses were tied.

"Thank you for not letting Grandfather insist that he was more than capable of taking a room on the second floor. He can be very stubborn. He should probably not even have taken this trip, but he was adamant about visiting his daughter, my aunt."

"Glad to accommodate. Any likes or dislikes concerning meals that I should know about?"

"Grandfather is especially fond of fresh fruits and vegetables. Would not be opposed to nuts either," Chance told the innkeeper, thinking of Ashu.

"That can be taken care of. Ah, here is one of my lads who will help you with the horses."

Chance gathered his pack off the back of his saddle hoping that Ashu would remain inside and out of sight long enough for him to get the pack to their room. He also removed several packs off the packhorse, and the two walking sticks. He then told the innkeeper's lad he would meet him at the stable in a few minutes. Once Chance had deposited their belongings in the room, he went to the stable to help settle the horses in.

When all of his chores were finished, Chance returned to the inn. As he entered through the inn's side door, he heard two men talking in a room just beyond the small entryway where he was standing. Their words caused him to stop walking forward. Standing very still, he listened.

"You sure no one of that description has signed in here over the last few days?"

"I've not had a seeker stay with me since I took over this inn several years ago, nor have I had a big man and a lad sign in lately. Mostly, I get either families to enjoy the waters hereabouts or folks of some means. Only man and lad pairing I've had lately arrived today, but they don't fit who you are looking for. Was a grandfather and grandson."

"When did they arrive?"

"Just a short while ago, but the grandfather is not a big strapping fellow, and his grandson is not a young lad."

"You're sure the pair is not the ones we seek?"

"Look, Blaxton, you can check for yourself. They're staying several days."

"You do know how important this is to Lady Farcroft, and what you owe her."

"I'm not likely to forget."

Not wanting to be caught listening, Chance eased himself back toward the door he had entered and exited. Trying to look nonchalant, he wandered through the garden back to the stable. When he entered the stable, the stable lad asked if he needed anything. Chance, trying to keep his voice casual, said he had forgotten something from one of the packs and went into the stall where he had left them. Seeker Eshana's horse moved aside just enough for Chance to open a pack, take a small bag out of it, and then refasten the pack. He did not have to worry about anyone being able to search their gear for Seeker Eshana's horse was trained to prevent that.

Not wanting to run into the speaker or the innkeeper, he strolled through the garden, and then, headed toward the front door. Upon entering the inn, he was hailed by the innkeeper.

"Ah, lad, glad I caught you. This gentleman here, Blaxton by name, thinks he knows your grandfather. Your grandfather did say his name was Sennett, did he not?"

Chapter Twenty-Two

"Yes, sir," Chance replied. He began to have a very bad feeling about the man standing before him. Though the man appeared to be friendly and interested in whether Chance's 'grandfather', a man named Sennett, was someone he knew, Chance had the uneasy feeling that this was the man, Blaxton, who he had overheard.

"Perhaps you will take me to him, so I can see if it is indeed the Sennett I know."

"Ah, sir, well, you see, sir, my grandfather is most likely asleep in the chair I left him sitting in. Traveling just plain wears him out. I'm sure he would like to meet with you if you are an acquaintance, but perhaps later we could arrange a meeting. I really don't want to disturb his nap. You do understand?"

Chance tried to look as if waking Seeker Eshana would be a very bad idea. The man before him could either choose to think it would be bad for Seeker Eshana's health or bad for Chance's health. Chance did not really care either way, so long as he could postpone the meeting. He hoped the man would not insist.

"Ah, yes, I understand," Blaxton stated in a friendly manner. "It must be hard for a young man like you to be burdened with the responsibility to travel with an old man. Perhaps you would like to join me for a little libation while your grandfather sleeps?"

"That's a very kind offer, sir, but I really must return to our room. I still need to unpack and have other chores."

"Surely you can put them off for a little while."

"I thank you again, but I really must decline."

"Perhaps later then, when your grandfather has gone to bed for the night?"

"Once again, I thank you for your kind invitation, but I too am weary from our travels and think I will call it an early night."

With that said, Chance turned, and as calmly as he could, walked down the hall to his room. Once he entered it, he closed the door softly and just leaned against it, trying to calm himself down and stop his hands from shaking. He felt Ashu climb up his body and give his face a gentle pat. For some reason, that helped him steady his breathing and slow his heart down. Shifting Ashu to his shoulder, he walked through the sitting room to find Seeker Eshana standing at the bedroom window looking out at the lake.

"Trouble?"

"I think so, sir." Chance proceeded to describe what he had overheard, and also, the conversation with the man named Blaxton.

"You're sure he mentioned Lady Farcroft?"

"Yes, sir."

"So, she still has her hand in. Hmmm." Seeker Eshana continued to gaze out the window.

"I don't think I gave anything away, sir." Chance felt nervous once again.

"Oh, no lad, I think you did just fine. With this fellow Blaxton so curious about us, our task here will be more difficult. Getting out of the inn unnoticed will take some work." Just then a knock came at the door.

"Why don't you go answer it, lad. Hand me Ashu and close the bedroom door behind you as you go out. If it is that persistent Blaxton fellow, tell him I am still napping and you are not going to wake me. I suspect, however, it is our meal."

Seeker Eshana's suspicion was correct, and it was one of the servants with their meal. Chance did note that the servant took quite a bit more time than was needful to set their meal out at the little table by the window. He was relieved when the servant left.

Seeker Eshana came out of the bedroom, but Ashu was not with him, or at least that was what Chance thought at first, until he noticed that something was moving around in the side pocket of Seeker Eshana's robe.

"You might want to hold this fellow on your lap while we all have our meal. Anyone on the beach looking this way with the use of a good spy scope might spot him."

Chance did as the Seeker directed. Ashu did not seem to mind, as long as Chance was handing him bits of fruit, vegetables, or an occasional nut.

"I think for tonight we will stay in. After all, we are both weary from our travels. Tomorrow, we will take short trips out. A beach walk in the morning, and then perhaps, a ride to the market in the afternoon. I suspect we will find ourselves in a chance meeting with Blaxton. Hopefully, he won't know he is meeting Chance." Seeker Eshana began to chuckle at his own play on words. "Sorry, I just couldn't resist."

The night passed quietly without incident. In the morning, Chance and Seeker Eshana took what would look to others as a morning constitutional along the beach. Seeker Eshana shuffled along, relying on his walking stick for support, looking to be an elderly man getting the morning air. Chance had tucked Ashu in his day pack, and the little halekrets seemed content to curl up and nap. Chance wished he could let Ashu out.

When they arrived at the portion of the beach that fronted the house where Chance had grown up, he was surprised and appalled at its condition. What had happened here, he wondered, as he stared at the ruin of what had been his family's home. He had expected someone to have moved in after his family was forced to abandon their home and flee the country. His father, after all, had left the managing or sale of the house in the hands of a solicitor he trusted. Several years after they had left, word had reached them that the house had been sold, and the money for the sale held in trust.

"The house looks like it was hit by a raging storm," Chance commented to Seeker Eshana.

"I think man rather than nature had a hand in the destruction of what was once a fine house. We may never know what happened, and it would be best if we did not bring it to anyone's attention that we are interested. I suspect, however, folks have been very enthusiastically looking for the piece of the oppgave ringe. Let us see if we can find a local tea shop on our ride this afternoon. They are often the center of gossip. It might be interesting to hear what is going on hereabouts."

Upon arriving back at Hawser House, Chance asked one of the serving folk for directions to the local market, and where they could find a decent tea shop. That afternoon, the two rode out to take in the town. Because there was a very cool wind blowing off the lake, both Chance and Seeker Eshana had worn cloaks. That had allowed Chance to conceal Ashu in an inner pocket of his cloak once they were settled in the tea shop, and slip him bits of tea cake as they sat sipping tea.

The proprietor of the tea shop stopped at their table to inquire if their tea needed a bit of warming. "Are you visiting someone in Raskfoss?" she asked.

"No, just passing through. The journey has been a difficult one for Grandfather, so we are taking a few days to rest and enjoy the lake country."

"Had us a nice stroll down the beach this morning. Most pleasant, most pleasant indeed. Enjoyed looking at the beautiful homes along the way. Well . . . except for that one," Seeker Eshana remarked, hoping the proprietor might comment, which she did.

"That's an awful shame, isn't it? Nice family used to live there, but suddenly they were gone." She leaned in and said in a whisper, "It was during the really bad times under the Regent, you understand. Heard it was seized for back taxes shortly after, but no one ever moved in. Strange goings on were reported. You know, weird lights in the middle of the night, strange noises coming from the house. Pretty soon no one would go near it. Been pretty quiet until just recently."

"Oh?" Seeker Eshana said.

"Seems the strange lights and noises have started up again. Oh, excuse me, I need to seat the two that just entered."

"We didn't owe any back taxes, we sold the house. What was she talking about?" Chance asked, a look of confusion on his face.

"I suspect that, in truth, you sold the house, but whoever bought it spread the rumor about owing the back taxes. It was just a way to begin to change folks' view of your family," Seeker Eshana said in a quiet voice. Pitching his voice into a somewhat higher range and putting a bit of whine into it, Seeker Eshana said, "Why, they snuck out in the middle of the night. There must have been something underhanded about that family. Probably left with a batch of creditors hot on their heels."

Chance could feel himself growing angry and was about to say something when he felt someone walk up behind him.

"Excuse me, Gershón isn't it?" asked the man Chance had overheard in the innkeeper's office. "Name's Blaxton," he said to Seeker Eshana. "Do you mind if I join you?"

Having no reason to tell the man they did not want him to join them, Seeker Eshana motioned Blaxton to have a seat. Once Blaxton had ordered his tea, he began to ask questions of Seeker Eshana and Chance. Because they had expected this encounter, Seeker Eshana took the lead in the beginning and answered all of the questions. Chance was glad they had rehearsed what to say when it was his turn to answer questions. It was all he could do to keep Ashu still by continuing to surreptitiously slip him treats. Having a strange animal as a companion made trying to be disguised very difficult.

It was a relief when Seeker Eshana mentioned he was becoming very weary and wanted to return to his quarters at Hawser House. Blaxton appeared too solicitous and mentioned if Chance wanted to continue to explore the town, he would be glad to accompany Chance's grandfather back to their quarters. Chance respectfully declined.

Once back in their quarters, Seeker Eshana remarked, "That Blaxton fellow was much too interested in us for my peace of mind. I think it might be best if we retrieve what you came here to get and move as quickly out of town as possible. We should move this night."

Chance and Seeker Eshana had talked at length about how Chance would go about retrieving the piece of the oppgave ringe from where his father had hidden it. The rest of the day dragged by slowly, and it was a relief when it was finally time to put the plan into action.

It was close to the midnight hour when Chance and Ashu slipped out the window of their bedroom. When Chance had put one foot over the window ledge, Ashu had jumped on Chance's back gripping his shirt tightly. It would seem there was no leaving him behind.

Chance and Seeker Eshana had choreographed his exit with Seeker Eshana lighting a lamp in the sitting room. They hoped if anyone was watching their rooms, their eyes would be drawn to the lit window momentarily, allowing Chance's exit to go unnoticed. Fortunately, there was a thick hedge that ran along the wall of the building for a number of feet, which Chance could slip along behind. Once beyond the hedge, the landscape was dark, for there was a heavy cloud cover. A dense fog had also rolled in off the lake.

Moving swiftly down to the water's edge, Chance was careful to walk in the dry sand. A number of folks had strolled along the beach this day, and his footprints would not be all that noticeable. The fog was both a help and a hindrance. It would make it difficult for anyone to spot him unless they were within several feet, yet, on the other hand, it would be difficult for him to spot anyone, too. The fog also muffled and distorted sound, which again was a mixed blessing.

It took Chance a bit longer than he had anticipated to arrive at his old home. It saddened him that the home that held such good memories was now just a shell of its former self. He hoped his parents decided not to return to Raskfoss. Between what had happened to the family home and to the family's reputation, life in this town would not be the same as it had been before they had left.

Shaking those thoughts off, Chance continued down the beach. What he was looking for was a small one-person boat that he could borrow for a short while. From the time he had been just a wee lad, he had paddled the small narrow boats. They did not have a similar boat in the Havkoller Islands, so Chance could only hope he would remember how to handle such a boat once he found one.

It wasn't until five houses down from the family home that he found what he needed. He had found other boats, but the paddles had been removed. Chance rolled up his pant legs, and lifting the small boat, walked into the water. He had forgotten that getting in and out of the boat had always been the trickiest part, and almost dumped Ashu and himself into the lake, before he finally got them settled in. A brisk wind had come up, and the fog began to thin. The clouds had also begun to break up, leaving Chance more exposed on the open water. Fortunately, the moon had not risen yet, but it would soon.

Chapter Twenty-Three

It did not take Chance long to slip into the rhythm of paddling, using the J-stroke that allowed him to move the little boat through the water swiftly while maintaining a straight course. Ashu, once again, had settled himself at the very tip of the bow, despite the occasional wave that splashed over him. It took just under an hour of hard paddling before Chance arrived at the craggy cliffs of a rock formation that rose thirty to forty feet out of the lake. By that time, he was sure his arms were going to fall off and his back was screaming in pain. Well, it could not be helped, as it had been a while since he had paddled.

Chance could only hope the landmarks his father had told him about were still there, and he would be able to find them in the dark. Before he had left the Havkoller Islands, his father had reminded him what to look for, and had had him repeat the directions back to him several times to make sure he would remember them correctly. Letting the boat drift, Chance began to look up toward the top of the cliff.

"You want to paddle to the side of the rock opposite the town," his father had told him. "You'll see an arch coming from the cliff out to a column of stone that rises up from the water. Tie your boat up to the column. Once there, you're going to have to slip into the water and swim up to the rock face. Here's where it gets a bit tricky. About five or so feet down, there is an opening in the side of the rock face. You'll have to swim through the opening, go another ten feet or so, and then swim upward. You'll find yourself in a small cave." He had then gone on to tell Chance what he needed to do next.

Chance reached his hand over the side of the boat to check the temperature of the water. He was surprised it felt warm. The water that he had stepped into when putting the boat in the water had been icy cold, as had the occasional splash from his paddle. Removing pants and shirt and placing them on the seat, Chance turned and spoke to Ashu.

"Stay with the boat now. I'll be gone only a little while." Chance could only hope the halekrets did as asked and did not decide to climb up the column the boat was tied to.

Taking a steadying breath to calm his nerves, Chance slipped over the side of the boat and swam the short distance to the rock face. Finding the opening his father had told him about was not as simple as it had seemed in the telling. Time and time again, Chance pushed himself under water only to surface when his air ran out, and still he had not located the opening. He hoped the cave had not collapsed, or that a large rock had not fallen from above, sealing the opening. Finally, just as he knew he should return to the surface, he located the hole in the side of the rock face.

Pushing himself to the surface, Chance took a number of deep breaths, and dove. Swimming as quickly as he could, he pulled himself through the underwater tunnel. Just as he felt he could go no farther before he ran out of air, he broke through the surface of the water in the small cave. At first, he just treaded water and tried to take in what he was seeing. The cave was filled with translucent glowing columns of rock that cascaded down from the ceiling. Never had Chance seen anything so beautiful. As his eyes adjusted to the dim light, he became aware of something paddling in the water next to him.

"Ashu, I told you to stay in the boat," Chance admonished, but his heart was really not in the scolding. "Ah well, as long as you are here, we had best get on with our task."

Chance's father had told him he needed to slip behind the third column on the left side of the cave. Once again, he would need to submerge himself and feel along the column until he found a hollow. If he reached his hand in and down, he should find a metal box within. The box would have a ring on the top that he could use to pull it up and out.

Again, the task was harder than it had sounded when his father had given him the instructions. In the first place, the column was slippery. Once he located the hollow, he had to keep himself under water and, at the same time, pull the box up and out. Unfortunately, the ring on the box was also covered with a slippery substance, making holding onto it difficult. Once he finally surfaced with the small box in hand, he realized it was going to be difficult to carry it back out through the tunnel. Treading water, he took some time to think through what he needed to do next.

Finally, he put his back to the cave wall and brought his legs up and pushed his feet against the column. After several tries to steady himself, for his feet kept slipping, he felt he was secure, at least momentarily. He placed the box on the top of his legs and carefully unhooked the latch. Chance was worried that the lid would be sealed shut, given the metal box had been in the water for a number of years, but it lifted up without the slightest problem. He was surprised that the inside of the box was almost completely filled with a block of wood. There was a circular opening in the center, and there on a post was the piece of the oppgave ringe Chance had come to retrieve. Pushing extra hard with both his back and his feet to assure he was stable and steady, Chance reached in and pulled the ring out of the box.

Warmth spread throughout Chance's body the moment he took hold of the ring. The sensation startled him, almost causing him to drop the ring, but he kept his wits about him. Chance closed the lid to the box and carefully balanced it on his legs as he reached up and drew the golden pine spider silk pouch cord over his head. He opened the pouch, placed the ring in it, pulled the cord tight, and put the cord back over his head. Once that was done, he grasped the box in one hand and dropped back under the surface of the water. After placing the box back in the hollow, Chance resurfaced, and beckoned to Ashu who was clinging to one of the columns.

"We had best be getting back, Ashu."

At the sound of Chance's voice, Ashu launched himself off the column and landed in the water on his belly, causing a splash. Chance laughed, which went a long way toward relieving the tension he had not been aware he was feeling. Ashu made a beeline toward the cave wall and ducked under water. When he did not resurface, Chance followed, took several deep breaths and dove. He found the opening that led out of the cave and was quickly back on the surface of the lake, trying to catch his breath.

It took several attempts, and almost swamping the boat, before Chance pulled himself belly first into the boat. Unfortunately, in the process, he had dumped his clothes into the waterlogged bottom of the small craft. Ashu, of course, had no problem getting into the boat. Now that Chance was out of the warm water, the cool air blowing across the lake on a brisk breeze began to chill him quite quickly. Pulling on soaking wet clothes would not help, so he retrieved them from the bottom of the boat, wrung them out, and placed them on the small bow seat. He hoped he would warm up paddling.

While he had been in the cave, the moon had begun to rise, but the clouds had returned somewhat. As the wind blew the clouds across the moon, the lake surface became a kaleidoscope of light and shadow. One moment there were moonbeams dancing across the lake's surface, the next moment the surface was dark, with only a line of light along the shoreline. Chance began to paddle, gliding across the dappled lake surface as silently as he could. He could only hope no one else was up at this hour watching the lake.

By the time Chance had paddled to the beach and pulled the boat up, he was quite warm. Having to put on his still overly damp clothes was not something he was anxious to do. He knew, however, it was not in his best interest to try to make his way back to his lodgings barely clothed. By the time he had managed to pull his clothes on, his teeth were chattering. The only warm spot on his body was where Ashu clung to his chest.

The way back to Hawser House was a series of sprints and stops. When the moon went behind a cloud, Chance would move as quickly as he could across the loose sand beach. When the moon would come out from behind the clouds, Chance stopped, crouched low to the sand, and waited until the beach was covered in darkness once again. Finally, he ducked behind the thick hedge next to the inn. He waited there for several long moments, listening. He could hear no movement, either from outside the window he was near, nor from inside the room he wanted to enter. Cautiously, Chance eased himself down and crab-walked his way to just below the open window he had exited several hours before. Slowly, he reached up and felt along the windowsill. The window was still open.

When Chance silently eased his leg over the windowsill, he became aware of an unnatural stillness in the room. Chance froze with indecision, one leg inside the room and one leg still outside the room.

"Get in lad, and quickly. Close the window quietly now and draw the curtains," Seeker Eshana whispered.

Chance did as directed, bringing his other leg inside the room. He turned and slowly, quietly eased the window down, locked it in place, and closed the curtains. The only sound in the room was the chattering of Chance's teeth. Whether the chattering was due to being cold, or the night's tension catching up to him, was hard to tell.

Seeker Eshana crossed swiftly to the settee, grabbed a throw, crossed back, and threw the throw around Chance's shoulders.

"Let's move you over to the fireplace and try to get you warmed up. There is not much fire left, but it should help. I also left the kettle in the coals, so I can at least give you a cup of warm water to try to warm your insides. Now get yourself out of those wet clothes while I grab another blanket."

Once Chance was in dry clothes and pulled up next to the dying embers of the fire with his hands wrapped around a warm cup of water and Ashu wrapped around his hands, Seeker Eshana asked if he had been successful.

"Yes," Chance said. "Everything was just as my father had described it to me, and I got what we came for. What next?"

"I think we will leave after the morning meal. We don't want to look like we are scurrying off. You and I will take our morning walk before breakfast, just like we did yesterday. When we get back, we will inform the innkeeper that we are intending to head out, that I am anxious to get on the road again, anxious to get to my daughter's. Now it is best we get some sleep, for morning will be here all too soon.

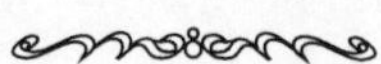

"Well?" Blaxton asked the man who had knocked at his door just before the break of dawn. "What do you have to report?"

"The man you had stationed at the family's old house stated that he caught a glimpse of the lad called Gershón passing the house shortly after the clock tower struck midnight. Was just luck he saw him going by, because the fog was quite thick at that point. Our man slipped in behind him and saw the lad take a boat and head out on the lake. He lost sight of him in the fog, so he could not tell where the lad went."

"And?" Blaxton asked barely containing his impatience.

"Our man hunkered down and several hours later, the lad Gershón returned. It appears that at some point he either had dumped the boat over, or he had been swimming. Seems a mighty strange thing to do at that time of night. Go swimming, I mean. Our man reported the lad seemed to be carrying something, but it was too dark to tell just what it was."

"What happened then?"

"The way our man tells it, about halfway toward morning, Gershón made his stealthy way back here and climbed in the window of their rooms."

"Post someone outside their windows to make sure no one leaves that way again this day. Keep me informed."

"Yes, sir," the man replied, and he slid silently out of Blaxton's room.

Several hours passed before a knock came on Blaxton's door. He opened it to find the innkeeper on the other side, hand raised to knock again.

"I have just been informed by the man calling himself Sennett that he and his grandson will be leaving today. They intend to take a walk on the beach, eat the morning meal, and then depart. He asked my cook if she would pack a midday meal for them."

"So, if these two are who I think they are, they have gotten what they came for or are heading toward it today. You have, once again, done well. Lady Farcroft will not forget your loyal service."

The innkeeper left, and Blaxton swiftly crossed his room and began to pack.

The ride out of Raskfoss was uneventful. It was one of those beautiful cool days, the sky a brilliant blue. They were heading south and west, the direction Seeker Eshana had indicated his 'daughter' lived, the direction folks would expect them to go. They did not rush, but looked, for all the world, like two folk who were intent on traveling a far distance this day.

No one seemed to be following them. When the sun reached the noon position, Seeker Eshana had them pull off the road.

"This looks like as good a spot as any to give the horses a rest and have a bite to eat. It will feel good to stretch our legs."

His legs were not the problem, Chance thought to himself. It was his arms and back that were stiff and sore after his unaccustomed paddling the night before. Sliding down off his horse, he stretched his arms and back, shook his hands out, and massaged his neck. Even the slight weight of Ashu on his shoulder was painful.

Their noon meal over, the pair was just about to mount up when they became aware of the sounds of pounding hooves. Ashu leapt from Chance's shoulder and scampered up the low branched tree the trio had been sitting under. The riders came swiftly up the road, and soon, Chance and Seeker Eshana were surrounded by four men with drawn knives, or swords, including the man called Blaxton.

"I would suggest you stand véry still," stated Blaxton. He and the others dismounted and surrounded Seeker Eshana and Chance.

"Tie their hands behind their backs," he instructed, holding a sword point to Chance's throat and suggesting to Seeker Eshana it would be in the lad's best interest to cooperate. "Search their gear."

Blaxton himself rifled through Seeker Eshana's clothing, including having him take off his boots. When he reached inside Seeker Eshana's shirt and flipped out the seeker's medallion, a look of triumph crossed Blaxton's face.

"Your little disguise almost fooled us, but not quite."

Crossing over to Chance, Blaxton searched the lad's clothing, checking pockets and pouches. He then reached beneath Chance's collar and pulled out the pouch made of golden pine spider silk. He held the pouch up, only to have his look of victory turn to one of dismay, when Ashu, hanging down from an overhead branch, snatched the pouch out of Blaxton's hand.

Chance watched in horror as Ashu swiftly climbed up the tree trunk, and one knife after another flew from Blaxton's hands, each time thunking into the trunk of the tree, thunk, thunk, thunk, thunk, thunk, just a hair away from where the halekrets' ringed tail had been.

Chapter Twenty-Four

Blaxton whirled, grabbed Chance by his shirt front, shook him, and then shoved him hard. Chance lost his balance and landed on his arms, which were tied behind his back, causing considerable pain to shoot up into his shoulders. Blaxton stalked away from him, yelling at his men to try and locate the ring-tailed animal who had snatched the pouch. Striding back to Chance, Blaxton pulled him up by his shirt and shook him once again, pushed him up against a tree trunk, and demanded to know if the animal belonged to Chance.

"No, sir," Chance answered through clenched teeth, for it was hard to respond when being violently shaken. Chance was not lying to Blaxton, because in truth, Ashu did not belong to him in the strict sense that he owned Ashu.

"Great, just great. To think I almost had in my hands the means to end this stupid challenge, and it is snatched away by a forest animal."

"Begging your pardon, sir," one of Blaxton's men said.

"What?" Blaxton shouted, rounding on the man.

"Well, sir, if the two here don't have what we came for, and we don't have what we came for, doesn't that accomplish the same thing? It's not like that little animal is going to deliver the object to the interim ruling council, now is it?" the man stated, chuckling at his own perceived cleverness. "We could just tell La . . . ." The man stopped speaking when Blaxton held up a hand and glowered at him.

"Quiet, I need to think."

Chance continued to search the branches of the trees above him but could not see any sign of Ashu. He was so worried about the halekrets that he was not really aware of what was happening around him, and almost missed a tug on the rope binding his hands behind his back. He felt small paws working on the knots of the rope. Part of him was excited he would soon be free of the rope. Another part of him was very nervous that any one of the men would notice that Ashu was behind him. When the rope was untied, Ashu placed the golden pine spider silk pouch in Chance's hand.

Ashu scampered up the tree trunk, and then ran from branch to branch, making quite a bit of noise doing so. All four of the men looked up, several of them pointing, trying to follow the halekrets' path through the branches. As they looked up, several things happened at once. Chance slipped the pouch containing the piece of the oppgave ringe back around his neck, tucking it in. Seeker Eshana made a move that Chance could hardly follow, which caused one of the men to crumple to the ground. And Seeker Eshana's horse came seemingly out of nowhere and bowled over two more of the men. Seeker Eshana quickly collected their swords and knives. In the ensuing confusion, Chance slipped passed the three downed men, grabbed the two walking sticks off the pack horse, and moved to stand next to Seeker Eshana's side.

"Well now, that evens up the odds quite a bit, don't you think?" Seeker Eshana stated, all the while keeping close watch on the four men. The two who had been knocked down by Seeker Eshana's horse were still on the ground, trying to recover their collective breaths. The one Seeker Eshana felled was still lying motionless on the ground. Only Blaxton was standing.

Chance was not sure quite what Seeker Eshana did, but he seemed to grow bigger and stronger with each passing minute. His voice was deeper and became more commanding. The walking stick he held almost appeared to glow.

The two men on the ground began to inch away from the Seeker, until he told them to halt.

"Pick up your companion, and then, I would like you to move on down the lane in the direction you came from. No, don't go near your horses." The men hurried to do as they had been instructed. "Chance, I want you to go and take the saddles and gear off their four horses. Just dump it in a pile next to that maple tree."

Chance did as he was told. He noticed that Seeker Eshana had placed himself between him and Blaxton.

Blaxton stood rigid, sword in hand, but so far had made no move to stop his men from following Seeker Eshana's instructions or to try to change the situation.

"Are you going to tell the lad to go through our belongings looking for valuables and coins now? I thought seekers were above petty thievery," Blaxton said, and there was a definite sneer in his voice.

"No, I have no intention of taking anything other than your horses, but . . ." Seeker Eshana held up his hand to stop Blaxton's next remark or protest, ". . . I intend to release them about an hour down the road. I don't want to make it easy for you to catch up with us again. Come, lad, bring those horses with you and mount up."

"But . . . ." Chance began to protest.

"I don't know what these ruffians thought you had in your pouch, but we have no time to look for it now. I'm sorry, lad. I know that small medallion you carried in your pouch had sentimental value, but it just cannot be helped. We need to put as much distance between ourselves and these men as possible. Come along now."

Chance played along with what Seeker Eshana said, since he knew that the pouch neither held a small medallion of sentimental value, nor was the pouch missing. He also was not worried about Ashu, for he had seen him slip into the carrying pack on the back of his horse. Trying to look sad over the loss of his sentimental medallion, Chance mounted his horse.

As Chance and Seeker Eshana left Blaxton behind, they heard him shout, "This isn't over, not by a long means. Do you hear me? This isn't over."

As promised, an hour later, Seeker Eshana called a halt and sent the horses they had taken on their way. It was the first time Chance and he had an opportunity to talk.

"I'm sorry, lad, about having to leave Ashu behind. We will go back for him, but we will have to be very careful when we do. I can only hope he has not dropped the pouch, or hung it up on some branch we can neither see nor climb up to, if we can locate it."

"That won't be necessary . . . ." Chance started to say, but Seeker Eshana interrupted him.

"No, Chance, I know this journey has been really difficult for you, but you can't give up now."

"I have no intention of giving up," Chance stated with some heat, surprising even himself. "There is no need to go back, because I already have the pouch and its contents. In addition, Ashu is at this moment curled up asleep in his place behind me. He has been a really clever fellow today. It almost feels like he had help, but from who or what?"

Seeker Eshana was momentarily speechless, and then, he just smiled and told Chance to mount up.

"Well, in that case, let's see how much distance we can travel yet this day."

Seeker Eshana then remounted and urged his horse forward at a fast ground eating pace. He did not call a halt for several more hours. After walking the horses to cool them down, Seeker Eshana motioned that Chance should join him at the pack horse.

"Here, hold down the other side of this map," he instructed Chance. "We need to figure out a way to get you to the capital unharmed and undetected. The Regent's followers are not going to give up. They also must be getting more desperate, or much bolder, or both. There was a clear message at the Well of Speaking when the Gylden Sirklene challenge was called that we seekers were charged with trying to locate the parts of the oppgave ringe. All heard the warning that we were not to be detained or harmed. It was very clear that there would be dire consequences to those who attempted to do so. Those men who tried to detain us would have had no qualms about dropping both of us into the deepest well they could locate. This is not good. We are going to need some help."

"But sir, won't involving others increase the risk?"

"Yes, but I think we need to take that risk. I suspect those men we left back there will shortly be after us and will also have gotten the word out to others to look for us. I think they will think we will head directly to the capital. I don't think they will expect us to double back."

"You want to go back to Raskfoss?"

"No, I want to go back to pick up your skiff."

"But sir, even if we sail to the port of Litenhaven, Skipper Nereo will not be there for at least a fortnight. Wouldn't staying in one place be a greater risk than moving across country by horse?"

"And here I thought I had heard you loved the sea."

"I do, but . . . ." Chance started to say, and then he took a look at Seeker Eshana's face. Seeker Eshana's face had a very crafty look on it. "You have a plan, don't you?"

"I think so. We are going to travel back toward Tverdal as fast as we can. Not far to the west of where we are now is the village of Vegger. I have several friends there who I think I can talk into accompanying us."

By the time Chance and Seeker Eshana reached the village of Vegger, Chance was not sure he would ever get the feeling back in either his legs or hands. The weather had turned cold and damp, and Chance just felt numb. He was so tired, he almost missed the fact that the village of Vegger was a walled village, which was quite unusual. Walled towns were common in Sommerhjem, but not walled villages.

Seeing the puzzled look on Chance's face, Seeker Eshana explained that Vegger, a very, very long time ago, had once been the home of a very talented Günnary gem cutter. His gems had been much prized in the land. That was, of course, before the Günnary had all but disappeared from the landscape. Because there were always folk who covet that which is not theirs, or which they could not afford, raids on the village of Vegger became all too frequent. To protect themselves, the villagers built a defensible wall around their homes. In present time, the village of Vegger is a place where folk can deposit their valuables and bank their coin. The village is essentially a fortress and has its own troop of guards.

"I have a few friends here," Seeker Eshana told Chance. "They are very loyal to the Crown, and I think, will be willing to help. They have trained all of their lives to protect both what is stored in Vegger and also to guard against robbery if a valuable needs to be transported either to or from Vegger. I think a bit of misdirection is called for in order to get you to the capital."

Chance and Seeker Eshana were stopped at the village gate, which was heavily barred. Someone had to be called from the interior of the village to come and verify that it was alright for Seeker Eshana and Chance to enter the village itself. They were escorted down a small side street to the barracks of the traveling guards. There Seeker Eshana was welcomed by the commander, one Captain Manipal.

"Ah, my old friend, have you come to deposit some rare find or take one out?"

"Neither. Is there a place we can talk in private?"

"Yes. Let me arrange for some refreshments. We can get comfortable and talk in my office."

Captain Manipal's office was like a vault. The door, Chance noticed, was at least ten to twelve inches thick, and the room had neither a fireplace nor a window. When Captain Manipal closed the door, he slid a thick board down into brackets, effectively keeping the door from being opened from the other side by anything other than a very determined crew with a battering ram and a great deal of patience. The three settled and the refreshments that had been set on a low table next to their chairs were passed around.

"Now then, why don't you tell me what brings you to Vegger, and how we might be of service?" Captain Manipal asked.

"I have need to get a very important item to the capital undetected, and I need a young man who is similar enough to pass for my apprentice here in height, build, and coloring, who doesn't get seasick."

Chapter Twenty-Five

"I have just the man in mind who could pass as your apprentice, and he is a fair sailor, also. We can get into that in a moment, but first, I think you need to tell me who, or what else, you have smuggled into this room. Your apprentice's cloak seems to be moving."

Chance did not hear any alarm in the Captain's voice, only curiosity. Chance reached into his cloak and coaxed Ashu out.

"Well now, is this who you want to get to the capital?"

"Yes, Ashu here needs to go to the capital, as does my apprentice Chance, but they are only partly why we need your services. There are a great many folk who would like to get their hands on Chance, due to what he carries."

Captain Manipal merely raised a quizzical eyebrow and waited for Seeker Eshana to go on.

"Chance has in his possession one of the pieces of the oppgave ringe. As I said, there have been a number of folks who have tried to prevent him from getting to the capital. I realize you are thinking that you and your guards would have no problem making sure he arrives there in one piece with all of his possessions. You are known for making that happen, and I am going to trust you to do that. However . . ." Seeker Eshana said holding up his hand to indicate he was not through speaking. ". . . however, I think a bit of misdirection is also needed for those who have tried to stop Chance have also tried to stop me."

"These folks would interfere with a seeker?"

"Would and have."

"This is just not right. What do you have in mind?"

"I suggest that your stand-in for Chance and I travel back toward Tverdal and retrieve Chance's skiff. We will sail it down the Travers River to open sea and from there go to Litenhaven. At that point, your man will change back into himself and return here. I imagine you can have transportation awaiting him, yes?"

"Most certainly. We often deliver and pick up valuables from seaports."

"What will you do then?" Chance asked, entering the conversation for the first time.

"I intend to wait for a ride to the capital on a ship that I know will be there in a fortnight."

"But what of your horse and all of your possessions on your pack animal?" Chance asked.

"You'll be riding my horse, and I think the Captain will have some type of transportation to carry all of my gear. It will be the precious cargo that his guards are guarding. You'll just be another one of the guards."

"What of Ashu?"

"Well, I don't think we have a guard uniform small enough to fit him, but he could ride in the small wagon, which I think will work for this trip," stated Captain Manipal with a perfectly straight face.

"Or he can ride behind you, as he has up until this point. Unless those trying to get what you are carrying are extremely desperate, the closer you get to the capital, the less and less chance they will try to attack your escort. You will be traveling on the royal road, which is more heavily patrolled the closer you get to the capital. It's just in this area that I think the search for you is concentrated, at the moment, so I want to throw them off just a bit by our ruse."

Captain Manipal, Seeker Eshana, and Chance spent the next hour talking over the plan, looking at maps, and exchanging ideas. It was decided that they would put the plan in motion the next morning. The Captain suggested they settle in and stay in the room he assigned, to give him time to put together the folks he wanted for both parts of the plan.

Once Chance and Seeker Eshana had settled in their room, Chance had a chance to express his concerns.

"Wouldn't it be better if you just rode to the capital with me?" Chance asked. "I worry that you might be captured again."

"I thank you for your concern, lad, but I need to find out who has been after you. I strongly suspect one of the parties trying to stop you, and perhaps other ring bearers, is Lady Farcroft. I also suspect she was not the one who had you picked up in Marinel. I'm hoping to get some clues about that while I wait for Skipper Nereo's ship to return to Litenhaven."

"What happens once I get to the capital?" Chance asked.

"Your escort will take you directly to the Glassmakers Guildhall and to your cousin, Master Clarisse. She will know what to do then."

"And after I take care of putting the ring in its proper place?" Chance inquired, for he truly wanted to know what might happen next.

"If you are set on becoming a seeker, my apprenticeship offer is still open."

"Yes, sir, I would very much like to do that."

"Good, then you will need this," Seeker Eshana said, reaching into his pocket and pulling out a medallion hanging from a brilliant blue colored cord. "Keep it tucked away for now, but you will have need of it when you get to the capital. I sent a message on asking that a seeker meet you at there. She will be there to stand with you, since I will most probably arrive at the capital several weeks after you do. Her name is Seeker Zita. Now, I have a question for you. Will you need to travel back to the Havkoller Islands?"

"Much as I might want to see my family, I think that is not a trip I would make at this time. I will need to get word back to them that I'm well, and about what I hope to do. I also need to let them know that our house and place in Raskfoss will never be as it was. I wonder if, upon hearing about what has happened in our former home, they might not want to remain on the Havkoller Islands."

"Time will tell. First things first, however. We will leave early in the morning, each going our separate ways, but I will meet up with you at the capital. Now, let me tell you what you need to know about my horse."

Chance thought about the next leg of his journey and all he had discussed with Seeker Eshana before they had blown the candles out. With all that on his mind, he thought he would have a difficult time getting to sleep. He was surprised when he felt Ashu patting his face and he opened his eyes to sunlight streaming in the room's window. Seeker Eshana was not in the room, but Chance saw that there was a guard's uniform laid out across the chair beside his bed. After washing up, Chance dressed. It felt odd to be in the uniform, and he hoped he could carry the disguise off. Just as he finished, Seeker Eshana appeared at the door.

"It's time, lad. Here's hoping that Neebing luck rides with you."

Chance didn't quite know what to make of that statement by Seeker Eshana, but he tucked it away along with having been called Neebing blessed. Someday he vowed to himself, he would know what both of those statements meant.

After breakfast, Captain Manipal drew Chance aside and introduced him to the Lef'tenant, who would be in charge of the guard that would be riding with and protecting him.

"This is Lef'tenant Kilinda. She will be in charge of your guard and will also be in charge of you. Her group will keep you safe. Just follow their lead. You are of the lowest rank, so know you will probably get the worst of the jobs. If they treat you any differently than a new recruit, people on the road will notice. I will apologize ahead of time," said Captain Manipal.

"It will probably seem just like being with my family," suggested Chance with a deep sigh. "I'm the youngest of many brothers and sisters. I'm used to the worst of the jobs and a great deal of bossing around and teasing. I might even get homesick."

"Sounds like we'll get along just fine," suggested Lef'tenant Kilinda. "We will leave shortly, so make your farewells."

Chance turned to Seeker Eshana and found he was very reluctant to say farewell to the Seeker. Part of the difficulty he was having, he knew, was due to worry for both himself and Seeker Eshana. Part of it was worry about the road ahead. He tried to speak, but the words seemed to get stuck in his throat.

Seeker Eshana drew him aside. "Now lad, a seeker always looks like he is in control and knows what he is doing, even if he is shaking in his boots. You need to project confidence and an aura of command. A good piece of advice if you want to look like you really belong with this group of guards. I know you are worried about a few things. Just keep telling yourself that everything will work out in the end. After all, despite all odds, you have made it this far."

Chance was not sure whether Seeker Eshana's words left him reassured or not. The first part of the advice made a great deal of sense to him, and the ideas had been reinforced by watching how Seeker Eshana presented himself to folk during their time together. The second part of what the Seeker had said was somewhat less reassuring, if true. Much of what had happened to him since he had left the Havkoller Islands had only been partially resolved by his own actions and quick thinking. He had had a great deal of help along the way. Keeper Odette, Skipper Nereo, and Seeker Eshana had had a great part in getting him to this point in his journey. However, he would never have even gotten away from the Shadow Islands if it had not been for Ashu. He wondered if there were such a thing as halekrets luck. Chance did not know from Neebing luck riding on his shoulder, but he knew Ashu had been.

The command came to mount up. Seeker Eshana gave Chance's shoulder a reassuring squeeze, and then, turned to mount the horse he was riding. As the guards rode out of Vegger's gate, Chance glanced over his shoulder and saw Seeker Eshana tip his hat to him in farewell. That gesture made Chance want to turn his horse around and ride back, rather than face the unknown of the coming days.

Chapter Twenty-Six

Lef'tenant Kilinda drew her horse up and signaled her patrol of guards to halt. The group had been traveling on the royal road for several days, and so far, it appeared that the plan Seeker Eshana and Captain Manipal had devised was working. The patrol pulled into a camping area that was beginning to fill up with fellow travelers. She had not felt there had been anyone overly curious about her group, nor had she felt as if anyone had been following them. She had also been impressed with the lad Chance. If he were not so determined to become a seeker, he would make a good addition to her guard unit, she thought. The lad had pulled his weight, and taken all the ribbing by the other guards with good grace.

"We'll pull off here and halt for the night. Private recruit, you are on cook detail tonight. Try not to burn the water this time," Lef'tenant Kilinda said, directing her remark to Chance.

Chance heard snickers coming from several of the guards, along with a few moans. He probably deserved the ribbing, Chance thought, since his first time at cooking had been an utter disaster. He noted that Lef'tenant Kilinda had once again chosen a camping spot that was easily defendable. He had really grown to appreciate how very clever she was. Anyone really looking at this patrol of guards would notice that all of the guards' attention was focused on the small wagon they had been traveling with, as if this was what they were guarding, rather than Chance.

Ashu had been content to travel either in his pouch behind Chance's saddle or in the wagon. He seemed to understand he needed to be out of sight. When the guards camped, Ashu would often scurry up the closest tree and remain there until it was dark. It was probably best for Ashu that they usually camped near trees, for the food the guard traveled with was mostly dried and certainly lacked fresh fruits and vegetables. Ashu was probably eating better than the guards, since he was good at finding food in the forest.

Each morning, the guards efficiently packed up and were on the road shortly after dawn. The days passed swiftly. Finally, the morning dawned when Chance and his escort were close enough to the capital that they would arrive late in the afternoon. Chance was not sure how he felt about their imminent arrival. He felt relief, but he also did not know what to expect once he got there.

Chance really did not have any time to worry, for Lef'tenant Kilinda had assigned Chance the job of driving the small wagon this day, and he needed all of his concentration because the road became more and more crowded the closer they came to the capital. Finally, he found himself tightly surrounded by the rest of the guard as they pulled up to the capital gates. Once through, Lef'tenant Kilinda ordered him to turn over his wagon driving duties. Ashu had chittered at him when he had passed by the side of the wagon on his way to mount up, so he sent an inquiring look toward the Lef'tenant. She indicated he should let Ashu out. When he mounted Seeker Eshana's horse, Chance felt a great deal better that Ashu was once again riding on his shoulder.

Lef'tenant Kilinda had sent a rider ahead to the Glassmakers Guildhall to alert them of Chance's arrival. His cousin, Master Clarisse, was waiting for him when they arrived.

"Chance, I cannot begin to tell you how relieved and happy I am to see you." Turning to address Lef'tenant Kilinda, Master Clarisse invited her and the guards to ride around back of the Guildhall to the stables.

"I thank you for your kind offer, but we need to check into our headquarters here and get our next assignment. Chance, it has been an honor to escort you to the capital. Should you ever decide to become a Vegger guard, you would be welcome in my patrol."

"I thank you for my safe passage here," Chance told Lef'tenant Kilinda. "As for rejoining your patrol as a private recruit, well . . . ."

As the patrol wheeled and began to move away, one of the guards yelled back, "You had best not let him have cook duty." Laughter followed the patrol down the lane.

At a questioning look from Master Clarisse, Chance replied, "Please don't ask."

"Before we head inside, I have a few questions for you. First things first. Were you successful in the task your family sent you to Sommerhjem for?"

"I was."

"That is good. Now to my next question. Who or what do you have on your shoulder, and where does he, she, or it come from?"

"This is Ashu, and he's a halekrets. I found him adrift on a piece of flotsam while I was sailing here." Chance hated to lie to his cousin, but he could not reveal where Ashu had really come from.

"How did you get to Sommerhjem after the smugglers dropped you off at the Shadow Islands?"

Chance and Seeker Eshana had discussed how to handle this question, so Chance was prepared.

"The story of the smugglers dropping me off at the Shadow Islands is a rather big fib on the part of the tellers." Dumping me overboard with the intention of drowning me would be more accurate, Chance thought to himself. "My being snatched in the port of Marinel and taken aboard a smuggler's ship is true. Fortunately for me, after I was thrown overboard, I was rescued and transported to Sommerhjem on a ship, whose captain and crew were good honest folks. I acquired a small skiff, sailed down the coast to the port of Willing, and then, up the Travers River as far as I could. I thank you for sending Seeker Eshana to find out what happened to me. Without him, I might have made more of a mess of the task I was sent to do by my family than I already had."

"I don't think you should be so hard on yourself. Your task should have been an easy one. No one should have known you were coming. The fact that someone did, and was waiting for you, has caused no little concern here. It suggests either we need to be much more discrete in our conversations so that they are not overheard, or someone whom we think is loyal to the Crown is playing a double game and getting information to those who are not loyal to the Crown," Master Clarisse stated. "We should have been more vigilant. It would seem that those who would wish to either put the former regent back in power, or wish to keep the Gylden Sirklene challenge from happening, are both more knowledgeable and more organized than we ever suspected. A disturbing turn of events, to say the least. Well, we had best head inside. As I said, others are waiting to greet you."

Chance had not liked lying to his cousin. He felt even worse about lying about Ashu's origins, since she was being so kind and understanding. He was not looking forward to meeting those who were waiting for him, since he knew there were going to be more questions. Squaring his shoulders, Chance followed his cousin through the doors into the Glassmakers Guildhall.

The Glassmakers Guildhall entrance was filled with color and light. It was a place Chance would have liked to stop and take a moment to enjoy the beauty of the stained glass windows and dome, but his cousin moved briskly through the entrance and straight up the stairs to the second floor. She finally stopped just outside the entrance of a set of double doors.

"This is the Guildhall's library. Before you arrived, I arranged to have refreshments set up and sent runners off to gather the others who need to meet you. Some are here already, and we will await the rest before we begin to discuss what to do next. I am sorry this does not give you any time to catch your breath from your ride here. The sooner we have a plan in place as to what needs to happen next, the less likely it is that those who have tried to prevent you from getting here will have time to cause any more trouble."

Chance followed his cousin through the double doors. It took him a moment to register that there were others in the room, because his eyes were immediately drawn to the floor to ceiling bookshelves. Books of all sizes filled the shelves, and Chance could see that some were very, very old. It took him a moment to bring his attention back to what his cousin was saying.

"Chance, I'd like you to meet Master Rollag," Master Clarisse said, introducing a man whose size could almost rival that of Seeker Eshana, seated at a table set in the middle of the library. "Seated on his right is Seeker Zita and on his left is rover Thorval Pedersen. We are waiting on Lady Esmeralda, Lady Celik, and either Lord or Lady Hadrack. We have chosen to have our meeting here in a more informal setting because it is probably more secure than the palace, until we can determine how information we do not want to have in the hands of those who oppose the Crown is getting out."

"Perhaps you would like to introduce us to your companion," kindly suggested the rover Master Clarisse had introduced as Thorval Pedersen.

"My apologies to Ashu," Master Clarisse said. "Go ahead, Chance."

"This is Ashu. He's a halekrets."

A look of interest flashed across Seeker Zita's face. "I'm not familiar with Ashu's kind and don't think I've run across any halekrets in my wanderings. Where did you find him?"

Chance did not want to go into where he had found Ashu once again. He thought he might be able to shift the attention away from having to lie again to what he had learned.

"I was told by a forester elder, Elder Nelda, who is the Smale Stier forest clan's keeper of their history, that halekrets used to live in the quirrelit groves of Sommerhjem a very long time ago. She had an ancient book that had a picture of one. She did not know where or when they had last been sighted in Sommerhjem."

Before Seeker Zita could respond or ask more questions, others began entering the room and introductions were made. Chance's cousin, Master Clarisse, did the honors.

"Chance, may I introduce you to Lady Esmeralda, Lord Hadrack, Captain . . ."

"Sorry, am I late?" asked a young man who rushed in the door.

". . . and Lord Hadrack's nephew, Aaron Beecroft, fondly known as Beezle to his friends. And once again, I have forgotten Ashu. Chance's companion, who is making great inroads into the fruit and totally ignoring us, is Ashu, a halekrets," Master Clarisse said, chuckling. "I think he has the right idea. Let us all get something to drink and eat before we settle down to hear Chance's tale about how he got here, and then decide what needs to happen next."

Once everyone was settled, Chance told the group the version he and Seeker Eshana had cobbled together as to what had happened to him since he had left his family in Havkoller. He could only hope the folks assembled in the library of the Glassmakers Guildhall did not ask too many questions. He tried to read the faces of those gathered around the table to see if he was convincing enough about how he had found Ashu on a piece of floating flotsam and how the two of them had been picked up by a passing ship. Chance also told them about his encounter with the two men near Tverdal and meeting Seeker Eshana. He concluded his tale by telling them about their passage through the Smale Stier forest, once again recounting what the forester Elder had told him about halekrets.

"We finally made it to Raskfoss, and from there to Vegger, where Seeker Eshana arranged to have the Vegger guards escort me here. He headed back to Tverdal with a Vegger guard, who is about my size and coloring. Seeker Eshana and the guard, Orman I think his name was, were going to pick up my skiff and sail on to Litenhaven. Seeker Eshana thought this might confuse those who were looking for me. He should be here in several weeks, and suggested we not wait for him to get what I carry into its proper place," concluded Chance.

"Perhaps we can see what you are carrying," stated Lord Hadrack.

Chance looked at his cousin who gave an approving nod of her head. Pulling the golden pine spider silk pouch out from under his shirt, he opened the drawstring and tipped the ring into his hand. No one moved or reached out for it, so he laid it in the middle of the table. Chance felt a bit of a loss when he laid the ring down, but when Ashu left his small dish of fruit and swiftly climbed up onto his shoulder, he felt immensely calmer.

"Certainly looks like the two that Nissa carried and placed in the vesstebok s," exclaimed Beezle.

"And also, like the ones Greer and Meryl placed there," agreed Master Rollag.

"Do you know the history of how your family came to possess the ring, and where has it been hidden all this time?" asked Lady Esmeralda.

Once again, Chance was a bit at a loss. Here he was being questioned by one of the members of the interim ruling council, and he did not know what was proper to do. He had already lied to those assembled in the library, which had left him feeling awful, especially lying to his cousin, but was he supposed to tell them where his father had hidden the ring? Before he could answer, a sharp urgent knock came at the door.

Chapter Twenty-Seven

Seeker Eshana and the young guard had very little trouble returning to Tverdal. They stopped by the Glassmakers Guildhall to request someone to ride with them to just short of the fishing village where Chance had left his skiff. They were going to send their horses back to the Guildhall, where they would be stabled until Captain Manipal sent someone to retrieve them.

Once they had reached their destination and the horses had been sent on their way, Seeker Eshana and the young guard Orman began to walk toward the fishing village and go over their plan.

"You had best put that sling on your arm, and I'll wrap the bandage around your head. Remember to keep your head down. We want folks to think you are Chance and spread the word that we were here. We are early enough that the fishers probably have not set off for the day. Once we get to the village, head right to the skiff. Let me do the talking."

Seeker Eshana's timing was good, for the fishers were just beginning to push their boats into the water. Chance's skiff was tied up on shore, so Orman headed right toward it. Seeker Eshana spotted the female fisher Berrimilla right away. He headed toward her and introduced himself.

"I am Seeker Eshana, and the lad Chance wishes to thank you for looking after his skiff," Seeker Eshana told the fisherwoman. "He had a slight accident on his walkabout. Broke his arm and banged himself up some. I, fortunately, came upon him shortly after he took his tumble, out of a tree of all things, and thought I would get him home."

"He's lucky that you came along when you did. What happened to that cute little ring-tailed animal he had with him?" asked Berrimilla.

"He's the reason young Chance has a broken arm. Seems the little animal he called Ashu decided he liked quirrelit trees and disappeared up one. Chance tried to coax him down, but he had disappeared. The lad stayed in the grove several days and never caught another glimpse of him. He decided he would climb a tree and set a trap up, hoping to lure Ashu in and capture him. That is when he fell. Never did get the little animal to come back. Added heartbreak to his other injuries."

"Poor lad," Berrimilla said sympathetically. "Do you need help putting the skiff in?"

"I thank you for your offer, but I can handle it. I suspect you are anxious to get on the water yourself. Looks to be a good day for fishing."

"Aye, that it will be. I'll just be off then. Tell the lad I'm sorry for his troubles."

"I'll be sure to do that, and thank you again on Chance's behalf."

Seeker Eshana made quick work getting the skiff into the water, stowing their gear, and setting the sail. Orman kept his head down, and once they were underway, lowered himself to the bottom of the skiff and tried to look like he was sleeping. There was a steady wind blowing, and the pair made good time.

Seeker Eshana hoped to be well down the Travers River and out to sea before Berrimilla or her husband took their fish to Tverdal docks to sell. If he was any judge of character, the fisherwoman would probably tell the fishmonger about the lad Chance returning with a seeker, about Chance's adventures, and about him not having the little halekrets any longer. In fact, Seeker Eshana was counting on her to do so. Now, all he needed was for the weather to hold and the wind to blow steady, so they could make it to Litenhaven before the word got out. One of Orman's fellow guards would be waiting for him with a spare horse, and they would return to Vegger. Seeker Eshana would wait for Skipper Nereo's boat. Of course, this plan depends on weather, gossip, and a great deal of luck, Seeker Eshana thought, as he adjusted the sail.

"Come," said Master Rollag, responding to an urgent knock on the door. A noblewoman entered the room. "Ah, Lady Celik, glad you have been able to come. This young man is Chance, and he has brought the fifth piece of the oppgave ringe to the capital."

"How glad I am that you and what you carry have made it safely here. There have been a number of reports that the activities of the former regent's agents have increased in the last few weeks. I am glad they were not successful in finding you," stated Lady Celik. "Now who, or what, is that who has just snatched a piece of apple off your plate?"

Chance, once again, introduced Ashu and was bracing himself for the next questions he did not want to answer, when Lady Celik begged his pardon.

"I am sorry I am late. I am sure you have discussed what has happened to you since you disembarked in the port of Marinel. Much as I am curious to know what happened, I think we need to get on to the discussion on what to do next, and how to keep you, Ashu, and the ring safe until you can place the ring in the vessteboks. With this, the fifth piece out of nine of the oppgave ringe being brought safely to the capital, those loyal to the former regent are getting even more bold and restless. It is causing me no little measure of concern."

The Captain of the royal guard spoke for the first time. "My patrols have also reported noticing more activity in and out of the capital by elements that we would label anywhere from misguided to dangerous. I've called for extra guards to be posted here tonight and to escort whoever assembles here tomorrow to the Well of Speaking."

"Thank you, Captain," said Lady Esmeralda. "I have sent word out to the rest of the interim ruling council to be prepared to meet at the Well of Speaking midmorning tomorrow. I hope that is agreeable to all of you." Turning to Chance and Ashu, she said, "I am sure if you are like the others who have been the bearers of pieces of the oppgave ringe, you might just as soon skip all the pomp and ceremony of placing the ring in the vessteboks in front of a great crowd of folk."

Chance had not really been aware that he would be doing anything in front of a great crowd, and once he thought about what Lady Esmeralda had just said, he was in total agreement with her.

"Is there a reason I can't just wander over there now and take care of placing the ring in the, what was it called, the vessteboks?"

"Much as that would be easier on you, and perhaps simpler to manage," Chance's cousin, Master Clarisse, replied, "it is better to have more people witness the event." When Chance gave her a questioning look, Master Clarisse went on. "A lot of people have been skeptical about the Gylden Sirklene challenge. With more and more folk witnessing the placing of the rings, more and more folks are becoming convinced that there is really something to this challenge. Your being a hero for a day or so is a small price to pay for the goodwill and tales that will come out of the Well of Speaking tomorrow. Now, I think we need to firm up our plans, and then give Chance some time to relax."

As if that is likely to happen anytime soon, Chance thought to himself, as the conversation swirled around him. He was not even really aware that the meeting had broken up, until his cousin tapped him on the shoulder and he realized the room had emptied out.

"Chance," Master Clarisse said.

"What? Oh, sorry, I was lost in thought."

"You look troubled. Shall we take a walk in the garden and stretch our legs?"

The two descended the stairs and went out a side door of the Guildhall into a small, but secluded, walled garden. After wandering silently for a few minutes, Master Clarisse suggested they sit on a bench in the sun.

"Is something troubling you, Chance?"

Chance was silent for several minutes trying to gather his thoughts before he began to speak. For all of his deep thinking, when he finally opened his mouth, he blurted out, "I'm not a hero. I'm the furthest thing I can think of from a hero. I'm just a bungler at what I thought was going to be a grand adventure."

"Now Chance, why would you think that?"

"All the heroes or heroines I have ever read about have been clever, brave, and able to get through any challenge by themselves. I didn't even last an hour off the ship in the port of Marinel before being picked up. All along the way, others have rescued me when I got in a tight spot. Ashu, Seeker Eshana, the Vegger guards . . . ." Chance's voice trailed off and his body slumped.

"Of course, heroes or heroines in stories can do great and daring feats. In real life, most of us need friends and boon companions to help us when times are difficult. A true hero is one who knows when to accept the help of others to get the task done. You had been given a very difficult task to complete by your family. They could have sent any one of your brothers or sisters, yet they sent you. Through it all you have never given up and have been wise enough to accept help and good counsel along the way. I have a feeling that your journey to this day has not been an easy one. I, for one, am very proud that you are my cousin."

"Thank you."

"You are very welcome. Now then, tomorrow is going to be a busy day, and Seeker Zita asked if she could have some time with you."

"Could we sit here just a little longer?"

"Of course."

The two sat in companionable silence for quite some time. Ashu had curled up on Chance's lap and was asleep. The garden was quiet except for the hum of various insects going about their business. There was a light warm breeze causing the flowers to sway gently. Finally, Chance roused himself from his thoughts.

"Seeker Eshana has asked me to become his apprentice, to train to be a seeker."

"And how do you feel about the idea?"

"It was a foolish childhood dream I once had . . . ."

"And now?"

"And now, it doesn't feel so foolish."

"And are you worried what your family will have to say about your not returning and joining the family business?"

"Not really. My parents have always encouraged all of us to find what would suit us best. All of my brothers and sisters seem to like being traders, either by land or water. For me, it was just alright, not something I had any overwhelming fondness for."

"I think your parents would be very proud to have a seeker in the family. The Høyttaier clan has been proud to claim a number of seekers among us over the years. Hopefully, you will be able to add to our knowledge of the old language in your seeking. I think bringing the ring to the capital was just the first step in your journey."

As they rose to walk back into the Guildhall, Chance continued to think about what Master Clarisse had had to say. Was he about to embark on another journey, and where would that take him? Would looking for more information about the old language become the direction of his seeking? Could seekers even choose what knowledge they wished to seek out?"

Chance and his cousin parted ways at the door to the room Chance had been assigned. She said she would send Seeker Zita on up. Before the Seeker was to arrive, Chance took the time to look around his chambers. He had a sitting room, and as he could see through an open door, a sleeping chamber. His and Seeker Eshana's gear had been neatly piled up against one wall of the sitting room.

Chance found he really wished that Seeker Eshana were here right now. He had grown comfortable with the Seeker and had come to rely on him. Chance walked over to their gear and picked up both of their walking sticks. He knew it was foolish to feel somewhat better just by holding both of them, yet they represented a connection between Seeker Eshana and himself. A little part of Chance worried that once Seeker Eshana arrived, he might take back his offer of having Chance as an apprentice. Chance leaned the walking sticks against a chair and went back to the packs to find a cleaning rag and some beeswax. He thought that while he sat there he could polish the walking sticks up a bit. Chance had just settled into one of the comfortable chairs in his sitting room when a soft knock came at the door.

"Yes?"

"It's Seeker Zita. May I come in?"

"Please enter."

Chance looked up and noticed that Seeker Zita was carrying a bundle and her walking stick.

"We need to get you prepared," Seeker Zita stated, setting the bundle down.

Chapter Twenty-Eight

"Prepared?" squeaked Chance, and he was embarrassed that his voice did not seem to be under control. Clearing his throat, Chance tried again. "What did you mean by saying I need to get prepared?"

"Seeker Eshana's brief message stated that you posed as his apprentice during your travels. Is that correct?" Seeker Zita inquired.

"Yes," answered Chance, who had begun to worry that the offer to be Seeker Eshana's apprentice had been just for the purpose of a disguise and not the real thing, that the Seeker had not really wanted him to be his apprentice. He had become so concerned with that thought that he almost missed what Seeker Zita said next.

"A second message from him clarified that he really has asked you to be his apprentice. The governing body of the Order of the Seekers has responded to his request that you be accepted into the Order. I'm here to make sure you are properly dressed for tomorrow, since you will be representing us."

"Prop-prop-properly dressed?" Chance was simultaneously trying to hold onto his elation that Seeker Eshana had really meant it when he had asked him to apprentice with him, and a great bit of awe. Governing body of the Order of the Seekers, indeed.

"For the most part, we seekers generally dress in comfortable clothes that are suitable for travel, having little need for fancy fripperies. On those rare occasions when we need to make an impression, we have robes. I have brought you one. I need you to try it on, so I can make sure it is the right size and you don't embarrass either yourself or the Order by tripping down the stairs at the Well of Speaking tomorrow."

"I'm so glad I now can add tripping down the stairs at the Well of Speaking to the huge number of fears and concerns I already have about tomorrow," Chance stated ruefully, while still trying to get his wildly out of control emotions in hand.

All that had happened to him since he had left his family in the Havkoller Islands was swirling through his head. Leaving home, being kidnapped, thinking he was trapped on the Shadow Islands, feeling like he had failed his family, the rite of passage, finding Ashu and then worrying that he had lost him, meeting Seeker Eshana, and all the rest. And now this news that he really did have the opportunity to become a seeker, but with that news came new responsibilities on top of what he had to do the next day. It was a good thing he was still holding his walking stick, for otherwise he might have just slipped to the floor.

Seeker Zita, being very perceptive, had noticed the lad had gone a bit pale. "You might want to relax the death grip you have on your walking stick, before you squeeze it in two, and sit down. I didn't mean to add more trepidation to tomorrow's doings than I think you already feel. Why don't you hand me the beeswax? My walking stick could use a good polish, too. Do you have another cloth I could use?"

Chance was glad to have something to do besides continue to dwell on the loop of thoughts that were going around and around in his head. He got up to rummage around in the pack for another cloth that could be used to clean up and polish Seeker Zita's walking stick. Handing her the cloth he had found, he sat back down and resumed polishing his own.

When Seeker Zita saw that Chance was calmer, she began to talk. "Most seekers acquire carved walking sticks somewhere in their journeys. Mine was given to me by a woman hermit who lived high up in the far southern mountains. It and my seeker medallion are two of my most prized possessions. How did you come by your walking stick?"

Chance really did not want to lie to this Seeker, so he stuck as close to the truth as he dared. "In my travels, I stayed for a while on an island. While there, the walking stick was left for me while I slept."

Seeker Zita felt there was probably much more to the story, but chose not to inquire further. After putting the final rub on her walking stick, she stood and suggested to Chance that they had best spend some time working on his robe. Moving over to where she had left the bundle she had set aside when she had entered the room, Seeker Zita unwrapped it and shook out a brilliant blue robe.

"I think this should be a fairly good fit. We seekers keep a modest set of rooms in the capital for when we visit and are studying in the royal library or royal history center. We keep a number of supplies there, including robes of various sizes, since we are sometimes called upon to attend official doings. Bunch of fuss and nonsense, if you ask me. I always feel like I'm playing dress-up whenever I don one of these robes. However, sometimes there is a need to impress or make a statement. Tomorrow is one of those occasions."

"Why tomorrow?"

"There is ever the fear that those who still support Lord Cedric Klingflug, the former regent, or those who have other ideas as to how Sommerhjem should be ruled or choose a new ruler, might strike back at those who have or are helping move the challenge forward. You being one of the four who have delivered a piece of the oppgave ringe to the capital are just one more specific folk that they see as thwarting their plans. Seeker Eshana, myself, and the others who favor the Crown want to make sure a clear message is sent that you are very off-limits for their revenge."

Seeker Zita continued. "At the great summer fair in the capital this summer, after Nissa the rover placed the first two rings in the vessteboks, your cousin, Master Clarisse, made it very clear that anyone who brought a piece of the oppgave ringe was not to be harmed. Master Clarisse also made it clear that those who would search for information about the rings for the Crown, such as seekers, should also not be harmed. I guess you had to be there, but when she made that declaration, there was great authority in her voice, as if something more was backing what she was saying. I don't quite know how to explain that, for I was not there, but that is what I heard. At any rate, by you being in the formal robes of a seeker, all who attend the gathering tomorrow at the Well of Speaking will clearly know you are now one of us and under our protection. So stand up, and let's see how this robe fits."

Chance stood as directed and tried on the brilliant blue robe. He thought he would feel foolish, but he did not. It surprised him that the robe felt both comfortable and, somehow right.

"Did Seeker Eshana give you a medallion?"

"Yes," answered Chance, and fumbled it out from beneath his shirt.

Ashu, not to be left out of the proceedings, quickly scampered up the front of the robe and settled himself on Chance's shoulder.

Upon seeing the halekrets make himself at home on Chance's shoulder, Seeker Zita remarked with a chuckle, "Definitely what the outfit needed, a small ring-tailed animal on the shoulder to complete the ensemble. Now all of us seekers will be envious and want one."

Seeker Zita's remark did more to calm the tension Chance had been feeling all day than anything else had. He smoothed his hands over the robe and discovered it was of a practical design, for it had side openings that allowed him to reach in and get at pockets in what he would wear under the robe.

"If it is alright with you, I will walk with you to the Well of Speaking and down to the sea wall. Your cousin, Master Clarisse, will be there to both support and coach you through what you need to do next. Do you have any questions?"

"What will happen after the Well of Speaking?"

"There will be a lot of fuss. You know, receptions, gatherings, folk wanting to talk to you, bask in your reflected glory . . . ." Chance gave her such a look that Seeker Zita became more serious. "After several days, things should calm down, and then you will be able to get on with your life. You will move into the Order's rooms to await the arrival of Seeker Eshana. Is there something you would like to do while you wait for him to get to the capital?"

"I wouldn't mind a chance to spend some time in the royal library," Chance said, somewhat shyly.

"Ah, a lad after my own heart. That can certainly be arranged. I will leave you now, for I have several tasks to take care of before tomorrow. Will you be alright?"

"Yes, my cousin is going to stop by so we can catch up. We didn't have much time earlier. Thank you for your time and the robe."

"Always a pleasure to help a fellow seeker out," Seeker Zita remarked, as she left the room and closed the door behind her.

"Well, Ashu, what do you think of this fancy robe?"

Ashu just patted Chance's cheek and climbed back down, settling himself comfortably in the chair Seeker Zita had been sitting in.

"Less than impressed, are you? Ah well, I had best hang up the robe and figure out what to do next to keep myself occupied, so I don't think too much about tomorrow."

The rest of the day passed swiftly, as did the night, during which Chance alternated between sleep and wakefulness. He was grateful that the night had not been filled with dreams. The knock on his door the next morning was almost a relief. His cousin, Master Clarisse, was there and invited him down to breakfast. Chance did not think he could eat anything, for he felt very nervous. His cousin had talked to him the day before about what had happened when the previous three folks had placed their pieces of the oppgave ringe in the vessteboks, but that information had done little to lessen his nervousness this morning. However, when Ashu climbed up on his shoulder, a feeling of peace settled around him, and he found himself very hungry. All too soon after the morning meal, it was time to go and get dressed for his walk to the Well of Speaking.

His cousin was waiting for him at the bottom of the stairs, as were others who had gathered in the entry hall of the Glassmakers Guildhall. Chance stood at the top of the stairs, and part of him wanted to turn around, go back to his room, take off the robe, and . . . .

"Are you just going to stand up there, so we can admire you in your fancy new robe, or are you going to come on down?" said a melodic voice Chance never expected to hear in Sommerhjem.

Looking down at the folk assembled below him, he spotted another seeker dressed in a brilliant blue robe. Her deep tan contrasted with her white hair. He knew even from this distance that her eyes were the color of the sea that surrounded the islands of Havkoller, a brilliant deep aqua. When, how, why, were the questions that quickly passed through Chance's thoughts before he could even draw another breath. His next questioning thought hit him even harder. Keeper Odette is a seeker? He did not really have the time to sort through all his questions, for it took most of his concentration to get down the stairs on shaky knees while wearing an almost too long, unfamiliar robe.

When Chance reached the bottom of the stairs, Master Clarisse approached him first. "Are you alright?" she asked. "Is there something wrong?"

What could he tell her, Chance questioned. I'm fine, just a little surprised that the Seeker standing next to Seeker Zita is Keeper Odette of the mysterious Shadow Islands, those same islands I am pledged to never talk about.

"I'm really fine, just a bit overwhelmed and a lot nervous. Nothing is wrong." As a matter of fact, there was a kind of rightness that Keeper Odette was here, Chance thought.

"Then, we had best head to the Well of Speaking. Remember, there will be a large crowd of folk already there. The word gets out swiftly when a piece of the oppgave ringe is going to be placed in the vessteboks."

Chance just nodded his head, for the two seekers were heading his way.

"Chance, I would like to introduce you to a fellow seeker. This is Seeker Odette. Seeker Odette, this is Chance. No wait, that was incorrect. Seeker Odette, this is Seeker Chance, new to our order."

"It is a pleasure to meet you, Seeker Chance."

Chance's thoughts were split between being addressed as Seeker Chance and the fact that Keeper Odette was acting as if she were just meeting him for the first time.

"I look forward to having an opportunity to spend some time with you, once today's activities are over," suggested Keeper Odette. "I would be honored if you would allow me to escort you this day, along with Seeker Zita."

"I would be most grateful to have both of you with me," Chance answered sincerely.

The walk to the Well of Speaking was uneventful. Even though Master Clarisse had warned him ahead of time that there would be a crowd, Chance was still taken aback by the sheer number of folk that took up every available space in the Well of Speaking. When he reached the bottom of the long stairs down to the sea wall, he felt extremely relieved that he had not embarrassed himself by either stumbling, tripping, or tipping Ashu off his shoulder. He caught snatches of conversation that swirled around him.

"It's a seeker this time 'as brought the ring."

"What's that animal that's on his shoulder? Ever seen the like?"

". . . will happen when . . . ."

"It is time, Chance," Seeker Zita stated. "Seeker Odette and I can come with you if you wish."

"Thank you for your kind offer, but I think I need to do this next part by myself." Ashu made a sound at that moment, and Chance revised what he had said. "Correction, I think just Ashu and I need to go on from here."

Gathering himself, straightening his shoulders, gripping his walking stick more firmly in his hand, Chance stepped forward. His cousin had given him clear directions as to what he needed to do next, so he nodded to her he was ready. She stepped back. Chance leaned his walking stick against the sea wall, but the walking stick slipped slightly. Before he could reach it, however, it came to rest at a slight angle against the far edge of the rock next to the one holding the vessteboks. Since he had no excuse to delay, he pulled the pouch of golden pine spider silk from beneath his robe. Chance tipped the ring onto his hand. As he reached out to place the ring in the vessteboks, Ashu moved down his arm until his small hand was touching Chance's hand. Chance felt a rightness in Ashu placing the piece of the oppgave ringe in the small golden box with him. All of his nervousness and worries of the past several days disappeared, and he felt a great sense of peace.

Together, Chance and Ashu placed the ring in the box. A column of light slowly emerged from the vessteboks rising straight up. A very slight puff of wind came down from the top of the Well of Speaking and struck the column of light, which unfurled forming the shape of a skiff sail. The wind continued to blow gently, and the sail-shaped form of light filled, luffed just a little, and then seemed to be pulled into a close reach by an invisible hand.

Chance had stepped back. The thought struck him that his walking stick now looked like a bowsprit with the rocks of the seawall forming a boat heading south and the light forming its sail, but that was just fanciful thinking, he mused. His fanciful thinking was reinforced when Ashu leapt onto the seawall and went to stand by Chance's walking stick, leaning forward, looking just like he did when he was on a real ship. Chance was brought out of his musing by his cousin, who suggested they needed to move on.

As the sail made of light became bigger and bigger, it slowly began to move off in a southerly direction. Chance took one last look at the sail of light and noticed it had changed course once again. The wind had shifted slightly, and the sail of light was now heading slightly inland. Chance picked up Ashu and his walking stick, turned, and began to climb up the stairs. He wondered about the sail of light turning inland as he climbed up the steps.

Chapter Twenty-Nine

Several days later when Chance came down to get some breakfast, he found Keeper Odette in the kitchen, lingering over a cup of tea. The days following placing the ring in the vessteboks had been filled with receptions, gatherings, and a whirlwind of other activities, leaving little time for Chance to get even enough sleep much less talk with others for more than a few brief sentences.

"Good morning Kee-, ah, Seeker Odette." Chance glanced around the kitchen and into the hallway before going on. "I don't know how to address you."

"Here, it would probably be best if you called me Seeker Odette. Now come, sit down and have something to eat. I have sent Cook off to the market, and Seeker Zita is off on errands of her own. We are the only two here. I am sure you have plenty of questions, which is always a good trait in a seeker."

"I do have many questions, but I'm not sure where to begin." Taking a deep breath, Chance settled himself more comfortably on his chair and asked, "You can be both a seeker and a keeper?"

"When I was your age, I traveled a great deal as many seekers do. After a while, two things happened. I grew tired of the wandering, and the Shadow Islands seemed to be calling me back. During part of my travels, I studied under a skilled restorer of manuscripts and books, a keeper in his own right, you might say. He was working in the royal library that my sister now heads. After studying with him for several years, I returned to the Shadow Islands and became the Keeper there. There is some irony that my sister, the bookish one of the family, went on to head the royal library and I, the adventuresome one, now look after the archives. Interesting where our life paths lead us. But to answer your question, yes, I can be a keeper and a seeker, for to be a seeker does not always mean you have to travel to the far ends of the land. Much can also be found in books and scrolls."

Chance tucked that information away to be examined later. For now, he had other questions. "Can I come and go from the crater valley as I wish?"

"Of course. You are one of ours now, with the knowledge to return or leave anytime you wish. Your mentor, Seeker Eshana, returns now and then himself."

The two continued to talk for some time before Chance brought up one more question. "What brought you to Sommerhjem at this particular time?"

"I had some errands I needed to run and folks to see. I hoped to find you, or at the very least, find out where to find you. I knew all along how very important your task was, and not just putting you on a ship and sending you immediately on your way was the hardest thing I have ever done. I am glad you accomplished what you set out to do."

"I know you could not just let me go. I have no hard feelings about what happened to me on the Shadow Islands."

"There was another reason I came to Sommerhjem, hoping to cross paths with you. I went back into the archives to look at the journal you were reading concerning your little friend there, who, by the way, just snitched the last bit of apple off my plate. No, it's alright. Anyway, when I read the journal from beginning to end, I noticed that one of the cover's inside corners was loose. Upon closer inspection, I realized that something had been hidden away beneath the endpaper, the paper that is on the inside of the cover. When I gently peeled the endpaper back, I could see a slight outline where something thin had been stored. I became very curious and wanted to ask you if you had discovered something there, or whether whatever had been there had been long gone."

While embarrassed that he had not told Keeper Odette about the loose endpaper when he had discovered the note that Laron Karmoris had hidden there all those many years ago, he had not known then he could trust Keeper Odette. He knew he could now.

"I found a note hidden there by the journal writer. Though I thought at the time that the note was probably a colossal joke on anyone who would find it, as time has gone by, I have begun to wonder."

Chance went on to explain what the note had said, and about the possible clue to a missing piece of the oppgave ringe. He had wondered if maybe he and Seeker Eshana might travel on to Tårnklokke and follow up on the possible clue hidden in the really bad poetry.

"Bad poetry?" Keeper Odette inquired.

"I memorized the poem. Judge for yourself. Laron Karmoris wrote: 'as the clock strikes the midday hour, before the cat can devour the mouse, slip unnoticed into the musical tower, and snatch the clue from inside the mouse's house'."

"I agree with you that Laron Karmoris would not have won any prizes for poetry. I am unfamiliar with the town of Tårnklokke, but perhaps my sister Eluta, the royal librarian, will have more knowledge about the town. She said that Seeker Zita had dropped off a damaged journal, and if I remember rightly, it was written by a Karmoris. She told my sister Eluta that she picked up the journal at a farm near the Fjell Skoj forest. The journal was smuggled out of Høyhauger, the Bortfjell border town across the pass from northern Sommerhjem. It is very battered and worn. Some of the pages are stuck together, due to water damage. What you found might just go along with what Seeker Zita suggested might be in the journal. Now, I am doubly curious about that journal. Shall we head off to the royal library? Would that suit you?"

It suited Chance just fine. It was a fine day for a walk, and they arrived in short order at the royal library. Eluta was there to greet them.

"Since you all appear to be very serious and want to talk to me about what I would suspect are weighty matters, might I suggest we move this discussion to the walled garden off my office? It is private, and I don't think we will be overheard there. Follow me, please."

Eluta led Chance, Ashu, and Keeper Odette through her office and into a beautiful garden filled with small pathways, laid out flowerbeds, and surrounded by a thick hedge that hugged the high garden walls.

If this was a small garden, Chance thought to himself, he wondered what a large garden would look like. It took him a moment to realize he was being called to come sit in a bench area. Once they had all settled, upon Keeper Odette's urging, Chance told Eluta about the note he had found in the journal. He did not tell her where he had found the journal and she did not ask. Once again, he repeated the poem he had found in the note.

"Tårnklokke, you did say Tårnklokke, didn't you?" asked Eluta.

"Yes," Chance answered.

"There is a clock tower in Tårnklokke containing an amazing clockworks that can be seen from the street. At the striking of the hour, figures move into view. At noon, there is a cat and mouse, and as the clock strikes the noon hour, the mouse moves toward his hole, and the cat follows. Of course, the cat never quite catches the mouse, but each day at noon the cat tries. The cat and mouse only appear at noon. It sounds from what you have told us, Chance, that Laron Karmoris placed a clue in the mouse hole as to where he hid the piece of the oppgave ringe."

"I imagine that someone should probably go and check out that mouse hole," suggested Keeper Odette.

"Or perhaps not. What I have been able to decipher so far from the journal Seeker Zita left, it appears to be written by another member of the Karmoris family. What you have told me just now, Chance, makes what I have read so far in that journal begin to make sense. Apparently, one of Laron's cousins, one who lived in Tårnklokke, somehow found out that Laron had taken something from his family's home and that Laron had left a clue about it in the clock tower. This cousin then removed the clue and left another one, thinking it was going to be a big joke on Laron. Meanwhile, the cousin of Laron followed Laron's clues and retrieved the ring. The clues the cousin left as a prank would have eventually led Laron back to the cousin, who I suspect anticipated a good laugh."

"I can tell you that Laron Karmoris never returned to Tårnklokke nor knew what his cousin had done," stated Keeper Odette gravely. "Now, the question is, what happened to the cousin?"

"That is just one of the many questions that are not answered. Another is how did the journal end up in Høyhauger? And I have to admit, I have only managed to get through about a third of the journal, for I have not taken the time to separate the stuck pages in the last two thirds of it. What is going on with your ring-tailed friend, Chance?" Eluta asked.

Chance looked over to see Ashu disappear into the bushy hedge. He stood up to make his way over to the hedge to check on the halekrets, but Eluta suggested that there was nothing in the garden that could harm Ashu. Chance sat back down, but continued to watch where Ashu had entered the hedge. Several minutes later, Ashu reappeared and came back to where Chance and the others were sitting.

The conversation went on for several more minutes. Eluta promised she would try to get to the damaged journal over the next several weeks. It was a busy time at the library right then, so she was working on it in her spare time. She would inform Seeker Zita if there was any more information to be found. Also, she thought she could do some research in the rolls, the documents that were compiled every ten years as to who was living where in the country of Sommerhjem, and try to find out what had happened to the journal writer.

Chance thought about the conversation with Keeper Odette and the royal librarian, Eluta, off and on over the next few weeks, but with Seeker Eshana's arrival, he had other things to concern him more. Seeker Eshana informed him that it was time to begin his formal and proper seeker training, and to do so, they needed to travel to the Order of the Seekers holding. The time had come for them to leave the capital. Chance's cousin had made arrangements to inform his family that he had been successful in his task, and that he was well. She would include the letter he had written to them, explaining where his life was about to take him.

On the morning of leave-taking, Master Clarisse, had drawn him aside for a private chat.

"I think your family would be very proud of you, not only for getting the ring to the capital, but also for making the choice to become a seeker. I think your journeys have just begun. You take care, and keep Ashu close. I'll see you when you come to the capital once again. Safe travel."

Chance thanked his cousin for her kind words and found himself somewhat reluctant to leave her company, but he needed to mount up. Half of him was very nervous as to what awaited him at the Order of the Seekers holdings, and half of him was more than ready to find out.

PART TWO

Chapter Thirty

Yara froze when she heard folks enter the garden. She knew she should not be there in the first place. It was, after all, the royal librarian's garden. Now mind you, the royal librarian had never said she could not be in her garden, Yara thought to herself, but then again, she had not said Yara could be there, either. Yara did not know what she should do. Step out of the bushy hedge she was hiding behind and give away her secret, or stay hidden?

Looking through the dense leaves of the hedge, Yara could see that three folk had entered the garden, but it was difficult to see just who they were. Cautiously, she moved a few branches aside to get a better view. Two of the three did not surprise her, for they were the head royal librarian, Eluta, and the woman who had been introduced as her sister, the Seeker Odette. The other one was a surprise, for he was the young man who had just brought the fifth piece of the oppgave ringe to the capital. Maybe not so much a surprise on second thought, considered Yara. He was a seeker, also. She was just about to move out of the hedge, so as not to eavesdrop, when she heard one of them mention the name Laron Karmoris. Her whole body stilled, and she listened in amazement to what both Seeker Chance and Seeker Odette had to say.

They were talking about her great-something uncle who had disappeared, never to be heard of again, the one her great-something grandfather blamed for all the troubles her family had suffered after Laron left. Now, it would seem there was some justification to the stories, but not in the way her family thought. Her father was always talking about how the Karmorises used to be a great merchant family, who had had great wealth and who had fallen on hard times, due to some past treachery within the family.

"It all started when that Laron disappeared. Took the family's luck with him when he went, he did," her father would say, bemoaning their present circumstances, which had become worse under the rule of Regent Cedric Klingflug.

Now it seemed, from what Yara was hearing, that Laron Karmoris had not taken the family's luck, but had taken a piece of the oppgave ringe that the family had been charged with keeping safe. Then it seemed, another relative, some great-something cousin, had taken the ring from where Laron had left it and left a trail of clues that led back to the great-something cousin. No wonder her family's fortunes had declined, considering those who were in charge of it at the time, Yara thought with disgust. Laron's father had made several really bad decisions and had lost much of the family's fortune. His remaining sons, including her great-something grandfather, had tried to recoup the family's fortune by taking up smuggling, but they were not very good at it. Yara's father conveniently forgot that part of the family history.

As Yara remained silent behind the hedge, a plan began to form in her mind. She needed to do two things. One was to look in the rolls to see if she could trace what had happened to the cousin who wrote the journal and where any of his family had gone. Second, she needed to get her hands on that journal. The first, looking in the rolls, would not be easy but doable. Getting a look at the journal would be much more difficult. For now, she was safely hidden, with none of the three the wiser that there was someone listening in on their conversation.

Yara's only worry was that Tokala would begin to stir and give away their position behind the hedge. Tokala was the reason Yara was behind the hedge in the first place. She had found the half-grown, half-starved red fox kit shivering and cold, huddled under a crate behind her rented room, being tormented by several neighborhood dogs. She knew foxes lived in the parks scattered around the capital. Rarely were they found in the part of town she lived in. No matter how Tokala had come to be in the alley, he would not have lasted long if she had not chased the dogs away. Since she knew she could not keep a fox in her room, she had sneaked him into the royal library, and then into the royal librarian's garden, where she had been looking after him ever since. She had rigged together a makeshift pen for Tokala, and he had seemed content, but he was getting stronger each day, which had had her worried. Quite frankly, Yara was surprised she had gotten away with having Tokala here for this long.

Yara was concentrating so hard on hearing every word the three in the garden were saying that at first she did not hear something moving into the hedge she was hiding behind. Slowly leaning back, and putting a protective hand on Tokala's still-sleeping body, Yara looked up into two huge gold-colored black ringed eyes which almost overwhelmed a small red furred face. Pointed tufted ears on the top of the animal's head twitched several times, as if seeing her hiding behind the hedge was a cause of amusement to the little animal. Yara did not have time to dwell on that idea, for just then, Tokala woke up and his hair bristled under her hand.

Fear gripped her almost as tightly as she gripped Tokala. Yara worried that the strange animal that had joined them might harm Tokala, or vice versa. The little ring-tailed animal then did the unexpected. He reached out and touched her hand. Just as suddenly as the fear had risen in her, it disappeared. Tokala settled back down at the same time. The little ring-tailed animal looked at Yara for several long moments, and for some unexplainable reason, Yara felt as if she were being measured. Then the little animal nodded twice, reached out and stroked her cheek with his soft hand, turned, and left the hedge. Yara was too shaken by the encounter to move for a long time. When she did, the three, no four, who had been in the garden had left.

Just as she was about to move out of the hedge, she gave a good glance around the garden and the garden walls to make sure no one was watching. It was then that she caught movement near the second entrance to the garden, the one that was always kept locked. Pulling back into the hedge, Yara tried to get a look at who else had been in the garden, but only caught sight of the back of a man as the door closed behind him. Knowing that someone else may have heard the recent conversation made Yara all the more determined to find the information she needed. She was going to have to move fast, since there might now be three parties who knew about the mystery left behind by Laron Karmoris.

Moving cautiously out of the hedge after settling Tokala, Yara moved to the door she had seen the man leave by. It was locked. Turning and heading the other way, Yara checked to make sure Eluta, the head royal librarian, was not in her office. Seeing that her way was clear, she slipped silently to the door and checked the hallway. No one was about so Yara headed toward the room she knew held the rolls. Hearing her name called startled her.

"Yara."

Yara turned to see Eluta heading her direction down the hall. She could only hope the panic she was feeling did not show on her face.

"Oh, good, I caught you. Would you mind staying a bit late today? I need some research done, and I need it done quickly. Come into my office so I can explain."

Yara dutifully followed Eluta into her office. It would have looked odd if she had refused. After all, it had been Eluta who had given her a job after her former employer could no longer pay her. Three years prior, she and her brother, who were the oldest in their family, had left home in search of any kind of job they could find, since there were too many mouths to feed at home. The former regent's taxes and fees had left her family barely surviving. Yara had found a job as a downstairs maid in the home of Mendel Bevare. He was a very eccentric gentleman, who spent all of his days either in his library or wandering about the countryside in search of old and rare books. One day, when she was sent to build the fire up, light the lamps in the library, and then bring him his afternoon tea, she had become distracted watching him work on a damaged book. Mendel Bevare had noticed her interest. Rather than scolding her or having her dismissed for not doing her job, he had called her over and had begun quizzing her concerning her education. Could she read? Could she write? Was she handy with needle and thread?

Yara could still remember how astonished she had felt when he had commanded that she pull up a chair and watch what he was doing. That had been the first day of her education on how to repair old and damaged books. Yara had trained under him for two years. At the end of that time, Mendel Bevare suffered a reversal of fortune and had to dismiss most of his staff. He could no longer afford to keep Yara. He and Eluta had been long time colleagues, however. He had talked the royal librarian into finding a position for Yara at the royal library. Yara had continued her training under Eluta. Yara was pulled out of her reflections when Eluta told her to sit down.

"I have grown to trust you over the last year," Eluta said. "You have shown great skill in repairing damaged books and also, helping to preserve them. I have noted your research skills, and I need someone to discreetly do some research for me."

All Yara could think was that this was the very worst time to come to the head librarian's attention, just when she needed time to do her own research. It was obvious to her from the conversation she had overheard in the garden that one of her ancestors had once been charged with keeping a piece of the oppgave ringe, and that several other of her ancestors had been responsible for causing the ring to disappear. One branch of the family had continued to have good fortune, but not hers. If she could get her hands on the ring, who knew what that might do to change her family's fortunes. Who knew what a piece of the oppgave ringe was worth? Her attention was brought back when she heard the royal librarian mention the Karmoris name.

"I beg your pardon. Could you repeat what you just said?"

"I know that this will entail you putting in long hours, but I would like you to research a branch of the Karmoris family. I'm hoping to find out what happened to one Kinza Karmoris, who resided in Tårnklokke about two hundred years ago. Did he stay in Tårnklokke? Did he marry, have children? I need you to trace his descendants to today, if you would," requested Eluta.

Yara could not believe her good fortune. Here she was being given permission to do what she wanted to do. She had not known how she was going to do her work and also do research on the sly. Now she was being given not only permission, but a means to the end she sought. It was all she could do not to get up and dance a jig in the head librarian's office. Schooling her face and damping down her emotions, Yara told Eluta that she was honored to be a trusted member of the staff and would be happy to do the research.

"Here is a key to the room that houses the rolls. I have told the librarian in charge that you will be doing some work for me after hours. He is aware that the work you will be doing is not to be mentioned to others. I can tell you that he is not happy that you will be in what he considers his domain after hours, but I have assured him you will be careful and will certainly not be holding any wild parties in the room."

It was all Yara could do not to stare at Eluta in astonishment, for she had not been aware that the head librarian had a sense of humor. The woman had always seemed as dry and dusty as the books and scrolls she worked so hard to care for.

"I'm honored that you asked me to do this research, and I will try to refrain from having any wild parties in the room that holds the rolls."

"That's good then. On a less jovial note, I again must mention that I need you to be very discreet, and also not mention to anyone what you are researching."

"I will not have any trouble keeping quiet about what you have asked me to do."

"Here is another key you will need. Stand up and follow me."

The royal librarian led Yara through a door that led not to the garden or the corridor, but to a second room off the head librarian's office. It was a small cluttered room, with floor to ceiling book shelves on all four walls that were filled to capacity with books. The center of the room was taken up by a large table, which had a reasonably clear surface holding only those tools needed to repair damaged books.

"This is where I work on books that are either extremely rare or need delicate handling," Eluta said.

Skirting the table, Eluta moved to the book shelf opposite the door they had entered. "Now then, watch closely. You will notice that this back wall of book shelves is divided into seven sections. You will need to count over from the left three sections. Then you will need to count down seven shelves. Are you following me so far?"

"Yes, ma'am."

"Good. See this green leather bound book?"

Yara nodded her head to indicate that she was following what Eluta was trying to show her.

"You need to tip it out from the shelf from the top, like this."

When Eluta tipped the green leather bound book out, Yara heard a click. Eluta pulled the green leather bound book toward her and the six books to the right of the green book followed.

"As you can see, there is a small locked door behind the books. Use the small key I gave you and open the door."

Yara did as asked. Behind the door was a fairly deep opening.

"You can store any notes you take concerning what you find out in the rolls in here, once you are done each night. I will meet with you midmorning each day to discuss with you what you have discovered. Now then, let's lock this up, put the books back, and then I want you to practice several times, so I know you know how to find and open the locked door."

Yara went through entering the room, finding the green leather bound book, pulling it toward her from the top, swinging the connecting books out, and unlocking the door. When Eluta was satisfied with Yara's ability to lock her research away each night, the two went back into Eluta's office, where Eluta gave her a key to her office to go with the other two keys.

"Just one more thing before you leave. It's about the small red fox in my garden . . . ."

Yara froze in the doorway and took a moment to compose herself. Taking a deep breath, hoping her face would give nothing away, she turned and faced Eluta.

"Fox?"

Chapter Thirty-One

"Yes, that half-grown scrawny red fox that you have been hiding in my garden. Don't you think it is high time you let him out and gave him free run of the garden?"

"Ah yes, that fox. Well, you see . . . ."

"It's quite alright, lass. You've got a good heart, but you are not too trusting, are you?"

Yara was not sure how to answer the head librarian. These last three years away from home and family had taught her many lessons, some of them very painful ones. She was no longer as naive as she had once been.

"Actually, I thought you showed quite a bit of ingenuity using the wall, there where it juts out, and the hedge as a place to pen the fox. With two sides taken care of by the wall and the hedge, you only needed to block off one side to form a pen. It would not have held a healthy fox, but from the looks of that little fella, he was not in very good shape when you brought him here, was he?"

"No, ma'am," Yara answered. It would be foolish to deny knowledge of the fox at this point, Yara concluded to herself.

"Since you will be working late for me, I suggest you take a break late afternoon. Take the time to go to the staff kitchens and pick up something to eat. I have talked to Cook, and he is saving meat scraps and a few bones for your fox. Told him I had one in my garden who was on rat patrol, not that he has been in any condition to catch a snail, much less a rat. Now off with you. You have work to do."

"Yes, ma'am. Thank you, ma'am," Yara said, as she exited the head librarian's office. Since it was clear that very little escaped the head librarian's notice, Yara realized she would need to be extra careful with what she needed to do with the information she had learned in the garden, and with whatever she gleaned from the rolls.

Nathair stood very still just inside the doorway, hidden in the shadows. He had been walking down the corridor and had almost missed noticing the door was slightly ajar. He had meant to just pull the door closed, but his curiosity had gotten the better of him. He found himself standing in a beautiful walled garden. It would certainly be a wonderful place to come and read, but that was not why he was here at the royal library.

Just as he was about to step just a little farther into the garden, he heard voices from the other side. He knew he should either step forward and let whoever had entered the garden know he was there, or he should leave. He had just decided to leave when he heard one of the three mention the name Laron Karmoris. That was the very name his father had sent him to the capital to the royal library to find in the rolls.

As Nathair listened, he began to realize he had been on a fool's errand. He could look and look in the rolls until his eyes blurred, and he would never have found a trace of Laron Karmoris. The lad had simply disappeared, and the woman he recognized as a seeker was very convincing when she stated that Laron would never have returned to Tårnklokke to retrieve the piece of the oppgave ringe he had stolen. However, what he had stolen from Nathair's family had not disappeared with him, according to what the three in the garden were discussing. It would seem that Laron's cousin Kinza had played a practical joke on Laron, but Laron never returned to the clock tower to find out.

At least now Nathair had a real place to start in finding what had happened to the piece of the oppgave ringe that his line of the Karmoris family had been responsible for. His father had told him the story of how their branch of the Karmoris family had fallen out of favor a number of generations back. His ancestor had been picked by his ancestor's father to carry on a family trust and to be the next keeper of the piece of the oppgave ringe, a misshapen golden ring that had deep scratches in it. When the ring had gone missing, his ancestor had been blamed, became the black sheep of the family, and was sent packing. While he had not turned to smuggling as had some of his brothers, he had also not fared well as a trader.

From one generation to the next, the story had been passed down to one chosen member of the family that their branch of the family had been entrusted with a piece of the oppgave ringe. The loss of the family fortune and standing occurred because Nathair's ancestor's father had been unwilling to listen to reason. He had been unwilling to accept that his youngest son, Laron, might have known about the ring, much less might have taken it. No, he had placed the blame on Nathair's direct ancestor. He had said that Nathair's ancestor had lost the family's luck.

As Nathair's family had passed the tale down, much knowledge had been lost as to what it was that had truly been lost. They knew that the object that was supposed to be kept secret and guarded was a piece of the oppgave ringe. Over time, no one quite knew what the oppgave ringe was, or its significance, but they knew it was a sacred trust. It was not until the events that had taken place over the last few months that Nathair's father had discovered just what it was that his family had held in trust. Since Nathair's father was convinced that their direct ancestor had been telling the truth, he strongly suspected that Laron had been the culprit. He had sent Nathair to the capital to try and trace what had happened to Laron.

Maybe I was meant to find that open door to the garden at just this time, so I could find out I was on a wild goose chase that would lead me nowhere, Nathair thought to himself. Maybe the Karmoris luck is not entirely gone. Nathair continued to listen closely to what the three were discussing. He had a slight moment of panic when the small ring-tailed animal moved away from the group and headed into the hedge. He was worried that the animal might roam even farther away from the three who were talking and discover Nathair. He felt a great deal of relief when the animal returned to Seeker Chance.

What would it be like to come into the capital with a piece of the oppgave ringe, Nathair wondered. All that attention and fame would be his, if he could discover a piece of the oppgave ringe. He also thought about what other options he might have. They would only come about if two things happened. He needed to get to the rolls and do his research before anyone else. Second, he needed to get his hands on Kinza Karmoris' journal.

Researching the rolls would be fairly easy. The librarian in charge of that particular set of rooms had not bothered Nathair so far. As long as Nathair wore gloves and was gentle with the ancient material, the librarian did not seem to pay too much attention to what Nathair was looking up.

Nathair found himself growing impatient. He wanted to leave the garden, but he dared not while the three were still there. Now that he had a place to really start, he wanted to get at it. It sounded like Eluta, the head librarian, was going to work on the journal herself, but not for a while. That gave him a little time to try to figure out how to get his hands on it. It also sounded like she was going to be very busy for the next week, so that would give him a head start finding out what had happened to Kinza Karmoris.

Once the folks in the garden concluded their conversation and left, Nathair wasted no time leaving the garden. He turned and quickly went back through the door, closing it behind him. It took him several steps before he realized he had made a major blunder. He had automatically pulled the door closed behind him and thought he had heard a click. Did that mean the door had merely latched, or had it locked? Nathair retraced his steps and tried the door. It had locked.

How stupid can you get? I should have made sure I could get back into the garden, and then into the head librarian's office to look for the journal, and now I have lost that chance, he thought, disgustedly. Getting into her office would now be more difficult.

Muttering to himself, Nathair continued down the corridor and headed to the rooms that held the rolls. It was time for some serious research now that he had a lead. When he arrived at the room containing the rolls, he was further frustrated to discover that the door was locked. The sign on the door stated that the librarian in charge of the room had been called away and would not return until the next day. The librarian apologized for any inconvenience.

"Sorry for the inconvenience, my foot," Nathair mumbled under his breath, as he turned and headed back the way he had come.

It was close to closing time for the royal library, at any rate, he thought. Just as he turned the corner to head out, he heard footsteps coming from the other direction. Something caused him to halt just out of sight. As he listened, he heard the footsteps slow down, and then, stop. Then he heard the sound of a key turning in a lock. Thinking it was the rolls room librarian returning, Nathair looked around the corner hoping to ask the librarian if he might work in the rolls room for a little while, even though it was close to closing time. Nathair was surprised when he peered around the corner to see not the rolls room librarian, but a young woman instead. He drew his head back just as she turned his way. For some unexplained reason, he hoped he had not been seen.

Nathair waited until he heard the rolls room door close, and heard the sound of the lock clicking, before he dared move. He took a deep intake of breath, for he found he had been holding his. As quietly as he could, Nathair walked back the way he had come, and soon found himself exiting the royal library.

Nathair needed to get a message off to his father and find out what his father might know about Kinza Karmoris. Nathair had established a message box with a messenger bird merchant, so he could send and receive messages from home. Now, he was glad he had done so.

The next day was a more successful day at the royal library than any day previously had been for Nathair. Now that he knew who he was looking for, he began making progress. Very slow progress to be sure, but progress nonetheless. He was thankful to the ancient scholar who had set up the rolls in the first place. Not only were the rolls a system of keeping track every ten years of who lived where in Sommerhjem, but over time, a coding system had been established which made finding specific folk among the myriad of records easier. In addition, others had used the rolls to develop charts and volumes containing family generational lists. Nathair hoped he would be lucky and find someone before him had researched the Karmoris family. He had been concentrating so hard on a particular paragraph in a roll from Muggen Myr that he jumped when he was tapped on the shoulder.

"It's closing time, young man. You will have to put everything you have dragged out back where you found it, and leave."

Nathair knew there would be no arguing or pleading with the rolls librarian to have more time. The man was a stickler for rules. He would also be watching him like a hawk to make sure he put everything back in its proper place. For someone who did not much care what you looked at, the rolls librarian was very strict about where everything went. Nathair dutifully put everything he had been looking at back, gathered up his notebook and other materials, put them in his day pack, and left the room. He did not leave the library right away. Instead, he left the rolls room and walked just a little way away, stopping where he had the day before. He was curious as to whether the young woman who had come at the end of library hours would return again this night. Unfortunately, he did not have a chance to discover that, for his luck ran out when the head royal librarian turned down the corridor where he was standing.

"Is there something I can help you with, young man?"

"No, ma'am, I was just heading out."

Nathair hoped that if he began to move on down the corridor, the head royal librarian would be convinced he was leaving. He thought he might still be able to double back and see if the young woman returned again this day. It was not to be.

"You, young fellow, where are you going? Come with me," said the head royal librarian, motioning that Nathair should follow her.

Chapter Thirty-Two

Yara woke abruptly, and at first did not know where she was. She was so tired. She had been putting in her usual hours at the library, and then spending half the night in the rolls room tracing what had happened to Kinza Karmoris and his descendants. Each night, she had taken her notes and hidden them in the secret opening in the head royal librarian's work room. Every day, she had shared what she had found with Eluta. Each day, she had felt worse and worse, knowing that the head royal librarian Eluta trusted her, and did not know that she was having Yara do for her what Yara would have done anyway. Yara felt like she might be taking advantage of Eluta, but then she would tamp down that feeling, for she knew what was at stake for her and her family. She also did not know if she was going to tell Eluta what she had found out this night. Before she would make any final decisions, Yara knew she had to get a good night's sleep. It had gotten to the point that she could no longer think straight or make good choices.

Not really knowing what the time was, Yara gathered up her notes and put them in her day pack. She then took care replacing all of the books and other items she had looked through this night. As she began to replace the last item, a thought occurred to her. She realized her eyes had been taking in some information, but her mind was just a little slow in putting together what she had seen. Someone else, very recently, had been looking at the same material she had looked at. The old tomes and other items should have been dusty, but were not. Coincidence, she wondered. Was someone else interested in the Karmoris family? If so, who, and why now?

She was still pondering those questions when she entered Eluta's office, so deep in thought that she did not see the shadow detach itself from behind the door before it was too late. She was shoved hard from behind. It was so unexpected that Yara barely had time to put her hands out to break her fall, her head just missing the corner of Eluta's desk. Lying on the floor trying to catch her breath, her hands and knees stinging, Yara heard the sounds of running footsteps moving away, for which she was grateful. Rolling over and sitting up, she leaned her back against Eluta's desk, drew her legs up, and rested her head on her knees. It was in this position that Eluta found her when she entered her office early the next morning.

"Yara?" Eluta said softly, gently touching the sleeping lass' shoulder, hoping she would not startle her.

"What, ah, um, oh, ouch . . . ." Yara answered, moving a bit too quickly and finding herself very stiff and sore.

"What happened? Are you alright?"

"I'm not sure. I lost track of time last night in the rolls room. To be honest, I fell asleep. When I woke up, I put everything I had been working on back, and then came here to lock up my notes. The room was dark, which I thought was unusual, for you usually leave a turned-down lamp burning. I really had not had much time to think about the lamp when someone pushed me very hard from behind. I heard someone running away from here just after that. I guess, when I sat up to gather my wits, being very tired and hurting, I just fell asleep where I sat. As to how I am, I think, except for being very stiff and sore, I'm fine."

"Do you need help getting up?" Eluta asked, reaching out a hand. After she had helped Yara up, Eluta asked, "Do you still have your notes from last night?"

Yara quickly checked, only to find her day bag was still slung over her shoulder. Looking inside confirmed that her notes from the night before were still there.

"I want you to tuck your notes away, and then go home. Get some decent sleep, and don't come back until tomorrow."

"But . . . ."

"No buts. You are doing a great job at both your day duties and at the task I asked you to do. Burning your candle at both ends is all well and good, but I think you may have just run out of wax last night, so to speak. A good rest will make you all the sharper at both tasks. Go on, now. It never does to argue with the head royal librarian."

After Yara left, Eluta sat down to think about the implications of someone being in her office long after the library had closed. No one should have been in the library after hours, with the exception of other librarians or the watch guard. She would have to check with the other librarians to see if any had stayed, or if any had seen someone who did not belong there. In addition, she felt that she needed to increase the number of watch guards for the next few days, to see if they could spot an intruder.

While Eluta sometimes had very rare and valuable volumes in her office, if she was inspecting or working on them, she did not have any here at this time. The only thing she had new was the journal of Kinza Karmoris, and that was not here in her office. It was in her workroom at home. Eluta was not worried about anyone breaking into her home and finding the journal, for it was well-hidden there. This journal was not the first book that Eluta had worked on in private for the Crown, nor was it the first one she had worked on for a member of the Order of the Seekers. Yara is not the only one who has been burning her candle at both ends, Eluta thought to herself.

The more Eluta began thinking about the dedication that Yara was putting toward her assignment concerning the Karmoris family, the more she began to wonder. Was Yara overworking herself because she was trying to impress Eluta, or was there some other reason the young woman was staying much longer than expected. What was driving her? Eluta made a note that she needed to talk to Yara's former employer again.

Eluta had another concern. She had noticed several times that her office was not as she had left it. A less observant, or more absentminded, folk would not notice that things were not quite where they had been the day before. At first, Eluta thought she was just imagining that a book here or a pen there had been moved. Wanting to test her theory, Eluta had positioned a number of items in a certain way. Each morning after she had set her trap, Eluta had found that some of the items had been moved during the night. Had Yara been searching for something in Eluta's office, or had last night's intruder been there other nights?

Nathair was having trouble concentrating on the chart on the table before him. He was still thinking back to the night before, when he had almost been caught in the royal librarian's office. He had not thought he was taking that much of a risk to stay behind after the library had closed. One day while wandering the library corridors stretching his legs, he had discovered an alcove behind a tapestry. It was a perfect spot to settle in and wait until he thought even the most dedicated librarian would have left for home. Unfortunately, it had been a very quiet and surprisingly warm place, and Nathair had fallen asleep. He did not know what time he had awakened, but the jingle of the watch guard's keys as he passed by where Nathair had hidden himself had roused him.

Nathair had listened to the watch guard's retreating footsteps before he emerged from his hiding place. He had stealthy crept down the library corridors, until he reached the head royal librarian's office. It had not taken him long to pick the lock and enter, closing the door and locking it behind him. Using a small shielded lantern, Nathair had begun a very careful search of the royal librarian's office. He had actually not gotten very far in his search when he thought he heard the sound of footsteps approaching. He had barely had time to blow out his lantern, extinguish the low burning lamp on the head librarian's desk, and hide beside the door. He had become unnerved when he heard the key being inserted into the door to the royal librarian's office. He could not afford to be caught. When the folk had opened and stepped through the doorway, Nathair had panicked, shoved the folk, slipped out the door, and run as fast and as quietly as he could back to his hiding spot, hoping against hope that an alarm did not go out. He had not known if his hiding place would be safe, or if an all-out search would be called.

Nathair had stayed hidden all the rest of the night. When an alarm had not been sounded and a search had not been mounted, a more terrifying thought occurred to him. What if he had seriously harmed the folk he had shoved in his panic to get away? How could he find out what had happened? If he asked any questions, he would give himself away. He could only hope no one had seen him or could identify him. That would just not do, he thought.

When the sounds in the corridor indicated it was morning and the library was open, Nathair had slipped out from behind the tapestry and purposefully strode down the hallway to the room that held the rolls. No one had stopped him, or even paid much attention to him. Now, here he was several hours later, still no more informed than he had been all morning. Nathair decided he needed to get away from the library for a while, so he began to put his materials back. Just as he was about to put the last book back, another librarian entered the room and began to speak to the librarian in charge of the rolls.

"Did you hear the latest? They are increasing the watch guard. Seems we might have had an intruder in the library last night. Bunch of fuss and nonsense if you ask me. Probably someone who fell asleep in the back stacks and got lost in the maze of corridors. I just don't know . . . ."

Nathair did not hear the end of the sentence, for the two librarians had headed into the next room. That the watch guard was being increased meant he would not be staying hidden in the library this night. It would be far too risky. Getting caught and questioned would not help forward his plans. No, he would need to bide his time and be extra careful for a while, until things settled down a bit, Nathair thought.

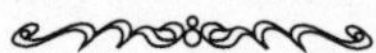

"You're home late tonight. Long day at the library?" Keeper Odette inquired of her sister.

"Had a break-in at my office last night. That nice young restorer Yara was attacked. I wanted to make sure the watch guard had sent enough folks over to really cover the library this night. I also personally checked out a number of hidden nooks and crannies that the watch guards might not know about. All seemed to be clear. Now, come with me and make yourself useful," Eluta said.

Keeper Odette knew better than to question what her sister wanted when Eluta used that high-handed tone, so she followed Eluta up a series of narrow back steps, which ended at a locked door.

Eluta pulled a chain out that hung around her neck and pulled it over her head. Using the key that hung on the end of the chain, she unlocked the door, stepped through the doorway, and lit a small lantern.

"Please close the door behind you and make sure it is locked."

Keeper Odette did as she was asked and found herself very curious as to where the short hallway where they were standing led to. She could not see very far, but thought she could see the outline of several doors.

"I have a complete workroom up here and use it when whatever I am working on is a bit too sensitive to leave where others at the royal library might see me working on it and ask what I am about. I have been working on Kinza Karmoris' journal up here. That is not why I wanted you to come up here, however."

"What is it that you need me for?"

"Why, to help me sort out what would be essential for me to take along on a walkabout, of course." Eluta ignored the look of surprise on her sister's face, turned, and continued down the hall. "Come along now, don't dawdle."

Now more curious than ever to find out what her sister had hidden in what had once been an empty attic, Keeper Odette followed her. Here again, the door was locked and had to be unlocked. It was the inside of the room that surprised Keeper Odette. The walls were lined with shelves full of neatly labeled boxes, bags, and bundles.

"What is all this?" Keeper Odette asked.

"Why, all the supplies one would need to travel about the country, of course. I may not have done the traveling you have done, but I have read every book on the subject and made a careful study of the essentials that would be needed to go on a walkabout. I have carefully gathered all I might need and stored it here."

Keeper Odette just stared at her sister before she asked, "And where have you stored the rover wagon to carry all of this?"

"Oh, do you think I might need one? Well, I guess I could try to find one but . . . ." Eluta then took a good look at her sister's face. "You're laughing at me, aren't you?"

"Only a little. Now, why do think you need to go on a walkabout at this time?"

Chapter Thirty-Three

Yara had been reluctant to leave the library, but she knew better than to argue with the head royal librarian. Common sense told her that Eluta was right, and Yara needed sleep more than anything else at this moment. She had been so close to the end of her research last night, before exhaustion had overcome her. All she needed was just a few more hours, and she would then know where to start looking.

Yara had the feeling time was running out. Someone else was looking at the same material she was. It just did not feel like a coincidence to her, especially not after last night. Yara had been very carefully searching the head royal librarian's office for Kinza Karmoris' journal each night after she had locked up her notes. She had not found the journal. Had that also been what the intruder who had pushed her was after? There had been that other listener in the garden, when she had overheard the discussion about the journal, and what it revealed.

Now that Yara had had some sleep, her thinking was much clearer. Tomorrow, she should find the last of the information she was seeking, and then, it would be time to move on. Since it was now midafternoon, she would have to hustle if she were to get the supplies she needed and get packed up. She was glad she had a carrying case already made for Tokala, for she did not want to leave him behind.

Yara felt both guilty and sad about what she needed to do, but it had to be done. She needed to find the piece of the oppgave ringe that had been left to her family. That feeling of urgency had not gone away in recent weeks. In fact, it had increased to the point that the hunt consumed every waking hour. At night, Yara dreamed about finding the piece of the oppgave ringe.

Since she was not required at the library this day and was feeling rested, it was time to head down to the docks and make sure everything was prepared on her skiff. Yara certainly had been lucky concerning the sailboat. Normally, someone of her station and means would not have been able to own a skiff. Fortunately for her, her father had an old friend who was a shipwright. Her father had suggested she and her brother make contact with him when they had come to the capital to find work. Her brother had signed on with the shipwright and had learned his craft so well that he had headed home to build boats. Her last letter from home had been filled with how successfully his fledgling business was doing. Her brother's gift to her before he had left the capital had been to give her the first skiff he had built on his own. The little sailboat had been her joy on her days off, when she could let all her cares blow away with the wind as she sailed the open water beyond the capital's harbor. Now, it would be her way to travel where she suspected she needed to go in order to follow the trail of Kinza Karmoris' descendants.

The shipwright was deep in a discussion with someone when she arrived at the boat works, which was fine with Yara. She waved in his direction, as she stepped over a coil of rope and tried to avoid the smoke from the fire under the pitch pot. Yara breathed a little easier once she reached the dock and her skiff. She really had not wanted to get into a conversation with the shipwright this day. She liked the man, but since her brother had left, the shipwright had decided to step in and "look after" her in her brother's stead. However well-intentioned both of them were, why neither of them thought she could not look after herself was a sore point. Just because much of what she knew came from books did not mean she was not able to figure things out on her own. Being bookish did not mean she had no practical experience or knowledge.

Yara spent the rest of the afternoon checking the skiff over, making sure the lines, halyards, and stays were all in good repair. She had been bringing supplies to the skiff each time she visited. She never brought much, so no one would suspect she might be leaving, but she had always known the day would come when she would have to leave. When everything was shipshape and stowed away, Yara headed back to her rented room. What little she owned was packed either in the skiff or at her room. Her rent was paid up to the end of the month. Now, all she had to do the next day was to find the last of the information she needed, and then, she could be on her way.

"All of our lives you have been the adventurous one traveling hither and yon as a seeker," stated Eluta. "Once you got all that traveling out of your system, you went home to the Shadow Islands and now find your adventures and contentment in the archives. I have only traveled in books. In my youth, I was not as courageous as you and was content with my life, maybe too content. I have become increasingly restless these past few years. The events of this past summer shook me up a bit."

"And because of this, you think, at your age, you should do a walkabout?" asked Keeper Odette. "And with all this equipment? I can see that you have every known item and gadget for camping in comfort, but . . . ."

"I know, I know. I may have gone a wee bit overboard."

"A wee bit?"

"Alright, a lot overboard, but you never know what you might need."

"You are determined to do this? Why?"

"I have my reasons."

"You think life is passing you by, and now is the time to do something about it? You are needed here, Eluta. The Crown needs your skills and wisdom, your leadership and knowledge. You can't just run off irresponsibly."

"Actually, I think the Crown needs me to do the walkabout. Now, are you going to help me sort through all of this stuff and pick out what I really need, or not?"

"I will help you, if you can give me even a clue as to why you think the Crown needs you to leave the capital on an adventure."

"Alright, now listen up, and hand me that box that's just above your left shoulder. You are taller than I am."

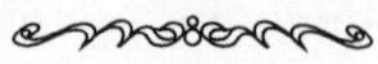

When Yara returned to the library the next day, she worked to finish repairing a book she had almost completed the day before the head librarian had sent her home early to get some rest. Knowing she would be leaving, Yara did not want to leave behind a reputation of someone who did not finish her tasks. Tidying up her workspace, she headed to the room that held the rolls. When she arrived, she was surprised to find the rolls room librarian still there. He was muttering and fuming.

"You, lass, come here," the rolls room librarian commanded. "There is a book of rolls for the southern region of the Muggen Myr area missing. There has been a young man in here every day looking at different rolls and family books. I have been watching him like a hawk. I know he did not take the rolls out of this room, but he certainly did not put it back where it belongs. He came in earlier today after I discovered it missing. I gave him a piece of my mind. He is no longer welcome here. Well, don't just stand there. Come along."

"Which year of Muggen Myr rolls has been misplaced?"

"Why, the last one, didn't I tell you?" the rolls librarian said absentmindedly. "You check the shelves holding the Muggen Myr rolls. Maybe a fresh set of eyes can discover something I have not."

Yara felt her heart sink upon hearing that the very rolls she had come to study this night was the one that was missing. It also concerned her that the rolls was missing, just at this time. She was now doubly convinced that someone, in addition to herself, was pursuing the same information she was. This latest turn of events was not good, especially since she was so close.

At first glance, everything seemed to be in order on the shelves she was looking at. Yara ran her eyes over the shelves and noted that the rolls were shelved there by year. Muggen Myr had never been a very populated area, due the fact that much of it was saltwater marsh. The rest of the area consisted of ridges created by rivers, and streamlets that ran in great profusion through the inland marshes, bogs, and swamps.

After she had gone over the rolls for the fourth time, Yara noticed a set of books was placed forward on the shelf just a bit more than those on either side. She also noticed that these volumes were from a time much earlier than the records indicated that the Karmoris descendants had moved to the Muggen Myr area. After putting on her gloves, Yara gently began removing the rolls that were slightly out of place. Tucked in behind was the missing rolls.

"I found the missing volume," Yara called out to the rolls librarian in the next room.

He came back to where Yara was and demanded to know where she had found it.

"Someone tucked it behind this set of rolls here," Yara answered.

"Well, that young man is no longer welcome here, I can tell you that. Oh bother, I am now late. Put that back where it belongs and make sure you lock up tight. Don't let anyone in after I leave. Either the head librarian or I will discuss this issue with you tomorrow, but I really must leave now."

Without waiting for an answer, the rolls librarian turned and stalked out of the room, complaining about irresponsible folks and how the library should not be open to everybody. Only serious scholars should be allowed.

Feeling more urgency now than ever, Yara pulled out her notebook and began her search once again. As the hours dragged on, Yara realized she had been mistaken. Her search did not end in the Muggen Myr salt marshes, or even in the area that bordered it. She had thought so at first, and had been about to put the book back, when she noticed a footnote. At first, she had thought the star next to the name was just a smudge, but holding her lamp closer, she noted she had been mistaken. Looking to the back of the rolls, she found a small notation scrawled in a tiny crabbed hand that suggested she had one more place to look.

Apparently, there was a very small bit of land at the foot of the mountains that formed the edge of the boggy land of Muggen Myr. On that small bit of dry land could be found a very small village, which produced finely crafted baskets, woven from reeds found in the bog. This small village, called Sivkurv, was not actually part of the Muggen Myr rolls. Yara found the rolls for Sivkurv for the time period she wanted. At first, she was tempted to blow the dust off the slim book, but decided against it. No sense in letting anyone else know that the slim book had been looked at recently. Instead, Yara very carefully eased the book out, trying not to disturb the dust.

If I were in charge of this room, I would keep these volumes dusted, she thought to herself, after she had sneezed several times. Very carefully, Yara paged through the volume until she came across the name she was looking for. What she discovered was not conclusive, but gave her a place to start. Anything could have happened in the intervening years in the tiny village of Sivkurv, from the time of the last rolls to now.

Yara, once again, carefully put all of the materials she had been looking at back, except the rolls from the village of Sivkurv. She left the book sitting on the table and wandered farther back into the rooms holding the rolls, until she found herself in a back section that was little visited. There, she found a couple of books that had a goodly amount of dust on them. Yara removed them and walked back to the table she had been working on. Propping the slim book up against one of the books she had carried back to the table, she blew the dust off the second book onto the slim book. When she felt it look sufficiently coated and would look undisturbed, she gingerly carried the slim book and placed it back where she had found it. For added measure, she took the time to blow a little more dust onto the slim book, now that it was back on its shelf. Putting the two dusty volumes back where she had found them, Yara wiped the excess dust off the table where she had been working, glanced around to make sure she had not forgotten anything, and left, locking the door behind her.

When she reached the head royal librarian's office, Yara was very cautious. The door was locked, and she could see a slight glow under the door, indicating the lamp had been left lit. Unlocking the door, Yara moved into the room and locked the door behind her. To her great relief, no one else was there hiding this night. Moving quickly into the royal librarian's work room, Yara opened the hidden area and took out her notes. She replaced them with notes that were slightly altered and did not add her notes from this night.

Once the hidden area was again locked and closed up, Yara moved to the door that opened onto the royal librarian's garden. Slipping quietly through the doors, she headed straight toward where Tokala was penned. Sliding between the branches of the hedge, Yara began to talk softly to Tokala.

"It's alright, Toki, it's just me. It's time for us to move on."

Yara shook the carrying case open that she had brought with her. Picking up the sleepy red fox, Yara gently put him in the case and closed it up. Backing out of the hedge, Yara was unaware that there was someone waiting on the other side.

Chapter Thirty-Four

Yara's progress was slowed when her long dark hair caught in a branch of the hedge. Grousing quietly under her breath, Yara set Tokala's carrying case down and untangled her hair. Picking the red fox's carrying case back up, she backed out of the hedge. When she straightened up and turned around, she almost dropped Tokala's carrying case.

"It's about time you showed up. I have been waiting half the night. Know where we are going now, do you?" asked Eluta.

"Going? I, um, you mean Toki and me?" Yara asked, stalling for time and trying to gather her wits about her. What was the royal librarian doing here in her garden at this time of night? More importantly, what was this "we" business?

"No, I do not mean just you and Toki. I mean, where are you, Toki, and I going to find your long lost relative and a piece of the oppgave ringe?"

Eluta's words froze Yara to the spot. How could Eluta know that she was related to the Karmorises, Yara wondered, or that she was on the hunt for a piece of the oppgave ringe?

"Come along, youngling. Someone else has been following the same trail you have, and we are just barely ahead of him. Time is a wasting, and this night is not getting any longer. My supplies are already stored on your boat. Do you need to stop by your room to pick up anything?"

"Wait, I think there might be a bit of a misunderstanding here," Yara suggested, halting to catch her breath.

"A mistake that you are not a Karmoris, or a mistake that you are not leaving to search for a piece of the oppgave ringe? I don't think so. Now hurry on, lass, don't dawdle. We need to be away before daybreak. Time enough for talking when we are out to sea."

Yara was getting the feeling she now knew what it would feel like to be run over by team of horses and dragged down the lane. Not knowing what else to do, she followed Eluta through the corridors of the royal library. Soon she was following Eluta through a maze of corridors that were unfamiliar. Just when Yara was feeling almost hopelessly lost, they came to a door situated at the end of a hallway. Yara watched as Eluta produced a key and unlocked the door. The door opened with a soft screech.

Eluta motioned that Yara was to follow, and when she stepped through the door, it was into a dark alley. What surprised her more than stepping outside was the fact that there was a small closed carriage waiting.

"About time you got here, sister dear," stated Keeper Odette, somewhat testily. "All this skulking about in dark alleys lost its appeal years ago."

"Oh, quit your whining. You had a cushy carriage seat to wait on. I have been sitting on a cold stone bench. Yara, remind me when we get back that I need to put some comfortable chairs in my office garden. Now then, you had best get on board. Do you need help getting Tokala's carrying case into the carriage?"

"No, ma'am, I can handle it." What I cannot handle is what is happening right now, Yara thought. Even if I did try to make a break for it, the two would probably make it to the docks faster in the carriage than I could on foot lugging Toki's carrying case, and then what? Reluctantly, Yara concluded she had no other choice at that moment but to climb aboard the carriage and keep alert.

The quick stop at Yara's room to pick up the last of her belongings had not given Yara a chance to escape, for Eluta had gone with her. When they arrived at the shipwright's dock, Eluta climbed out of the carriage first and had Yara hand Tokala's carrying case down. When Yara stepped down out of the carriage, Eluta did not hand the case back. Eluta turned and headed toward the dock where Yara's skiff was tied. Keeper Odette, meanwhile, had climbed down off the carriage, tied the horse to the hitching ring, and taken up a position at the end of their little procession.

"Permission to come aboard, Yara," Eluta asked.

"Permission granted," Yara stated, less than gracefully, since she knew she really did not have any other choice.

Eluta turned and handed Tokala's case to her sister, and then, nimbly stepped aboard the skiff. Yara followed. The woman Yara had heard called Seeker Odette then handed Tokala's carrying case aboard.

"You three get settled. Let me know when you want me to cast the lines off."

Yara opened the hatch that covered the opening to the very small cabin. Climbing down the few short steps, she turned around and pulled Tokala's case in, setting it on her bunk. Glancing around the small area, she noticed Eluta had been telling the truth about having already stored her gear aboard. There was nothing to be done about it now, so Yara went back on deck.

What she found happening on deck was not anything she had expected. In the brief time she had been below, Eluta had taken the coverings off the sails, had straightened the lines and was coiling them up. Yara did not know why she was surprised that the head librarian knew her way around a sailboat, but she was. It was then that she realized that she knew very little about the woman and had pigeonholed her into a nice neat category: older woman, head librarian, about as dry and dusty as the books she was in charge of, with no life outside of the library.

"Well, lass, it is time to batten the hatches down, as they say, and set sail. Are you ready?" Eluta asked.

No, I am not ready, Yara wanted to shout. Instead, she nodded her head, hoisted the sails, and asked the Seeker to cast them off.

"I can't talk you out of this, can I?" Seeker Odette asked her sister Eluta.

"Nope."

"Since you are bound and determined to do this, then I wish you good sailing and safe journey. Send me a message when you get back. I need to get back home. You take care now, the both of you."

Keeper Odette swiftly uncleated the lines and tossed them to Eluta. Yara adjusted the sails and settled in at the helm. With a fresh wind filling the sails, it did not take them long to maneuver out of the harbor. Only after they had left the harbor, and adjusted course to head south, was there time for Yara to be able to ask the questions that had been gnawing at her since they had left the head librarian's garden. Unfortunately, once out of the capital's harbor, the wind picked up and kept shifting directions. All of Yara's concentration was needed to maintain her course, leaving her questions unanswered for the time being.

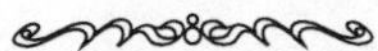

Nathair could not remember a time he had been this frustrated and this angry. When he had arrived at the rolls room in the royal library, he had been informed by the librarian in charge that he was no longer either welcome or allowed in the rolls room.

"Your blatant disregard for following procedure to return books and scrolls to their proper place cannot be tolerated," Nathair had been informed. When he had questioned just what the snooty librarian had been talking about, he was told that taking a book and hiding it so others could not find it was just not done. Nathair had protested he was innocent, but to no avail. It was probably that lass he had seen entering the rolls room, after the librarian had locked up for the night, who had hidden the book, for it had not been him.

Nathair had certainly been aware that someone else was pursuing the same line of questioning as he was. Someone else was looking for what had happened to the Karmoris family. There was nothing left to do but hide himself away and hope the lass returned this night. While he did not want to tip his hand by confronting the lass, he could at least follow her when she left the rolls room in the early morning hours.

It had been a long uncomfortable time for Nathair as he waited for the lass to finally leave the rolls room. He was correct in his guess that she would proceed to the head librarian's office. What surprised him the most was to see not only her leave the head librarian's office, but to see the head librarian accompanying her. He wondered what the lass was carrying in the case. It was all he could do to duck into a dark alcove to keep from being caught, for the two did not head out of the library the way he had thought they would.

Keeping well back, hoping he would not lose them in the corridors, Nathair just barely missed being seen when he cautiously rounded a corner and watched the two of them slip out a door. Nathair rushed to catch the door before it locked. He waited a moment to catch his breath, then peeked outside. He almost missed the departing carriage turning the corner. Running to the end of the alley, he saw the carriage heading down the road. Since the carriage was not moving swiftly, Nathair managed to keep it in sight. After one quick stop and quite a jaunt, he was surprised to see the carriage turn into an area of the docks where several boatyards were located.

Trying to remain undetected, he crept closer and closer to where the carriage had stopped. Hiding behind an overturned boat hull, he could see what was going on, but the folks were talking too quietly for him to hear what was being said. He watched the lass and the royal librarian climb aboard a skiff. They loaded on board the case the lass had been carrying and several small packs. It did not take very long before the sails were being raised, and the lines cast off. The woman who had driven the carriage stood on the dock until she could no longer see the skiff's sails, then turned and drove the carriage away from the boat works.

Only after she had left did Nathair come out from his hiding place and begin to pace. He had his suspicions that the lass and the royal librarian were heading south to Muggen Myr, for his research, at least as far as he had gotten, had pointed in that direction. Muggen Myr was a big place, however, and so he could not pinpoint just where in the swampy lowlands they were heading. He was blocked from getting back into the rolls room to get more information, and now, the two he had followed would be a good quarter of a day or more ahead of him. The quickest way for him to get south would be by boat. Unfortunately, his boat was moored on the other side of the harbor. It would take him a while to get there and make sure he had all the supplies he needed. His father was going to be less than pleased when Nathair informed him of the latest developments.

Yara and Eluta had been sailing for several hours when Eluta spoke up and suggested Yara might want to go below and get some rest.

"That fox of yours might want to get out of his carrying case and stretch his legs. Has he ever been on a boat before?"

"No," Yara answered, all the while still trying to figure out just what was going on. She was still reeling from the idea that Eluta not only knew she was a Karmoris, but also knew she had a skiff. Not only had a skiff, but where it was tied up. How had Eluta known all these things? How did she know that Yara was searching for what had happened to one of the pieces of the oppgave ringe? Eluta had not been forthcoming on any information during the several hours they had been sailing. She had spent most of the time watching their back wake.

"Well, lass, unclench your fingers from the helm and go rescue the poor wee fox. I can handle things here."

"Do you know how to sail?"

"Why, I was practically born on a boat. I've been sailing all my life, and on boats a great deal more complicated than this one. Run along now. I promise, I will not capsize us or run us up on the reefs. Go now, scoot. The weather is fine, the wind has finally picked a steady direction, and as far as I can tell, no one followed us out of the harbor." In a gentler voice, Eluta said, "Get some rest, lass. Get some rest, and let an old sailor enjoy once again the feel of the sea under her."

Yara could not come up with an argument that would keep her at the helm, so she gave it over to Eluta and went below deck. Toki was more than overjoyed to get out of his carrying case, and did not seem to have any trouble with the movement of the boat. Yara decided she might as well just lie down for a brief rest, and was asleep almost before her head hit the pillow. It was Toki pawing at her hours later that finally woke her up. It took her a moment to figure out where she was. Once she realized she was on her skiff, her second realization was that the boat was not moving, but rather was rocking gently.

Yara quickly scrambled up the short steps to the deck and peered out. Eluta was standing at the rail, a fishing pole in her hand. From the position of the sun in the sky, it was late afternoon.

"Ah, you're awake. Good. If I'm right, there is quite a storm brewing to the west, and we really do not want to be out sailing in it tonight. This cove seems quite sheltered, and we should be fairly snug and safe. Get the brazier going, would you? Fresh fish for dinner."

Yara, now that she had had some sleep, also had her wits about her. Looking straight at Eluta, she said, "Before the day gets one minute older, I think you owe me some answers."

Chapter Thirty-Five

"You have a point, and I am more than willing to answer your questions. My question to you, however, is do you want your answers right now, and then have a cold dinner in the cabin with the rain pounding down, or do you want a warm dinner out in the fresh air, and then retire to the cabin for answers while the rain pounds down? I estimate we have less than an hour before the storm hits."

Yara had spent enough time living next to the sea, or sailing on the sea, to know Eluta was right. Grumbling only slightly and under her breath, she set about getting a good set of coals in the brazier. The meal was delicious, and Yara discovered Toki really liked the fish, which was a good thing since her supplies were at a minimum and included little to feed the fox.

They had just cleaned up from their meal when the first of the raindrops began to fall. After making sure the brazier was out and rechecking the anchors, Yara followed Eluta and Toki down into the cabin, closing the hatch behind her. The cove Eluta had found provided good shelter from the wind and rain, but Yara could hear the storm increasing. She was glad they were not out on the open sea.

"Now then, I know you have questions, and certainly had not anticipated having a passenger on your venture south. I can understand that you might be confused and unsure as to just what is going on. I hope I can set your mind at ease."

Yara said nothing and waited for Eluta to continue.

"I've known for quite some time who your family is. Your former employer, Mendel Bevare, while a fine book restorer and a good mentor to you, was a very cautious man. While his teaching you all he knew about the care and repair of books and scrolls may have seemed like a spontaneous gesture to you, know full well that he knew exactly who you were and where you came from before he ever let you touch anything in his office. He shared some of that information with me when he discussed my hiring you at the royal library. It was not important information at that time. More recently, upon my request, he shared more details."

"Well, that explains how you might know I'm a Karmoris, but it does not explain how you knew I was looking for information that might lead me to the piece of the oppgave ringe that once was in the possession of my family. Or for that matter, how you knew about Toki."

"I knew about your fox in the garden for, after all, it is my garden. I was pleased you had a companion, for you've seemed happier since Tokala came into your life. I also knew you were in the garden when Chance, Seeker Odette, Seeker Zita, and I discussed the journal written by your ancestor. I took a chance that you would keep the information to yourself, mainly because you would consider it family business. I have to confess I took blatant advantage of you by asking you to trace what had happened to the cousin who played a trick on Laron Karmoris. I felt you would be motivated to find the answers. I was right. I know you, and someone else, looked for the journal in my office."

Yara almost started at that nugget of information that Eluta had so casually dropped into her monologue. She thought she had been so careful in her searching.

"Oh, don't look so worried. I admire someone who is enterprising, and you had no reason to trust me then, nor do you have any reason to trust me now. Let's review the facts. You are descended from the Karmorises who were charged with keeping safe a piece of the oppgave ringe. That little piece of family history has remained with at least your branch of the family. Were you aware of what the oppgave ringe was?"

Yara thought for a moment about whether she wanted to answer the head librarian with the truth and decided there was no sense making anything up at this point.

"The significance of what had been lost by my ancestor was not clear until this past summer. The oppgave ringe was always associated with the family luck. Once the ring was lost, so too, it would seem, was the family's luck at trading, and most branches of the family lost their fortunes."

"As far as I can tell, from what all any of us have been able to find out about the oppgave ringe, none of the information suggests that the rings have anything to do with imparting luck. Circumstances and bad investments had more to do with the downfall of the Karmorises' fortunes than anything else."

"I would have to agree with you. It seems my ancestors made a series of bad decisions, and then blamed it on the loss of the family 'luck'."

"It would seem, based information found in Laron and Kinza Karmoris' journals, it was more brotherly jealousy, and then family pranks, that caused this whole chain of events and the disappearance of the piece of the oppgave ringe," Eluta suggested. "I did manage to get through all of Kinza Karmoris' journal and found nothing else that would give us any clue as to where to go next. As I am sure you already know, he stayed in Tårnklokke for only a few more years, and then he and his family moved south to establish a branch of the family's trading business in the coastal town of Sandet Cove. The rest of the journal is just periodic musings by Kinza. Not very helpful, I'm afraid. I think you know more than you have shared about what happened to his descendants."

Royal librarian Eluta's statement hung in the air between them, and Yara knew she was becoming increasingly uncomfortable sitting on her bunk with the air of the skiff's cabin filled with expectancy. She did not think that trying to dump the royal librarian overboard at the first convenient moment was going to be an option, so Yara needed to determine just how much she should tell Eluta. Clearly the woman would know where they were and where they were going, since they were traveling together on a small boat.

Letting out a deep sigh of resignation, Yara said, "The last known descendant of Kinza Karmoris that I could find lives in a small village in the foothills of the mountains that border the bogs of Muggen Myr."

"Ah, the skiff will take us only so far into the salt marsh, and then we will have to find another means of travel. I will have to think on that. Now, if we were at the library, we could look up a book which would tell us how to construct a reed boat. Yes, that would be just what we would need. You don't happen to know how to build a reed boat now, do you?"

"'Fraid not."

"Pity. Well, it can't be helped. I am sure we will figure it out when we get there. Of course, in addition to needing to find transportation through the salt marsh, once we get to this small village, there is no guarantee that the descendants of Kinza Karmoris will still live there. Nor is there any guarantee that this folk will have any knowledge of the oppgave ringe. We may be on a fool's errand."

Yara sat on her bunk stroking Toki's fur, trying to gather her thoughts and remain calm. It would seem she now had a partner, whether she wanted one or not. Yara was at a loss as to why the head librarian had chosen to insert herself into what Yara felt was a private family quest. A loud clap of thunder brought her attention back, and she realized that Eluta had begun speaking again.

". . . so I owe . . . . Oh my, that was a close one. What I started to say was, I think I owe you an apology. I am sure you are quite capable of handling all this by yourself, and quite frankly, my being here is just a matter of pure selfishness on my part. Now mind you, I have never regretted the choices I have made, or the path I followed in my life. The quiet life of being a librarian has been rich and fulfilling. However, just once, I wanted to go on an adventure myself, rather than just read about the adventures of others. This seemed like the perfect opportunity."

Another loud clap of thunder, followed by a series of rumbles, made talking difficult. When it was relatively quiet once again, Yara started to speak, and then paused. Finally, she asked a question. "You're here because you want to go on an adventure, or you're here because you want to find the piece of the oppgave ringe?"

"Both. The idea of an adventure aside, anyone loyal to the Crown wants all of the pieces of the oppgave ringe found and put in the vesstebоks. I think, however, what you are really asking is: have I bullied my way onto your boat and into your family's business so I can claim the oppgave ringe for myself?"

Yara was somewhat taken aback by both the truth and the bluntness of Eluta's statement.

"The answer to that question would be no. I would neither desire, nor do I have any claim to, the piece of the oppgave ringe. I suspect I would not even be able to handle it. No, Yara, as I said, this was just an opportunity to get out of the library and go on an adventure. I can only hope that I can contribute a little and not be a burden. Now then, enough of this weighty conversation. I think I had best go check the anchors, and then, we should get some sleep."

Eluta moved briskly off her bunk, put on her rain gear, and moved swiftly topside, leaving Yara sitting there. The lass needs some time to think through what I have just said, Eluta thought to herself. Eluta took time to make sure the skiff was not dragging its anchor, and that all the lines were tight. She noticed that a bit of the sail had worked itself loose and fixed that. When she returned down below deck, she saw that Yara was settled in and either asleep or pretending to be asleep, for she did not stir as Eluta removed and hung up her wet gear. Enough talk for tonight, Eluta thought. Tomorrow would undoubtedly bring more questions.

If I did not have bad luck, I would not have any luck at all, Nathair groused to himself, as another heavy wave crashed over the bow of his boat. It had taken all his skill to keep his boat upright in the stormy seas for the last hour, as he sought a safe cove or harbor in which to anchor out of the storm's fury. He had finally spotted a decent-sized inlet that he hoped would accommodate his boat and was fighting his way there. It took him another fifteen minutes before he reached the mouth of what appeared to be a fairly wide river. Fortunately, there was a bend in the river fairly soon after entering the mouth, and the high dunes and scrub trees blocked much of the wind. Not far ahead Nathair could see several lanterns swinging over a short dock. It was with great relief that Nathair pulled in and was able to tie up. Though he could hear the continuous rumble of thunder overhead and see the streaks of lightning lighting up the sky, the water in this sheltered place was considerably calmer.

When the lightning lit up the sky, Nathair could see that there were a number of buildings on the shore, though all were dark. He thought he caught a hint of wood smoke in the damp air. Not willing to venture off his boat in the dark, Nathair took time to furl the sail to the boom, make sure everything else was tied down, and then went down into the cabin. He was wet to the skin and cold to the bone. It was time to change into dry clothes, look over his charts, and then get some rest. He could only hope that the boat he was trying to catch up with had had to pull into a sheltered area to wait out the night, too. It was hard to say this time of year. Storms came up so quickly and were gone just as fast. For all he knew, the boat he followed had not been affected by the storm he was in at all, and they had lengthened their lead.

Nathair knew he was sailing a faster boat than the skiff the lass and the librarian were on. With a good wind and good weather he felt he could, at the very least, catch up with them or even beat them to the Muggen Myr area, not that that would do him all that much good. If only he had not been banned from the rolls room before he had been able to find that one last clue he thought he would need. He wished he knew who had hidden the book he had been blamed for hiding. There was nothing to be done about it now. Now, he just needed to get some rest, so he could depart at first light and get on with the business of catching up with the lass and the librarian.

The storm had blown itself out by the first light of dawn. Nathair wanted to be away as quickly as possible. Several of the folk who lived in the very small gathering of cottages had come down on the dock, inquiring if he needed anything. Nathair had asked as to whether they had seen a small skiff pass by the previous day, but none had. They had been fishing quite a far bit off the coast, so if a small boat had passed by close to shore, they would not have seen it. He had thanked them politely for their offers of help and information. Once the sail was up, they cast off his last lines, and Nathair was on his way.

What he did not see as he sailed down the river was the blond haired man who had emerged from one of the cottages and had stepped out onto the dock to watch Nathair's boat disappear around the bend. There was a look of deep concentration on the man's face. If Nathair had turned around and seen that look, he would have been very concerned.

Chapter Thirty-Six

Yara had read about the salt marshes of Muggen Myr, but she was quite unprepared for the reality of the marsh. After having looked over the charts that Eluta had brought along, the two had determined that they needed to pull into the first of the two natural harbors located on the edge of the salt marsh, which extended for miles down the coast. Eluta, it would seem, had gathered some information about the two harbors, and the first one was considered the safest. The one much farther down the coast, which would have put them closer to their eventual goal, was also quite close to the border of Rullegress, the country to the south of Sommerhjem. Rumors abounded that that harbor was a fairly chancy place to put in and appealed to a rougher trade.

While the harbor master had assured them that Yara's skiff would be safe tied up to the Sikkervik town dock, she was reluctant to leave it. Packing up what they would need to head into the salt marsh provided some comic relief. Yara had no idea that any one folk could cram so much stuff into the nooks and crannies of a skiff. She had not even been aware of some of those nooks and crannies. Eluta had brought along enough gear to supply a small expedition, certainly more than two folk would need. It had been interesting, to say the least, trying to get Eluta to pare down what she was going to take.

"Since we are going to be traveling in a small reed boat, we will be very limited in what we can take before our gear becomes too heavy, and we just sink before we leave the harbor," Yara had told Eluta. It had been difficult to keep the frustration out of her voice.

"But we might need this book on flora and fauna of the salt marsh region."

"While true that it might be very enlightening to know what we are seeing as we travel through the salt marsh, may I remind you that our sole purpose right now is to try to get to the village of Sivkurv still afloat, without getting hopelessly lost."

"What about this handy gadget?"

"No."

"Or . . . ."

"No. We need to pack several changes of clothes, raingear, food, and other necessities like cookware, fire starters, tent, water bags, well, you get the idea. It all has to fit into these four waterproof packs. One pack each for personal gear, and the other two packs for the rest of the gear. Remember, we have to leave room in the reed boat for the two of us and Toki."

It was midmorning by the time the three were ready to leave Sikkervik. It did not take very long after entering the salt marsh that Yara began to get worried. The salt marsh was not like traveling on the sea where one could move in a straight line, or on a river which might bend here and there. The salt marsh turned out to be a series of switch backs. Yara and Eluta would travel along the channel running between marsh grass on either side until the channel looked like it would run out. It would not, however. Instead, just at the end would be a turn which would take them to another long straight channel that ran parallel to the one they had just turned out of.

"At this rate, we could travel for days and not really get very far," Eluta remarked, as they made yet another turn.

"The reed boat builder we purchased the boat from assured me that while the salt marsh is extensive, we will run into some channels that run east west rather than the one we are now traveling which is running north south. Eventually, we will get out of the salt marsh and be able to travel by river. Our last leg of the journey will be on foot."

By midafternoon, the three were still traveling in the salt marsh, switching back and forth. They were hot, sweaty and very tired, but continued to push on, hoping to find the outlet. When dusk arrived and the sun had sunk below the horizon, both Yara and Eluta expressed how worried they were to each other.

"It is getting harder and harder to see and still no sign of any outlet from the salt marsh," stated Eluta wearily.

"We are going to have to stop soon, so we don't become hopelessly lost in the dark," suggested Yara. "We will have to spend the night in the boat, for I don't think there is any solid land under the marsh reeds. This place looks like as good a place to stop as any."

"This place looks like as good a place to stop as any, indeed," Eluta suggested, and then began to chuckle as she turned around in her seat. "This place looks like all the rest of the salt marsh."

"Well, true . . . ." What Yara was going to say was not forthcoming. Toki had stood up, was looking beyond Yara, and began to make a gekkering sound.

"I've never heard a fox make that sound before," Eluta commented. "It sounds like someone is gently hammering on stone. What do you suppose it means?"

"When the foxes who lived near us back home made that sound, they were either fighting or playing. I'm hopeful that Toki is making a playing sound and not a fighting sound since, well glance over your shoulder. Since Toki is not making a warning bark, screech, or scream, it is hard to tell what he is trying to tell us."

Eluta turned around and saw what the two behind her were looking at. Hovering about a foot above the water was a small ball of pale greenish light. Just as Eluta was about to comment, the light winked out. Farther down the channel, a new greenish ball of light appeared and hovered again about a foot above the water. This one too winked out, and a third greenish ball of light winked into existence even farther down the channel. The third one winked out, and one appeared again where the first one had been. As Eluta watched, the small balls of greenish light repeated this pattern over and over again. She was interrupted in her watching when Toki clambered over the side of her seat and placed his paws on the bow of the boat.

"What are they?" Yara asked.

"I've heard of them. Some folks call them will-o'-wisps or hinkypunks. Stories suggest that if we follow them, they will not allow us to catch up with them, and they will lead us astray. Other legends suggest if we were to follow the lights, they would lead us to great riches."

"If my choice is between being led astray and great riches, I would choose great riches."

"These lights are not acting the way I have read about them. Usually, there is one light, and it beckons you to follow. Once you do, it leads you on until you are hopelessly lost, and then winks out. I have never heard of three will-o'-wisps winking out and winking on in a pattern. I wonder what would happen if we approached one?"

The moment Eluta suggested approaching one of the pale greenish lights, Toki stopped gekkering and settled back on his haunches.

"Why not? Shall we try and see what happens?" Yara answered.

The two quietly stuck their paddles into the water and began to move forward toward the first pale greenish light. It held steady and did not disappear as they moved slowly ever closer to it. Just as they were within a few feet of the will-o'-wisp, it swooped not away from them but toward the boat, coming to rest just inches from Toki's nose. The red fox tilted his head, as if he were listening, yipped several times, and then turned and pushed his head against the paddle Eluta had placed across her knees. When Eluta did not immediately respond, Toki again pushed his head against Eluta's paddle.

"I have the feeling I'm supposed to start paddling again. What do you think?" Eluta asked Yara.

"I'm not sure. Let's see what Toki does if we do begin to paddle again. For that matter, let's see what that greenish light does."

Both put their paddles in the water and began to slowly paddle forward. Toki climbed back over Eluta and settled down in his spot in the middle. The greenish light moved aside as the reed boat started forward, but did not wink out. Rather it drifted up another few feet, lighting the way forward. The greenish light ahead of them also drifted higher and seemed to brighten.

"It's as if they are lighting the way, but to where?" Yara asked. "Toki seems to be totally relaxed. I guess he either didn't feel the need to fight the will-o'-wisp or settled back down when he figured out it was not going to play with him. He seems to want us to paddle. I wish I knew what's going on."

"Let's see what happens when we paddle up to the next one," Eluta suggested.

Slowly paddling the reed boat forward, the three approached the next pale greenish light. It, like the previous one, shifted to the side as they moved past. Eluta looked over her shoulder and remarked to Yara that the first one had disappeared.

"I suggest we stop for the moment, and see what the lights do next."

As the reed boat drifted on the quiet water, a new pale green light winked into existence beyond the one ahead of them. The one they had just passed hovered several feet higher than their heads, once again lighting the way. Toki stirred, stood up, and crawled back over their stowed packs to nudge at Yara's paddle, which she had draped across her knees. The sound of thunder could be heard in the distance.

"Toki is certainly trying to be skipper of this small boat," Eluta remarked. "Do you suppose we should follow his orders?"

"Since he is now beginning to nip at my fingers, it might be a good idea. Also, while that thunder is quite far away, getting caught out in the open during a storm is going to be, at the very least, unpleasant and could become dangerous. No matter what, we need to find shelter. The advantage of following the wisps is that they light up the way. Otherwise, we would be paddling in almost complete darkness, since the clouds that have moved in have covered the moon. Go settle back down, Skipper Tokala, I'm paddling."

Yara and Eluta began paddling at a steady pace, hoping that they would find a way out of the salt marsh that would lead them to solid ground and some type of shelter. With no better plan, they followed the will-o'-wisps, for they provided light. The channel through the salt marsh continued to turn back on itself, which meant that distance was traveled, but it did not take them quickly away from the coast. Further complicating their progress was an ever thickening fog.

"Even with the light from the will-o'-wisps, it's getting harder and harder to see where we're going. You are going to have to let me know what is ahead, or if I'm going to run us into a wall of reeds," Yara told Eluta.

Oddly enough, just after Yara had made the statement about having difficulty seeing what was ahead, a second will-o'-wisp joined the one just ahead of them, adding more light.

"Now, that is just a bit disconcerting," Eluta stated. "You mention that we are having trouble seeing in the dark, and now we have six wisps lighting the way instead of three. Kind of gives you the willies, doesn't it?"

"Just a wee bit," Yara replied.

Time began to blur for the two paddlers as they continued to follow the salt marsh channel. No side channels could be seen, even though they paid close attention, trying to find any break in the reeds. The sound of thunder increased and grew louder. The slight mist that they had been paddling through had changed to a drizzle. Other than the sound of their paddles dipping into and pulling out of the water, there was little sound.

"How are you doing up there?" Yara asked Eluta.

"I hate to admit it, but I am beyond tired at this time. If we go on much longer, I am afraid I will not have much power behind my paddle strokes."

Yara was not doing so well herself. While she tried to stay active, her days had been spent hunched over damaged books. Out of shape was out of shape, no matter one's age. She could feel the muscles in her shoulders beginning to burn and knew that blisters were forming on both hands. Soon, no matter how much Toki insisted, neither she nor Eluta were going to be able to paddle. The storm would surely catch up to them shortly.

Fatigue had begun to dull Yara's senses to the point that she did not notice that as she passed a pale green light, there was not one ahead of her. Eluta had to call to her twice to get her attention.

"Stop paddling,"

"What?"

"You need to stop paddling, and we need to back up."

"Why?"

"Because the wisps are no longer ahead of us. They have turned down a side channel."

Yara looked over her shoulder and saw that two of the will-o'-wisps were floating side by side a good twenty or so feet back. She began to paddle backwards until she came alongside the two wisps. Eluta had been right. Yara could see the other wisps ranged out down a side channel, which was wider than the channel they had been paddling in.

"I wonder if this is the way out of the salt marsh, or the way into danger?" Yara asked. "Or both?"

Chapter Thirty-Seven

The drizzle had turned to a steady downpour. The sounds of thunder grew closer, and the lightning was now lighting up the sky every other minute. While the current of the channel Yara and Eluta were now paddling against was not strong, it added to their increasing fatigue. The channel they were now following wound and twisted and had frequent side channels leading off of it. It would be very easy to become hopelessly lost. In addition, the wind had begun to pick up, making staying on course more difficult. When the reed boat did bump up against the dense reeds on one side of the channel, and Yara tried to stop and rest there for a moment, the closest will-o'-wisps would swoop closer, and Tokala would become agitated, barking a warning bark, and moving to get up. In addition, the reed boat was gradually taking on water from the rain.

Yara was bent over, trying to readjust one of the packs, when Eluta shouted. Her words were lost in a clap of thunder. Still bent over, Yara shouted back, asking her what she had said.

"I said, look up ahead. Lights!"

Straightening up, Yara looked and could see that the wisps had gathered in a cluster about one hundred yards ahead. In addition to the pale green light of the will-o'-wisps, there was the yellow-orange glow of lantern light.

So this is it. For good or for bad, this is where the will-o'-wisps have led us, Yara thought. "What do you want to do?" Yara asked Eluta.

"I think we cannot stay on the water much longer. We are soaked, and I'm not sure how much strength I have left to keep paddling. If the rain gets much heavier, it will continue to slow our progress. I think we need to take a chance."

"I think you are right. Yes, Yes, Toki. Hush now, we're going on," Yara told the red fox, who had begun to bark again.

It was with some trepidation that the two started forward toward the gathering of will-o'-wisps. Yara noticed what appeared to be a second yellow-orange glow had joined the first, but this one seemed to be moving. It took her a moment to realize that what she was looking at through the rain and fog was the light from two lanterns, one stationary and one being carried by someone.

As the reed boat drew closer to the light, it became clear that there was a short pier sticking out from the channel wall of reeds. When they were a scant fifteen feet from the pier, a voice called out.

"Halt, who dares enter the land of the Venn this night?"

"I ask your pardon if we have trespassed," Eluta stated calmly. "I also ask for hospitality, for we are beyond weary and soaked to the skin. We have followed the pale green lights to here in hopes of safety and shelter."

"The wisps led you here, you say?"

"Yes."

"But you are not of the Venn."

"No, we come from the capital in search of a long lost relative."

"Marleigh!" the man standing on the dock yelled. "Marleigh!"

A woman in a flowing rain cloak came striding out of the darkness onto the dock.

"What are you bellowing about, Kellen?"

"The woman in the reed boat there said that they followed the wisps here, but you can tell they are not of the Venn, so that can't be possible."

"There are a few rare exceptions. If the wisps brought them here, there must be a reason." Directing her attention to Yara and Eluta, she said, "Please bring your boat to the other side of the dock. Once there, paddle parallel to it. You will see a narrow channel that will take you to the boat house. You can pull your boat in there to get you, it, and your gear out of the rain. We'll meet you there."

It was a relief to be out of the rain and wind. Yara, however, became more anxious than she had been out in the elements when she heard the boat house door drop down behind her. Just before she heard the door splash into the water, Yara caught a flash of pale green light out of the corner of her eye. One of the will-o'-wisps had followed them into the boat house and was now hovering between her and Toki.

"Fascinating," stated Marleigh. "Toss your gear up on the dock. It's a covered walkway to the cottage so your packs should stay fairly dry. We will help you carry them. Well, come along you four, the night is not getting any younger."

Four? What four, Yara thought to herself, for Kellen had gone on ahead carrying two of their packs. Had this woman the man had addressed as Marleigh counted wrong, or had she included the wisp who had remained hovering near Toki?

The back door to the boat house led to a covered wood plank walkway. It was not until they reached a set of stairs that Yara realized the cottage they were about to enter was raised up off the marsh on posts. The interior of the cottage was warm and inviting. The coals of a peat fire glowed in a brazier, and the floor was covered with a beautiful woven marsh reed mat. The furnishings were of a simple design, but very well cared for. The roof overhead was made of woven mats of marsh reeds.

After introductions were made, Marleigh invited Yara and Eluta to have a seat by the brazier to dry out and get warm. A short while later she joined them, offering them each a mug of hot tea. Tokala had made himself comfortable curled up next to Yara, and the wisp continued to hover close to him.

"Have you come to Muggen Myr to return the fox?" Marleigh asked.

"Return the fox?" Yara repeated, not knowing why the woman would ask that question.

"You said you were from the capital. The fox seems comfortable with you, so I assumed you had not just found him in the marsh. Logic would then tell me you are trying to return him to where he belongs. He is, after all, a bog fox. Tell me about where you found him."

Yara took a moment to think through what Marleigh was saying. First, she took a good look at Toki. He looked just like the red foxes from back home, she thought, but then Yara looked more closely. Now that she had taken a really good look, she was not so sure that he really did look like the foxes from home. His tail was bushier, and his belly was tan rather than white. She wondered why she had not really noticed the differences before.

"I found him in the alley behind my rented room. He was cornered by several dogs. Since he was not in good shape after I chased the dogs off, I kept him and cared for him. I thought he was just like the red foxes from home, or the red foxes that can be seen upon occasion in the capital parks. I had not noticed a difference until now. So no, I'm not here to return him to Muggen Myr. He is just newly strong enough to be on his own, and I would not hold him if he belongs here," stated Yara with less conviction than she felt. She realized she had grown attached to the young fox and had not really thought through what would happen when he was strong enough to be on his own.

Just as Yara had finished speaking, Toki got up, stretched and jumped into her lap, circled around three times, and settled himself. The will-o'-wisp drifted over to hover just to the left of Yara.

"Fascinating, just fascinating," Marleigh whispered so quietly that neither Yara nor Eluta heard her. Addressing her guests, she said, "You are welcome to spend the night. Kellen has put your packs in the guest cottage. I will show you the way."

Marleigh led Yara, Eluta, Toki, and the wisp out a side door, along an elevated walkway to another cottage raised up off the marsh on posts. It was smaller than the one they had left, consisting of a single room. The room held several bunk beds, and a couple of chairs. A brazier was giving off a welcoming warm, dry heat.

After Marleigh had left, Yara turned to Eluta and said, "There was something about Marleigh that made me a little uncomfortable. I'm not sure how to explain it. I wonder if we might have been better off taking our chances with the other Muggen Myr harbor. We might have been better off taking our chances with the smugglers and other unsavory characters there than with these Venn. When I was studying the rolls, groupings of folk were listed as living here and there in Muggen Myr, but I don't recall a clan called the Venn and I have never really heard about them."

"I have heard of the Venn."

"What do you know about them?" Yara asked.

"Very little, I'm afraid, very little. I know they see themselves as the guardians of the area we know as Muggen Myr. I think at one time they held a more official role, but mostly this area was seen by the former regent as not worth much, and so he paid little attention to it. In that way, this area was not as affected by Lord Cedric Klingflug's rule as was most of the rest of the country. I do not know at this point where their loyalties lie. I'm not sure they are loyal to anyone other than the Venn."

"So, we don't know if we are in good hands, or if we have jumped from the boiling kettle into the fire," Yara remarked.

"No, we don't. If I recall from what I have read about the Venn, they are a very closed and somewhat mysterious clan. There is some suggestion that they were late comers to Sommerhjem. Late comers, mind you, is a relative term, meaning only that they did not arrive with the first settlers. There has never been any conflict between the Venn and any other clan in Sommerhjem, or any conflict with the Crown that I can recall. Like I have said, Muggen Myr has never been an area that anyone has coveted. It is not good farm land, obviously. It does not lure people here to find their fortunes. It has no vast forest, and very little buildable land."

"How do the Venn live here then?"

"Just because it does not look like an ideal place to live, Muggen Myr has enough plant and animal life to sustain those who live here and know the swamps, bogs, and salt marshes. It is a place rich in a different sort of beauty and life." Yawning, Eluta said, "Much as I would like to continue this conversation, I must confess I am extremely weary."

Yara, looking at Eluta, realized the royal librarian looked pale and haggard. Feeling upset at herself for not noticing sooner, Yara briskly set about finding their sleeping rolls and getting the beds ready while Eluta washed up. Once Eluta was settled into bed, Yara blew out the lantern light and crawled into bed herself. She did not go to sleep right away, but lay staring at the underside of the top bunk for quite some time. When she turned on her side to get more comfortable, she realized that the wisp was still in the room, but instead of floating near Toki, it was hovering just to the side of her bunk. It was not as bright as it had been when they were on the water, if it was even one of the ones that had led them here. It was now emitting a very faint soft glow. Yara fell asleep wondering about the wisp.

Yara was awakened the next morning by a small wet fox nose in her face. Moaning, because every muscle in her body ached from the long and rigorous paddle of the day before, Yara pulled the covers up over her head and tried to ignore Toki. When poking his nose in Yara's face did not work, Toki began to paw at the covers. Yara gave up, got up, and dressed. Since

Eluta was still sleeping, Yara quietly let herself out of the guest house. Toki and the wisp came with her.

Standing on the walkway, Yara took time to look around. Having arrived after dark the night before, it had been difficult to get a good look at where the will-o'-wisps had led them. In the early morning light, it was clear to Yara that there were more buildings here than the boat house, main cottage, and guest cottage. The walkway she stood on interconnected with other buildings besides the boat house, and what she assumed was Marleigh's cottage. Some of the buildings lined the channel and had docks of their own.

Toki had wandered a little way away and was studying something just over the edge of the walkway. After a few moments, he wandered farther down the walkway toward what Yara could see might be a meadow. The walkway ran straight across the meadow toward a stand of trees, which indicated that there was higher and more solid ground ahead. Toki continued on the walkway, heading toward the trees.

Yara stood, indecisive as to what she should do next. Should she follow Toki, or let him go on his own? Marleigh had said that Toki was a bog fox and probably from the Muggen Myr. He belonged here, and after all, he really was a wild animal. Should she just let him go?

Chapter Thirty-Eight

As the days wore on, Nathair had worried about the sail he had glimpsed off and on behind him. He had not been certain if someone was following him, or if he had just been seeing glimpses of sails from different boats that sailed these waters. As he had drawn closer to Sikkervik, there were more boats, which had only added to his concerns. His journey south since the storm had been one of smooth waters and fair winds, but the look of the clouds moving in from the west suggested that another storm was on its way. Nathair was glad he had tied up at a safe mooring in Sikkervik's harbor before the skies opened up.

Just before he had needed to return to his boat and batten everything down before the storm hit, Nathair had had a chance to wander the docks. He had located Yara's skiff. It did not seem occupied when he casually strolled by it, and the storm coming in would prevent him from checking to see if Yara and the royal librarian were there this night. He would have to wait until morning to try to discretely track them down.

Tired from the long days of sailing, Nathair retired early. The howl of wind and the pounding of the rain did not wake him, and he slept the night through. Anxious to be on his way to finding out if Yara was still in the area, Nathair quickly dressed, climbed up the ladder, and unlatched the hatch. As he stepped through the opening, a large hand clamped down on his shoulder.

"Good, you're awake. No, now, don't try anything foolish. I'm bigger than you and more skilled at fighting than you will ever be. That's better. I have heard tell you're a smart fellow."

"What do you want? I have no great riches for you to rob," said Nathair. He was trying to keep his voice steady and strong, but was not sure he was being successful.

"Why, I want to have a very quiet talk with you about the Karmoris family luck," the man stated.

Nathair started at the mention of the Karmoris family luck. How did this man know?

"You aren't the only one who has been looking for what happened to Kinza Karmoris' descendants. I, too, have been searching the rolls. It is unfortunate that your distant cousin has the jump on us."

Distant cousin, what distant cousin, Nathair wondered, trying to concentrate and really take in what the man was suggesting.

"Ah, I can see by the look on your face, you did not know that the lass who was locking herself in the rolls room was a relative of yours. You two have actually been quite helpful, for all I needed to do was to follow behind you both and find the books you had been looking at. That rolls librarian was most helpful, especially after you hid that Muggen Myr rolls book," the man stated with a smirk in his voice.

"But I didn't hide the book, I . . . ." Nathair's voice trailed off. "You hid the book. It was you who got me banned from the rolls rooms."

"See there, I knew you were a smart fellow. Now then, I suggest you tuck that indignation away somewhere and listen to what I propose. I know where Yara and that librarian woman are heading. They have chosen to travel through an area of Muggen Myr protected by the Venn. I don't think it would be in either of our best interests to travel in that direction. There are more expedient ways of getting to where we all want to go, but once there, it would be easier if a member of the Karmoris clan did the inquiry. We could help each other out. I have the knowledge you need, you have the family connection. Think about it. If you want to join forces, I will meet you here at noon."

Having made his offer, the man stepped off the boat and headed up the dock. Nathair just stood there, silent for a moment, and then on shaking legs went to sit at the helm. What was he to make of what had just happened?

Nathair began to think about what the man had told him. The lass he had seen entering the library room that held the rolls, according to what he had just been told, was his distant cousin. She had been looking for the same information that he had. He wondered what branch of the Karmoris family she belonged to, and what her angle was. Was she looking for the piece of the oppgave ringe, too? What were her intentions if she found it? For that matter, who was the man who had just left his boat, and what did he really know? The more immediate question, Nathair thought to himself, was should he move on and try to find out where Yara and the royal librarian Eluta had gone, or should he take the man up on his offer? Before making any decision, Nathair needed to do some discreet inquiring about both the two he was trying to catch up with and about the Venn.

Nathair returned to his boat several hours later, no closer to a decision as to what to do than when he had left his boat. He had found out that Yara, Eluta, and of all things, a red bog fox had paddled off in a small reed boat heading into the salt marsh. His informant suggested that they would eventually cross into the territory of the Venn.

Nathair had gone to a dockside eatery to get breakfast. There he had casually asked about the Venn. Folks had been more than willing to talk, but he was not sure, even now, if they had been telling him the truth, or if they had been pulling his leg, seeing as he was a stranger in town. Nathair suspected it had been a little bit of both. In sorting through what folks had told him, it seemed to Nathair that the Venn were most probably guardians of a portion of Muggen Myr. Now, about the rest of what he had been told, he was not sure. Either they were very mysterious folk or just a very close clan. He did not put much credence in the tall tales he had been told about folks going into the Venn's territory never to be heard of again, or about strange lights and goings on in the marsh.

Just fanciful tales to be told to gullible strangers. The Venn might even be smugglers who made up tales to keep the curious folk out of their business. Yes, that must be it, Nathair thought to himself. The Venn were either guardians who did not want folk messing up their part of Muggen Myr, or smugglers who did not want folk being too inquisitive as to what they were doing.

Now, he had a decision to make. Did he go into the marsh alone hoping to find some trace of Yara and Eluta, or did he join forces with the stranger, who claimed to have the information he needed about the Karmorises. If he chose to head into the marsh in hopes of finding those he sought, there was no guarantee he would find them, and then what? How would he pick up their trail? On the other hand, he was not all that anxious to take up with the stranger. He did not know what the man really wanted. If he actually had the information Nathair needed, then why did he need Nathair? Why did the stranger think it would be better to have Nathair along? An even more important question was: what would happen if they actually found Kinza Karmoris' descendant, and that folk had the piece of the oppgave ringe? Would the distant relative give up the oppgave ringe, and would the stranger try to take it from Nathair?

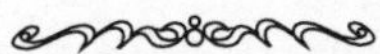

Toki had wandered on about twenty more feet away from Yara, and she stood watching him go. Suddenly he stopped, turning his head to look over his shoulder. Then, he came scampering back to Yara. Yara squatted down and reached out to ruffle Toki's fur, but before she could, he grabbed her hand gently in his teeth and pulled. Yara had to put her other hand down to steady herself. Toki then released her hand and moved back several feet. When Yara remained where she was, Toki moved back and tugged on the bottom of her pants leg and moved off again.

"Do you want me to follow you?"

Toki turned and trotted a bit farther down the walkway.

"I'll take that as a 'yes'," Yara stated, only feeling a wee bit foolish as she brushed away a single tear that had slipped down her cheek. It seemed that Toki, at least for the moment, was not running off without her. Just as she started to follow him, she caught movement out of the corner of her eye. Turning to her left, at first she could not see anything that might have moved past her. It took a few seconds for her to realize there was a very, very faint pale green glow hovering just off and slightly ahead of her left shoulder. Toki's bark brought her attention back to the red fox, who had moved farther down the walkway.

"Well, wisp, come along. Seems Toki is getting impatient." Or maybe she was the one who was supposed to come along, since both the wisp and the fox were in front of her.

Yara noticed that what she had thought was a meadow was actually a bog, and not solid ground. She appreciated the walkway, for while she knew from her reading that she could walk on the bog, she was glad she did not have to this day. Her boots were just drying out from getting wet in the rain the night before.

Toki seemed content to scamper ahead, exploring and then running back to Yara, as long as Yara continued to follow him, which she did at a leisurely pace. It was a warm sunny morning. It was peaceful in the bog, which held its own beauty and fascinating plant life. Insects buzzed, birds sang, and there was a slight breeze carrying the different smells of the bog. Yara had expected the bog to smell of rotting vegetation, and it did not. The smell was pleasant.

When Yara reached the trees she had seen from the cottage, she noticed the walkway ended at a well-worn path. It was at that moment that she realized that she might be trespassing. She had not asked anyone's permission to wander around. Because she had left Eluta sleeping, Eluta would wake and not know where Yara had gone. When Yara tried to turn around and head back, Toki barked sharply twice, and the wisp hovered just in front of her face. Yara was not sure if she turned back around because of the urgency in Toki's bark, or because she did not know what the wisp would do if she tried to go back.

"Fine, into the woods it is then," Yara said, turning and following Toki.

The trees were unlike any Yara had ever seen. At first, she thought they might be a young grove of quirrelit trees, but when she really took a look at them, she realized that they were similar to but not the same as quirrelit trees. Maybe a smaller variety, she thought to herself. Once under the boughs of the trees, the air was considerably cooler. The farther she walked, the denser the trees became, cutting out the sunlight.

The wisp that had accompanied them into the shade of the woods was now much more distinct, and seemed to have taken the lead. As the path twisted and turned through the trees, Yara began to get nervous. She had just about decided that she needed to turn around and go back, when the sight that greeted her when she looked over her shoulder knocked that thought right out of her head. Behind her, darting in and out of the trees were dozens more wisps. They would form up in groups, and then break apart. Some would zip up into the branches, others would hover close to the path. Some would wink out, and others would wink in to take their places. In a swirling kaleidoscope of pale green light, the wisps were now everywhere she turned to look, except ahead on the path. Only the one she had been following was in front of her.

What amazed Yara the most was that Toki did not seem bothered by the wisps at all. He just kept following the single wisp down the path, as if he were out for a leisurely stroll. She knew he was aware of the wisps behind and to the side of them, but he paid them no attention at all. That Toki was unconcerned about the wisps helped with Yara's uneasiness, but did not altogether remove her concern that, in a sense, she was being herded forward.

Yara was so busy paying attention to the wisp that she was not paying attention to the rest of her surroundings, and it took her a brief moment to realize she had come to a halt at the edge of a large clearing. The wisps began to gather closer to her. When she stepped into the clearing, the wisp who had been guiding Toki and her began to move again, leading the others in a slow clockwise circle around Yara and Toki. As Yara watched, the wisps began to pick up speed, and soon became a blur of pale green, until suddenly they all winked out with the exception of one.

It took a few moments for Yara's eyes to adjust once the whirling ring of pale green light was gone. She found herself standing just inside a ring of trees whose boughs provided shade for most of the glen. The center of the glade, however, was bathed in sunlight. She thought she heard someone say "fascinating," but that may have been just her imagination.

Chapter Thirty-Nine

"I think you and I need to have a talk," stated Marleigh, as she strode out of the shadows of the trees surrounding the clearing where Yara and Toki had come to a halt.

Yara wasn't quite sure how she should take Marleigh's statement. She wondered if she had done something wrong, or if she had somehow trespassed. Yara had not seen any warning signs suggesting she should not walk on the boardwalk, or be in the woods.

"My apologies if I've wandered where I shouldn't have," Yara said sincerely.

"No apologies are necessary. All are welcome in this grove, as long as they do not intend any harm to the trees. You have done nothing wrong, lass. I'm sorry if I gave you that impression. No, we need to talk about you and the will-o'-wisps. From what little you have told me of yourself, it would appear that you are not of the Venn."

"No, my family is definitely from much farther north with the exception of one branch that moved to . . ." Here Yara paused, for she did not know just how much she should tell this woman. ". . . moved to this area, but from what I can determine, lived on the border."

"Yes, I remember you mentioning looking for a long lost relative. What was the family name?"

Marleigh had asked a perfectly normal question, which Yara was not sure she wanted to answer. It would look odd if she did not answer, and since she had never been very good at convincingly telling tales, she knew she had to give a truthful answer. Giving the family name would not really reveal why they were looking for her lost kin, so Yara told Marleigh that she was looking for descendants of the Karmoris family.

"Ah yes, the Karmorises. Used to be a family by that name in Sivkurv. They were fair basket makers, and even better traders."

"Were?" Yara asked.

"Swamp fever is a constant threat to those who live in or near Muggen Myr. Unfortunately, some folk are more susceptible than others. Sivkurv was particularly hard hit a number of years back. Decimated the village. We tried to help, but there has always been an uneasy and tenuous relationship between the Venn and the villagers. All but one of the Karmoris family was struck down by the fever."

"Only one survived?"

"Only one, and before you get your hopes up, her body survived, but I am afraid her mind was never the same."

"Nevertheless, I need to find her," Yara stated.

Marleigh gave Yara a long measuring look. "Yes, I think perhaps you do. Please do not think too unkindly of the villagers of Sivkurv, but they banished the poor woman, took her into the Tåkete Bog, and dropped her off. They did not want to be responsible for her, and thought they might still catch the swamp fever from her, even though she had survived."

"She survived the fever, but they banished her from her village. Is she still alive?" Yara asked, even as her heart sank, thinking that anyone who was not quite right in their mind would probably have perished in the mist-shrouded bog.

"The area the Venn hold dear borders the Tåkete Bog, and from time to time, there have been reports of a lone woman being spotted. She appears to be in good health, but no one has been able to get very close. We have invited her to join us, to live with us, but to no avail. When anyone tries to enter the bog where she has been seen, they are warned off by a skulk of red bog foxes like the one sitting patiently at your feet. She is called Russhell by our people, due to her fox-colored hair. I don't know what her real name was, for the villagers do not speak of her. I think they are ashamed of how they treated her."

"I have a great need to find her."

"Why would that be?"

"Well, she is kin, after all," Yara said, but could see the look of skepticism in Marleigh's eyes.

"I can hear the truth in your first statement, that you have a great need to find her. I have a feeling there is more to this search for lost kin than you are telling, but no matter. The wisps seem to accept you, so who am I not to lend aid to a wisp friend? We can guide you to where she was last reported as having been seen, but then it will be up to you."

"I will take you up on your kind offer. I had best get back, for Eluta will most likely be awake by now and wondering what has happened to me."

"About your companion. Is she also related to the Karmorises?"

"No," Yara said, before she could think her answer through. Why, she wondered, was it so difficult sometimes to forget to put one's brain in gear before putting one's mouth in motion? Her feeling that she might have given the wrong answer was confirmed when Marleigh spoke.

"I suspected as much. It would be best that Eluta not travel beyond this point." Before Yara could protest, Marleigh went on. "Finding Russhell will be difficult at best. If you do find her, getting past her skulk of red bog foxes will be a challenge. Assuming you accomplish those two tasks, getting her to talk to you and say anything intelligent will also be hard. Having someone else with you will only add to your already difficult task. Russhell might see two folks as a threat, whereas she might, and I stress the word 'might', she might let you get close to her."

"So, what you are proposing is that I let you guide me, and only me, to the Tåkete Bog, which is usually foggy or mist covered, drop me off somewhere there in hopes that I might find this elusive Russhell woman, get past her skulk of bog foxes, get her to trust me, get her to talk to me, and then hope she says something rational."

"That sums it up very nicely," declared Marleigh, over her shoulder, as she turned and headed back out of the grove of trees.

The conversation with Eluta went pretty much as Yara had expected. She protested and argued, but in the end, Eluta conceded that Marleigh had probably made a correct assumption when she suggested two strangers entering the Tåkete Bog and trying to make contact with Russhell, who had good reason to mistrust folk, would have little chance of success. Marleigh extended an invitation to Eluta to stay with her. Eluta accepted the invitation, thinking she would be able to add more to her knowledge of both the Venn and the Muggen Myr.

"Now don't you fret over me, lass. I'll be right as rain here. I'll worry about you, mind you, but I have to reluctantly agree with Marleigh. Two strangers wandering the bog seeking a woman who has not been treated kindly by her own kind might make finding her and talking with her much more difficult. You do realize, however, even if only you go, the woman Russhell will certainly know the bog better than almost anyone at this point, and if she does not want to be found, you won't find her. I have a good feeling about this venture you are about to make, however."

"Why is that?" Yara inquired.

"While I do not know much about will-o'-wisps, actually nothing for that matter, I get the impression that the fact that one has been hovering over your shoulder since we arrived here is somewhat special. It certainly has surprised our hosts, and in a positive way. I will be here when you get back. Now, we had best look in our packs and see what you are going to need," Eluta suggested.

The next morning Yara bid a reluctant farewell to Eluta and took up the bow position in a reed boat. Marleigh was in the stern. Yara had been worried that Toki would either choose to stay behind with Eluta, or would wander off, but he jumped in the boat before either Marleigh or Yara could. Once settled, Yara looked around to see if the wisp who had been her constant companion lately was still with her. At first, she could not spot the pale green glow and found herself very disappointed. Then as she faced forward, and was just about to dip her paddle into the water, she spotted the wisp ahead of her. For some reason, seeing the wisp in front of her made her feel better.

The trip to the Tåkete Bog took several days. Yara began to appreciate the area they were traveling through and was glad her guide was someone who knew the territory. The Muggen Myr would never be an easy place to live and held a myriad of dangers for the unwary. It was midmorning of their final day of travel when Yara became aware that the air had grown cooler and held a slight haze.

"We are getting close to the border of our land," Marleigh stated calmly. "We should run into one of our border patrols soon."

No sooner had she spoken than Yara heard the slight whisper of paddles being pulled from the water. Looking behind her, she could see several reed boats approaching.

Marleigh greeted those in the boats and inquired as to whether they had seen any sign of Russhell in the area.

"Funny you should ask. She is so rarely seen at all these days, and it is even less so for this area, but we have seen her several times in the last few days just up beyond that bend. It has almost felt as if she were waiting for something, or someone. Struck us as odd."

"Lead the way."

It did not take long for the boats to reach the place that Russhell had last been seen. The boats pulled in, and Yara disembarked. Toki was handed up to her, along with her gear.

"You're sure you want to do this?" Marleigh asked. "There is no guarantee that Russhell is still anywhere in the area."

"I thank you for your kindness and concern, but I feel like I need to find her."

"Good luck to you then. A patrol will be by here several times a week. When you need a ride back to my place, wave one down. They will know to keep a lookout for you. Be safe."

Yara stood on the bank of the waterway for a long time after she could no longer see either Marleigh's boat or the patrol boats. She found herself reluctant to leave the relative safety of the water's edge and venture into the thickening haze that hung over the bog.

Toki did not seem to have any reservations about heading into the haze. He had been sniffing about and, with one sharp bark, had begun to nose along what appeared to be a faint path. The will-o'-wisp that had been their constant companion was hovering just ahead of Toki.

Not wanting to be left behind, Yara reluctantly turned away from the water and began to follow them. She knew she needed to watch very carefully where she put her feet, for the bog might look solid, but it was not. The floating vegetation, which made up the bog, was deceptive. Some places felt very solid, and the bog underfoot sank only an inch or two when stepped on. Other places could look just as solid, and then quite abruptly yield beneath one's foot, so one would find oneself sunk up to one's knee or beyond.

Having no better plan, Yara continued to follow the two ahead of her farther and farther into the bog. The farther they moved away from the waterway where they had been dropped off, the denser the haze became, transforming into a patchy, misty fog. At times, the way was almost clear, and at other times, Yara could hardly see several feet in front of her.

Yara began to wonder how anyone could survive in the bog, for she was afraid to stop for very long and afraid to sit down. The wisp and Toki had been leading her along an animal trail, but Toki weighed considerably less than Yara. After several hours of carefully placing one foot in front of the other, and testing each new place she was about to step with her walking stick to make sure she would not sink, Yara's legs were beginning to tire. Just as Yara began to question the wisdom of her choice to try to find one lone woman in a mist-shrouded bog, she found herself stepping under the low hanging branch of a tree, which provided some shelter, and to her surprise, also provided solid footing. To make sure, Yara tapped the walking stick she had been using on the vegetation under the tree, and it did not sink in.

"I think we need to stop here for a few moments," Yara stated, addressing the fox and the wisp. "I need to catch my breath, get a sip of water, and give my legs a rest."

Toki sat down abruptly on his haunches and began vigorously scratching his neck with his hind leg. The will-o'-wisp settled on a nearby branch, its pale green light dimming to almost nothing. If Yara had not noticed where it had come to settle, she would have thought it was gone.

While Yara was grateful to be able to sit for a moment and rest, the general uneasiness she had been feeling over the last few hours did not ease at all. In fact, it began to increase. The patchy fog had begun to gather and thicken around her, so she again could no longer see very far in front of her. She became aware of sounds she had not noticed before. The slight breeze rustling the branches in the trees was certainly not very threatening. Skittering and slithering sounds were another matter.

Chapter Forty

As Yara stood quietly listening, she became aware that Toki had also stilled and looked to be listening, too. Her imagination, she knew, was beginning to work overtime, conjuring up all sorts of dangers. Shaking herself, Yara took a step forward, and then another. When nothing horrible slithered or stalked out of the fog, she moved forward some more. The wisp had taken up the lead once again, and so she and Toki followed. Yara did wonder at the wisdom of following the pale green light, but she had nothing else to direct her as to where she would find Russhell.

Yara kept a careful eye out for anything that could indicate that a woman alone, or a woman with a skulk of red bog foxes, had been where Yara was walking, but she could see no signs. While she had read books about folks who could track anything anywhere using only the smallest of clues, Yara had no practical experience, so the knowledge was of little help. Even if she found a broken branch or a squashed pitcher plant, she had no way of knowing what had caused the damage. She could just as well be following a deer path, which she most likely was. What she did not know was if Russhell had walked the path before her.

As the day wore on, the more tired Yara became. She was determined that if she found a solid piece of ground, she was going to stop for the day. Yara knew she could not continue to wander the bog after the sun went down. It was much too dangerous. She would not be able to see where to put her feet, and she had no intention of accidentally ending up in a watery hole.

Yara was beginning to feel desperate as the sun sank lower and lower in the sky. Just as the last rays of light hovered on the horizon, she spotted a grove of trees ahead and quickened her pace. Fortunately, the grove was in the direction both Toki and the wisp were heading. Yara did not know what either would do if she veered away from the direction they had been leading her. It was deep dusk when she arrived at the first tree in the grove, only to discover to her dismay that the ground beneath her feet was not solid. Cautiously walking a bit farther into the grove, she halted abruptly when she saw the glow of the wisp reflecting off water.

The wisp veered to Yara's left, and Toki followed. Unless Yara wanted to spend the night alone with her feet slowly sinking in the spongy bog, she needed to follow them. The two ahead did not go far. It took Yara a little while to pick her way cautiously to where they were. Upon arriving, she was surprised when the darkness around her slowly began to lighten. It took her a moment to realize that the wisp she had been following had been joined by others. In the pale light, she could make out what looked like a low stone wall. As she came closer, she realized what she had thought was a wall was really just one side of a stone platform. Three shallow steps led up to the top.

Yara warily climbed the steps, for she was not sure what to make of finding a stone platform in the bog. Who had built it, and for what reason? Had it been the floor for a wood or reed cottage that had long ago fallen down and rotted away? Had it been built by bog dwellers to provide a solid place to spend the night, Yara wondered, or was it a trap of some sort to beckon in the weary traveler? Yara realized that she really had only two choices. Either she continued to wander around the bog in the dark, or she could take advantage of the only solid ground she had set foot on since midafternoon. She opted for the platform.

When Yara awoke to the early dawn light, she was surprised she had slept so well, despite the hardness of the platform and the dampness of the air. The night before, as she had been sharing her dinner with Toki, she had begun to relax and had felt calm and safe, for reasons she could not explain. That same feeling lingered as she stretched and climbed out of her sleeping roll. Gathering her cloak around her, for the misty morning air held a touch of chill, she was able to take a good look at where Toki and the wisp had led her the night before. She was standing on a platform that was set squarely in the middle of a clearing surrounded by trees.

Taking a good look at the platform on which she stood, Yara marveled at the craftsmanship. The platform top was made up of stones carefully placed in a beautiful spiral pattern. The stones were placed so closely together that Yara did not think she could have stuck a thin knife blade between them. When she stepped down off the platform, Yara saw that the sides of the platform were built of flat stones that fit together so well that they did not need mortar.

Yara was abruptly brought out of her musings by a sharp bark from Toki. She looked up to see a number of red bog foxes glide into the clearing and ring the platform she had scrambled back up on. While it was disconcerting to have at least a half dozen red bog foxes staring up at her, they did not advance, nor make any threatening moves. They sat on their haunches watching Toki and her with an air of waiting expectancy. Before Yara could make up her mind as to whether she was going to stay on the platform or try to walk down the steps past the foxes and out of the clearing, all of the foxes stood up.

Yara looked up to see a woman striding toward her. She was surprised at the appearance of the woman, who had now stopped no more than fifteen feet away. She was much younger than the silver white hair suggested. While not overly tall, she had a commanding presence. Her clothing was strange, for it was not made of any material Yara had ever seen before. It took her a moment to realize that it was made out of finely split and woven reeds. Yara did not take much time to study the garment further, other than to admire the artistry, for her eyes were drawn to the short bow the woman was holding, and the arrow notched and ready.

Holding out her arms, hands outward and palms up, Yara addressed the woman. "I mean no harm to you and yours. I apologize if I have trespassed. I have come looking for the woman the Venn call Russhell. I think we are kin."

Several things happened all at once. At the sound of Yara's voice, the foxes quickly withdrew from around the platform and drew in close to the woman. The woman raised her bow, aiming it toward Yara. Toki stepped in front of Yara and screamed, causing Yara to jump, for she had never heard such a sound out of Toki before. The woman drew back her bow string. Yara prepared to drop to the platform. Suddenly, the space between Yara and the woman was filled with blinding pale green light.

The stranger returned to Nathair's boat promptly at noon, as he had promised. Up until the moment the man stepped aboard, Nathair had not been sure what his answer to the man was going to be.

"Well, lad, are you going to try to do this on your own, or are you going to join forces?"

"Join forces," Nathair said reluctantly. If this man knew the whereabouts of the last of the Karmorises in this region, he had more information than Nathair did at the moment. Nathair had weighed that information against what he had learned about venturing into the area overseen by the Venn. He decided taking his chances with one stranger was a better decision than trying to find his way through the salt marshes, bogs, and swamps of Muggen Myr alone, with little or no hope of discovering where those he had been following had gone.

"Excellent choice. We'll take your boat, then," the man said, as he reached down and picked up the sea bag he had dropped at his feet. "Are you ready to set sail?"

No, Nathair thought, I am not ready to set sail with a stranger I do not know or trust, but he did not say that out loud. Instead, he just nodded his head and began to hoist the sail.

They were soon underway. The wind was brisk, and the stranger seemed to know his way around boats. Once they were out of the harbor and had set the course south, Nathair began to ask some questions.

"What should I call you?" Nathair asked.

"Ah, how absolutely rude of me not to have introduced myself. I am called Bertok by some. You may do the same."

It took a minute for Nathair to really think through what the man had said. He was called Bertok by some. Did that mean he had other names, or was called something else by others? Nathair didn't have time to dwell on that thought, for the wind had quickened and was shifting directions. He needed to concentrate on his sailing, and so he put the thought of the stranger's name on the back burner. He thought he had heard the name before, but he just could not put his finger on where.

"Where are we heading?"

"Farlig Brygge."

At the mention of Farlig Brygge, Nathair began to regret his decision. He might have been better off taking his chances in the salt marsh. Farlig Brygge harbor had the reputation of being a place where one did not want to venture, unless forced to do so due to very, very bad weather.

"Is that going to be a problem for you?" Bertok inquired.

"N-n-no," Nathair stuttered.

"Worried about your boat once we dock there?"

"I have heard tales . . . ." Nathair replied.

"Not to worry. I have friends there who will make sure it remains tied up at the dock, and not stripped of everything valuable or not valuable, if you get my meaning."

That statement only added to Nathair's worries, for he was concerned about the fact that the man he had joined forces with would have friends who held enough power in a place such as Farlig Brygge to guarantee the safety of his boat. Just who was this man?

The trip took a bit longer than anticipated because of a number of squalls, which had sent them tucking into coves or dropping anchor on the lee side of islands. If they had tried to sail during those brief but dangerous squalls, it could have torn their sails to shreds.

His traveling companion had not inspired either trust or camaraderie on their journey, having been silent for the most part. Once again, Nathair began to question his choice of going with Bertok, for the looks of Farlig Brygg's docks caused Nathair to feel even more unease than he had felt over the last few days. The wood was weathered and barnacle encrusted, the buildings next to the dock looked tumbled down and in disrepair. The town stretched up the low hill away from the dock, exuding a feeling of gloom and desperation. The darkness of the clouds overhead added to the feeling of desolation. The good changes wrought by the interim ruling council did not appear to have reached this far south.

Once they had tied up at the town wharf, furled the sails, and coiled all the lines, Bertok turned to Nathair and said, "You need to go below and lock yourself in. I need to make some contacts to assure that your boat is still here when we get back. Don't let anyone in, no matter what they tell you. Do you understand?"

Nathair answered in the affirmative, more than willing to lock himself in the cabin and not come out at all. Descending the short ladder down to the cabin, Nathair settled himself on his bunk and ate a cold meal. Unfortunately, during the ensuing hours while he waited for Bertok to return, his imagination began to work overtime. Just what had he gotten himself into? Had he made the right decision to go with Bertok? What if something happened to Bertok, leaving him here alone, wondered Nathair.

The hours seemed to drag on and on. When Nathair looked out the cabin porthole, he noticed a heavy fog had drifted in, and he could see no more than three feet beyond the boat. Anything or anyone could be out there creeping up on the boat, he thought, which made him feel even more frightened and less secure than he had been feeling. He would have liked to be able to pace to work off some of his nervous energy, but the cabin offered very little room. There was nothing to be done but to lie down and try to sleep.

Crawling into his bunk, Nathair lay there, listening to the sounds of the night, trying to relax. He could hear the boat gently knocking against the wharf. There were the sounds of the waves lapping against the boat and the creak of wood. Nathair heard the occasional call of a seabird. Other sounds were muffled by the fog, and it was hard to tell what direction they were coming from. Finally, Nathair drifted off to sleep.

In what only seemed like minutes, Nathair awoke and sat straight up. He was not sure what had awakened him. He tried to still his harsh breathing and listen over the sound of his heart beating rapidly. At first, he heard nothing but the noises he expected to hear. Straining, he listened even more intently. No, he was not mistaken. Someone was quietly walking on the deck above him.

Chapter Forty-One

Yara quickly closed her eyes against the blinding bright pale green light, and as an extra added precaution, dropped to the floor of the platform. No sense in taking chances when someone is aiming an arrow at one, she thought to herself, as she tried to make herself as flat as possible. The bright pale green light was beginning to fade a bit, and while Yara still had spots before her eyes from the initial flash, she knew she needed to get herself off the platform. Sliding herself backward, she quickly made it to the edge of the platform, when it occurred to her that if she slid down off the platform that might provide some shelter from an arrow, but it placed her on ground level with a skulk of foxes. Neither the prospect of being shot by an arrow or gnawed on by foxes was appealing.

As the spots before her eyes began to dim, Yara chanced a glance at where she had last seen the woman with the bow and really took a good look at her. The woman did not fit the description of her relative Russhell. Yara should have realized that earlier. Russhell had been described as having fox red hair, thus her name. The woman before her had hair the color of spun silver. Yara also noticed that the woman had lowered her bow.

"Who are you that the blekbrann would protect you?" the woman holding the bow asked.

"Blekbrann? Oh, do you mean the will-o'-wisps? I'm Yara, and I can't explain what just happened."

"Only the ignorant, or the Venn, call them wisps. The Venn have never understood the blekbrann," the woman retorted in disgust. "But that is neither here nor there. I have never seen the blekbrann do what they just did. I have never even heard of it happening. This will take some thinking on, and by folk wiser than me. Another question then. Why are you here in the Tåkete bog?"

"I have come looking for the woman the Venn call Russhell. I think she is my long lost kin." Yara could see no reason not to tell the woman what she was doing in the bog.

"Are you from those ignorant folks of Sivkurv, come to ease your conscience that you abandoned your kin to the bog? You want to make sure she has survived?" the woman asked Yara.

Yara could hear the anger in the woman's voice.

"I'm not from the village of Sivkurv. I've come from the capital. The Venn told me the sad tale of the woman they call Russhell, who, as I said, I believe is kin. I'm trying to find her."

"You are from the capital, you say."

"Yes."

"Just recently come to Muggen Myr?"

"Yes," Yara answered, wondering where this questioning was going.

"How then did you capture a red bog fox?"

"I didn't capture him," Yara said, and then went on to explain how she had come to have a red bog fox accompanying her. "And before you ask, no, I did not bring this fox back to Muggen Myr so he could return home. I didn't even know Muggen Myr was the home to bog foxes. For that matter I didn't even know Toki was a bog fox. And again, before you ask, he is free to leave my company any time he chooses, but so far he has chosen to stay with me. Now, I have a question for you. Am I still in danger of being shot?"

"My apologies, no, you are no longer in danger of being shot. We are a small group of folk that live here in the Tåkete bog, and very cautious. It's easy for folks to get lost, or in trouble here, as I suspect you are aware. In addition, at times, some very unsavory folk have tried to hide out in the bog, and that has caused no end of trouble for us. Please come with me. I will take you to Russhell."

"Just out of curiosity, what changed your mind?"

"The blekbrann. I have never seen them do what they did moments ago. In fact, I have never seen so many in one place before. We honor the blekbrann here, and you seem to be under their protection. I have never seen the like, nor heard of that happening. Others wiser than I may be able to explain it. Perhaps introductions are in order. My name is Terentia. And yours?"

"As I said, I am Yara, and I call the fox Toki, short for Tokala. Do the foxes with you have names?"

"Yes," Terentia said, but did not elaborate. After introductions, Terentia had said nothing more, and so they traveled farther and farther into the Tåkete bog in silence.

As they walked, Yara had time to reflect that for someone who had spent a rather quiet life so far, and would be considered very cautious and sensible, she had certainly been following others willy-nilly, which was so unlike her.

Midday, Terentia veered off the path they had been following onto a side path, which led to a small grove of trees. In the center was a platform similar to the one where Yara had spent the night. Yara was more than ready to stop moving for a while. Her guide had held to a quick and steady pace all morning.

"Are these platforms scattered throughout the Tåkete bog?" Yara asked.

"Yes."

"Did your folk build them?"

"No."

"No?"

"No." Terentia seemed to unbend a little and went on. "These platforms have been here for time out of mind. No one knows who built them. As you will see once we reach our destination, there was once a village in the very center of the bog. We will rest here for a short while, and then continue on."

As they sat in silence, Yara reflected back on what she had learned when researching the rolls. She had thought she had searched through all of the areas of Muggen Myr looking for her relatives, but she did not recall that there were any folk listed as living in the Tåkete bog. She began to second guess her decision to follow Terentia. Were she and her folk not in the rolls because no one had taken the time and effort to track them down, or had they somehow eluded the rolls taker? Why had there been no record of Terentia's folk? Before she could figure out a way to ask, or even if she should ask, Terentia had stood and indicated it was time to move on.

By the time they stopped for the night, Yara had another concern, which she voiced once the spare and cold meal was done.

"The woman I'm looking for, Russhell, will she be at your village?"

"I do not know the answer to that, but someone there will know where she is. We know she needs to come and go as she pleases, but we do keep track of her, in case she has need of us."

That seemed like an odd statement, but before Yara could question further, Terentia indicated she was going to turn in for the night. Terentia's foxes had returned at this point from their hunting and had joined them on the platform, forming a protective ring around the edges.

Yara was relieved that Toki, who had gone off with the skulk, had returned also, and was now cozied up next to her. The wisps, or what Terentia referred to as the blekbrann, were still with them, but not in as great a number as earlier. The one who had been her companion since leaving the Venn, or at least she thought it was the same one, hovered just above her still, though its light was damped way down.

The fog grew thicker and thicker the next day. It had started as a ground fog, but as the day progressed, rather than dissipating, the fog had grown more and more dense and risen higher. By midafternoon, Yara was hard pressed to see Terentia ahead of her. At times, all she was following was the wisp. As she picked her way along, Yara became aware of the sound of water lapping against something. She almost ran into Terentia, who had stopped ahead of her. A slight break in the fog showed Yara that she was just several feet away from a river or a lake, she could not tell which.

"Wait here. I will signal the watch that we are here."

Signal the watch? That did not sound good, Yara thought. Why would they need a watch? She soon found out, when Terentia returned and led her along the shoreline until they came to a ferry landing, but not a ferry landing like she had ever seen before. There was a substantial gate blocking the stone landing. At first, Yara did not think a gate would keep folks from getting on the ferry, until Terentia cautioned her to be careful to not fall off the stone landing. She had told Yara that the bog on either side of the landing was very unstable, and could swallow a person whole in a matter of moments. Yara was not sure if Terentia was telling the truth or just trying to frighten her, but she decided not to test it out.

Yara did not know how they were going to find their way in the fog, but the folks poling the ferry did not appear worried at all. She began to notice that the fog was beginning to thin within minutes of leaving the ferry landing. She could see that they were traveling across a fairly wide body of water, but she was not sure if it was a river or a lake. Yara could see the landing on the opposite shore. The land was grassy and flat for a while, and then turned to forest. The forested land sloped up, and Yara could see bluffs in the distance.

"Is it an island then, where we are headed?" Yara asked.

"No," Terentia answered, but did not elaborate.

As the ferry continued to move across the water, Yara was aware that the four folks poling the ferry were giving her more than cursory glances. Or maybe they are just checking out Toki, she thought to herself, for Toki had chosen not to stand with the rest of the foxes, but with her. Or maybe, it is not usual for a stranger to be accompanied by a blekbrann. Whatever the reason, they continued to surreptitiously glance her way, and it was making her feel uncomfortable. It was a relief to finally reach the other shore and step off the ferry. It took Yara a moment to realize she was standing on solid ground. At least her feet were on solid ground, she thought, if not her being here among strangers.

Terentia beckoned Yara to follow her. "We are about a half day walk from home," she had told Yara.

The flat grassy land was an easy walk on a well-worn path. Once they reached the trees, the air around them cooled considerably. The path through the woods was also well established and easy walking, though as they moved higher and higher, the path became rockier. Finally, toward late afternoon, they came out of the trees onto a flat open expanse, which had the look of land that had long been farmed and grazed. In the distance, Yara could see a bluff. After crossing a field of what had once been a grain crop that had been recently harvested, they came to a lane that they followed to the bluff. As they came closer and closer to the bluff, Yara began to realize that the houses she had been seeing from a distance were actually built into the side of the bluff.

When they arrived at what on closer examination was a small village, Yara saw that a number of folks had gathered and were waiting for them. They did not look happy.

"Terentia, what is this? You have brought a stranger to our homes," an austere older woman scolded Terentia.

"This lass claims to be long lost kin to the one the Venn call Russhell. She has come looking for her."

"Come to ease your conscience, are you now? Well, we will not have that poor lass subjected to any more harm by you from Sivkurv. Haven't you done enough? Set her off in the bog because of ignorant fear. Do you really think she is going to be glad to see you? Are you going to take her home? No, you aren't, are you? Get her out of my sight," the woman said, and those around her nodded their heads in agreement.

"Ah, Bidelia, she is not from Russhell's village. She says she is from the capital."

Before Bidelia could remark on what Terentia had just said, a small lad broke through the throng that had now surrounded Yara, Terentia, and Toki. Terentia's foxes had disappeared when they had been walking through the woods, but Toki had stayed with Yara.

"Did you bring a new fox home, Auntie Terentia? Did you bring him for me?" the young lad asked.

"No, nephew, the fox chooses to travel with this lass."

The look of disappointment on the lad's face would have been comic under other circumstances, but gained him little notice, for the group had once again turned toward Yara.

"I say seize her and march her right back to the ferry," said a large burly man, who had been standing back in the group, as he pushed his way forward, heading directly toward Yara.

"I would strongly advise against that action, Uncle," Terentia advised, "because . . . ."

Suddenly, a wall of bright pale green light formed around Yara and Toki.

Chapter Forty-Two

Nathair reached under his pillow and grabbed the knife he had put there before he had settled in for the night. Whoever was walking quietly on the deck was heading straight for the hatch that led down to where he was sitting stiff and still.

"Nathair, open the hatch cover, and quickly."

Nathair could hear the urgency in Bertok's voice. He scrambled off his bunk and swiftly climbed the short steps to the hatch cover. The moment he opened the lock, several things happened. The hatch cover was snatched open, Nathair was snatched up, and Bertok propelled Nathair down the ladder. Bertok then turned and swiftly secured the hatch cover.

"You need to be still and very, very quiet if you hope to live through the rest of the night," Bertok admonished.

"What . . . ."

"Sh-h-h!"

The two stood still listening. They could hear men shouting to each other, but their words were muffled. At one point they heard someone come aboard, walk across the deck, try the hatch cover, and then disembark. Finally, a quiet descended on the area.

"We need to get out of this harbor as fast as we can," Bertok whispered.

"Won't someone setting sail in the middle of the night be a little noticeable?" Nathair whispered back, with more than a tinge of sarcasm in his voice. "If the night is clear, if anyone is watching, they are certainly going to notice."

"A thick fog has moved in, and there is a heavy cloud cover."

"Just how do you expect us to sail out of here in a thick fog on a dark, dark night?"

"I don't expect us to sail out of here, I expect us to row," Bertok answered.

"I am not leaving my boat behind, and besides, just how far do you think we are going to get on the open sea in a rowboat?"

"I'm sorry, let me clarify. We are going to row out of here, pulling your boat. We are going to borrow a rowboat, row like crazy, pulling your sailboat behind us."

"In a heavy fog, on a densely cloud-covered night?"

"That's the plan. Do you have a problem with that?"

"Oh, let me think a moment. Well, yes, I have a number of problems with the plan. First would be theft, as in 'borrowing' a rowboat. Then again, there is the problem of trying to navigate ourselves out of the harbor without running aground, rowing in circles until dawn, or hitting large objects such as wharfs, and other boats. Also, there is the little fact that once, and if, we reach the open sea, we still have to navigate our way through the reefs. Other than that, I can see no problem," Nathair replied.

"Oh ye of little faith. The rowboat in question comes with another rower who knows this harbor like the back of her hand. So that takes care of one of your objections. Secondly, we will only be borrowing the rowboat, for my friend will return it after we have used it. As for navigating through the reefs, the light towers are set high enough that we should be able to see them, once out of the harbor, for the fog is a low one tonight, according to my friend. Any more questions?"

"Yes. What if I don't want to leave? After all, I've not gotten to where I want to go, and haven't gotten the information I came to find."

"I'm afraid the alternative to leaving is going to be very painful for both of us, for there are folks here who are not so happy that I'm in the area. Wait, before you raise more questions or objections, I have the information you need, and going on to the village of Sivkurv is only going to be a waste of time." Bertok became very still for a moment, listening. When he heard the two sharp raps against the side of the boat, he began moving toward the hatch. Turning back to Nathair, he said, "Grab your foul weather gear, for that fog is very damp, and come topside. There is no time to lose."

Nathair was directed to climb into the rowboat that had drawn alongside his boat. He reluctantly did as he had been told. He had been directed to move to the bow of the rowboat, ahead of the folk who had brought it alongside. She was in the stern seat, holding the tiller. He could not get a very good look at her, for her hood was pulled up, which left her face in shadows. Bertok, meanwhile, cast off the lines, and then nimbly climbed aboard the rowboat, settling in the middle seat. Rowing their way to the bow of Nathair's boat, the woman at the stern snagged the bow painter and tied it to the stern of the rowboat.

For a moment, it seemed as if they would not be able to get enough momentum to pull Nathair's boat away from the dock, much less out of the harbor. Once they really put their collective backs into the process, the sailboat began to move. While the progress was slow, they moved at a steady pace. Both Nathair and Bertok were trying to row as quietly as possible, and fortunately for them, if they did make a noise, the fog muffled most of it.

Nathair had not been convinced that anyone, no matter how well they knew the harbor, would be able to get them to the open sea in the fog. The longer they rowed, the more confident he became that they might make it. Finally, he was given the signal to stop rowing and had a chance to really look around. The fog, he noticed, was a bit thinner where they were, and he could see the glow of the signal lights in the two towers flanking the harbor.

"You are now beyond the mouth of the harbor. The way to get safely through the reef is for one of you to sail and the other one to watch your stern. You need to stay squarely between the two tower lights. I will leave you here."

"You're sure you'll be safe, my friend?" asked Bertok.

"Not to worry. This old rowboat is going to drift into the harbor on the tide. Just give me a moment to untie my reed boat from the stern of the sailboat. I'll be long gone in my reed boat into the salt marsh before those who were overly interested in either of us notice we are no longer in Farlig Brygge. Safe sailing, my friend."

"Be safe yourself. Thanks for your help."

"Me and mine will always be there for you."

"Once again, I am indebted to you."

"There is no debt." When Bertok started to object, she went on, "We will argue about it another time. Again, safe sailing. You had best get moving, for the tide is turning."

"One can only hope," Bertok replied cryptically.

Yara stood perfectly still within the circular wall of pale green light. She wondered why she did not feel frightened, but all she felt was an overwhelming sense of calm and peace, as if nothing bad could happen to her. Slowly the light began to fade, but still Yara did not feel afraid. In the lingering light, Yara could see that the villagers who had gathered had taken about ten steps back. The looks on their faces, even the look on the face of the burly man who had been moving aggressively toward her, had changed. Now, there were looks of confusion.

"As I was saying, Uncle, it's best not to threaten Yara. For some reason, which I certainly can't explain, she is under the protection of the blekbrann. Ah, Mother, I was hoping you were here. Maybe you can explain what is going on."

"My apologies for our less than warm welcome. I am Narada, Terentia's mother and head of our village. Perhaps we can start over again and try a civil greeting to our guest here," Narada suggested, giving an especially pointed look toward Terentia's uncle. "Perchance we could put on our more civil faces and discuss what just happened over tea." Turning to the woman who had confronted Yara, Narada said, "I know you are only trying to protect Russhell from more hurt, but give this one who the blekbrann have chosen to safeguard a chance. Come, Bidelia," Narada said, placing her arm around the woman, "let us go set the kettle on and get to the bottom of what is going on. Come along, all of you, to the meeting room."

Though there were still mutterings and whispers among the group, they all followed Narada's request, Yara and Toki included. It was a short walk up to the huge doorway that led into one of the buildings built out from the bluff. The doors were ornately carved, but Yara was not allowed to linger long enough to study them. What she did notice was that the doors could be closed and barred on the inside, making it very difficult for anyone to get in.

Once inside, it was clear to Yara that the room she had entered only served as a large foyer to another set of very sturdy doors, these a bit smaller and very plain. She noticed they were doubly thick and reinforced with metal bands. These too could be closed and barred from the inside. Why did these folks have need of such sturdy doors, Yara wondered. Who did they want to keep out? Yara was pulled out of her musings when she was invited to take a seat at one of the tables arranged on the side of the room.

Once everyone was settled, Narada turned to her daughter Terentia. "When the blekbrann formed a protective circle around Yara, you did not flinch or react as one might expect. I take it you have seen this happen before."

"Yes, Mother, when I made a threatening gesture toward Yara . . . ." Terentia's mother cocked an inquiring eyebrow. "She was a stranger who had spent the night on one of the platforms. She was asking about Russhell. I jumped to conclusions," Terentia replied ruefully, raising her shoulders and holding her hands out palms up in a 'what can I say' type of gesture.

"There seems to be a lot of conclusion jumping," Narada suggested, giving a hard glance at her brother and Bidelia. "Now, Yara, tell us why you are looking for your long lost relative."

Yara and Eluta had discussed what Yara should say if she were asked why she was looking for her long lost relative. Eluta had cautioned her to stick as close to the truth as possible.

"Several generations ago, my family, the Karmorises, were a strong trading family. Something happened, and each branch of the family went their separate way. Nothing good seemed to happen after that to the family fortunes. Recently a journal arrived at the royal library where I work, which shed some light on what happened. It made me curious, so I set off to find out what might really have transpired. I spent hours and hours in the rolls, looking for what had happened to the journal writer's branch of the Karmoris family, and that led me here."

Narada was not the only one who gave Yara a skeptical look.

"So, you just left your work at the library and set off alone to find this lost branch of your family," Narada asked.

In for a copper, in for a silver, Yara thought to herself. "Well, actually I set off with the head of the royal library. Seems she had gotten itchy feet and had decided to go on a walkabout. Her sister asked if I would accompany her, to keep an eye on her. Seemed she had no clear direction she wanted to go, so I suggested we start our adventure by looking for my lost relative. She agreed."

"And just where is this royal librarian now?" Bidelia asked.

"She is at the residence of the Venn named Marleigh. Marleigh suggested, and the royal librarian named Eluta agreed, that it might be better if just one of us tried to approach Russhell. Eluta was very tired after our travels in the salt marsh and was looking forward to resting and studying."

"Marleigh, did you say?" Narada asked.

"Yes."

"Hum-m-m. Interesting. Go on."

"That's about it. I was dropped off on your border where the Venn had last spotted Russhell and . . ." Here Yara paused. ". . . and then, I followed one of the wisps, ah, one of the ones you call blekbrann."

"Why would you follow a blekbrann?" Bidelia demanded.

"They led us to shelter before a storm when we were caught out in the open in the salt marsh. One of them has been with me ever since. As I had no better guide, I just kept following it and Toki. I think I would have angered the blekbrann if I had tried to wander off on my own. Just a feeling I had. I also think it might have been leading me here, for it did not object to my following Terentia."

"Fascinating," Narada remarked. "Rumors have been filtering our way that the Neebing blessed are abroad, that change is in the wind. This protection of one by the blekbrann has not been heard of for generations, but it has occurred before. It was back when . . . ."

Narada was interrupted when a young lad entered the foyer. "Elder Narada, you need to come right away. It's Russhell."

Chapter Forty-Three

The urgency in the young lad's voice had everyone turning toward him. He repeated his request. Narada stood abruptly and headed toward the door. Others stood and followed. Upon reaching the door, Narada turned and motioned that Yara should come along, too.

Yara did not know what she had expected since Marleigh had told her that Russhell had been affected by the swamp fever. Standing amid at least two dozen red bog foxes of all sizes and ages, was a young woman. At first glance, she looked just like the other folk who lived in the Tåkete bog. She was dressed as the others were, but there was something very different about her. Not her physical appearance, but there was something, Yara thought. She wished she could put her finger on just what it was. Maybe it was the faraway look on Russhell's face, as if she were seeing a different world than the rest of them.

As Yara tried to take in what she was seeing, Toki slipped by her and cautiously approached the other foxes. Worried that he would be hurt, Yara began to take a step forward, but Terentia put a restraining hand on her shoulder.

"Your fox will be alright. You, however, would not be, if you tried to approach them."

"Why?" Yara questioned.

"For some reason, foxes gather around Russhell, but never before in this number. I wonder what has caused this gathering? The group I travel with is mingled in with the ones who are always with Russhell. There are several other skulks here, too. Ah, look."

Yara watched as a pair of foxes moved away from the others and approached Toki. After what seemed an excessive amount of sniffing of each other, one of the foxes made a sharp bark, and two other foxes about the same size as Toki broke away from the others. Soon, the three young foxes were wrestling and playing.

"It would seem that your Toki is indeed from here. Those two adult foxes standing by and watching the three playing are part of those who travel with Russhell. Coincidence? I wonder. This might complicate things."

"Why?"

"Russhell is both very attached to the foxes, and fiercely protective of them. She is bound to ask how Toki returned here. She might think you stole him and are now returning him. She will not welcome you with open arms as a long lost relative if that is the case."

"I have never expected to be welcomed with open arms as a long lost relative, since I don't know under what terms our ancestors parted, nor what family stories have been passed down over time. I can only hope she will let me tell how I came to be traveling with Toki before she dismisses me, or is angry with me. I hope she will listen to reason that I may have saved Toki's life."

Watching Toki wrestle and play with what must be his litter mates, Yara felt her heart break just a little bit. She realized that no matter the outcome of her meeting with Russhell, Toki would probably choose to stay with his family, now that he had been returned to them. She wondered briefly if she would have brought him along, had she known that she was bringing him back home. Yara dismissed that thought almost as soon as it formed, for she knew she was being very selfish.

Suddenly, several things happened at once. Russhell started toward Toki walking at a rapid pace, Terentia again gently restrained Yara when she started to move forward, and Toki broke away from his littermates and scampered back to Yara.

Russhell stopped walking forward, and there was a look of confusion and sadness on her face. Slowly, she sank to the ground, drawing her knees up to her chest, and began rocking back and forth. Tears began to stream down her cheeks.

"Oh, dear," Terentia murmured softly.

Yara, seeing the young woman in such distress, gently but firmly removed Terentia's hand where it still rested on her arm and began to walk forward toward Russhell, Toki at her side. When Terentia moved to stop her, Narada cautioned her to remain where she was.

A hush fell over the group gathered there. There was little sound other than that of the wind in the trees. Yara very slowly and cautiously approached Russhell. Toki walked alongside her, and the wisp, who had been Yara's constant companion, hovered just off her left shoulder.

When Yara got to within about four feet of Russhell and the gathering of foxes, she sat down cross legged on the ground. Toki sat down next to her. Yara did not speak, nor did she make any move. She just sat and waited. She could hear whispers behind her, and some movement, but still she did not move.

The foxes who had been surrounding Russhell soon began to drift away, until there were only six left. Yara thought that some of the foxes who were left might be Toki's family, but she could not be sure.

Not wanting to startle the young woman in front of her, Yara spoke softly. "I named the young fox who sits beside me Tokala, but I call him Toki. I found him in the alley behind my rooms in the capital. He had been cornered by several dogs. He was being very brave, but he was certainly outnumbered. I chased the dogs away. Toki was not in very good shape. He looked like he needed food and a safe place, so I took him and hid him in the royal librarian's garden."

As she spoke, Yara noticed that Russhell had stopped rocking, and her tears were less. She decided to continue to speak. Using her most soothing tones, Yara said, "Toki is free to come and go as he pleases, for I know he is a wild animal and should never be caged. Before I came to Muggen Myr, I didn't even know he came from here. I thought he was just a young fox who had somehow found his way into the capital. Right now, he seems to want to stay in my company just as yours seem to want to stay in yours. I would not hold him if he wanted to return to his family."

Something in Yara's quiet words must have gotten through to the distraught woman, for she looked up and held Yara's gaze for the longest moment before she reached out to Toki. Toki remained seated by Yara's side.

In a voice barely above a whisper, Russhell asked, "How can I trust you who command one of the blekbrann? You must also be commanding the one you call Toki."

"Ah, I can see where you might think such a thing, but rather I think it is the blekbrann who command me, for they have led me here," Yara said, with a slight chuckle in her voice.

"But I saw them surround you, protect you."

"While I am extremely grateful that they have come to my aid, not once but twice, the choice has been solely theirs. Before I came here, I had never even heard of the blekbrann, or seen one. I can't explain it. The point here is I don't command Toki any more than I could command the wind. I came here to Muggen Myr looking not to return Toki, but to find you."

Russhell looked both startled and afraid. She began to stand up and looked ready to flee.

"Wait," Yara said in the same soft voice. "Please, don't go. I mean you no harm." What had those villagers of Sivkurv done to this young woman that made her so terrified? "I have come looking for you, for it would seem we are very distant cousins. I, too, am a Karmoris."

"You are kin?"

"I think so, but only distantly."

"All of my family are gone, all gone, all gone . . . ." Russhell murmured, as she once again curled in on herself and began rocking.

"I am so sorry," Yara said softly, hoping she had not caused Russhell pain.

Yara also hoped Russhell would not withdraw completely into herself, or that the folks standing behind her would think she had hurt Russhell. It would not do to have one or more of the villagers step forward and try to move either of them away. Glancing over her shoulder, Yara asked the folks behind her to please wait, to give her a little more time, for she saw that several of them were inching forward, about to intervene.

Turning back to Russhell, Yara said again in a soft voice, "I am so, so very sorry. You lost your family and your home all at once. You lost all who were and all that was familiar."

Something in Yara's sympathetic voice must have gotten through to Russhell, for she stopped rocking and looked up.

"I have something still. The foxes know," Russhell stated in a whisper. "The foxes know, the foxes know," Russhell continued to say over and over in a sing song voice.

Yara felt like she was losing Russhell's attention, so she asked Russhell what the foxes knew.

"Can't tell, no, can't never tell," Russhell murmured, and began rocking once again.

Yara became aware of a commotion going on behind her, which had become less quiet and more heated while she sat there. Finally, she heard Narada speak quite authoritatively, telling the rest of the villagers to go about their business. She assured them she would watch over both Russhell and Yara. Terentia's uncle and Bidelia protested the loudest, but eventually gave in. Soon a silence fell over the area, but Yara could still feel folks watching. She gave a startled jump when a hand touched her shoulder.

"I think it would be best if we moved away from prying eyes," Narada suggested to Yara. Turning to Russhell, Narada urged the young woman to get up and come and have some tea. Russhell complied.

As Yara followed Narada, she had to wonder what the folks she knew in the capital would think of the procession she was in. Here she was with two other folk, calmly walking along, completely surrounded by red bog foxes. The addition of a wisp hovering off her left shoulder only added to the strangeness.

Narada opened the door of her home and invited all to enter. Russhell had calmed down a bit and entered, followed by her foxes. Yara entered next, with Toki and the wisp, followed by Narada.

"Please make yourselves comfortable while I put the kettle on for tea."

Yara removed her pack and settled into a chair across from Russhell. It was not a comfortable silence between Yara and Russhell, as they waited for Narada to return. Russhell kept giving Yara furtive glances and looked ready to bolt at any minute. Yara could think of nothing to say or ask, for fear that she would upset Russhell once again.

"It seems as if I have run out of tea," Narada said as she walked back through the sitting room. "I'll be back in a little while. No, Russhell, you stay here with your cousin. It will be alright."

As Narada closed the door behind her, Russhell began to get to her feet, a panicked look on her face. Toki stood up from where he had settled and ran over to her. His action distracted her, and she crouched down to pay attention to Toki.

"Russhell, I'm not here to harm you. I just wanted to find you and talk to you," Yara said softly.

Russhell did not say anything. She kept running her hands over and over Toki's body, as if she was determined to make sure he had not been harmed. Toki was enjoying the attention so much that he flopped over on his back.

While Russhell continued to rub Toki's stomach, Yara noticed that the inside of the sitting room was getting brighter and brighter. It took her a moment to realize that there was more than one of the blekbrann in the room. As she watched, more and more of the pale green lights began drifting through the open windows into the room. None of Russhell's foxes paid them any mind, nor did Toki.

When Russhell finally looked up and noticed the ingathering of blekbrann, there was a startled look on her face. "Who are you, who are you, who are you?" she repeated over and over, as she sank once again into a small heap.

Before Yara could answer, the door banged open.

Chapter Forty-Four

Standing in the doorway was a young man, sides heaving, as he tried to catch his breath. He held onto the doorframe, steadying himself, trying to gain his composure. Once he had control over both his breath and his composure, he quietly walked across the sitting room and knelt beside Russhell, taking both of her hands in his.

"What did you do to her?" the young man demanded harshly, looking at Yara.

Yara felt her anger rise and had to tamp down a desire to stand and stomp her foot. "What is it with you folk, always accusing, always thinking the worst? I've done nothing to Russhell, other than to quietly and softly speak to her. However, ever since I have entered the Tåkete bog, I have been threatened with arrows and by words. You are the most unwelcoming and suspicious folk I have ever met. Even the Venn, which I take it you have little liking or use for, treated me better."

"You are right," stated Narada apologetically from the doorway. "We have not treated you well. I think we need to start over. First off, introductions are in order. The young man kneeling beside Russhell is my nephew Redding. He is very protective of Russhell, as you can clearly see. Redding, this is Yara. The fox with her is Toki, and . . ." Here Narada paused, for she had finally taken the time to really take in the sitting room. ". . . and it would seem we have a number of other guests."

Redding glanced up at his aunt with a questioning look in his eye, which changed to astonishment when he became aware of the number of blekbrann who had gathered in the room.

"Ah, Aunt, ah, um, are you referring to the blekbrann as our other guests?"

"That would seem appropriate, don't you think?" Narada answered.

"Why are so many here in your sitting room?" Redding questioned.

"That is a good question for which I have no answer, other than Yara seems to be the cause."

"The blekbrann are gathering around her. Surely that is cause for alarm."

"Only if you try to threaten her, I can assure you," Narada stated dryly, and there was a slight hint of amusement in her voice. "You should have seen your father's face when . . . but that is a story for another time. We are neglecting our guests. I was about to make some tea a while ago. The water should be hot now. Perhaps you could give me a hand, Yara? Redding, could you see if you can calm Russhell down and get her off the floor?"

Yara followed Narada into the kitchen area, and at Narada's direction, began to assemble mugs and spoons.

"I think if you know a little bit more about those who live here, you might think less poorly of us. My family has lived here for several generations. Many of the others who now live here are relative newcomers. For one reason or another, they found refuge here during the reign of Regent Cedric Klingflug. Because of their sometimes terrifying experiences outside the bog, many of those who live here now are very cautious of strangers, to say the least. They may not have started life as wary, suspicious folks, but time and circumstances have made them so. Like Russhell, they have not been treated well by others, and so often suspect the worst in folk they don't know."

"I just want a chance to talk to Russhell. I can only repeat that I have not come here to harm Russhell, or any of you here."

"I know that, lass. The blekbrann would not be so protective of you if that were not so. Come now, gather that tray and follow me."

For a while, the only sounds in the sitting room were the sounds of folks sipping hot tea, and the soft breathing of half a dozen sleeping foxes. Finally, Narada broke the silence.

"Russhell, are you feeling calmer now?"

Russhell answered yes, in a shaky whisper.

"This lass has come a very long way to find you."

"She is not from my village. Why would she come to find me?"

"You are related."

"How?"

Yara explained to all who were gathered in the sitting room that she and Russhell were distant cousins, and that the family had moved apart due to a number of misunderstandings a long time ago. Yara had explained that not one but two journals, written by two Karmoris cousins, had turned up at the royal library recently and explained part of what had caused a long ago rift in the family. It had made her curious, Yara had gone on to explain, and so when the opportunity had arisen for her to come here, she had taken it.

"I really would like a chance to talk with Russhell without angry uncles or doors slamming open. She seems so frightened, and just when I think we have become comfortable, something I say, or someone interfering, causes her to withdraw. I'm open to suggestions."

"You're not going to let her be alone with Russhell, are you, Aunt?" questioned Redding.

"I would suggest you look around you, nephew. Between over a half dozen foxes and several dozen blekbrann, the two would hardly be alone. But more importantly, we are forgetting one important consideration."

"What?" Redding asked.

"It's really up to Russhell to make her own choices. It really is not up to us, but up to her, as to whether she wishes to even talk to Yara. Russhell, do you wish to talk to this lass, who claims to be distant kin?"

"I will talk with her. I need to be outside," Russhell answered, as she rose and headed toward the door.

"Thank you for the tea and for your help," Yara said to Narada, as she too rose, grabbed her pack, and followed Russhell.

"Where would you be more comfortable?" Yara asked.

"I would go to the grove," Russhell answered. Not waiting for any response from Yara, Russhell turned right and headed east out of the village.

After an hour of walking, Yara began to doubt the wisdom of following Russhell. After all, Yara did not know the area, nor did she know the young woman she was following. Russhell could lead me anywhere, and then just abandon me, Yara thought to herself.

All the while, Russhell, Yara, Toki, the other foxes, and a gathering of blekbrann had been walking, they had been following the bluff. Suddenly, Russhell stopped, at what first appeared to Yara as a crack in the rock wall. Russhell squeezed through the crack followed by her foxes, Toki, and the blekbrann. Not wanting to be left alone, Yara followed.

Once through the crack, the passage widened out and was open to the sky high above. Straight ahead was a stairway carved out of the rock. Yara followed the others and began to climb. The stairs eventually came out at the top of the same bluff the Tåkete bog dwellers' homes were built into. The small plateau was covered with vegetable gardens and fruit trees. In the distance, Yara could see several folk who were bent over weeding and tending to the crops. Russhell, however, did not head in their direction, but instead continued toward a grove of trees. Yara followed.

The grove was made up of ancient quirrelit trees that had withstood time and the windswept storms that came off the sea. Once within the grove, Yara felt the tension and uneasiness of the last few days fall away. She also noticed that a feeling of peace settled over her. In addition, Yara noticed that Russhell looked less tense.

"There is a great feeling of peace in this grove," Yara said in a hushed voice.

"Yes, that's why I come here. I feel safe here."

"Are you afraid when you are in the Tåkete bog?" Yara inquired.

"Sometimes. It's not like where I grew up. The foxes, though, seem to like my company and warn me of danger."

"Are you afraid of those who live in the village below?"

"No, they have been kind. It's just the time right after the fever, when those who were of my village, those who had been friends with my family and me, turned away from me and threw me out to live or die in the bog. That was a very frightening time. The fog, being all alone, not knowing . . . I, I, I . . . ."

Yara started to reach out a hand in comfort, but then pulled it back, not knowing how Russhell would react. At least this time when broaching a subject, Russell had not folded in on herself and started rocking.

Thinking that changing the subject might prevent Russhell from withdrawing, Yara asked, "What else is it about the grove that you like?"

"Its age. These trees have stood over time. I wish they could talk," Russhell said wistfully.

"Do you think we could find a place to sit and talk?"

"Yes. There is a clearing within the grove and benches. We can sit there. It's just a little ways."

Yara was surprised when they entered the clearing to find that there were not just a few benches. Ahead of her was a small amphitheater with ornately carved stone seats. Like the grove of trees, the amphitheater had the feeling of great age. Despite the solemn gravity, the grove was one of great peace. Yara noticed two things. Russhell had visibly relaxed, and the blekbrann had settled on the lowest branch of one of the quirrelit trees. It struck Yara as somewhat strange that the blekbrann would all gather in one place, but before she could think further on that thought, Russhell brought her attention back with a question.

"What did the journals say?"

"I can only tell you what the royal librarian Eluta told me, for I have not read the journals myself. The one that was written by your ancestor suggested he had played a trick on one of my ancestors. It was a harmless and rather clever trick at the time," Yara quickly assured Russhell. "Our ancestor Laron had his feelings hurt when his father showed something to Laron's brother, but did not trust Laron with the knowledge. Laron then stole the item and hid it, meaning to return it, but for some reason was unable to do so. I didn't have a chance to read his journal nor find out what happened to him. Your ancestor Kinza somehow found out that Laron had something he had taken from his family, and where he had hidden it. Kinza then took the object from Laron's hiding place and left him a note with a clue to follow as to where to find the object. He had intended for Laron to end up finding him and then have a laugh over the whole thing. Since Laron's father didn't know Laron knew about the object, he thought my great-something great uncle, Laron's brother, had taken it, and blamed him. He said that my great-something great uncle had lost the family's luck."

Upon hearing what Yara had said, Russhell looked as if she were about to stand and bolt out of the grove. The foxes, sensing her agitation, stood and moved closer to her.

"Wait," Yara said softly. "I'm not here to blame you for something that happened a long, long time ago, nor am I mad at you for what our ancestors did. Please don't go. I just wanted to ask you if your family had any stories about a family heirloom, or tales about family luck."

Russhell settled back down, pulling her knees up to her chest and wrapping her arms around her legs. She was silent for several minutes.

"I know little of my family's history. I know we have always been traders, but I know very little else. My grandfather met my grandmother as a young man and settled in the village of Sivkurv after marrying her. She was an excellent weaver, and he was a very good trader. He would take the baskets and rugs that the villagers wove and get good trade for them. He trained my father to carry on the business after he was no longer able."

Russhell was very silent for a long while. Yara waited patiently for her to go on.

"Even though my family helped the others in the village to be successful, we never quite belonged, were never quite accepted. No matter that we had lived there a long time, we were still outsiders, never quite of the village. It didn't help that our family was a bit more prosperous. When the swamp fever hit and all of my family succumbed to it, a few of the villagers who had been most jealous of my family convinced the others that I was bad for the village. They just wanted what we had. The taxes, fees, and licenses the Regent imposed had taken most of the profit out of any sales we made from our baskets. Most of us didn't know from day to day if there would be food or other things we needed. Times were very bad. In addition, many of the villagers are very superstitious and began rumors that the swamp fever was my family's fault."

"You don't have to talk about that time if you don't want to," Yara said gently.

Russhell began to rock again slightly, and tears began to stream down her face. Abruptly, she stopped rocking and angrily wiped the tears from her face.

"I had no family left, and then they took what my family had built and threw me out. They didn't get everything, oh no, they didn't get everything. Hurt him it did, hurt him," Russhell stated with conviction and just a bit of satisfaction in her voice. "The foxes know." A feverish look came into Russhell's eyes as she drew up her knees and hugged herself close.

Yara was beginning to once again question the wisdom of following Russhell away from the village. Even though there were others on the plateau, Yara did not think they would hear her if she shouted, for they were too far away.

Suddenly, Russhell lunged to her feet, and the foxes that accompanied her rushed to her side.

Chapter Forty-Five

Yara became more than a bit concerned over the somewhat feverish appearance of Russhell. She was not sure which was worse, the terrified Russhell who closed in on herself, or the angry Russhell. Standing herself, she held out her hands in an appeal of peace.

"I'm sorry the Sivkurv villagers were so cruel and hurtful. I'm glad you survived. From what I saw in the village down below, there are many here who care for you and are very protective of you, especially Redding and his father."

Russhell blushed at the mention of Redding and reached down to pet the fox resting nearest to her.

"I won't leave here. Just because you are kin, I won't leave with you," Russhell declared.

"And I wouldn't want you to. As I said, it is very apparent to me that you have a home here among the villagers, and they care for you. I came here to find you and to ask you a few questions."

"You won't make me leave?" Russhell asked in a quiet trembling voice, her manner switching again.

"Even if I had the authority to make you leave here, which I do not, I wouldn't ask you to leave," Yara assured Russhell. "You have found a home here. No, as I said, I just want to ask you a few questions."

"Alright. What are your questions?"

Yara cautiously sat back down, hoping Russhell would do the same. Toki came to lean against Yara's leg. Russhell finally sat back down, and her foxes settled down also. Thinking that starting with a question about what Russhell's foxes knew might set Russhell off again, Yara decided to start with other questions.

"Did you have any family stories passed down about your great-something grandfather?"

"Nothing comes to mind."

"No stories about being a practical joker, or doing something in his youth that he might have regretted?"

"No."

Yara was beginning to feel discouraged. She wondered if she had come all this way for nothing. Trying again, she asked, "Did your family ever talk about family luck?"

"No, not that I remember. Father always said that people made their own luck."

Yara decided to change tactics. "Did you hear what happened at the capital's summer fair when the Regent was made to step down?"

"Only that the Regent is no longer the ruler. The villagers here told me. I didn't pay much attention, for those outside Tåkete bog pay very little attention to us."

"The former princess, now Lady Esmeralda, called the Gylden Sirklene challenge. The challenge is the way we of Sommerhjem have chosen our new king or queen, up until the last several hundred years. In order for the challenge to proceed, all nine pieces of the oppgave ringe need to be in the capital, by a year from the day the challenge was called. So far, five of the pieces have been found and brought in."

"Interesting, but like I said, it really makes no matter who rules. The bog is of no interest to those outside of the bog. What does this challenge have to do with me anyway?"

Well, in for a copper, in for a silver, Yara thought to herself. Taking a deep breath, glancing around to see if she could spot anyone lurking in the shadows of the trees surrounding the glade, Yara answered Russhell's question.

"Our family was charged with keeping safe one of the pieces of the oppgave ringe. It was a family secret passed down from one generation to the next. Our great-something grandfather gave the information to Laron's older brother. As I said, according to what I've been told, Laron overheard the conversation and was angry that he had not been included. Because he was jealous, he took the object and hid it, thinking that when his father found out, he would blame Laron's older brother. Unfortunately, his plan worked too well, for Laron never had a chance to tell anyone what he had done before he disappeared. The family's luck turned at about the same time, and Laron's older brother was blamed for losing the family luck. They thought the object that Laron had taken was the family luck. Since it was a secret, I imagine Kinza, your ancestor, never knew what he had taken as part of a practical joke. I came here, hoping your family might still have the piece of the oppgave ringe that Kinza took. It needs to get to the capital."

Very cautiously, Russhell asked, "What does this piece of the, what did you call it?"

"The oppgave ringe."

"What does this piece of the oppgave ringe look like?"

"It's described as an irregularly shaped ring with scratches on the outer surface. It's made of gold."

"And this was a family secret you say?"

"The way I understand it, once the challenge is concluded, the nine pieces of the oppgave ringe are sent out of the capital, and certain folk are charged with keeping them safe until they are needed to fulfill the challenge when a ruler dies. It seems that only a few chosen individuals can handle them. If it was handed down in your family, then you probably can handle it, and are most likely the one who should take it to the capital."

"No."

"No to what?" Yara asked.

Russhell did not answer, but had once again pulled into herself and was rocking. "The foxes know, the foxes know," she kept repeating over and over.

"What do the foxes know, Russhell?" Yara asked gently.

The question, asked so quietly and simply, caused Russhell to look up.

"What do the foxes know?" Yara asked again.

"Can't tell, can't tell, I, I . . . ." Russhell stammered and then buried her head in her arms.

"Maybe it's time to tell someone. Whatever it is, whatever happened, maybe it's time to tell someone," Yara said, in soothing tones, and then sat back trying to look calm and relaxed, so as to not frighten Russhell any further.

Russhell looked up at Yara, tears streaming down her face. "It's my fault."

"What's your fault? Surely you don't think the swamp fever was your fault."

"No, the swamp fever was not my fault but . . ." Russhell hesitated before going on. ". . . but a man from Sivkurv was hurt because of me."

"Why don't you start from the beginning?" Yara suggested.

"There were two groups of folk who gathered when it was decided that I was to be banished from the village of Sivkurv. Those who protested weakly against my banishment, but were insistent that I be allowed to take some possessions with me, and those who felt I should be thrown out with nothing. After much arguing, I was allowed to enter my family's home one last time and gather some clothes, a few blankets, a little food, a knife, and little else. The head of the villagers' son, a man called Shomari, stood over me the whole time to make sure I took very little of value." Russhell's voice trailed off, as she became quiet and lost in remembering.

"So, they let you take very little from home," Yara summarized.

"Some of the women of the village protested, but the head man told them I didn't even deserve what I had taken, since the swamp fever had been my family's fault. He said the sooner I was gone from the village, the better."

"So, then what happened?"

"Shomari was given the task of escorting me to the Tåkete bog. Once we arrived at the edge of the bog, he insisted I dump everything out of the bundle I had wrapped my possessions in, to make sure that I hadn't taken anything he might think was of value. I did as he demanded, and then . . . ." Russhell shuddered and stopped talking.

"If this is too hard to talk about, you don't have to, but maybe talking about that time, getting it out, might help," Yara said.

"Be-be-before my father died, he gave me something to keep safe. I wore it around my neck in a pouch. When I bent over to pick up my meager possessions, the pouch slipped out, and he saw it. He demanded I give it to him. When I tried to tuck it beneath my shirt, he grabbed me and ripped the cord over my head. He opened the pouch and tipped its contents into his hand, and then . . . ."

"And then?" Yara inquired leaning forward, for Russhell had been speaking more and more quietly as her tale went on.

"He opened the pouch and tipped the contents into his hand. There was a flash of light, and he flung away from himself what had been in the pouch, flung it into the bog. I will never, never forget the look of fear in his eyes when he looked at me, all the while clutching his hand as if he had been burned. He began backing away and then turned and ran."

Yara felt her heart sink. There had been a tale floating around the capital about how only a very few could handle the oppgave ringe pieces. On their sail to Sikkervik, Eluta had told her what she knew about how the other pieces of the oppgave ringe had come to arrive at the capital. She remembered the story Eluta had told concerning the lad, Greer, who had brought one of the pieces of the oppgave ringe to the capital. Yara thought she recalled that in his story, someone who had tried to steal the piece of the oppgave ringe had also had a hand injured. The two stories were too similar for her to think that what the man called Shomari had flung into the bog was not one of the pieces of the oppgave ringe. How would it ever be found now? Lost in her thoughts, Yara did not realize at first that Russhell had begun to speak again.

". . . all was lost . . . ."

"Sorry, I wasn't listening. Would you start again?"

"I thought all was lost, since being able to find what my father had placed in my care was surely lost in the bog, but then the foxes came. Six of the red bog foxes came. It was as if they had been called. I was terrified. All I had to defend myself against six wild red bog foxes was a small knife. I was sure my life was about to end."

"What happened?"

"The six foxes formed a circle around me, but were facing out rather than facing me. It looked like they had formed a protective ring around me, but at the time, I thought that was just my imagination. Then, the strangest thing happened. A seventh fox appeared out of the fog. At first, I didn't see it, for it was not a red bog fox like the others, but the color of the fog itself." Russhell paused, and then said in a whisper almost too soft for Yara to hear, "Maybe the fox was made of fog . . . ."

By now, Yara was thoroughly intrigued by the tale Russhell was telling and leaned even farther forward, slipping to the very edge of the bench where she was sitting.

"The seventh fox approached me slowly and stopped where my gear was still lying on the ground. I was afraid to move. I was almost afraid to even breathe."

Yara continued to listen intently, holding her breath.

"The fox, the color of fog, bowed to me, at least it looked that way. I didn't understand what was happening, but I found I wasn't afraid. The fog-colored fox then bent her head down, opened her mouth, and dropped the contents of the pouch on the unfolded blanket at my feet. I could not believe it, for I had thought the ring had been lost forever."

Yara took a swift intake of breath, upon hearing that the fog-colored fox had dropped a ring.

"I was afraid to pick it up. I had never held the ring myself. I had only seen it in my father's hand, when he had shown it to me and told me to keep it with me always and to keep it safe. I didn't know why, and I'm not sure he did either, but since it was the last thing he had asked of me before he died, I had tried to do what he had asked."

"What happened next?" Yara asked, finding it hard to contain both her excitement and her curiosity.

"The fog-colored fox had such an air of expectancy and urgency that before I could stop myself, I reached down to pick up the ring."

Chapter Forty-Six

Nathair was very grateful that the fog had begun to dissipate the farther they got out to sea. It had been nerve wracking, to say the least, trying to navigate in the fog through the reefs beyond the harbor of Farlig Brygge. Trying to keep the boat equidistant between the two watch towers had been tricky. He had only heard the hull scrape twice, and as near as he could tell, the boat was not taking on water. Nathair hoped that the only things that were scraped off the hull were barnacles.

Fortunately, when they had been leaving Farlig Brygge, the wind had been enough to gently fill the sail, and not a brisker wind, for that would have made maneuvering through the gap in the reef much more difficult. The wind had picked up considerably once they were farther away from shore, and now, they were heading north at a steady clip.

Nathair felt he had been very patient waiting for an explanation as to why they had left Farlig Brygge so abruptly, but his patience had run out. "What was all the rush to leave Farlig Brygge all about?" Nathair asked Bertok.

"Some old acquaintances found out I was in Farlig Brygge and wanted to ask me some questions that, let us say, I was reluctant to answer. I was there long enough to find out that the ones you seek are no longer in Sivkurv. According to my source, all but one member of the family died of swamp fever. The one surviving member was thrown out of the village and left to die in the Tåkete bog."

Nathair felt his heart sink at the news. His whole trip had been for nothing, it would seem. How was he going to break this news to his father?

"This last remaining distant kin is dead, then?"

"No, my source said she is still alive and well."

"Why are we not heading to the Tåkete bog? Isn't it closer to Farlig Brygge than to Sikkervik?

"Pretty much the same distance from either place, when you look at the map, but that really is not the issue here. Those who live in the Tåkete bog are very wary of strangers. Many who have ended up living there in recent years have not been treated very well by the Regent or his agents. If they don't want to be found, they won't be found. They seem to be very protective of your distant kin, so it stands to reason, that if they don't want her to be found, she will not be."

"You are suggesting that if I went to the Tåkete bog, I would have a slim chance of finding my distant kin?"

"Yes."

"Then, just what is it that you are proposing?"

"I would suggest that we head to Sikkervik and see if your cousin has been more successful. If she has, then somehow I think the two of us can manage one lass and one elder, don't you think?"

Yara waited anxiously to find out what had had happened to Russhell when she reached for the ring the fog-colored fox had dropped. Yara knew she was close to finding the answer to what she had sought ever since she had begun her search all those months ago. It was obvious to her that after Kinza Karmoris had taken the piece of the oppgave ringe from where his cousin Laron had hidden it, thinking it was a grand practical joke, that when Laron had not come after it, he had kept it. Had he kept it because he thought Laron would eventually show up, or had he kept it because he had become too embarrassed by his youthful prank to send it back to Laron's family? Yara wondered if he even knew what he had had in his possession. Maybe the idea that the ring was a secret family trust had less to do with it being a piece of the oppgave ringe and more to do with holding on to it in case someone from Laron's family came looking for it. Yara anxiously waited for what Russhell would say next.

"I didn't have time to be afraid that whatever had harmed Shomari would also harm me. I almost felt as if there were no other choice but to pick up the ring. When my father had given the ring into my keeping, he had tipped it out onto a piece of golden pine spider silk. He never actually touched it. When he picked it up he did so with the pouch turned inside out. I never thought about that before. Ever since it had been in my keeping, I had never taken it out of its pouch."

"What happened when you picked up the ring?" Yara asked.

"Since I didn't, at that moment, think about how cautiously my father had handled the ring, I didn't think to be cautious about picking it up. As I said, I really did not feel as if I had a choice. Fortunately, there was no flash of light, and the ring did not harm me. It just felt very warm to the touch. The fog-colored fox then went over and picked up the pouch, which had landed near me. She came back and dropped it on my blanket, pushing it toward me with her nose. I took that as a sign that I was to put the ring back in the pouch, which I did. The fog-colored fox then nodded her head twice, turned, and walked back into the fog. The six remaining foxes stayed with me. I told Narada about the fog-colored fox, but she said she had never heard of such a fox, and she has lived here all her life. She talked to a few of the elders. There are some legends but . . . ." Russhell's voice trailed off.

After waiting for Russhell to continue, Yara finally asked in a very quiet voice, "Did you tell Narada, or anyone, about the ring?"

"No."

"And the ring, do you still have it?"

"Father said to keep it with me always. He said I must take care of it. The foxes and I have done so."

"I'm glad that you have kept it safe, just as your father asked. As I said, our family generations back was given the charge of keeping the ring safe until such time as it was needed again. It is needed now. The piece of the oppgave ringe needs to get to the capital to join the others already there. No matter what happened a very long time ago between our two branches of the Karmoris family, the fact remains that the ring needs to get to the capital. Since you can handle it, it would seem that you need to get it there."

"No, no, no, I can't, I can't leave here. No, I can't leave here." Russhell moaned and began to rock again.

Russhell's foxes came and huddled around her, leaning into her to give her comfort.

Yara was torn between wanting to shake some sense into Russhell and wanting to comfort her like the foxes were doing. It was so important to both her family and Sommerhjem that the ring be returned to its rightful place, but in lieu of moving Russhell's foxes out of the way and tearing the pouch over her head as Shomari had, if she was even wearing the pouch, Yara was at a loss as to what to do next.

"I know you have little reason to trust folks outside the Tåkete bog and feel safe here, but the ring you hold in trust is needed," Yara repeated, putting as much urgency in her voice as she could.

"I can't leave, I won't leave here," Russhell stated with conviction.

Both were so intent on their side of the issue, so lost in their own thoughts, that they did not notice a heavy fog had crept into the quirrelit grove along the ground. Soon the grove was thick with fog. The only space without fog obscuring the surroundings was the amphitheater where the two sat with the foxes.

Toki's urgent pawing on Yara's leg caused her to glance up. She noticed the fog immediately, but even more unnerving than the fog obscuring her vision of the grove, was the increase in the number of darting pale green lights as the blekbrann zipped in and out of the fog.

"Ah, Russhell, do we have a problem here?" Yara asked, trying to get Russhell's attention, for along with the rise of the fog and the increase in the number of blekbrann, the foxes, including Toki, had risen and were standing at alert, looking out of the amphitheater.

Russhell looked up and took a good look at her surroundings. "I don't know."

"That is not a reassuring answer," quipped Yara.

"Fog hardly ever enters the quirrelit grove, and I have never seen so many blekbrann in one place. They seem to gather wherever you are. The foxes are alert, but are not giving warning."

A waiting stillness fell over the quirrelit grove. Yara could no longer hear the occasional rustle in the undergrowth, and the birds no longer sang. Despite the strangeness, Yara did not feel afraid. The feeling of calm and peace that had been present when she had first entered the quirrelit grove had not left with the rise of the fog. Underlying it all was a feeling of expectation.

As the fog swirled around on the very edge of the amphitheater, more and more blekbrann became visible, until the amphitheater and the edge of the fog glowed a pale green. The foxes stood facing outward, still, with nary an ear or a whisker twitching. Yara and Russhell sat frozen in place.

Listening with great concentration, Yara thought she could hear someone, or something, approaching down the trail they had entered the grove by. It did not sound like footfalls, but rather like something smaller heading their way. Suddenly, the fog swirled and the blekbrann moved aside. One minute there was nothing but fog, and the next minute, a fox the color of fog stood in front of them. Yara heard a sharp intake of breath, and for the life of her, did not know if she or Russhell had done so.

"Is this the fox you spoke of?" Yara questioned in a whisper.

"I think so," Russhell replied.

"Should we be concerned?"

"I don't think so."

Yara almost lunged off her seat when the fog-colored fox approached Russhell and pushed her muzzle against Russhell's neck. Yara was afraid the fox had been going for Russhell's throat. Just as Yara began to leap up, Toki placed himself directly in front of her. Had she tried to move forward, she would have tripped over him. Since it seemed the fog-colored fox was not intent on harming Russhell, Yara reluctantly sat back down.

Russhell reached up and tentatively laid a hand on the fog-colored fox's head. "What is it you want?" she asked.

In answer, the fox again pushed her muzzle against Russhell's neck. Russhell reached in the neckline of her shirt and drew out a pouch. When she did so, the blekbrann moved out of the fog and began to circle those gathered in the amphitheater. The fog-colored fox put her paw on Russhell's knee and bowed her head. Russhell placed the cord of the pouch over the fog-colored fox's head.

Yara was stunned. Before she could say anything, the fog-colored fox moved away from Russhell and walked down the steps of the amphitheater to the platform at the bottom. The other foxes turned and followed her down, including Toki.

Yara wanted to scream, wanted to stand up and stomp her feet, wanted to yell 'no' at the top of her lungs, but she did none of these things. Taking a deep calming breath, Yara slowly turned to Russhell and asked, "Why, why did you give the pouch to the fox?"

Russhell was quiet for a long moment before she spoke. "It didn't seem as if it was mine to keep any longer. It was as if a burden was being lifted and, well, I don't really know how to explain it. It just felt right. I'm sorry. I know you have come a long way to find out what happened to the ring. You might even have expected me to give it to you, since according to you, my branch of the Karmoris family took what was not their right to have. It seems, however, it is not my place to decide. Look."

Yara had been so focused on Russhell that she had not noticed what was happening around her. All of the blekbrann had ceased their circling and had formed a corridor by lining each side of the steps that led down to where the foxes sat. All of the blekbrann with the exception of one. That one still hovered off Yara's left shoulder. Once she noticed it, it moved to hover at the top of the stairs.

"I think, maybe, you are being invited to go down there," Russhell suggested.

"Why do you think that?"

"Because the blekbrann are lighting the way, and the one who is your companion seems to be indicating that you should follow. Maybe they have been leading you here all along," Russhell stated simply.

Yara was not sure why, but she felt a rightness in what Russhell had said. Not knowing what else to do, Yara began to walk down the stairs. She was surprised to see the fog-colored fox nudge Toki, who swiftly ran up the steps to the step Yara was on, stopped, turned, and settled in at her side.

"Come to escort me down, have you?" Yara asked Toki.

As Yara began to make her way down the steps, she began to wonder just what was going on here. How could Russhell have so easily given over to the fog-colored fox the pouch holding what Yara strongly suspected was the piece of the oppgave ringe, the very object she had traveled so far to find? How could Russhell have just draped the cord of the pouch over the fox's head after Yara had told her how important the ring was? For that matter, Yara asked herself, why was she so calmly walking down the stairs following a pale green light toward seven foxes? What would happen when she reached the bottom step?

Chapter Forty-Seven

Yara paused at the bottom of the steps, but was not allowed to remain there for long. Toki reached up, gently took Yara's hand in his mouth, and tugged her forward. She climbed the few short steps up onto the last step to the platform where Russhell's six foxes waited, forming a circle around the fog-colored fox. The blekbrann began to circle around all of them.

The fog-colored fox sat patiently waiting in the middle of the platform. Yara stood frozen on the top step, not quite knowing what to do. The fog, which had ended outside the amphitheater where Yara and Russhell had been talking, had now drifted down the stairs and thickened. All Yara could see was the platform. The blekbrann continued to circle. She jumped when she felt a hand on her shoulder.

"I think you need to go up on the platform," Russhell stated in a quiet voice.

"Have you changed your mind about giving the fog-colored fox the pouch?"

"No. As I said, I feel like a burden has been lifted from my shoulders. I didn't think the contents were mine to keep any longer, and it seemed right to place it in the fog-colored fox's care. I can't explain why. I repeat, you need to go up on the platform."

"You'll come with me?" Yara asked.

"If you wish."

Yara took a tentative step up onto the platform. When nothing happened, she took several more steps forward. The fog-colored fox continued to sit patiently in the middle of the platform. The gathering of blekbrann continued to circle around the platform, moving faster and faster, until they were just a blur of pale green light. As Yara advanced, with Toki on one side and the single blekbrann on the other, the six foxes widened their circle around the fog-colored fox so Yara could continue. Russhell followed behind. When Yara came within several feet of the fog-colored fox, she halted. Russhell stepped to her side and halted also.

The fog-colored fox turned to Russhell first and nodded in her direction. She turned to Yara and walked forward until she was within one foot of her. The fog-colored fox looked at Yara for a very long time, taking her measure. The fox stretched one of her front legs forward and bowed low over it. The pouch slid off fox's neck and came to rest in front of her front paw. Then the fog-colored fox moved back and sat down with an air of expectancy.

Yara moved totally by instinct, crouched down, and tentatively put her hand out to pick up the pouch. As her hand hovered over the pouch, she looked directly into the fog-colored fox's dark grey eyes and thought she saw permission in them. The fog-colored fox nodded her head. Slowly, Yara closed her hand around the pouch and picked it up, straightening up at the same time. The fog-colored fox stayed seated, waiting.

"What's next do you think?" Yara asked Russhell.

"Perhaps you should open the pouch to make sure it is truly what you seek," Russhell suggested. "I think if you are the one to hold it now, it should not cause you any harm."

Yara had known what Russhell was suggesting was what she needed to do, but she wanted to stall just a few moments longer before finding out a number of things. Yara wondered if what was inside the pouch was really what she had searched so hard for and come so far to find. She also worried that it might harm her in some way, like it had Shomari. With some reluctance and with shaking fingers, Yara untied the pouch cord and opened the pouch. Then, she tipped the contents into her hand, closing her eyes in case a flash of light happened, bracing herself for possible pain. When no flash of light occurred, and all she felt was a slight warmth in her hand, she opened her eyes and looked. There, resting in the palm of her hand, was an irregularly shaped gold ring with marks scratched on the surface. Yara glanced up and looked at the fog-colored fox, who nodded her head, turned, and faded back into the fog.

Yara's reverie was interrupted when Russhell asked her if the ring was what she had been seeking.

"Yes. It matches the description of what I have read and heard about the pieces of the oppgave ringe, and it looks like the ones that now reside in the vesstebok in the Well of Speaking in the capital."

"Even if the why we should keep it safe was lost in the past, my father made sure I knew how important it was to keep it with me and safe. I won't apologize for what my great-something grandfather did."

"There is no need. I'm grateful to your family for keeping it safe these many, many years. A question though. Did you think of just giving the ring to me?"

"Oddly enough, no. When Shomari took the pouch from me, it was the last straw. Everyone and everything else that had been important to me was gone. The only thing I really had left of my former life was the pouch and its contents, which my father had entrusted to me. I felt as if I were letting him down. When Shomari flung the ring away from him into the fog shrouded bog, I thought I had lost it forever. When the fog-covered fox returned it to me, the holding of it felt different. It became a heavy burden somehow. I don't know how to explain it. Now that you have it, I feel lighter, freer, or maybe set free. I'm not as afraid now. The fog is lifting."

"When you wore the pouch, you felt as if you were in a fog?" Yara asked.

"No, no, look around you, the fog is lifting."

Yara looked up from the ring and noticed that indeed the fog was receding.

"It's getting late. Perhaps we should head back to the village. The stairs down off the plateau are more difficult when it gets dark."

Yara readily agreed to head back, for she remembered that the climb up to the plateau had not been all that easy. Tucking the ring back into the pouch and putting the cord over her head, she followed Russhell up out of the amphitheater, and then, out of the quirrelit grove. As they walked, Russhell asked Yara to tell her about her family. When she ran out of things to say, the two walked in companionable silence surrounded by the foxes. The blekbrann, who had surrounded them in the amphitheater, had faded away with the fog, with the exception of the one who still hovered just off Yara's left shoulder.

There was no one else on the plateau as they crossed it, and their climb down was uneventful until they were halfway to the bottom. There they met a group of people coming up, headed by Redding, followed closely by his father and a number of others from the village. Before Redding could say anything, Russhell spoke up.

"Everything is alright. We are fine."

"But fog and flashes of green light in the quirrelit grove were reported," Redding recounted anxiously.

"I can't explain the fog, but the light came from a gathering of the blekbrann. This one," Russhell indicated by nodding her head in Yara's direction, "seems to attract them in droves."

"You sure you're alright?" Redding inquired again.

Russhell surprised them both by reaching out and taking both of Redding's hands. "Dear heart, I'm better now than I've been in a very long time. I thank you for your care and concern. Now, perhaps we could get down before we lose the light."

Reluctantly releasing Russhell's hands, Redding turned and relayed to the others that all was well, and could they please head back down to the village. While there was some muttering and grumbling, the others behind Redding turned and began to descend. It struck Redding that Russhell seemed different, stronger somehow, and she had taken his hands and called him dear heart. Whatever had happened in the quirrelit grove seemed to have been good for Russhell.

Yara's reception in the village seemed to be a bit warmer than when she had been there earlier in the day. The evening meal was held in the large gathering room that Yara had been in earlier. While not a gathering filled with laughter and merriment, it was a comfortable meal. Yara sat with Russhell, Redding, Narada, Terentia, and several others. They did not ask what had happened in the quirrelit grove that afternoon, and Russhell did not volunteer any information. Yara followed her lead.

When the meal was over, Russhell asked to be excused, for she felt the need for a walk in the night air. Redding excused himself also, and stood up to follow Russhell out the door.

"Our Russhell does not do well, even yet, with large groups of folk or being inside. She needs space and lots of it."

"It would seem Redding is of the same mind. Needing lots of space and fewer folk," Yara replied innocently, but there was no mistaking the twinkle in her eye.

"So, you caught that, did you? I hope, someday, Russhell will notice him as more than a friend. She seems changed tonight. Something is different. Stronger somehow, and well, I just can't put my finger on it. You both seemed different after you came down from the quirrelit grove," suggested Narada.

Yara knew Narada was fishing for information, but she felt it was neither a story she wanted to tell, nor did she feel it was her story to tell, so remained silent. Suddenly overcome by the events of the day, Yara bid farewell to Narada and headed toward the small empty cottage where Narada had told her she was welcome to stay. Glancing around, Yara saw that Toki was a little way away, wrestling with another young fox.

"You staying out here, or you coming with me, Toki?" Yara called.

Toki immediately gave one last tussle with the other fox, and then, ran to Yara's side. Yara knelt down and gave Toki a squeeze, as a wave of relief washed over her. She continued to be afraid that Toki would choose to remain with the other foxes. For tonight at least, he had chosen to be with her.

The next morning, Yara was just about to open the door to the cottage where she had spent the night, when she heard a knock. Opening the door, she saw Russhell, about to knock again.

"Good morning, kin," Russhell said. "I wonder if we might spend the day together, or do you need to leave? There is much I would ask you."

"I would be delighted to spend the day with you. There is much I would ask you, also. Please come in."

The day passed by quickly, as Russhell and Yara told each other what they knew about each of their families. By the end of the day, Yara felt as if she had formed a tenuous friendship with her distant kin. It did not escape her notice that Russhell seemed less afraid. She certainly was not acting like the woman Yara had first met, huddled in on herself and rocking. Yara wondered if the piece of the oppgave ringe had been the cause of Russhell's fear. Yara questioned whether she would turn into a huddled mess if she carried the ring for any period of time.

"You looked worried just now," Russhell remarked. "Is something wrong?"

"You have changed since our time in the quirrelit grove amphitheater. You no longer seem as fearful as you did when I first met you. Do you think your change has something to do with the fact that you are no longer carrying and protecting the ring?

"I'm not sure how to explain it. Carrying the pouch was a trust that my father placed upon me, but maybe I was not the one who was supposed to take on that task. I was the first to get the swamp fever, and I survived. I was recovering when one by one the rest of my family came down with the swamp fever, and one by one, they died. My father was the last to become ill. I wonder if one of my brothers or sisters was the one who was supposed to take charge of the ring when my father chose to pass it on. Until he gave it to me, I never knew he had it. After what the villagers did to me, I think I went a little crazy, and the knowledge that I was responsible for the last thing my father asked of me only added to the confusion and burden that had become my life."

Yara thought a bit about what Russhell said, and then, asked what Russhell thought was different now.

"When Shomari tried to take the ring, all I could think of was it was not right that someone from my home village would strip me of the very last possession belonging to my family. My trust in folk was shattered. When the fog-colored fox rescued and returned the ring, I knew I could trust the foxes even as I thought I could not trust folks. A part of me also knew I probably would not survive long in the bog without the help of others. The foxes led me to this village. The villagers have been kind, and between them and the foxes, I have been safe."

"But that still does not explain what has changed for you."

"I know. I think, like I said, I was not the one who the ring should have been handed down to. I have just been a temporary carrier. I did not realize how great a burden it was until yesterday. When the fog-colored fox stood before me, I just felt my time to have the pouch and its contents had come to an end. It was no longer my duty to protect and carry it. I felt strongly that the fog-colored fox would determine what was to happen next. I can't explain it, really. Oh, are you worried that something will change in you since you now carry the ring?"

Yara reflected on what had happened in the quirrelit grove when she had stood on the platform. She had felt as if she were being judged in those moments when she and the fog colored fox had faced each other. Without really thinking, she reached up and cupped the pouch in her hand. A feeling of warmth and peace flowed over her, and suddenly, she felt just a little bit foolish. Of course, being responsible for a piece of the oppgave ringe would change her, but it did not need to be something to fear.

A tentative knock sounded at the door, and Yara rose to answer it.

"I'm sorry to bother you both, but I have some disturbing news," Terentia stated.

Chapter Forty-Eight

Yara invited Terentia into the cottage and asked if she would like to join Russhell and her for a cup of tea. Terentia stood by the small fire in the hearth warming herself, for the morning was unusually cold, made colder by the ever present mist and patchy fog. Once Terentia had a cup of hot tea in her hands, she sat.

"I must have your oath on your honor that what I am about to tell you will not leave this cottage," Terentia stated quite seriously, looking at Yara.

"You have my oath, on my honor, I will not repeat what you are about to tell me."

"Good. As you know, the Tåkete bog is a difficult one to find your way around in, due to the ever-shifting fog. That makes it difficult for just anyone to find their way to our village. It provides those of us who choose to live here some measure of safety. However, wise folk do not rely on only one method of keeping themselves safe. Knowing what is going on outside of the Tåkete bog also helps ensure we remain safe. Some members of this community, who have contacts in Farlig Brygge, have let us know that there have been inquiries made recently about your family, Russhell. Fellow they say was part of the Raven's crew was asking about the Karmorises in the region."

At the mention of the Raven, Yara saw Terentia shiver slightly, and she knew it was not from the cold. The Raven, or those he commanded, were the ones the former regent Cedric Klingflug called upon to carry out his evil and nefarious deeds. They were the enforcers of the former Regent's many unpopular edicts. The Raven also helped remove those folk who opposed the former Regent. Yara had heard tales of the Raven's misdeeds. Any folk who had been a part of the Raven's crew was certainly not someone she wanted to cross paths with.

Russhell stood up upon hearing that one of the Raven's former men was looking for her. "I should leave. I . . . ."

"No, you don't need to leave. I'm sorry if I scared you. The inquiry was made, but once the fellow knew that only one of you survived, he did not stay in Farlig Brygge for more than a few more hours. Seems some folks were not all that happy that he had showed up in their territory. He slipped out in the fog. He certainly has not tried to take any known routes to here. Our friend could not tell us anything else about this man who was asking about your family, other than he thought this man's name was Bartel, or Bertrom, or some such. Was not close enough to the folks who were talking about him to hear it clearly. I don't think you need be overly concerned. Know that the others here will be extra vigilant."

Yara began to worry. She had been sure someone else had been looking at the same records in the room of rolls in the royal library as she had been. It was not good news that one of the Raven's men was looking for the same family she had been looking for. This does not feel like a coincidence or some unrelated inquiry, Yara thought. She knew from talk around the capital that the former Regent was getting more and more desperate to find pieces of the oppgave ringe, in order to keep the Gylden Sirklene challenge from coming to fruition. Knowing that someone was in the same region looking for the same folk she had been looking for was not good news, not good news, indeed.

"Russhell, can you think of any reason that one of the Raven's men would be trying to find your family in this area?" Terentia asked.

"I can't imagine. We were just a simple basket weaving and trading family. We paid all the taxes and licenses that the former Regent demanded. My father never got involved with what was going on in the area. We didn't have much to do with those outside our village for anything other than trade. We never spoke out against either the Crown or the former Regent. We kept to ourselves. It was safer."

"Well, I don't think there is too much to worry about from this Bartel, or Bertrom, but take a bit more caution," Terentia suggested.

"Thank you, I will."

When Terentia left, Yara turned to Russhell. "I'm worried that someone else is looking for your family just at this time. When I was researching the rolls trying to find out what had happened to the descendants of Kinza Karmoris, someone else was looking at the same material I was. I have worried that someone else knew that your branch of the family had at one time possessed a piece of the oppgave ringe, and that they were determined to find it. I hope I have not placed you in danger by seeking you out."

"They will not be able to find me in the bog if I do not want to be found," Russhell replied. "But what of you? You now have what this folk may be seeking."

"I have always known that if I found you, or another of your kin, and if you had the ring, I would try to convince you or yours to take it to the capital or let me take it to the capital. If you chose to give it into my keeping, then I knew that trying to return home with it could be dangerous. It was important enough for me to take the risk. It would seem that I have been chosen now to carry the ring. I will have to deal with any danger that comes with that charge."

Pretty brave words coming from someone who has spent most of her life reading about other folks' adventures and daring deeds, Yara thought to herself. Was she trying to convince Russhell that she had everything under control, or convince herself?

While Yara might have wanted to linger longer and spend more time with this newly-discovered distant cousin, with each passing hour she felt more and more compelled to leave. Knowing it would not be wise to leave toward sunset, Yara made plans to leave at sunrise. Russhell had told Yara that she would walk with her to the edge of the bog and wait with her until the Venn border patrol came by.

Narada, Terentia, Russhell, and Redding were waiting outside when Yara stepped out of the cottage early the next morning.

"We have come to see you off," Narada stated. "We thought we would give a more cordial send off than we gave a welcome. I hope you will not think badly of us and your stay here."

"What I think is that you are a close-knit folk, who have reason to be less than trustful of those who do not live here, and that you are very protective of those who do. I think my distant cousin here is very fortunate to have found a new home and family with you folks. I will leave here knowing that."

"Russhell, I think the blekbrann have been attracted to your distant cousin based in part on her ability to keep an open mind and her kindness. If you want to get a goodly distance today, you should get going," Narada suggested.

After saying goodbye and thanking those who had come to see them off, Yara picked up her pack. She was surprised to see Redding had also picked up a pack and was helping Russhell on with hers. When she shot Russhell an inquiring look, Russhell, with some embarrassment, explained that Redding had been insistent on accompanying them. Yara wondered if Russhell was the only one who did not realize that Redding's feelings toward Russhell were more than just protective.

The walk through the bog seemed faster than when Yara had been following either the blekbrann or Terentia. During portions of the day, the fog had thinned. It was beautiful in the bog with the sun shining on the drops of dew left on the plants by the fog and mist. It looked as if the plants were dotted with tiny glittering jewels.

When the fog or mist thickened, Yara could no longer distract herself with the sights and smells of the bog. She was worried about several things. While it did her heart good to see Toki be so accepted by Russhell's skulk of foxes, she worried that when she got to the border of the Tåkete bog, he would want to remain with the skulk and not with her. While in her heart Yara knew that Toki was a wild animal and belonged in the bog, part of her grieved at the thought of him no longer being with her. Yara was also concerned about what lay ahead as she headed back to the capital. She hoped it would be smooth sailing, and not just in her boat.

When they finally arrived at the area where Yara had first entered the bog, it was midday. Since they did not know how long they would have to wait, Russhell and Redding set about gathering the tough reeds that grew along the open waterway. Working together, they wove thick mats which allowed the three of them to sit, stay dry, and not sink into the bog.

The foxes had wandered off, and Yara began to worry that if the Venn border patrol showed up while Toki was off with the skulk, she would be forced to leave without him, assuming he wanted to go with her. Deep in thought about this dilemma, Yara did not notice that all of the foxes had returned and had formed a ring around the three folk sitting on the mats.

"Someone is coming," Russhell stated.

Yara looked up and down the waterway, but could see no one. She gave Russhell a questioning look.

"I keep telling you, the foxes know," Russhell replied.

Yara realized that what Russhell said could have double meaning. She also realized that there was a trace of humor or teasing in Russhell's voice, something she did not think had been there very much since the loss of her family. Though Russhell stood in watchful waiting, she did not appear to be fearful. When Yara really looked at Russhell, she could see a change. Here was a young woman who was no longer afraid. She seemed stronger somehow. Yara continued to wonder if no longer being responsible for the oppgave ringe piece was the cause.

It was another quarter of an hour before the trio spotted the lead reed boat paddling their way. When they drew closer, Yara could see that the man in the lead boat was the same one who had been in charge of the border patrol she had met when Marleigh had dropped her off. That would make things easier, for she would not have to explain who she was or why she needed a ride.

The head of the patrol greeted her and suggested her timing was really good. "It's time for us to head back to home base, for our time on patrol is up. Be most happy to give you a lift back to Marleigh's landing."

Yara said farewell to Russhell and Redding, and thanked them for their assistance and companionship. She stepped into the boat and settled in the middle, arranging her pack in front of her. Yara then looked toward the foxes, who had remained alert.

"So Toki, do you wish to stay? It is your home. I would certainly understand." Yara thought those words might have been the hardest she had ever had to say.

At the sound of Yara's voice, Toki glanced at the other foxes. He turned to the lead fox, and the two stood and stared at each other for a few short moments. The lead fox bobbed her head once, and Toki turned and walked to the edge of the bog. With a very graceful leap, he landed in Yara's arms.

Not until the patrol was well out of sight of Russhell and Redding did Yara release Toki and really pay attention to the members of the border patrol. It struck her then that the only one she really recognized was the Captain. The others did not look familiar. That seemed odd, since the Captain had said they were returning to home base, for their time on patrol was up. She had had the impression that the patrols were out for weeks at a time. She could understand the border patrol captain's statement if he had been accompanied by the same crew that she had met earlier, but these folks were different from the ones he had been with before.

Maybe there is a logical explanation, Yara thought. What do I know about the workings of a border patrol anyway? Maybe this group is just one of many that watch the border between the Venn's territory and the Tåkete bog. Maybe the Captain moves from group to group. Something cautioned her from asking the border patrol captain about his crew. In taking a closer look at those in the other two boats and the man in the bow of the boat she was traveling in, Yara noticed that they did not fit their uniforms well. She remembered thinking that the other patrol had looked well-disciplined and well-groomed. She was becoming more and more suspicious that something was wrong. Yara realized there was nothing she could do at the moment, since she was riding in a boat moving down a channel in the bog. She would need to remain vigilant and try to determine if she really was in trouble or not.

Another worry occurred to Yara on the tail end of her first one. The blekbrann who had been her constant companion ever since the night they had been led to Marleigh's place, was no longer hovering off her left shoulder. She did not know quite what to make of that fact.

When darkness began to fall, the boats were traveling across a lake. The border patrol captain told them to pull up to a beach ringing one of the many islands.

"We will make camp here for the night," he stated.

For a moment, Yara thought the man in the bow of her boat would object, for he had turned to say something. She had noticed an angry look on his face, which added to the unease she had been feeling with each passing hour.

Once camp had been established, a brazier was lit to provide heat to cook a meal, and the crew settled in to attend to routine chores. Yara sat down on a fallen log just at the edge of the evening meal preparation area. She had not been asked to help, and had been sternly cautioned not to move out of the campsite. Toki, she noticed, had kept very quiet and very close to her since they had left the boat, for which she was glad.

Yara opened her pack, intending to take out a warm shirt for the evening had grown cold, and immediately shut it again. When she had looked down into her pack, she had been surprised by the very unexpected, very dim pale green glow coming from a blekbrann hiding there.

Chapter Forty-Nine

Dinner was a quiet one, there being very little conversation among the members of the border patrol. Yara's concern that something was not quite right did not ease with the passing of the hours. To a casual observer, the Captain of the border patrol looked as if he was the leader, but Yara had been concentrating on watching the others and had begun to realize that the man who had been in the bow of their boat was actually the one in charge.

Watch was assigned, and the fire banked. Yara curled up in her blanket roll and was glad Toki had decided to come with her. Having him curled up next to her gave her a small measure of comfort and warmth. She did not think trying to sneak off during the night was going to be the correct decision, for she did not think she would get past the watch. Yara's other concern was what she would find at Marleigh's, if that in truth was where they were heading. She hoped Eluta was alright.

Yara did not know whether to be relieved or worried when the boats finally did arrive at Marleigh's landing. Kellen met them at the dock.

"Good, you're finally here. Now, maybe we'll get some answers. That old woman hasn't been cooperative at all, and Marleigh returned sooner than expected, causing another complication. Now, get her out of that boat, and you, lass, hand up the fox."

Before anyone could follow either of the orders, Yara picked Toki up and lofted him up onto the dock. "Run, Toki, run," she yelled.

Toki hesitated only a second before he dashed right between Kellen's legs and down the walkway, heading toward the grove of trees.

Rough hands reached down, yanked Yara up out of the boat, and shook her. "I'll not be having my orders disobeyed, is that clear?" Kellen shouted, but did not wait for an answer, as he whirled and stalked off the dock, yelling over his shoulder to bring both Yara and the border patrol captain along.

Yara hugged her pack to her, which she had fortunately managed to hold onto when she had been pulled so abruptly out of the boat. She looked around frantically, trying to spot Toki, worried he would come back and be harmed. Yara stumbled when she was pushed from behind.

"Youse best 'urry along now. Kellen don't likes to be kept waitin'."

Once the procession from the dock reached Marleigh's cottage, they were escorted inside. Upon seeing Eluta, Yara rushed to the royal librarian's side, dropped her pack, crouched down, and took both of Eluta's hands in her own.

"Are you alright? Have they harmed you?" Yara asked with great concern coloring her voice.

"I'm fine, lass. Just a bit weary. I'm a tough old bird, you know. Now, sit down next to me," Eluta suggested.

When Yara stood up and looked behind her, she became aware that Kellen and those who had escorted her and the border patrol captain had not remained in the room. She could see them outside on the front stoop. Looking further around the room, she saw the border patrol captain and Marleigh sitting together quietly conversing.

Turning back to Eluta, Yara asked what was going on. Who were these men who obviously were not border patrol, and what did Kellen want?

"I imagine the men who brought you here are part of Kellen's gang. As near as I can tell, they're smugglers, or at least those who would earn their living doing things the Crown would not approve of. Kellen does not believe that you and I are just on a walkabout and have no nefarious purpose for being here. Thinks we are members of a rival gang or spies from the Crown. Imagine that, he thinks an old bird like me is a spy, for gosh sake. The Crown must be pretty desperate to send elderly librarians out into the countryside to spy on the likes of Kellen. I denied that I was either a member of any group that wanted to take over his business in the salt marsh, or that I was a spy for the Crown. I told him the truth."

"What truth did you tell him?" Yara asked. Her heart was racing just a bit faster now, worrying that Eluta had let Kellen know the real reason Yara had come to Muggen Myr.

"Why, I told him I was feeling dusty and musty after all those years in the royal library and was taking a walkabout to clear the cobwebs out. I told him I had asked you to come along, and we were in Muggen Myr because you had done some research and found out that a branch of your family may have settled in Sivkurv. I told him that once we got here, we discovered that your one remaining distant cousin had been spotted in the Tåkete bog, and you had gone on to find her, while I stayed here to study the surrounding area and talk with Marleigh. Like I said, I told him the truth."

Eluta had been clever, Yara thought. Yes, she had told Kellen the truth. She just had not told Kellen all of the truth. Yara was pulled out of her thoughts when Eluta asked her a question.

"Where you successful in your search?"

"Yes, I found what I was looking for," Yara replied, and hoped Eluta got her meaning, since she had said she had found what and not who she had been looking for.

"Ah, . . . good."

Yara could see the light of understanding in Eluta's eyes.

"And how was your distant cousin?"

"She is well, and well cared for. She did not want to leave the Tåkete bog, so we parted with the understanding that I would try to return someday to see her."

"Your pardon," Marleigh stated, interrupting Yara and Eluta's conversation. "I'm sorry this has happened to you. I had no idea that Kellen was connected to this group, or believe me, he would not have been working here. I think we need to put our collective heads together while we have a chance."

On the surface, the request seemed reasonable to Yara, but she was not quite sure she was ready to trust either Marleigh or the border patrol captain. They might be innocent victims in Kellen's schemes, or they could be in cahoots with him.

"What would you suggest?" Eluta asked.

"The Captain here said Kellen's men overpowered his patrol by surprise. They didn't harm any of the patrol, but left them deep in the bog with few supplies. He is confident that they will eventually be able to make their way back to their base, and will then send out patrols to look for him, but that will take time that we might not have."

"It is unfortunate for you that you turned up to be picked up when you did. A few more days and Kellen would have had to give up his scheme, for my men would have probably made it back to base, and then, have set off to find me. At least, I hope they would have made it back and would have been searching for me," the border patrol captain suggested.

"Do either of you know why Kellen and his men have such an interest in either of you, and you in particular, Yara?" Marleigh asked.

"No, ma'am, I do not."

"Kellen seemed particularly interested in the fact that the wisps led you here in the storm."

"Is that so unusual?" Eluta asked.

"The wisps have been known to be helpful to the Venn upon occasion, but yes, it was unusual for them to help those who are not of the Venn. In addition, he also followed you when you walked to the grove and saw the gathering of the will-o'-wisps."

"I take it that was also unusual," Yara suggested.

"Not only unusual, but almost completely unheard of. It got his curiosity up."

"And the rest of it is my fault, I'm afraid. Marleigh mentioned the incident in the grove to me, and as you know, librarians are just inquisitive by nature, so I began asking questions. That got Marleigh even more interested, since she is one of the historians of the Venn."

"Now, Eluta, don't go taking all of the blame. Even if you had not been here, I would have gone searching in the old records to see if I could find out if this phenomenon had happened before."

"Did you find anything?" Yara questioned.

"Yes. The records are very old and are not well preserved, but from what I could read, there have been other times when the will-o'-wisps have gathered in great numbers. Seems they have been attracted to and protective of a few individuals in the past. Unfortunately, the records gave very little insight as to why. Something to do with being Neebing . . . ."

Kellen chose that moment to enter Marleigh's place with several bundles of supplies. He dumped them on the table, and strongly suggested that they had best get cooking, for his men were hungry.

"And I'll be watching what you're doing so there will be no tricks," Kellen remarked, as he leaned against the doorjamb with his arms crossed.

It was not until after the dinner chores were complete that Kellen left Yara, the border patrol captain, and the two women alone again.

"Is anyone finding it odd that Kellen went to all the trouble to capture the border patrol, await my return, and yet has basically left us alone?" Yara asked.

"Now that you mention it, that is odd," Eluta replied.

"Might I suggest that he is probably listening to our conversation and waiting for you folks to reveal something," suggested the border patrol captain.

"Listening to us? How?" Yara asked.

"You are right. Why didn't I think of that?" Marleigh said in disgust. "Our cottages are built on stilts to keep the floor well above any flooding, and so some of our not so friendly marsh dwellers don't come in. All one would have to do is stand beneath the cottage and put their ear to the floor, so to speak."

"What in yours and Eluta's conversations might have directed his attention toward me?" Yara wondered out loud.

"Oh dear, do you think Kellen might have been eavesdropping when we were discussing the wisps and the ancient tales of lost treasures?" Eluta inquired of Marleigh.

"Wait, so my being picked up by the false border patrol has nothing to do with his suspicions about us being spies or rival smugglers. He thinks because the wisps gather around me in numbers that I somehow might know where some lost treasure of legend is located? Have I got that right?" Yara asked.

"It is something we could surmise," Eluta answered.

Yara started laughing. "Oh, that's rich. I hope you are listening," Yara yelled toward the floorboards. "All this skullduggery has been for nothing. I'm exactly who Eluta said I was, someone who works at the royal library. The only thing I came looking for was a long lost distant cousin. I don't know why the wisps even come near me, and I certainly don't know about any ancient long lost treasure. I don't know if you have noticed, but there aren't any wisps hovering anywhere near me now."

Suddenly, Yara could hear the stomping of feet on the stairs to Marleigh's cottage. Kellen entered the room and glowered at the four. "Think you are so smart, do you? Think I'm fooled by your laughter and lies? We'll see how much humor you find in being tied to a tree here at night. We'll see how long it takes you to scream for help when the animals that live in the marsh discover you can't defend yourself. To them you will look just like a tasty meal. Do you want to be responsible for your friends and acquaintances here being harmed? All this can be prevented if you just lead me to the treasure. And don't think you can save these others by offering to go alone with me. They'll be coming, too."

"I don't know how to convince you I really have no idea where to find any treasure. I don't know why the wisps are attracted to me. Maybe they were attracted to Toki, the red bog fox, and not me," Yara told Kellen.

"Enough of this nonsense! You'll tell me what you know about the treasure, or all of you will suffer," Kellen shouted, his face turning an alarming shade of red.

"On my honor, I can't tell you what I don't know," sighed Yara.

"So, you're going to stick to that story, are you? We'll see how long you'll last." Kellen then yelled for his men to come in and bring coils of rope.

No matter what Yara said, Kellen could not be convinced that she really knew nothing. Nothing about the will-o'-wisps, and nothing about any long lost treasure. She was grabbed and roughly shoved out of the cottage. There was no chance to break away, for two of Kellen's men had a grip on her arms and were marching her down the walkway toward the grove of trees. She could hear the others behind her being admonished to keep moving.

Kellen called a halt just at the edge of the trees. "Tie them up to the trees. Line them up, but put Yara on this tree so she can see all of the others. Remember, lass, their fate is now in your hands. Ah, now that is even better. Do you feel that? It's starting to rain. Remember to scream loud, so we can hear you, since we're not going to stand out here in the rain with you."

"I can't tell you what I don't know. No matter what you do to us, I can't help you," Yara once again told Kellen.

"You keep singing that tune, lass. You'll tell me what I need to know when them critters start biting."

Chapter Fifty

Yara had more to worry about than the soft drizzle that had begun to fall. Since she did not know how to find the alleged treasure, she could not call Kellen back and give him the information so they could be rescued. She did not think she would be able to convince Kellen that she and the others did not know anything, even if she did scream. In addition, she was worried that she and the others would not survive the night, between the threat of critters and a very angry, dissatisfied Kellen. Amid the other worries, she was also worried about Toki. What had happened to him after she had told him to run? The other thought that passed through her mind concerned the wisps. Twice before they had protected her, and yet, since the false patrol had picked her up, they had been conspicuously absent, with the exception of the one who had hidden in her pack. Why had it hidden, she wondered. Why were the others nowhere around?

"I feel like such a fool," Marleigh stated. "I have worked with Kellen over the past few years and never once suspected he was connected to anything unsavory. He came to me wanting to learn more about our folk's history, the history of the Venn. I'm one of the history keepers. I was thrilled to be asked to share my knowledge, for I often worry that the next generations down are just not interested in our past. I'm more disappointed than you know that he was just here trying to get any information that might lead him to some profit. I should have suspected, I should have known, I . . . ."

"No sense wasting time on regrets," Eluta said. "What we need to do now is figure out how to get untied and away from here. Any ideas, Captain? Yara? Marleigh?"

"The ropes are tight, and unfortunately, they took my knife," the border patrol captain replied.

"I'm tied up so tight that breathing is an issue," suggested Eluta.

"I have a little wiggle room, but not enough to help," Yara answered.

"Perhaps I can help then," said a voice behind the four.

"Russhell?" queried Yara.

"Yes."

"How did . . . ?" Yara began, only to be interrupted by Russhell.

"Be happy to answer all of your questions, but I need to get you away from here quickly. Redding is quite literally sitting on the man who was set out near here to watch over you. We need to get back to them. Should I release all of these folk with you?"

"Yes, please." Yara stood and began shaking her hands, trying to get some circulation back to them. When she felt something nudging her knee, she looked down and was overjoyed to see Toki.

When all of them were released from the ropes that had held them, Russhell signaled that they should follow her. She headed them deeper into the woods. Once they had gone a goodly distance from where they had been detained, they came upon Redding and Russhell's foxes. Russhell tossed Redding some rope, which he used to tie up the man he had down on the ground.

"I know you have many questions, but I need to tell the border patrol captain something quickly." Turning to him, Russhell said, "Your men are fine and not far from here. One of our patrols chanced upon them shortly after you had been separated from them. They sent another of our patrols ahead to try to find out what happened to you and caught up with us shortly after you and Yara had left. We volunteered to come on ahead and try to determine the situation here. Both your and our border patrols are not far from here, and are awaiting our report. We'll take you there."

With that said, Russhell turned and moved swiftly along a path that Yara could hardly make out. The foxes, including Toki, moved quietly in and out of the trees on either side of them. Their progress was unhampered, and soon they arrived at a channel. A number of reed boats were waiting. After a meeting of the two patrol captains, Russhell, Redding, Marleigh, Eluta, and Yara, it was determined that Kellen and his crew needed to be rounded up and detained.

It was interesting to Yara that the two patrols, one of the Venn and one from the Tåkete bog, despite their difference, at least in this instance, were united in their goal. They split up and set about approaching Marleigh's home from both land and water. The element of surprise and the cover of rain held them in good stead. Kellen and his crew were quickly subdued.

Afterward, Yara stood with her back to the fire, trying to dry off. Russhell, Redding, Marleigh, and Eluta had also pulled up close.

"You can't imagine my surprise when I heard your voice behind me when I was tied to the tree. I thought you would never ever leave the Tåkete bog."

"You are kin, you were in trouble," Russhell stated simply.

Yara did not know what to say to that, other than to thank her distant kin for coming to her rescue.

In the morning, Redding drew Yara aside. "I want to thank you."

"For what?"

"Before you came, Russhell was always afraid and very disconnected from anything and anyone except her foxes. Since your arrival, she has changed. I don't know what you said to her, or what happened between the two of you the afternoon you spent in the quirrelit grove, but she is different, and the change is all to the good."

Once again, Yara did not know what to say, but for a different reason. She certainly could not reveal just what had happened in the quirrelit grove without giving away that she now carried a piece of the oppgave ringe. She suggested that maybe Russhell was stronger or more confident because she no longer felt alone, that she had kin. Knowing she had family maybe left her open to exploring more relationships with folks other than her foxes.

It was with mixed feelings that Eluta and Yara took their leave the next morning. Yara was glad to be heading back to the capital but was sad to be saying goodbye to her newfound kin. Eluta and Toki settled in the boat as Yara said her last farewells.

Before picking up her paddle, something prompted Yara to check in her pack one last time, and she was surprised to see a blekbrann was still nestled inside. "Coming with us then?" Yara whispered.

"Did you ask something?" Eluta asked.

"No, sorry. I guess we had best shove off. We have a long way to go."

Yara and Eluta paddled in silence for the first several hours. Finally, Eluta broke the silence with a question.

"I didn't want to ask straight out before when there were so many people around, but I gather you were successful then?"

"Yes."

"Good. Then let's hope we have a strong wind at our back that will carry us swiftly home."

"And we don't run into any more trouble."

The way back to Sikkervik seemed to take a lot less time than the way out, but then that always seemed the way, Yara thought to herself. She had been somewhat concerned about leaving her sailboat all those many days ago, so was quite relieved when she saw it tied up where she had left it. It did not appear to be any the worse for wear.

Due to the lateness of the day and squall clouds on the horizon, Yara and Eluta decided they would spend the night on the boat in Sikkervik harbor and leave at dawn the next day, weather permitting.

"I'm looking forward to being home and sleeping in my own bed," Eluta admitted. "This walkabout has certainly been an adventure so far, but I think from now on, I will take my adventures between the pages of a book."

"I, too, will be happy to be back in the capital. I . . . ." Yara stopped speaking and put her finger to her lips, signaling Eluta to be still and quiet. Yara cupped one hand around her ear, indicating they should both listen. "Someone's up on deck," Yara whispered.

Eluta nodded her head that she, too, had heard the stealthy footsteps crossing the deck toward the hatch. "Did you latch the hatch?"

"Yes, but it will not hold anyone out who is determined to get in."

Just as Yara finished talking, the two could hear someone trying to open the hatch. Whoever was out there yanked and twisted the hatch handle to no avail. Just as abruptly as it started, the noise stopped, and the two below listened as the footsteps retreated. They felt the slight sway of the boat as someone stepped off onto the dock. A number of minutes passed, but they heard nothing more.

"I'm going to head up and check out topside," Yara told Eluta.

"Do you think that's wise?"

"We can't spend hours trapped down here. We need to leave in the morning. I'll give it a little while longer before I go up."

After a time, having heard nothing more, Yara cautiously unlocked the hatch and poked her head out of the opening. She had no sooner done that when she was lifted bodily up out of the opening and set none too gently on the deck.

"You had best tell the librarian to come up, if you value your safety. Nathair," Bertok yelled, "get back on board."

Yara looked over toward the dock and saw a young man climb on board. Something about him looked familiar, but she could not quite put her finger on what. She was distracted from that thought when Eluta climbed up on deck. Yara watched as Eluta took in what was happening. Yara thought she saw a flash of recognition in Eluta's eyes when she looked at the man who had so casually plucked her out of the cabin, but it happened so quickly she could not be sure.

"Now that I have your attention, I think I don't want to attract anyone else's, so we are all going to go below deck and have a little talk. Move," Bertok directed, giving Yara a slight shove.

The thought of diving overboard quickly came into Yara's mind, and just as quickly left, for she was not about to abandon Eluta, Toki, or her boat. Protesting loudly and yelling for help also occurred to her. She just as quickly abandoned that idea, since she knew no one in Sikkervik, and was not sure who might crawl out of the woodwork at this time of night.

"Your plan worked just like you said it would," commented Nathair, once all of them were below deck. "Walking together across the deck so it sounded like only one of us was here was pretty clever. When I left the boat and you remained still, they thought they were safe and came out to check, just like you predicted. Don't you think introductions are in order? Hello cousin, I'm Nathair Karmoris, and I'm wondering if you have something that belongs to my family? Oh, where are my manners? This gentleman here is Bertok."

Once Nathair had introduced himself as a cousin, Yara realized why he looked familiar. There was a slight family resemblance. Before she could reply to his introduction, Eluta spoke up.

"You! I recognize you. You are the young man who I escorted out of the library. I would guess that the watch guards and I may have missed escorting you out of the library several other times after it closed. Was it you who searched my office and pushed Yara down?"

"You're not the one in charge here, old woman. You had best sit down and be quiet," Nathair stated angrily. "I know what you came here for, and I want what is rightfully mine."

"I really don't know what you are talking about. I have nothing of yours," Yara bluffed. "I came looking for a distant kin, and I found her. I found out a little more about our family that I would be happy to share."

Nathair advanced toward Yara until his face was just inches from hers. "I was in the garden and overheard this old woman talking to others about having found the journals of two of our great-something relatives. Kinza followed the clues that Laron left and found the piece of the oppgave ringe. Kinza then left clues for Laron to follow, which would have led back to Kinza, but Laron never returned. It was hoped by those gathered in the garden that if descendants of Kinza could be found, that one of them might still have the ring. I would have gotten to Sivkurv before you, but Bertok caused me a great deal of trouble, and got me banished from the room of rolls before I could find the present location of the Kinza Karmoris' descendants. Seems he has an agenda of his own."

Nathair gave Bertok a look of loathing before he went on. "Now then, I'm going to give you a little time to think over what you said to me about your visit with our distant kin. To help with your memory, I'm going to take your friend here to my boat, and in the morning we are going to set sail north. You will be following me. As you sail, know that if you try to deviate from my course, I will very cheerfully dump your fellow librarian overboard. It would actually give me great pleasure, since I am not all that fond of librarians at this moment. At the end of tomorrow's sail, we will anchor and have another little talk. You had best be prepared to come up with honest answers. Do you understand what I am saying? Oh, and as an added incentive, I will also be prepared at that time to throw your wee fox overboard, too. Now, all of you move."

The next day it was a good thing that the wind was fair and steady for Yara's mind was on more than paying attention to keeping the sail trim and the boat on course. She was not sure if she would be willing to risk Eluta's life by trying to change course and trying to out sail Nathair. She suspected it would be a very difficult task, for his boat was certainly built for speed whereas her boat had been built more for comfort. Yara was also fearful that Nathair would carry out his threat to throw Toki overboard if he caught up to her. The option of giving him the piece of the oppgave ringe was also not one she wanted to choose.

So distracted by her thoughts, she was at first unaware that Toki was sitting at her feet, or that he had dragged her pack up the stairs, across the deck to where she sat. Once Toki noticed he had Yara's attention, he began pawing frantically at the front flap.

"Alright, alright, I will open the pack, Toki. Just settle down," Yara told the fox, as she reached down and lifted the pack onto her lap. Working the buckle open with one hand while she continued to keep the boat on course with the other, Yara finally managed to open the flap. The blekbrann that had been hidden inside flew out and hovered just off Yara's left shoulder. For some reason, having the wisp there gave Yara her first sense of calm since she had been so abruptly plucked up out of the hatch opening by Bertok.

As the day wore on, Yara was no closer to an answer as to what she should do once they found a place to anchor for the night. She was not sure what she, a red bog fox, and one small wisp would be able to do against two men who were holding Eluta captive. The fog-colored fox had entrusted the piece of the oppgave ringe to her. Was she just supposed to hand it over to Nathair, or was she expected to sacrifice Eluta and try to get away?

Chapter Fifty-One

When Yara saw Nathair's boat begin to tack and head toward the leeward side of an island, she was no closer to an answer than she had been hours before. Did she sacrifice Eluta in hopes of getting away? Was the cost of even one life worth keeping the oppgave ringe out of Nathair's hands?

The wind was beginning to pick up, and Yara thought, if she timed it just right, she might be able to break away and get enough of a lead on Nathair that she could get away. When she began to break away, which would take her away from Nathair's boat, the blekbrann shot forward over the side of the boat in the direction of his boat, hovering over the water.

Yara felt a great deal of relief as she corrected her heading and began to follow the same tack that Nathair had taken. The wisp returned to hover off of Yara's left shoulder.

"I couldn't have gone through with it, you know," Yara said, feeling a little foolish that she was talking to a very small pale green light. "I was about to turn back just as you zipped over the side."

Yara carefully maneuvered her boat upwind to bring it coasting to a halt alongside Nathair's anchored boat. She was relieved to see Eluta sitting on the deck talking with Bertok. Her relief soon turned to concern. The two seemed to be having a very friendly talk, and that worried Yara a great deal. Had she been wrong about the head royal librarian? What did she really know about her anyway? She certainly had pushed her way onto Yara's boat and into her life. Had Yara been set up by Eluta? The head librarian had said she knew Yara was a Karmoris and knew about what had happened to one of the pieces of the oppgave ringe. Eluta had told her she had known Yara was in the garden when the journals were being discussed.

How convenient it now seemed to Yara that Eluta had just happened to ask her to do the research on what had happened to Kinza Karmoris' side of the family.

"Good, you've made it. Catch the line my friend here is going to toss you, and we will pull you closer, so you can come aboard," Eluta said cheerfully.

When it looked like Yara was going to pull away and try to make a break for it, Bertok leapt easily across the narrow gap between the two boats and very quietly suggested Yara drop anchor and drop sail. She did as she was told while he tied the two boats together.

Toki, sensing Yara was upset, scrambled forward and clamped his teeth down hard onto Bertok's pant leg. The wisp began swooping and darting at Bertok's eyes.

When Yara glanced up from lashing the sail to the boom, she noticed that Bertok neither kicked out at Toki nor swatted at the wisp, which surprised her. She also noticed Eluta was standing at the rail, chuckling to herself. How very odd, Yara thought.

"Would you be so kind as to ask your friends to stop pestering me? I really mean you no harm. And you, Eluta, might want to curb your mirth at my dilemma," Bertok suggested.

"Sorry, but you have to admit that there is some humor in being attacked by a fox and dived at by a wisp, all the while trying to hold on to some dignity. Yara, it's alright. No, I have not gone mad and switched sides. Finish up there and come over here. I'll try to explain."

"Heed her words, lass," Bertok stated quietly. "No harm will come to you."

More than words, Bertok's actions convinced her she should step across to the other boat and try to keep an open mind. The fact that he made no move to disengage Toki from his pant leg, nor did he do anything other than duck his head when the wisp zipped close, said more than his words.

Crouching down, Yara called to Toki. "Toki, you can let him go. It's alright. No harm here."

Toki gave Bertok's pant leg one last shake and then walked back to Yara. The wisp also ceased flying about Bertok's face and took its usual position off Yara's left shoulder. With some trepidation, Yara stepped across the gap onto Nathair's boat. She noticed Nathair was conspicuously absent from the deck. The man called Bertok picked up Toki and followed her.

"I think we should all sit down and straighten up any confusion there may be concerning what is happening here," Eluta proposed. "Elek, would you be so kind as to fetch Nathair?"

Elek? Why was Eluta calling this man Elek? Yara watched in confusion as Elek opened the hatch and went below. She heard Nathair protesting long before she saw his head poke out of the hatch.

"You currish knotty-pated wagtail, you pribbling, plume-plucked jolthead. Unhand me and untie me right now. You have no right, you, you, you . . . ."

"You might get all you wish, if you would stop calling me names and quit fighting me every step up onto the deck," Elek stated dryly.

Finally, Elek just lifted Nathair up and carried him across the deck, set him down and swept Nathair's legs out from under him, plopping him down on the deck.

"Now, if you would be so kind as to refrain from spouting off any more colorful vocabulary, we might be able to clear up any questions and misgivings either you or Yara have. Why don't we all pull up a piece of deck and have a calm conversation? Introductions are probably in order, don't you think, Eluta?"

"That might help Yara, who I am sure is a bit confused at this moment."

That might be the understatement of the year, Yara thought to herself.

"The gentleman you and Nathair have known as Bertok has indeed been called that in the past, and he was indeed once part of the Raven's crew. You were quite up there in rank, weren't you?" Eluta inquired.

Yara could not believe how blasé Eluta was being about the man she had been told about and who had been introduced to her as Bertok. This man had been part of the Raven's inner circle, and certainly on the side of the former Regent, and yet, Eluta was not showing any concern.

Elek acknowledged Eluta's statement with a nod of his head. "I am much reformed at present, my dear librarian, as you well know." Elek doffed his hat and gave an elaborate bow.

"Oh, get on with you, you rascal."

"You would call the feared Bertok a rascal?"

"Would and did, but we had best get on with our explanations before Nathair hurts himself muttering, sputtering, and trying to loosen his bindings. Yara, please excuse our bad manners. The gentleman who stands before you has indeed gone by the name of Bertok, but he is in reality Lady Celik's son, Elek. He is not now, and never has been, loyal to the former Regent or any of his followers. He has always served the Crown. When asked by his mother to try to work his way into the Raven's trust, he did so at great risk to his own life. He is here now at the request of the interim ruling council."

Now Yara was feeling even more confused than ever. Why would the interim ruling council send one such as him to Muggen Myr? Was it because of her, or Nathair, or for some other reason?

"It came to my attention that two of you were researching what had happened to the descendants of the once strong Karmoris trading family," Eluta explained. "What I did not know was what your intentions were. Were you looking for Kinza Karmoris' descendants because you were curious and wanted to find family, or was there another reason? I felt I could keep a handle on what you were finding out, Yara, and then somehow I would figure out how to bully my way onto your boat when I suspected you were going to leave, but I could not be two places at once. You see, I was also aware that Nathair here is a Karmoris and was doing the same research. What none of us knew, at the time, was exactly why both of you were so interested as to what had happened to Kinza Karmoris in particular. We surmised that you might have suspected, as we did, that one branch of your family had or had had a piece of the oppgave ringe at some point in time. With time moving so swiftly by, the need to find the four remaining pieces of the oppgave ringe becoming more and more urgent, it behooved us to keep a close eye on those we thought might know where to locate one."

"I was asked to shadow Nathair, and try to make contact," explained Elek. "That way we could keep track of both of you. I made it so Nathair would have to be dependent on me to find Kinza's descendants."

"You see, dear, we were not sure where either of your loyalties lay," stated Eluta truthfully. "It was important for us to make sure, if one of you found the piece of the oppgave ringe, that you would do the right thing and return it to the capital."

"It belongs to my family," yelled Nathair, pounding both feet on the deck in anger. "My great-something grandfather passed the ring to my branch of the family, and Laron stole it. Kinza Karmoris then played a joke on Laron, and his family kept the ring instead of giving it back to whom it rightfully belonged. The family luck changed for the worse because of the loss of the ring. If the ring has been found by her," he said with great loathing, looking at Yara, "then she needs to give it over to me."

Yara began to speak very calmly, before either Eluta or Elek could respond to Nathair's demand. "The ring belongs to neither of our branches of the family. And while I agree that Kinza's joke on Laron was not the right thing to do, I'm grateful to his descendants for keeping the ring safe all these years. What you are forgetting is, that at one time, our great-something grandfather could have entrusted any one of his children with the keeping of the ring, including his daughter, Kinza's mother. I also think that we make our own luck, and the loss of the ring was only coincidental to the loss of the family fortune. Our descendants made their own bad luck when they made bad choices, including taking up smuggling, which they were not very good at."

"But, but, but . . ." Nathair sputtered.

"But nothing. The ring does not belong to our family. The ring was placed in safekeeping with our family. The Karmorises failed. Through jealously, trickery, and bad fortune, we failed. Your branch of the family having possession of the ring, or my branch of the family having the ring at this point, is not going to change the family luck or bring great fortune."

If Yara had not been looking at Nathair at that moment, she would have missed the sly and greedy look that swiftly crossed his face.

"You thought you could make a fortune by selling the ring, didn't you?" Yara accused Nathair.

"What are you going to do with it?" Nathair countered back, not answering Yara's question. "I assume from your answer that you have somehow stolen or tricked our distant cousin out of the ring."

"I'm going to take it to the capital and put it in the vessteboks where it belongs. And no, I did not trick our distant cousin or steal the ring."

"Yah, right. How are we to know you're telling the truth, and not just blowing smoke, waiting for the first chance to skip out on your supposed librarian friend here?"

"Quite frankly, you don't." Yara sighed. "At this moment, I would be hard-pressed to know what is the truth here. Quite frankly, I'm not sure that I can trust any of you."

"I certainly can understand how you might feel that way, Yara," Eluta said, shaking her head sadly. "I, for one, am most anxious for you to get that ring to the capital and where it belongs, nestled in alongside the five already there. Anything I can do to help that happen, I will. My first loyalty has always been to the Crown. And, quite frankly, I've had about as much adventure as I want."

"And I will assure you, on my honor, if you would trust my oath, that I, too, have always been loyal to the Crown and will also do anything you need to deliver you and that piece of the oppgave ringe to the capital," pledged Elek.

"Bunch of fancy words from folks who have not been upfront or truthful to one or the other of us in the past. You really think you can trust them? If so, then you are a big fool," Nathair sneered.

"Could you do something for me?" Yara asked Eluta.

"Anything within reason."

"Could we all go down into the cabin for a moment?"

Eluta agreed and asked Elek if he would escort Nathair down. Nathair continued to protest all the way down the ladder into the cabin, suggesting it was all a trick, and Yara was going to somehow lock them all in and escape.

"I'm sorry to disappoint you, but I will not be locking you all in. I want to instead offer any one of you the oppgave ringe piece I now carry."

"Yara, no, you can't," Eluta protested.

Chapter Fifty-Two

"Actually, I can," Yara stated. "I can just hand it over to anyone I choose, but I don't really think that is going to be a problem, because I don't think any of you will be able to handle the ring. We might think that we choose who the ring is carried by, but I suspect the ring chooses."

"Rings can't choose who has them," Nathair scoffed.

"Believe what you will. I will warn all of you that if you choose to handle the ring, you do so at your own peril."

"I'm not afraid of handling the ring. I'm the rightful descendant to have the ring. Untie me so I can take charge," Nathair demanded.

"Bertok, can you keep Nathair secure and release one of his hands?" Eluta asked.

"That should not be a problem." Turning to Nathair, Elek said, "If you give me any trouble, I will not release you. Is that clear?"

"Whatever you need to do. I will prove to all of you that I'm the rightful owner of the ring," Nathair jeered.

Yara very calmly took out the golden pine spider silk pouch from beneath her shirt and untied it. She tipped the ring out onto the palm of her hand and held it out to Nathair.

"Please know that I don't want anyone to get hurt. I don't want you to get hurt, Nathair. Know that I think if you try to take the ring from me, it will not be an easy or pleasant occurrence. Are you sure you wish to try?"

"It belongs to me and mine, so move closer."

When Yara moved close enough for Nathair to reach her hand, he did not snatch the ring right away. He slowly reached out his hand and let it hover over Yara's hand for a short moment. Yara could see that Nathair's hand trembled slightly. He is not so sure of this, she thought.

While the four folks stood still, each holding their breath in anticipation as to what would happen next, no one noticed that Toki had moved to lean up against Yara's leg, and the wisp was growing brighter.

"Go ahead, Nathair. If the ring is meant to be in your possession, there should be no problem. If not . . . ."

A determined look came over Nathair's face, and he moved to snatch the ring out of Yara's hand. Several things happened at once. Toki began making threatening noises, the wisp flared, a flash of light arced around the ring, and Nathair howled with pain as he dropped the ring back into Yara's hand.

"Would any of the rest of you like to try holding the ring?" Yara asked. When no one moved to take the ring, Yara tucked it safely back into the golden pine spider silk pouch and slipped the pouch back under her shirt.

"Neither Elek nor I ever had any intention of trying to take the ring away from whatever Karmoris descendant was in possession of it, should any of you have it. No, our charge was to first try to convince you to get the ring to the capital, and our second charge was to help you achieve that goal. I hope you can believe me about this," Eluta said sincerely.

"If those were your true intentions," said Yara to Eluta, "then your first goal has been accomplished, for I always intended to head to the capital. If you are sincere in helping me accomplish that, then I would welcome the assistance."

Yara then turned away from Eluta and stepped toward Nathair, who was curled in on himself, quietly sobbing. Before anyone could object, she crouched down and began untying the rope that still bound him. When Elek moved to object, Yara waved him back.

"Nathair," Yara said softly, "I'm going to untie the rope. I'm sorry you got hurt. The ring does not belong to you or your side of the family any more than the ring belongs to me and my side of the family. The ring does not belong to the Karmorises. Rather, I think all of the pieces of the oppgave ringe belong to Sommerhjem, and a long ago member of our family was entrusted with one piece of the oppgave ringe for safekeeping. We were never intended to keep it, for it was never ours to keep. If tradition had been followed when King Griswold died, who knows if the Karmoris family would have been given back a piece of the oppgave ringe for safekeeping until the next ruler needed to be chosen?"

Nathair began to quiet down as the rope was removed. Elek had rummaged around in a cupboard and found some salve and a strip of semi-clean linen. He helped the young man up and had him sit on his bunk. Elek applied the salve and wrapped Nathair's hand in the linen, tying the ends together in a knot to keep it from becoming unraveled.

"How's that feel now, lad?" Elek asked.

"It's, it's better."

"What happened to you sort of gives new meaning to taking the wind out of your sails, doesn't it, lad?"

"Yes, sir," stated a very subdued Nathair.

"Would you folks mind if Nathair and I had a chance to talk, just the two of us?" requested Yara of Eluta and Elek.

"Are you sure that's what you want?" Eluta questioned back. Looking to Elek, she inquired as to whether he thought Yara would be safe.

"I think all this conversation and drama has worked up a mighty hunger, so why don't we go topside and see which one of us can catch dinner first?"

As the two of them climbed up the stairs to the hatch, Eluta could be heard suggesting it was going to be quite the day if Elek thought he could out fish her.

Yara and Nathair sat in silence for a long time, broken only by an occasional sniffle on Nathair's part. Finally, Yara broke the silence.

"Is your hand feeling better?"

"A little."

"I'm glad. Do you understand that I really can't give you the ring, and even if I could, to sell it would just not be right? What had you hoped to accomplish by gaining the ring?"

"I don't want to talk about it."

"You don't have to. It was just my curiosity getting the better of me. You went to a whole lot of time and trouble to get a hold of the piece of the oppgave ringe."

"Alright, you really want to know?" Nathair said angrily. "All my life, I have had to listen to my father and his brothers, my uncles, complaining how life was not fair. They would bemoan how we used to be a wealthy trading family with a great fortune, but when what they called 'the luck' was lost, everything had fallen apart. They were convinced that if only they could get their hands on 'the luck', they would be rich again. Of course, they would sit around all day doing nothing but talk and moan about it. Most of them never did a lick of work. Expected their children to fetch and carry, do odd jobs. My mother took in washing to bring in what little coin we had." Nathair fell silent.

"Go on," Yara encouraged.

"I started gathering the bits and pieces of information about 'the luck'. I always was a pretty good scholar, not that I had much chance for schooling," Nathair said bitterly. "My father thought reading and learning were a waste of time. One day, he discovered I had made some progress finding out about where to look for 'the luck', and so he and the uncles scraped up enough coin to buy this boat, for they concluded that any descendant in the Karmoris family would not be too far from the sea. Were they wrong?"

"Well, yes, Sivkurv, being in the foothills of the mountains near the salt marsh, not to mention the Tåkete bog, is a bit far from the sea."

"My father told me to go to the capital and find out which of the Karmorises had 'the luck' and get it back."

"You never intended to bring it back to your father, did you?"

Nathair looked at Yara in surprise. "No, I didn't. I figured out I might be able to sell it to the highest bidder and make a great good fortune. Then I could return home with the family fortune restored. Being a scholar would have to be respected by my father, then, wouldn't it?"

"Yes, you probably could have made a great good fortune from certain folk, but at what cost to Sommerhjem, if the buyers were the ones who wanted to stop the Gylden Sirklene challenge from happening?"

Nathair was quiet for a very long time, head down, picking at a hangnail. When he looked up, he said in a very quiet voice, "I just wanted my father to respect me."

Yara was silent for some time, thinking about what Nathair had said. What extremes Nathair had been willing to go to because he thought so little of himself, because his father did not value his skills. She could not imagine growing up in a family like his. It sounded like his father and his uncles took advantage of their children, and yet, Nathair set off on this journey, which could have proved to be quite dangerous, just to please his father.

"Do you think you can buy respect, even from one such as your father?" Yara asked gently. "Even if you had been able to get a hold of a piece of the oppgave ringe and sell it, even if you had been able to return home with a great good fortune, how do you think that would have changed your life? Do you really think your father and your uncles would have sent praises out to the far corners of the land about what a brilliant scholar you are?"

"I don't like your questions. Leave me alone," Nathair shot back.

"Just one more question. Did you ever think of leaving home, striking off on your own, and finding someplace where folks would appreciate you?"

"Yah, like where?"

"Oh, I don't know, the royal library comes to mind."

Further conversation was interrupted when Elek hollered down the hatch opening to call the two to dinner. It was a quiet meal at first, but then Yara started a conversation with Eluta.

"I know that my present position with the royal library came about due to some luck. If my family had not sent my brother and me off to the capital to find work because there were too many mouths to feed at home, and the former regent's taxes and fees were making it difficult to put food on the table, I would never have looked for a job in the capital. If I hadn't been caught neglecting my duties in Mendel Bevare's home and become fascinated with what he was doing to repair books, he never would have trained me. If his fortunes had not taken a nose dive, he never would have talked to you about giving me a job at the royal library. I'm sure not everyone who works at the royal library takes such a convoluted path to find a position there."

"Before the former Regent took over the rule of Sommerhjem, there was a system in place where young folk who were interested in scholarly pursuits, but did not have the means, could work at the library, and we basically provided room, board, and a small stipend. Those who showed great promise in one area or another often rose up the ranks, so to speak. I was one of those scholars."

"Do you think that now that the Regent is no longer in power, the Crown might bring a program back such as you described?" Yara asked.

"It is already under discussion. The royal historian and I have been pushing for it. We can't afford to go on the way we have been over the last decade."

Yara noticed that Nathair had paid close attention to her discussion with Eluta. The group broke up soon after, for dusk had fallen, and they wanted to get an early start in the morning.

When Eluta and Yara were back on Yara's boat and had settled in for the night, Eluta asked Yara why she had asked about the library.

"It had to do with my conversation with Nathair." Yara went on to explain what Nathair had told her as to why he had been so desperate to get his hands on the oppgave ringe piece.

"He can't be who he is not, and yet, he is trying to please a parent who will never be pleased with who he is. Quite a dilemma for the young man. A scholar in a family that does not appreciate scholars," stated Eluta.

"He has to be pretty good at research, for tracing the convoluted paths the Karmoris family has taken since Laron and Kinza's time was not easy, and I have had some training. It just seemed like the library could use someone of his talent."

"You have a good heart, Yara. You do know that he would not have had the same compassion for you."

"I wonder. He's such an angry young man, but I don't think he's truly a violent one."

"I'll think about what you have said. We had best get some sleep, for we still have to get that ring you carry to the capital. Let us hope we have clear skies and a fair wind tomorrow."

Chapter Fifty-Three

When Yara came up on deck the next morning, the skies were not clear. She could see white caps on the water beyond the island they were tucked behind. Even as she watched the sunrise to the east, she could hear the sound of the wind increasing as it tore through the trees of the island.

"Looks like we are in for a bit of a blow," stated Eluta, who had come up on deck to stand beside Yara. "Just a squall, do you think?"

"We could . . . ." The rest of Yara's sentence was lost due to the sound of a loud crash near the shoreline of the island behind them. A large tree had fallen.

"I think it was a good thing that we separated the boats last night and moored separately. Not a good day for a sail I'm thinking. And here comes the rain," Yara said, as she rapidly crossed the deck and went below. It was well after midnight before the storm subsided.

After a discussion the next morning with Elek, it was determined that the two boats would sail together back to the capital. Elek reported he had gained Nathair's word that he would no longer try to obtain the piece of the oppgave ringe from Yara, and even as importantly, he would not disclose to anyone that she had the ring.

While Elek's words were certainly welcome and reassuring, Yara felt a strong urgency to get underway. Even the wisp seemed to be behaving strangely, for it kept pacing, if wisps could pace, from its position off Yara's left shoulder to the bow of the boat and back. Toki, too, had taken up a position at the boat's bow. He came back to sit beside Yara once they were under sail.

"Spray over the bow too much for you, Toki?" Yara asked, her voice colored with humor, for Toki had been drenched when a wave had crashed over the bow of the boat.

Toki just gave Yara a look of disgust and shook vigorously, sending water everywhere, but especially splattering Yara.

"Oh, nice one, fox. I'm sorry I found humor in you getting drenched."

"We will have to make a note of that in our study of red bog foxes. Never find humor in a thoroughly drenched bog fox, for they know how to get even," suggested Eluta. "Looks like we will have a fair wind today."

As they headed toward the capital, Eluta and Yara discussed what needed to happen once they got there.

"We can't be sure what the former Regent's agents know or have discovered in our absence. While your absence probably caused a little talk among those you worked with at the royal library, it probably has gone totally unnoticed by those who watch for the former Regent. At least we can hope so. My absence, however, would have been noticed. I don't think anyone who might have been interested in my comings and goings would have seen me leave with you, since it was so spontaneous, but we can't be sure. I think we need to be prepared for anything," stated Eluta frankly.

"It would look odd if I docked anywhere other than at the shipwright's dock where I have kept my boat. I trust him, and I think he would help us get back to the royal library. I don't know whether Elek and Nathair should follow us through the harbor and dock there as well."

"When I was 'captive' and sailing with 'Bertok' and Nathair, Elek and I discussed what should happen when we reached the capital's harbor. He is going to sail to his family's dock and suggested we do that also. It does not matter at this point whether it looks odd that you sail into the harbor and dock other than at your usual place, should anyone be paying attention. What matters is that Elek's mother, Lady Celik, has posted folks at and near their dock to be on the lookout for either boat, and provide assistance and security should either of us pull up there. Once docked, her instructions to her folk are to get either you or Nathair swiftly up to a place of safety and get in touch with those who need to know of your arrival," Eluta told Yara.

Yara sat at the helm of her boat, working to keep it on course, and at the same time really thinking about what Eluta had just told her. Her idea that the Karmoris family either once had, or still had, one of the pieces of the oppgave ringe had been known by more folks that she had imagined. The fact that both she and Nathair had not just been looking for long lost relations but had been looking for more than that had set a number of wheels in motion. Hers had been such a slender thread of information when she first started looking, as she imagined Nathair's also had been. Yara wondered how many other slender threads of information the Crown was aware of and following. Once she placed her piece of the oppgave ringe in the vessteboks, there would only be three more to be found. How many other wheels within wheels were now spinning by those loyal to the Crown and by those loyal to the former Regent?

The rest of the journey back to the capital was smooth sailing. The winds were favorable, and there were no more storms. Neither boat had difficulty navigating the capital harbor to Lady Celik's dock. Just as Eluta had told Yara, folks had been on the lookout for either boat, and an escort was waiting to take them safely to Lady Celik's town home.

It was shortly after they arrived at Lady Celik's town home that others began to gather. Master Clarisse arrived with Master Rollag from the Glassmakers Guild. Lady Esmeralda, several other members of the interim ruling council, and the Captain of the royal guard, followed shortly after. Yara was surprised that not one of those assembled seemed surprised or questioned that a red bog fox or a wisp from the Muggen Myr salt marshes were also in attendance at the meeting. The news that Yara had found and was able to bring the sixth piece of the oppgave ringe to the capital was greeted with enthusiasm and joy.

"I think it would be best if you place the ring in the vessteboks in the Well of Speaking tomorrow morning. That will give us time to get the word out. Do any of you disagree?" asked Lady Celik.

"No, I think that would be wise. Are you comfortable with that, Yara?" Master Clarisse inquired.

"Are you sure we need to go to all that fuss and bother? Couldn't I just slip over there now and take care of it?" Yara asked the assembled group.

"Unfortunately, we need the fuss," Lady Esmeralda told Yara. "With the placing of each piece of the oppgave ringe, the more encouraged the folks of Sommerhjem become that the Gylden Sirklene challenge is real and not some myth. The tide of acceptance is growing stronger and stronger. So, much as you might like to just walk over there now and be done, we need you to wait."

"I do have one request, then."

"What is it that you wish?" Lady Esmeralda inquired.

"I would like Nathair to walk beside me."

Nathair, who had been sitting quietly wondering why he had even been included in the gathering and had not been locked away somewhere, abruptly looked up. "You want me to walk with you?" he asked incredulously.

"Of course. The piece of the oppgave ringe was placed in trust with the Karmoris family. Had Laron not been jealous of his brother, had Kinza not played a prank, had Laron not gone missing, who knows which present day Karmoris would now hold the ring? Time and circumstance placed the ring in my hands. Though distant, you and I are family and Karmorises. No matter what led us to this moment, we both stand for our different branches of the family. Though we had different reasons, we both followed the same clues to discover where the ring might be found. I think it is only fitting we see this to the end together."

Nathair just sat for a moment, looking stunned. He had tried to find the ring and had thought to sell it to the highest bidder. He had almost hurt Yara when he had panicked in the head librarian's office and pushed her down. He had been awful to her on the boat, filled with loathing and self-pity, and yet, here she was asking him to stand with her. Straightening himself up from his slumped position in his chair, he told Yara he would be honored.

The meeting adjourned shortly after that, and the rest of the day was spent in preparations. Midmorning of the next day found Yara, Toki, and Nathair standing at the top step leading down to the Well of Speaking. The wisp, barely visible in the bright sunlight, hovered just off Yara's left shoulder. Taking a deep breath, Yara began the descent down the stairs. When she reached the sea wall in which the vessteboks was set, she noticed Nathair had begun to step back. She reached out and pulled him forward.

"You don't get to get out of this that easily," she told him with mock sternness. "I want everyone to see that not one but two Karmorises were here. I want them to talk about it. I want the news to get back to your father and uncles. I want them to know your worth has been acknowledged by many important folk in the capital."

Nathair could only nod his head and stepped forward.

Yara then knelt down and placed a hand on Toki's head. Just having him with her was a comfort, but when her hand touched his fur, a great wave of calm flowed over her. After a brief moment, Yara stood and stepped up to the sea wall.

Master Clarisse had explained to Yara what had happened to each of those folks who had placed a piece of the oppgave ringe in the vessteboks before her. Knowing what to expect helped, so she reached out and opened the vessteboks. A silence had come over the crowd of folks in the Well of Speaking. Tipping the ring into her hand, Yara placed it in the box. For a moment nothing happened. Then a spiral of pale green light rose gracefully up out of the box. As it rose higher and higher, the green intensified, and strands of darker and darker green became interwoven with the pale green light. When the column had reached quite a height, the strands of green unraveled and arched out in all directions, finally fading from sight. The folks in the Well of Speaking remained silent for quite a long time before they began to talk and move to leave.

As Yara turned to climb the stairs, she noticed that the wisp she had become so accustomed to seeing off her left shoulder was no longer there. Yara had a feeling of loss. Toki pushed his muzzle against her hand, bringing her out of her thoughts, so she moved forward with the rest of the folks who had accompanied her to the Well of Speaking.

After several days of official gatherings and celebrations, Yara was quite glad to be able to find some quiet time. She was sitting once again in the royal librarian's garden with Eluta, Toki, Elek, and Nathair.

"So, young man, have you thought over my offer?" Eluta asked of Nathair.

"What offer?" Yara inquired.

"I have asked Nathair if he might like to apprentice, in a sense, with the librarian in charge of the rolls room. I have assured him that the librarian was only play acting when he banished Nathair from the room. In fact, he had been quite impressed with Nathair when Nathair had been doing his research into the Karmoris family. He had remarked to me, even then, how he wished he could have someone like Nathair to help with the requests he gets and to train for when he might want to take a less active role."

"So, what have you decided?" Yara asked.

"I'm humbled by the offer, considering my past actions. I fully expected to be locked up somewhere due to what I tried to do, and instead, I am being offered a chance to do something I truly want to do. I accept the offer, and I will work hard, so your faith in me is not misplaced. Will you continue to work here also, cousin?"

Yara looked to Eluta. "I have not even asked if my place here is still available. After all, I did leave without notice."

"Well, if that were the criteria for not having a place here at the royal library, then we both would be out on our ears. After all, I left without notice, too," Eluta suggested. "I do think you will no longer be working here, however."

When Yara looked at Eluta questioningly, with a confused look on her face, Eluta went on.

"We have done a great job of preserving the past at the library, but we are not doing such a good job of preserving the present. So much out there is being written and recorded and needs to be brought to the royal library. Also, so much older material has not been copied and made its way here. When I think of the books Marleigh had that are in need of preservation before they are totally lost, I shudder. We need someone to travel about gathering new material for the library. Can't think of anyone better to do the job. It would seem your journey has just begun."

"You want me to travel about for the library and gather material?"

"Can't think of a better folk to do so. If you find ancient scrolls or books, you certainly know how to handle them. You have experience concerning old and rare books. You certainly know how to follow obscure threads of information. No, can't think of a better folk to do so."

"Do you want to go with me?"

"No, lass, one grand adventure is enough for me. Now, scoot. It's time for you to be off and take that mangy fox with you."

Yara reluctantly stood up to say her farewells. It was then she noticed her daypack was not closed securely. Flipping the flap open to check to make sure everything was secure, she was surprised to see a pale green light glowing within. Ah, Toki, she thought, it looks like we will have company on the next leg of our journey.